Passion
With a
Vengeance

**When the search for revenge
leads to love...**

GW00542573

Acclaim for the authors

About Emma Darcy
"Emma Darcy delivers a spicy love story..."
—*Romantic Times*

About *Gamble on Passion*
"Jacqueline Baird burns up the pages with...(the characters') lusty sensuality"
—*Romantic Times*

About Sara Craven
"Sara Craven is an excellent storyteller"
—*Rendezvous Magazine*

Passion With a Vengeance

Emma Darcy
Jacqueline Baird
Sara Craven

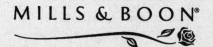

MILLS & BOON®

MILLS & BOON and MILLS & BOON with the Rose Device
are registered trademarks of the publisher.
Harlequin Mills & Boon Limited,
Eton House, 18-24 Paradise Road, Richmond, Surrey, TW9 1SR

PASSION WITH A VENGEANCE
© 1998 by Harlequin Books SA

The Sheikh's Revenge, Gamble on Passion and Flawless were first
published in Great Britain by Mills & Boon Limited.
The Sheikh's Revenge and Gamble on Passion in 1994
and Flawless in 1989.

The Sheikh's Revenge © Emma Darcy 1993
Gamble on Passion © Jacqueline Baird 1994
Flawless © Sara Craven 1989

ISBN 0 263 81130 1

05-9807

Printed and bound in Great Britain
by Caledonian Book Manufacturing Ltd, Glasgow

Emma Darcy nearly became an actress until her fiancé declared he preferred to attend the theatre with her. She became a wife and mother. Later, she took up oil painting—unsuccessfully, she remarks. Next came architecture, designing the family home in New South Wales.

Then she tried romance writing—'the hardest and most challenging of all the activities,' she confesses. Emma has now been successfully writing for Mills & Boon® since 1983 and has written more than 60 novels, which have been published worldwide.

THE SHEIKH'S REVENGE

by

EMMA DARCY

CHAPTER ONE

LEAH HAD the uncomfortable feeling of being watched. It was a strange, prickly sense of some strong presence menacing her peaceful solitude.

Absurd, she told herself. It was one of the perks of her job that this walled garden was completely private to her, a safe retreat where she could enjoy herself in her own way, without interruption or interference.

Nevertheless, she sat absolutely still for several moments, listening. There was no sound other than the soft splash of water bubbling from the fountain, supplying a cool tranquillity that blocked out the rest of the world. She ruefully decided her nerves were still on edge from all the emotional dramas of the morning. The whole palace was in a ferment in preparation for the month-long wedding celebrations. It was a welcome relief to get away from it for a while.

Perhaps the lingering feeling of something being wrong was still unsettling her. Samira had been so tense and agitated, natural enough for a bride-to-be who had never met her groom, Leah thought, but Leah had expected her to be more happily resigned, even excited about her imminent and highly prestigious marriage.

She heaved a dismissive sigh. If there was something wrong, there was nothing she could do about it. As an Arab princess, Samira had always been destined for this kind of marriage. It was not as though she was unprepared for it. She had been raised to it from birth. And the royal families certainly looked after their own.

Leah had learnt a long time ago to stand back from palace politics. She might be treated as one of the family, but she knew the indulgence depended on their approval of her behaviour and the way she carried out her job. Some self-protective instinct had urged her to distance herself from Samira this afternoon. If something went wrong... But it wouldn't, Leah assured herself. Everyone was hyped up, anxious everything be as perfect as it should be. That was all.

Beside her was a small table on which lay rows of the coloured wools she needed. In front of her stood the frame on which her tapestry was stretched tight. Having firmly put aside her concern for Samira, Leah worked the needle through the stiff fabric with nimble eagerness, wanting to complete the last remaining section of dark foreground so that she could begin on the more interesting flesh tones of the naked woman.

"Miss Leah Marlow?"

The softly spoken inquiry startled Leah. It was a male voice asking for her, and it was not the voice of her brother. No other man had the right to be admitted here. She jerked her hand up from the tapestry as her head spun towards the archway, the only entrance to the garden.

Her heart kicked in shock as she recognised the man who stood there, flanked by two fierce-looking soldiers, automatic rifles in their hands, the loose flow of their Arab robes disrupted by bandoliers.

Leah had seen his picture in the newspapers, watched him on television. The charisma of the man made him unforgettable. It was easy to understand why he had been the one to replace his uncle, who was shifted aside as 'not fit to govern.' Despite the simplicity of his plain brown robe and a soft white headpiece held down by black cording, there was no doubting his identity.

Sharif al Kader.

The Sheikh of Zubani.

The man Samira was to marry tomorrow.

Leah's brain clicked through these facts, yet stopped short of dictating some response to this unexpected and totally unheralded visitation. She stared at him, strangely unable to do anything else. Perhaps it was his utter stillness or the shimmering heat of the afternoon that made her feel he was a mirage, a representation of all man had been since the world had begun, hunter, warrior, zealot determined to conquer whatever needed to be conquered in forging the destiny of his choice.

A weird, fluttery sensation swept through Leah. It was as though the intense vitality of his life force had invaded her own, playing havoc with the inner serenity she had cultivated over the years. It was both exciting and unnerving, making her a stranger to herself. No man had ever had such an effect on her. After the messy and bitter divorce of her parents, Leah had developed an instinctive practice of blocking men out of her life. Except for her brother, of course.

"Miss Leah Marlow?"

The softly repeated question seeped slowly into her consciousness, then abruptly snapped the odd sense of unreality that had gripped her. "Yes, Your Excellency," she replied, automatically using the normal mode of address to a man of his status. She half rose to her feet before the tug of fixed thread reminded her of the tapestry needle in her fingers.

"Do not be disturbed, Miss Marlow. Resume your seat. Be at ease," he commanded as he stepped towards her, away from his bodyguards.

Leah was glad to comply. Her fingers trembled slightly as she slid the threaded needle into the spare fabric at the edge of the tapestry. It was good to subside into the safe comfort of her chair. She was acutely aware of the power emanating from this man, and it made her feel intensely vulnerable.

The sense of being watched was now explained. It was said that his eyes were like searchlights. Nothing escaped them.

She had not heard his approach and had no idea how long he had been watching her or what it portended. The silence of his arrival and the lack of any warning of it had to be deliberate. Yet why the sheikh of Zubani should intrude on her privacy like this was totally incomprehensible, completely outside normal protocol.

He was a man who made his own rules. He was also the type of man whose world was immovably centred on himself and his people. Since she was a Western woman, her personal rights were probably discounted in his mind.

Leah struggled to ignore her agitation, the rocketing beat of her heart. She folded her hands in her lap and kept her eyes lowered as he walked past the fountain. She could not imagine what he wanted with her, and it was not her place to ask, but her sense of danger was immeasurably heightened when he came to a halt beside her chair, apparently interested in viewing what she was working on.

"The rape of the Sabine women," he observed in a slightly mocking drawl, naming the famous Rubens painting imprinted on the fabric.

He moved behind Leah, picked up one of the garden seats and positioned it beyond the small table that held her wools. He sat down facing her, emitting an air of patient purpose, his lean brown fingers idly interlocking in his lap.

"Does such a subject interest you, Miss Marlow?"

"I enjoy doing tapestries, Your Excellency," Leah replied evenly, ignoring the silky taunt in his voice.

"You chose that one yourself?"

"Yes."

"Does it excite you? The idea of women being carried off and ravished by men of strange and foreign lands?"

The contemptuous sting in his words goaded Leah into meeting his eyes, dark, riveting eyes that impaled her with their sharp intelligence. His face was one of those that defy the ravages of time, austere in its beauty yet enticing in its refinement, the kind of face one wanted to touch or trace or hold. There was a stamp of hard, immutable strength on it, but it was the power of his eyes that made him a leader of men.

Sharif al Kader was both daunting and compelling, but Leah was not about to be intimidated into letting him nurse some undeserved contempt for her. "I find the idea absolutely revolting, Your Excellency. I have no desire to be ravished by any man. I couldn't imagine anything worse."

He raised his eyebrows quizzically.

"Rubens was a great artist," she continued coolly. "I was more interested in the composition of colour and shape than in the actual subject he chose to paint."

He smiled as though in approval, but his eyes gleamed cynical disbelief. His gaze drifted to the pale gold of her hair and travelled slowly down its shiny length. Leah had not bothered pinning it up since the thick mass was still drying from its recent wash when she had come out to the garden. She had simply rolled back swathes from each side of her face, clipped them together at the back of her head and left the rest to flow loosely over her shoulders.

Leah was aware that her fair colouring excited more than a passing curiosity and interest in the males of the Middle East. When she went out in public she wore a veil to protect herself from unwanted and unwelcome attention, but this *was* her own private garden, and not even the sheikh of Zubani should be viewing her appearance as less than modest. Her long-sleeved white caftan covered her from neck to toe, yet that didn't escape from critical appraisal, either.

It was all Leah could do to hold herself completely immobile as he virtually undressed her with his eyes, lingering on the high, firm roundness of her breasts before slowly following the curve of hip and thigh where the long garment was tucked under her. She told herself it was the feeling of helplessness that made her want to squirm. Impossible to get up and walk away.

When he began what felt like an insultingly intent study of the shape of her mouth, a surge of rebellious anger tilted Leah's chin higher and sent splashes of hot colour into her cheeks. It made the blue of her eyes more vivid as they defied the common judgement on Western women whose supposedly loose morals made them fair prey for Arab men who desired them. To Leah's mind, if any censure was deserved for *loose* behaviour, then both sides were equally at fault.

Sharif al Kader was reported to have been educated in England and France, and Leah was willing to bet he had not been celibate throughout all those youthful years in a more liberal culture. Yet, she had to admit that apart from his flawless English accent, the Western world did not appear to have scratched the surface of this man. Perhaps he had always held himself aloof from it.

"I do not know that you are at all suitable," he finally declared. "Indeed, my first impression is that you are entirely unsuitable."

Unsuitable for what? Leah wondered angrily. Pride in her self-worth was beamed straight at him, but she held her tongue, waiting for him to elaborate on his contentious statement.

He frowned in brooding disapproval. "I was expecting a woman who had put aside any hope of attracting a husband. A woman of no feminine allure
whatsoever. You do not fit that image, Miss Marlow."

Leah remained silent, disdaining any reply to his
prejudiced opinion that the only goal of an attractive
woman had to be marriage. It might be so in his
world, but she had other options. Attracting a husband was not on her wish list. A marriage certificate
promising forever love and loyalty and fidelity was
nothing more than dispensable paper, in Leah's experience. Having been through that disillusionment as
a child, she had no intention of inviting more of it as
an adult.

"I was informed that you have been both teacher
and companion to Princess Samira since she was
eleven years of age," the sheikh continued, still with
that air of brooding disapproval.

"That is so, Your Excellency," Leah answered with
cool dignity. "But as you must know, Princess Samira was sent to England for her formal education,
then to a finishing school in Paris. My responsibility
here is to supervise the learning of all the royal children and prepare them for schooling in other countries. For the most part, I have only been a companion
to Princess Samira during her vacations."

"I know all this," he said in curt dismissal. "What
I find disquieting, Miss Marlow, is that you were given
this position when you were only eighteen."

"My brother sponsored me. He is King Rashid's
personal pilot."

"A surprisingly high position for so young a man."

Leah bridled at his critical tone. "Glen has been here for ten years, Your Excellency," she pointed out.

"Against all normal procedure." The dark eyes stabbed some underlying accusation at her. "Few foreigners are granted more than a two- or three-year contract. Yet your brother has been here for ten years. And you for eight. Your contracts renewed again and again and again," he emphasised. "To me it adds up to one thing, and one thing only."

"What is that, Your Excellency?" Leah asked, struggling to keep calm under what felt like an attack on her probity.

"Someone of high royal blood wants to keep you here."

"I do my job with the children very satisfactorily," Leah said, reacting to the disturbing sense that she had to justify the longevity of her employment.

A flare of angry frustration burst from him. His hand slammed down on the table, scattering the neat rows of wools. "Whose concubine are you?" he demanded. "Do you have the king himself?"

Leah was shocked out of any guard on her tongue or manners. "I am not a concubine!" she retorted fiercely. "And never will be one! No man will ever get me to surrender myself to his pleasure!"

The sheikh threw his head back and laughed in utter disbelief. "You are a simple minder of children?"

"That is what I choose to be," Leah bit out, seething under his open derision and cursing herself for having revealed her deeply entrenched hatred of sex-

ual desire that overrode every other caring consideration.

"Has no man satisfied you?"

"None seems likely to."

Her eyes furiously defied the challenge in his, the
intensely male challenge that asserted he could do it
with his hands tied behind his back if he wanted to,
teaching her a pleasure that would have her begging
for more. He was, at that moment, the most sexual
man Leah had ever met, and the feelings he aroused in
her were quite frightening.

"And the Princess Samira. Have you corrupted her
mind with fanciful stories of how you believe love and
passion should be?" he mocked.

"Certainly not!"

"You have not talked to her of your frustration with
all the lovers you have tried and found wanting?"

"I have never once mentioned lovers to her."

"She has not asked?"

"It is not a subject I care to discuss. With anyone,
Your Excellency," Leah shot at him, bitterly resent-
ing his outrageous assumptions about her.

He eyed her wildly flushed cheeks with an air of
weighing her truthfulness, then relaxed in his chair,
apparently satisfied. He gave her a thin smile. "Your
discretion does you credit, Miss Marlow."

Leah glared, rejecting any credit from him. If he
expected her to thank him for the grudging compliment, he could wait until Doomsday. Perversely, her
stubbornly rebellious silence provoked a gleam of
amusement in his eyes.

"The Princess Samira…tell me your impression of her," he commanded.

Leah took a deep breath to calm her turbulent feelings. Common sense dictated that she reply to a direct command, however improper she felt the question was. "I'm sure you will find the princess a suitable wife, Your Excellency. She has been brought up to accept the duties of state."

"Meek and mild and resigned to her fate, Miss Marlow? Is that what you are giving me to understand?" he mocked.

It stung Leah into a further reply. "Princess Samira has the natural high spirits of her young age. I would not call her meek."

"So, she is a shrew."

"I didn't say that," Leah hotly denied. "It's only natural that a young woman of her broad education and lively intelligence should form opinions of her own."

"I hope the princess has not picked up your independent attitudes, Miss Marlow. It would not lead to domestic harmony."

"I'm sure your authority will hold sway, Your Excellency." Leah gave him a thin little smile.

His gaze flicked to her mouth, then back to the clear blueness of her eyes. "Perhaps you should have chosen a tapestry depicting a Leonardo da Vinci painting, Miss Marlow. It would seem that *Mona Lisa* is more your style. I always felt her smile deceptive."

"No doubt you are a greater expert on such matters than I am, Your Excellency."

He was amused by her tactic of agreeing with him with the same silky contempt he had used on her. Leah dimly recognised she was on dangerous ground, but he had riled her into a wild recklessness that demanded she give him back tit for tat.

"I like to make my own judgement of people, Miss Marlow, particularly where a position of trust and influence is involved."

"A judgement reflects the prejudices of the judge," Leah said tartly, still smarting from his distasteful cross-examination.

He raised an eyebrow. "You expect me to accept at face value that a woman of your beauty and intelligence is content to spend her life being a minder of other women's children?" He shook his head. "Something is wrong."

"I happen to *like* children, Your Excellency."

"Perhaps you mean you feel safe with them, Miss Marlow, because you are in control of the situation," he said with an insidious softness, slicing too close to an uncomfortable truth.

"I care about them," she defended.

"Then it will be no burden for you to care for mine. I have two daughters from my first marriage. They will be staying in the children's wing for the month of the wedding celebrations."

He paused, watching Leah intently as she absorbed the shock of this announcement. She had not been informed of any such arrangement for the sheikh's children, and while the reason behind this extraordinary meeting was now clear, the idea of being in any way responsible for this man's daughters had no appeal for her.

The manner in which he had inspected and cross-examined her demonstrated a lack of respect and trust that Leah found extremely offensive. And should any mishap occur with the children while they were in her care, Leah had no doubt the consequences would be equally unpalatable.

"Naturally I will do my best to make their stay here a happy one," she said, hating the fact that she had no choice in the matter.

"They will not be completely in your charge, Miss Marlow. My daughters are very close to my heart, and I would not leave them with a stranger. Their nanny, Tayi, will be looking after them for the most part. Tayi is a loyal and highly valued member of my household, and I place the utmost confidence in her."

"I see," Leah said dryly.

"I, also, shall see. You may teach my daughters some English while they are here, and I shall monitor their progress under your guidance. Nothing you do over the next month will escape my notice, Miss Marlow."

It was both a promise and a threat, and it was no pleasure for Leah to discover that the sense of her peaceful privacy being menaced was deadly accurate. While she had nothing to fear in being spied upon, Leah bristled at the thought of being constantly under this man's distrustful scrutiny.

He raised his hand, and one of his bodyguards instantly bowed then disappeared from the archway.

"You will now meet my daughters. Please remember, Miss Marlow, that from this moment on, I will be watching you with the eyes of a hawk. Whatever is wrong, I will know of it."

Something was wrong, all right, Leah thought with grim irony. It was suddenly clear to her why everyone had been in a state of nervous agitation this morning. It all sprung from the coming of this man. He had swooped in like a desert hawk, bringing all the uneasiness of a force that acknowledged only his way and his will.

Leah took another deep breath in an attempt to calm the storm he had stirred in her. One month and Sharif al Kader would be gone. Surely she could withstand whatever small pressures he might bring to bear on her. After all, her conscience was clear of any wrongdoing.

She sternly told herself she had nothing to fear from the sheikh of Zubani. Nothing at all!

CHAPTER TWO

AS THEY WAITED for his children, Leah watched Sharif al Kader's fingers drumming lightly on the armrest of his chair. They should look like talons, she thought, but they didn't. They looked strong and sensual, and the steady beat of their touch had a relentless rhythm. She wondered how Samira would feel tomorrow night when . . .

Leah swiftly repressed the uncharacteristic speculation. She did not want to think of Sharif al Kader as a lover. She did not want to think of lovers at all. Besides which, love didn't enter into this marriage. The sheikh of Zubani was simply taking a new wife to warm his bed and cement a political friendship with the royal family of Qatamah. The latter purpose was undoubtedly more important to him, since his rise to power was relatively recent.

It was said that one of the reasons he had moved against his uncle's rule in Zubani was the old man's refusal to use the oil wealth pouring into the country for the welfare of its people. His uncle's belief that their traditional way of life would be destroyed by too much too soon was not shared by Sharif al Kader.

His first wife had died from an infection after the birth of their second child. He had laid the blame for it on the ill-equipped and inadequately staffed hospital his uncle had done nothing to improve. Less than perfect medical facilities no longer existed in Zubani. Any problem that touched this sheikh's heart was obviously dealt with in a ruthless and very thorough fashion.

His fingers stopped drumming. Leah flicked a glance at his face and saw his whole demeanour change. The man of relentless purpose was transformed by a smile that radiated warm and loving indulgence. He rose to his feet and turned towards the archway. "My daughters," he said with deep paternal pride.

Leah rose more slowly from her chair, stunned not only by the change in her powerful antagonist, but also by the sheer magnificence of the woman who held the two little girls by the hand. A descendant of the highly valued Ethiopian slaves from the last century, Leah surmised. She stood at least six feet tall, her majestic figure enhanced by a silk robe coloured in vivid yellow and orange. A matching turban was wound around her head. The fine delicacy of her features was dominated by the striking beauty of large, velvety eyes.

"Thank you, Tayi." The sheikh spoke in Arabic. "Send them forward to meet Miss Marlow."

The little girls were released and given a gentle push. They walked forward shyly, staring at Leah with huge, wondering eyes. It seemed that she was as much a figure of awe to them as their nanny had been to Leah.

"My daughters have never met a woman of your fair colouring before," the sheikh explained with dry

irony as he moved to line them up for a formal introduction to Leah. "This is Nadia. She is five years old.
And this is Jazmin. She is three years old."

He touched them with love and there was love in his,
voice. For a moment Leah's mind spun to her own
childhood, when she had been close to her father's
heart. It had hurt so much when he had betrayed that
love and withdrawn the security of his caring, leaving
her and Glen with their mother who cared far more for
her new husband than she did for them.

She looked sadly at Sharif al Kader's daughters. As
beloved as they undoubtedly were now, they also
would be passed into the care of strangers when the
sheikh married them to men of his choice. But at least
they would be raised to accept that, and they would be
spared the feelings of betrayal.

They were beautiful children, and their innocent
appeal tugged at Leah's heart. She crouched to meet
them on their level, smiling to put them at ease. She
spoke the Arabic greeting that would be most familiar to them, and the elder girl replied in a rush of relief and pleasure. The younger appeared to be totally
tongue-tied. She tentatively reached out and touched
Leah's hair.

"Jazmin," her father reproved. "Where are your
manners?"

She looked up at him in wide-eyed confusion.

Leah smoothed over the awkward moment, speaking soothingly in Arabic. "It is strange to meet someone who looks different, but you will soon get used to
me, Jazmin."

"I wanted to know if your hair was real," the little girl said apologetically.

Leah gently caressed the child's soft black curls. "As real as yours."

"Can I touch it again?" she asked eagerly.

"Jazmin!" The pained patience in her father's voice held her in check. "You have not yet greeted Miss Marlow."

She rattled out the required greeting with somewhat irreverent obedience to her father, then breathlessly added, "How did you get blue eyes?"

"Enough!" the sheikh cut in brusquely. "Go off with Tayi now. You will see Miss Marlow again tomorrow."

They went, glancing over their shoulders at Leah, who smiled after them as she straightened up.

Sharif al Kader heaved an exasperated sigh. "Perhaps I have indulged Jazmin too much."

"Her curiosity is only natural, Your Excellency," Leah replied, amused at the thought there was one little female who was undaunted by the authority of this formidable man.

"Miss Marlow..."

The steely edge in his voice commanded her full attention. She turned to face him. Any trace of warm indulgence had been wiped from his expression. There was a gleam of mocking resignation in his eyes.

"I am a fair man. It is clear that you do have an empathy with children."

Leah's eyes scorned the concessionary nature of this statement. To her mind, he owed her an apology, not a grudging concession. There had been no reason for him to judge her differently in the first place. An apology, however, was obviously not forthcoming, and her silence evoked a thin little smile.

"I am told that Princess Samira is very fond of you, Miss Marlow."

"As I am of her," Leah replied, wondering how Samira would fare with him and feeling oddly ambivalent about the marriage. It might be right politically, but she hated the thought of Sharif al Kader's dominant personality crushing the sparkle out of Samira's lively nature.

"It is against my inclination to employ you, but I wish to make the Princess Samira happy in our marriage. Therefore, should you prove satisfactory to me, I will permit you to be some kind of minor companion for her. And you can make yourself useful by looking after my children and teaching them the English language."

The sheer blazing arrogance of this speech raised Leah's hackles. Did he expect her to thank him for such condescending beneficence? "I don't think I understand, Your Excellency," she bit out with barely controlled anger. "My position here . . ."

"Will be continued in my palace, Miss Marlow. You will accompany Princess Samira's retinue when we return to Zubani," he stated as though the decision had nothing at all to do with Leah.

Despite her fondness for Samira, everything in Leah recoiled from being in any way connected to this man's domestic affairs, let alone receiving confidences from the young bride about her new husband. She didn't want to hear, didn't want to know anything more of

Sharif al Kader, particularly not the kind of intimate
details Arab women bandied around between themselves. Just the thought of hearing about him in that
way made Leah feel sick.

Apart from which, to be in his employ, and therefore in his power, was only asking for trouble. He
didn't like her, and she certainly did not like him.

"Please pardon me for declining your generous offer, Your Excellency," Leah said strongly. "Thank
you very much, but I am happy here. I am also bound
by contract—"

"Your contract will be terminated."

"On what grounds?" she demanded.

His eyes glittered with amusement at her apparent
naivety. "Perhaps you forget you are not in your
country, Miss Marlow. You stay here at our will, not
your own. It is a simple matter to find you unsatisfactory. As an example, being rebellious against well-
meant advice is quite pertinent. Your contract would
be handsomely paid off, and you would be expelled,
never to return."

"The royal family has been pleased with my service," she argued. "King Rashid—"

"King Rashid will be more concerned for his
daughter's happiness than yours, Miss Marlow. Unless there is some personal reason for him to keep you
here?"

Leah flushed at the pointed implication. "The welfare of the children—"

"Can be attended to. Easing Princess Samira
through a period of adjustment is of more urgent
consideration."

"So I have no choice but to accept your offer."

"That's correct."

Oh, no it's not! Leah promised him. The sheikh of Zubani was dead wrong if he imagined she would submit to his power. She had suffered from a total lack of choice when her parents had divorced. She was not a helpless child now.

"Perhaps I have already stayed too long in the Middle East," she said in icy disdain of *his* plan for her.

He raised one eyebrow in derisive challenge to her show of defiance. "Perhaps your brother has also, Miss Marlow. You wish to cause his fall from favour?"

Leah seethed at the shameless blackmail, yet knew the Arab culture automatically linked family members together. Favour or displeasure flowed to all and affected all. It was because of Glen that she had been welcomed and treated so well. Because of her, Glen could be summarily dismissed from a job he loved.

"I shall consult with my brother," Leah said stiffly.

"Do that, Miss Marlow."

He gave her a cruel little smile then strode away, having shattered her peace and menaced not only her future, but Glen's, as well.

Leah stood staring at the empty archway for a long time, fighting a paralysing sense of disbelief that the secure world she had constructed for herself could be taken away from her with a mere snap of the fingers. Or more accurately, by an act of will. Sharif al Kader's will.

This was her home, she kept thinking. She had made it her home. What right did the sheikh of Zubani have to uproot her from it?

She would ask for an audience with the king. King Rashid liked her. Though not in the way Sharif al Kader had intimated.

But what if the king did put his daughter's happiness first? Samira had to leave *her* home. The only home she had known. Not an adopted home, as it was for Leah. Would the king argue that Leah would be made just as comfortable in Zubani as she had been made here?

Despite the heat of the afternoon, Leah shivered. Impossible for her ever to feel comfortable in Sharif al Kader's household. His manner towards her was not indulgently paternal, like King Rashid's. He made her feel . . .

Leah instinctively shied away from examining what he made her feel. She simply wanted nothing more to do with him.

Glen would intercede with the king for her. The Arab respect for family would surely hold weight if Glen invoked it on her behalf. It would be all right, Leah assured herself over and over again. It had to be all right. After all, Glen's skill as a pilot had saved King Rashid's life when they had been forced to crash-land due to engine problems. King Rashid wouldn't want to lose Glen's services. Her brother's nerves of steel were legendary.

A rueful smile flitted over Leah's lips. She doubted anyone understood her brother as she did. Glen was more wedded to an airplane than he would be to any woman. Women didn't figure in Glen's life any more than men figured in Leah's. The hurt and betrayal of their mother's many infidelities had left him with little regard for the female sex. Except for Leah, who had shared that miserable time with him.

Flying gave Glen all the satisfaction he wanted in life. He shared an intimate relationship with whatever aircraft he was piloting, and was instinctively aware of what it could do in response to his handling of it. If truth be told, he had probably been more attuned to saving the plane than saving his own life or King Rashid's.

Nevertheless, the incident had raised Glen to hero status in Qatamah. Did Sharif al Kader know that? Could he really override the king's favour with his demands?

Leah shook off the lingering influence of the power that had emanated from him. Since there was nothing she could do about this situation until she talked to Glen, there was no point in churning over it or standing around in a daze. Yet she could not dispel the fear that clung around her heart, despite making a determined effort to get on with what she'd been doing before the sheikh of Zubani had invaded her life.

She picked up the wools that had fallen from the table when he had slammed his hand on it. The idea of her being a concubine made Leah burn all over again. She sat down in front of her tapestry and fiercely wished she had chosen some other print. But the Rubens was a fine dramatic picture, with definite lines and areas to it. Since her last tapestry had been an impressionist print by Manet, Leah had wanted a sub-

ject that was more clearly defined this time. Just
because it was naked women being carried off by men
on horseback did not mean she fancied such a fate for
herself.

Men, she thought in disgust, had only one thing on
their minds when it came to women. It had been more
important to her father to give himself the pleasure of
having a new wife than to take custody of the daughter of his first marriage. And her mother had been no
better. She hadn't stood up for Leah against the mean
little cruelties of her new husband.

Sharif al Kader was right about one thing. Leah did
have an empathy with children. If it turned out she
had to leave her job here, Leah knew what she would
do. Go back to Australia and find work in a child-care
centre.

Calmed with these thoughts, Leah picked up her
tapestry needle and resumed stitching with a dogged
determination not to think of Sharif al Kader again.
At least, not until she had to. She finished off the section of dark foreground and was threading the lighter
wool to begin on the woman's foot when she heard her
brother's voice calling out for her from her apartment.

"I'm in the garden, Glen," she called back, leaping to her feet in pleasure and relief at his timely visit.

She ran to greet him and they almost collided in the
archway. He grabbed her upper arms to steady her and
spoke with urgent haste. "Leah, I haven't much time.
Come inside with me quickly."

"What's the matter?" she cried, alarmed to find her
unflappable big brother in a state of tense anxiety.

His handsome face wore none of the easygoing confidence she was accustomed to. It was tight and strained, with no trace of the sunny, carefree disposition that was as much a part of Glen as his sky-blue eyes and his gold-streaked hair. He had vowed at the time of their parents' divorce he was never going to let anything touch him deeply again. Roll with the punches and keep coming up roses was his philosophy.

But something had got to him today. He ignored Leah's question, virtually bundled her into her living room, swiftly closed the door behind them, then began pulling his shirt out of his trousers.

"Glen!" she protested. "What on earth are you doing?"

"Taking off this money belt." His eyes fastened on Leah's with a sharp intensity that commanded her attention. "It holds ten thousand American dollars, Leah. I'm leaving it with you."

"What for? What do you want me to do with it?" she asked, bewildered and deeply disturbed by his manner and actions.

His gaze dropped from hers as he unbuckled the belt and slid it from his waist. "Put it in your bank account."

"I don't understand. Why don't you put it in yours?"

"Taxation purposes," he said as he headed for her bedroom.

Leah followed him, her agitation increasing as she watched him put the belt under the pillows on her bed.

"Have you been doing something wrong, Glen? Flying in contraband or—"

"No." He straightened and gave her a fleeting smile that was supposed to be reassuring, but wasn't. "It's all legitimate money, Leah. Don't worry about that."

"Then why—"

"Haven't got time to explain. The king has ordered an unscheduled flight. I've got to get going." He busied himself tucking his shirt in again as he strode to where Leah stood in the bedroom doorway. He moved her aside and dropped a kiss on her forehead. "Wish me luck, Leah," he said thickly, then attempted a devil-may-care smile.

Something was terribly wrong. "Glen, does this flight have anything to do with all the unease there's been in the palace today?"

The smile froze on his lips. His hands curled tightly around her shoulders. His eyes flickered with... Could it be despair? "What unease, Leah?" he demanded in an urgent rasp. "What's been going on? What's happened?"

"Don't yell at me, Glen."

His fingers dug bruisingly into her soft flesh. "Tell me. It's important!"

"Nothing that I could put my finger on," she said. "Just a feeling. I thought it had to do with the sheikh of Zubani coming. He appears to unsettle everyone."

"Nothing substantial then?"

"No."

His relief was palpable. As much as she wanted to unload her troubles on him, Leah realised this wasn't the right time to tell him about Sharif al Kader's threatening visit to her.

"I truly need to talk to you, Glen," she said fervently. "As soon as you get back."

"Leah..." A pained look crossed his face. Then suddenly he swept her into a hug that clamped her body to his so fiercely she could feel his heart thumping madly against the wall of his chest. He rubbed his cheek over her hair with a ragged tenderness that twisted Leah up inside. Glen had never shown affection like this. Usually it was a kiss on her nose or cheek or forehead, a fond hug of the shoulders, a squeeze of her hand. Leah had the frightening sense he was taking some last farewell of her.

"Stay in this apartment tonight, Leah," he ordered huskily. "If there's unrest in the palace, keep well away from it."

"Glen—" panic swirled through her mind "—this flight. Is it dangerous?"

He drew back enough to chuck her under the chin and give her a crooked smile. "Is there any flying job I can't handle?" His arm slid away from her as he planted a last kiss on her nose. "Got to go. Be a good girl and do as I say."

She trailed him out to the living room, desperately wanting to stop him from leaving her yet feeling helpless to do so. There was resolution in the rigidity of his squared shoulders, driven purpose in his step. He reached the door, opened it.

"Glen." It was a desperate little cry, an appeal not to leave her alone.

He turned reluctantly, her golden big brother who was father and mother as well as brother to her, all the family she had. But he had already said goodbye to her. There was a faraway look in his blue eyes, as though his mind was already set on his mission. "I have to go, Leah," he said flatly.

Her heart squeezed tight at the finality in his voice. "You said to wish you good luck."

A wisp of a smile. "*Inshallah,*" he said softly.

He left her with that word, the Arab word for "I hope." It held out no guarantee for tomorrow. It expressed the desert philosophy of uncertainty, where man is not governor of his own fate. He has only a loose hold on the reins.

Leah was riven by the terrible feeling she would never see Glen again. What would she do if he didn't come back? How would she survive on her own? She had lived in the warm cocoon of his protection for so long. Without him...

A dreadful sense of isolation closed around her. The dark image of Sharif al Kader supplanted Glen's in her mind. How could she fight *him* without Glen at her side?

Why was everything happening today?

It felt so wrong, wrong, wrong!

Then a dreadful thought struck her. This unscheduled flight that had been ordered... was the sheikh of Zubani behind it?

CHAPTER THREE

LEAH FELT TOO CHURNED UP to settle to anything. She brought her tapestry in from the garden but could not pluck up the interest to continue with it. She needed some distraction to take her mind off worrying about Glen. She could find it easily enough in the children's wing, but Glen had told her to stay in her apartment tonight. As harmless as the company of children surely was, Leah could not bring herself to ignore his protective warning.

She played a video of her favourite movie, but it failed to captivate her.

She fixed herself a light meal but didn't have the appetite to enjoy it.

Her restlessness was so pervasive that it was a relief when a knock came on her door, providing her with some brief but definite direction. She opened the door, only to be plunged into more perturbation. The nanny to the sheikh's children, the majestic Ethiopian, stood in the corridor, her beautiful face expressionless, her dark, velvety eyes staring unblinkingly at Leah.

"Can I be of help?" Leah asked, prompted into speech by the other woman's silence.

Without uttering a word, the woman turned and moved off down the corridor, walking with a slow,

swaying grace that was almost hypnotic. Leah roused
herself to try to find some sense in the woman's actions.

"Tayi? Do you want me to follow you?" she called
after her.

There was no response. The woman kept walking
away. Was she deaf? Unable to speak? No, that
couldn't be right, Leah reasoned. Tayi had responded
to the sheikh's command this afternoon. In any event,
she could have tried some gesture to make herself understood. So why had she knocked on Leah's door?

The answer that leapt into Leah's mind sent a wave
of fury through her. She slammed the door shut and
raged around her living room. Sharif al Kader was
using Tayi to check up on her, finding out if Leah was
in her apartment and whether she was alone.

He was an abominable man! No way in the world
would Leah consent to being part of his household.
Not for Samira's sake! Not for the children's sake! Not
for anyone's sake! Glen had to come back and sort this
out for her.

But what if he didn't come back?

She was standing in the middle of her living room,
in an agony of uncertainty when a more peremptory
knock came on her door. Perhaps she had misunderstood Tayi, she thought hopefully, and the Ethiopian
nanny had come back to make herself more clearly
understood this time. Since the idea of being spied
upon was intolerable, Leah again felt a surge of relief
as she went to answer the summons.

It was short-lived.

Two guards stood in the corridor. Their faces were stern, their bodies stiffly alert. One of them spoke in harsh, clipped tones.

"The king commands your presence, Miss Marlow. We are to escort you to the throne room."

Alarm skittered through Leah's heart. She was accustomed to seeing the king in the children's wing or the women's apartments, but never had she received an official royal summons to the throne room. She had been there only once, the day Glen had presented her to King Rashid, eight years ago. It was where the king held his morning *majlis* for the men of Qatamah to put their petitions to their ruler or tell him of problems. It was the place of government. It was not a place for women.

Yet a royal summons was a royal summons and could not be denied or ignored. Mindful of proper courtesy and custom, Leah swiftly said, "If you'll excuse me for a moment, I must put on an *abba.*"

As she turned, a strong male hand grabbed her arm, detaining her. "Come now."

The curt command allowed no argument. There was a look in their eyes that promised she would be taken by force if necessary. She chose the more dignified path of submitting to their orders, her trepidation growing with every step she took. To appear before the king in his throne room with her head uncovered and her face unveiled was tantamount to showing disrespect. For such a consideration to be swept aside had to mean that something terrible had happened.

Glen, she thought in sickening panic.

The moment she entered the throne room Leah found herself the cynosure of all eyes. Conversation stopped. The groups of men who lined the long room stiffened into silent observation. The attendants around the king drew back, revealing his regal presence on the throne. Seated prominently beside him was the sheikh of Zubani.

There was no smile of welcome from either man as Leah was ushered forward, and she was acutely aware that the atmosphere around her was not one of friendly sympathy. Something was very badly wrong, and Leah had never felt so frightened in her life. She kept her eyes trained on the grave face of the king, afraid that her shaky legs might falter if she so much as glanced at Sharif al Kader. Whatever this crisis was, every quivering instinct told her that the sheikh of Zubani was at the centre of it.

She managed a deep curtsey.

"It is with deep sadness that I see you here, Leah," King Rashid said solemnly. "Until a few minutes ago, it was thought you had accompanied your brother on his flight out of Qatamah."

"I don't understand, Your Majesty," Leah replied in bewilderment. "I have been in my apartment since my brother visited me this afternoon."

"So! He did come to see you."

"Yes."

His dark, liquid eyes filled with sorrowful hurt and accusation. "After all these years of being amongst us, you felt no loyalty to this household? You conspired with your brother to bring shame upon us?"

"What shame, Your Majesty?" Leah cried. "My brother informed me he was to take an unscheduled flight for you. He gave me no details of it. As far as I know, we have both been completely loyal to you and your family."

There was a mutter around the room. The king's long, noble face remained impassive. The sheikh of Zubani leaned over and murmured something to him. King Rashid nodded and signalled an attendant forward. The man leaned down and received some whispered instruction, then hurried from the room.

Leah watched all this with intense agitation. Was there some plot to discredit her and Glen? What had Sharif al Kader suggested to the king? Whatever was happening had to be his fault, she wildly decided, trying to drown her fear with a wave of righteous anger.

The king addressed her again. "Once it was confirmed that you were still in the palace—"

Confirmed by the Ethiopian nanny, Leah thought in bitter resentment. *His* loyal servant!

"There was only one course to be taken, Leah, and I have taken it."

The grim authority on the king's face engendered a presentiment of doom. Leah desperately clung to the idea that justice had to prevail in the end.

"I have ordered out the air force with instructions to intercept your brother's plane. If he does not respond to the command to turn back, he will be shot down."

Shock paralysed Leah for several moments. Her premonition of dire danger, of seeing Glen for the last

time, was coming true. Before she knew it her arms
stretched out in frantic appeal.

"But why? Why would you do that? What has Glen
done for you t—" she swallowed hard as bile rose in
her throat "—to order him shot down?"

The king's face could have been carved from stone
for all the impact her plea had on it.

"He has betrayed the trust I placed in him."

"How?" Leah begged.

The king's face tightened. A muscle contracted in
his cheek. He looked past her as though her question
deeply affronted him and he would not reply to it.

Leah waited for long, agonising moments for the
king to acknowledge her presence again. She was left
standing in unbearable tension. No-one spoke. No-one
looked at her.

Except Sharif al Kader.

Leah could feel his eyes boring into her.

She could feel his powerful aura swirling around
her, drawing on her like a magnet. She grimly fought
the insidious force that commanded her to meet his
eyes. She would not give him the satisfaction of any
acknowledgement he had been proved right about her
and her brother.

He wasn't right.

There had to be some dreadful mistake. Glen would
never betray the king's trust.

Yet Leah could not dismiss the anguished feeling
that had poured from her brother this afternoon in his
farewell hug. Glen must have known he was flirting
with death in what he planned to do. And King Rashid
did not make impetuous decisions. She frantically

searched her mind for some reason that might drive her brother to put aside all normal considerations, to risk this fatal condemnation from the king.

Had he felt his life was under threat anyway? But if that was the case, why not take her with him? Why leave her behind? He must have known she wouldn't want to stay here if he was never to return. From the king's earlier words, it had been assumed that Leah *was* with her brother. And from other implications made, it would seem Glen might have been safe if she had gone with him.

Try as she might, Leah could make no sense out of the sequence of events. She was still floundering through improbable possibilities when the nerve-tearing silence was broken by the return of the attendant who had been sent off earlier. Leah barely withstood another shock wave as she recognised what he held out to the king. It was the money belt Glen had shoved under the pillows on her bed.

A sense of outrage billowed over her shock. Her private apartment had been searched. That was what the sheikh of Zubani had suggested to the king. Leah seethed in impotent fury as King Rashid stared at the money belt and listened to his whispering attendant. Finally the king returned his gaze to her, and there was condemnation in his eyes.

"You still protest your innocence, Leah?" he scorned in a harsh voice.

"Of what am I guilty, Your Majesty?" she replied, her chin lifting defensively, her eyes defying any false judgement.

"This money belt was found hidden in your apartment. It is your brother's. The amount of money it contains is proof of your complicity in his treachery."

"Is it a crime for a brother to give his sister money?" Leah argued strongly. "I have no knowledge of any treachery, Your Majesty, and I cannot believe—"

"Enough! You will wait here for your brother's return, dead or alive." His eyes blazed a fierce denial of any further defence on her part. "There is no more to be said. You were party to the abduction of my daughter, the Princess Samira."

The accusation thumped into Leah's heart, shattering the spirit to keep on fighting for her own and her brother's integrity. Her mind grappled weakly with all the things that had been wrong today. Slowly, inexorably, they fell into a straight, inevitable line.

Samira, so tense and agitated this morning.

The wedding tomorrow.

The arrival of the sheikh, her designated bridegroom, who set about imposing his will on what he considered suitable for their marriage.

Glen saying goodbye, making what provision he could for Leah against the consequences of his mad, quixotic decision to fly away with Samira.

Not an abduction. Leah didn't believe that for one moment. It was the king's pride insisting his daughter had been abducted. To admit anything else would be an intolerable humiliation in front of the sheikh of Zubani.

No way in the world would Glen abduct Samira, or do anything to hurt or harm her. Rescue her, yes. If

Samira had pleaded with him for help, begging him to save her from being married to a man she had never met and didn't want as her husband, Glen would have felt deeply touched by that plea, whether he liked it or not. Not only did he have a strong protective streak, but Samira had always been his favourite amongst the royal children.

He had flown her away to school and home again over the years, shown big-brotherly interest in her progress from childhood to adolescence to womanhood, treated her hero-worship of him with indulgent kindness. Leah understood only too well that Samira would see Glen as her white knight, the one person in Qatamah she could turn to who could effect her escape and set her free of a future she did not want.

When had she made her decision?

When had she contacted Glen?

Leah shook her head at her futile musing. Sometime today the die had been cast, and Leah knew in her heart neither Glen nor Samira would turn back now. The runaway princess and her white knight would fly to their death rather than concede defeat.

A fierce pride in her brother's abilities battled the fear that his plane would be shot down. Glen was the best pilot in Qatamah. He would give the whole air force a run for their money. She wondered which plane he had chosen. Was it fast enough to outfly his pursuers? Or had he gone for manoeuvrability? The Harrier, perhaps.

The waiting played havoc with Leah's nerves, but she kept telling herself that each passing minute meant Glen and Samira were closer to safety. There was only so far to go before the pursuing air force would be intruding on some other country's airspace. Impossible then to shoot down a plane without creating an international incident, and that would be anathema to the king. The last thing he would want was worldwide publicity about his daughter's defection.

Leah called on every last fibre of pride to hold herself erect throughout the long ordeal of standing before the king until the final outcome of Glen's flight was known. She would not bow her head in any supposed guilt. She was innocent of any wrongdoing, and she was not ashamed of what Glen had done.

Nevertheless, when the king's eldest son, Prince Youssef, strode past her to hold counsel with his father, Leah felt herself sway from the strain of holding herself together.

Please, God, let it be good news, she prayed with desperate fervour. Glen had taught Prince Youssef to fly. They had been the best of friends. He couldn't shoot his best friend and his own sister out of the sky, could he? Surely his father would not have asked it of him. Yet he was in his airman's uniform.

The message he delivered was spoken in low tones, impossible for Leah to make out. The king slumped forward, covering his face with his cloak. A collective moan ran around the room. Youssef stepped back and swung around, his handsome face drawn with grief. He looked at Leah with such pain that she cried out in anguished protest.

"No, Youssef. No..."

"Neither of them will ever return, Leah."

Her knees startled to buckle, and she half stumbled towards him. Youssef caught her and held her upright, giving her the support she needed.

"Why?" he rasped, his eyes begging hers for an explanation. "Why?"

"Samira must have asked him. Glen wouldn't..." The defensive words trailed into silent desolation as she felt some vital part of her dying inside. Her brother, her beloved big brother, shot down.

"It's done," Youssef said in bleak resignation. "All that we shared... it's over."

He withdrew the support he had impulsively given her and strode away, leaving her to his father's mercy. Or rage.

Leah felt so numb that nothing mattered. With Glen gone out of her life, lost to her forever, it was totally irrelevant what the king might decide to do with her. Somehow she remained standing upright, suspended in a vacuum of nothingness. All she could think of was that she hadn't hugged Glen back, hadn't kissed him goodbye, and it was too late now to tell him how much he meant to her.

At the first sign of movement from King Rashid, Leah instinctively straightened her shoulders and lifted her head high. She was innocent of any treachery, and she would wear the badge of innocence to her grave, if it came to that. Her own life held no significance to her now, and she would not shame her brother's memory by acting like some snivelling coward.

Very slowly the king drew his cloak back, uncovering a face that had sternly put sorrow aside. He rose to his feet with regal dignity and swept his gaze around the room.

"Be it known," he proclaimed, "that my daughter, the Princess Samira, is dead."

There was a rippling murmur of agreement.

The king turned to the attendant who held Glen's money belt. He took it from him and tossed it contemptuously at Leah's feet. "Take your blood money and go, Leah Marlow. I expel you from Qatamar. You will be taken from this palace within the hour and flown beyond our borders. You will take no farewell of anyone, and you are never to return. Go now and pack whatever possessions you wish to take with you."

The sentence of expulsion reminded Leah of the sheikh of Zubani's earlier threat to her. A sense of bitter irony penetrated the numbness in her heart. Glen was out of Sharif al Kader's reach. Samira was out of his reach. And now she was out of his reach. Forever.

She felt a savage desire to scorn his power, and turned her gaze to the man sitting beside the king. Their eyes clashed in a challenge that sizzled with deeply primitive emotions. Sharif al Kader acknowledged no defeat. Leah found herself shaken by the searing force of his will. She tore her gaze away, but burned into her mind was the impression that he meant to exact payment for this loss of public face. He had no intention of ending up a loser.

She did not pick up the money belt. As much as she might need the ready funds, to take the belt with her was tantamount to admitting guilt, on her own part and on Glen's. She would not give anyone the satisfaction of that implicit confirmation.

She did not curtsey to the king. Nor did she bow her head to his judgement. Leah walked down the long throne room with slow, determined dignity, acutely aware of everyone's eyes watching her. There was one gaze she felt burning into her back. It could burn as much as it liked, Leah thought vehemently. The sheikh of Zubani would never see her again.

He might make many demands in compensation for what had been done to him, but he could make no demand regarding Leah.

The king had spoken.

She was free to go.

CHAPTER FOUR

LEAH WAS FLOWN from Qatamah to Dubai, the closest international airport. A car was waiting to take her to the passenger terminal. It was a courtesy she had not expected, given the circumstances of her leaving, but her mind was too laden with grief to question it. The king probably meant to have her seen onto a flight that took her to some other part of the world, far away from the Middle East.

Leah had travelled the route to the terminal many times. When the Mercedes deviated from it and turned towards the city she felt a niggle of disquiet. "Is there some repair work being done to the road?" she asked, since that was the most obvious explanation.

The driver said nothing. The guard in the front passenger seat replied, "A slight detour. No problem. We will get you to your destination."

Leah began to feel more disturbed when the car kept heading into the city. "Where is my destination?" she asked, wondering if she was to spend the night in a hotel.

Perhaps she had been booked onto a flight with a specific destination. An air ticket to Australia, she hoped. But would King Rashid give her that much consideration when he had expelled her with such towering condemnation? Unlikely.

She frowned when she received no reply. "Where are you taking me?" she asked more sharply.

"The sheikh of Zubani desires your presence. We are taking you to him."

Dear heaven! Leah thought in dazed horror. Would this terrible day never end?

"You can't do that!" she cried in frightened protest. "King Rashid ordered that I be—"

"You are no longer under the jurisdiction of Qatamar," came the cutting reply. "That border was crossed some time ago."

"I'm not under the jurisdiction of Zubani, either," Leah argued. "We're in Dubai."

"And we will very soon be out of it." The man in the passenger seat turned hard, impassive eyes on her. "May I suggest you relax. We have a long journey ahead of us. If you look, you will see a similar car to this in front of us, and another behind us. We are now travelling in convoy. There is no hope of escape."

The underlying threat was not lost on Leah. Whatever she said or did would have no effect on the final outcome. Sharif al Kader had her neatly and securely trapped in his power, and there was no-one to rescue her. No-one who knew where she was.

She slumped back in her seat and closed her eyes. *Oh, Glen!* she thought in abject despair. *What have you left me to?*

Yet she could not blame her brother for what he had not known. Glen had gambled that the king would let her go, and he had been right about that. He had gambled that Leah would understand the choice he had made to set Samira free, and she did understand, however deeply that choice grieved her now.

The mistake had been hers. She had not told him about the wild card in the pack, the outside force that could break any predictable outcome. She had underestimated the will of Sharif al Kader.

She was now his prisoner, and the only question was ... what form would his revenge take?

Wearily she opened her eyes and found they were speeding out into the desert on the four-lane highway that linked the United Arab Emirates. How far was it to Zubani, she wondered, but couldn't find the spirit to bother asking. As inexorable as the sands of time, so, too, was her eventual arrival there.

Meanwhile, she had already exhausted all her reserves of energy. She told herself she didn't care what Sharif al Kader wanted with her. Nothing could hurt more than Glen's death. She wished she had been in the plane with him. Since that oblivion had been denied her, she settled herself more comfortably into the cushioned leather seat and invited the oblivion of sleep.

It was dawn when she awoke, and they were still travelling through desert. The vast stretch of sand looked strangely luminous in the half-light. Large dunes rose above the road, their flanks falling sheer on one side, on the other shaped and scalloped by ripples of wind. A visual eternity of subtly moving desert.

Was it moving over Glen's plane—somewhere out there—already covering up the evidence of two lives linked together in death? Leah shivered and quickly closed her eyes again, trying to wipe the painful image from her mind.

The voices of the men in the front seat woke her the second time. She sat up and found they had left the desert behind. There were date plantations on either side of the road. Irrigation ditches divided the land into squares. Beneath the date palms were fruit trees and crops of market garden vegetables. Pomegranates and bananas and oleanders and vines grew among them. Pigeons fluttered around the big clay dovecots beside the occasional flat-topped dwelling. Leah looked ahead and saw that they were approaching a village.

"Where are we?" she asked.

"The oasis of Shalaan," came the obliging reply. "It is the sheikh's birthplace and spiritual home."

Had the sheikh retreated here for some spiritual re-boosting after his wedding fiasco in Qatamah? Leah frowned as she saw nothing that remotely looked like a palace. The only large building was the mosque, dominating the centre of the village. Despite the many new concrete constructions, the place was clearly a quiet backwater where goats and hens roamed the streets.

"Is this our destination?" she asked.

"Soon," was the unhelpful reply.

Once they were through the village, Leah did not need any assistance in identifying their destination. The road led nowhere else, and her heart quailed at what she saw at the end of it. A massive stone fortress

stood at the edge of the desert, looking as bleak and
unwelcoming and impregnable as any prison could be.

It was a huge square creation, the high and heavily
blocked walls supported at each corner by round towers. It had clearly been built to withstand attack
against marauding forces in the days of warring tribes,
and it was still rock solid, despite the ravages of war
and time and natural elements.

It suited him, Leah thought, this birthplace and
spiritual home. Born and bred to survival of the fit-
test. It had been her first impression of him, a man
finely honed by poverty, heat, hardship and desert
loneliness, rising above every test of his mettle to lead
his people into the world of the future. Daunting, intimidating, formidable and invincible.

But he was wrong about her.

A bitter pride rose out of her desolation over Glen's
death. Sharif al Kader could imprison her beyond any
possibility of escape, but she would prove him wrong
in his judgement of her. And she would fight any
judgement he made against Glen. She would not have
her brother denigrated in any shape or form. He was
a hero to her and always would be.

The entrance to the fortress was guarded by two
massive iron doors, standing open for them to drive
straight into the paved courtyard. Within the walls was
a continuous building running around all four sides,
fronted by an arcade, which opened onto the courtyard and provided ready shade from the sun. Tubs of
fruit trees at regular intervals provided some colour,
but did little to break the grimly austere look of the
place.

In the centre of the courtyard was an ancient well, undoubtedly drawing on underground water from the oasis, ensuring a constant supply to last through the longest siege. The cars slowly skirted it before coming to a halt in front of a large arch in the far wall.

The men poured out of their cars and were met by other men emerging from inside the building. There was a short conference. Leah remained seated in the back of her car, mentally steeling herself for the inevitable confrontation with Sharif al Kader. Eventually her travelling companion from the front seat stepped back and opened her door, signalling her to alight.

Leah gathered up her courage and stepped out, glad she was wearing the traditional long robe and *abba*, since she was once more the cynosure of all eyes. She had planned to change into Western dress at the international airport, but since her kidnap, there had been no opportunity to do anything. She was in considerable discomfort from the need for a bathroom, but she grimly maintained control of herself as she was ushered through an avenue of men.

Two black-robed women waited at the main entrance to the building. "Your servants," her guide informed her. "They will take you to your apartment and see to your needs."

Leah breathed a sigh of relief. Perhaps the sheikh had not yet arrived from Qatamah. In any event, she had a reprieve from an immediate meeting with him, as well as time to refresh herself and become oriented to her surroundings.

The women led her along the arcade to the adjoining side of the square, then up a narrow staircase to the

next floor. They went along a corridor, and at the end
of it Leah was ushered into an amazingly rich and
luxurious sitting room, Oriental in its furnishings and
with a heavy use of red and gold. The room was all the
more exotic for being circular, and Leah realised this
was part of one of the corner towers.

Astonished to find such contrast to the outer aus-
terity of the fortress, Leah was more prepared for the
equally lush and exotic furnishings of the adjoining
bedroom. She might be in a prison, Leah thought, but
it was certainly gilded with every creature comfort.

"Is there a bathroom?" she asked.

She was shown into a spacious en suite. The
plumbing left nothing to be desired, either. When she
emerged ten minutes later, she felt considerably better
and tidier. The women had begun unpacking her luggage, which had been delivered to the apartment.
Their movements were arrested by the sound of an
approaching helicopter.

"The sheikh comes!" one of them murmured, and
gave Leah a hard, searching look. Then they herded
her into the sitting room before scuttling away. This
must be the appointed waiting place, Leah thought,
fighting against the tension that knotted her empty
stomach.

The beat of the helicopter blades grew louder and
louder. Leah moved over to the long, narrow windows. They were barred and looked out to a chain of
mountains beyond the desert. Wherever the helicopter was landing it was out of her sight, but she heard
the engine cut off and the blades gradually whine to a
halt.

She wondered if she should sit on one of the silk brocade sofas, but decided she preferred to stand until Sharif al Kader sat. The behaviour of the servants left little doubt he was on his way to see her right now.

She remained at the window, staring out at the distant mountains. They rose up mistily over the horizon, their peaks hazy and insubstantial, stretching away as far as the eye could see. She heard a door open and knew he had entered the room. There was nothing hazy or insubstantial about the presence of Sharif al Kader. He emitted a force that jolted Leah's heart into nervous palpitation. Her hands clenched as she fought his effect on her, but she made no other movement, flouting his power with her stillness.

"Turn around!" he commanded.

She stubbornly defied him.

"Rebellious to the bitter end?" he softly mocked.

"Why have you brought me here?" she asked, her back rigidly maintaining her scorn of his authority.

He came up behind her, his nearness stirring a turbulence inside her that was impossible to control. It took an intense act of will not to shrink away, to resist every shrieking impulse to put some defensive distance between them. Her skin crawled with awareness of his greater physical strength, the hard maleness that sought to dominate her softer femininity.

But he did not touch her.

He made no attempt to enforce a submission to his command.

He raised an arm, pointing past her to direct her gaze. "See the pigeons down there," he said, his voice low and resonating intimately in her ear. "Many times

when I was a youth, I captured them with my bare
hands. At first, there's a sense of exultation in holding them, stroking the softness of their feathers, feeling their helpless fluttering—''

"Does it give you pleasure to take even a bird captive?" Leah bit out, fighting the fear clutching at her
heart.

His arm lifted, and as though deliberately enforc-
ing the image he had conjured up, he gently slid his
fingers through the fine silkiness of her hair, a sensual caress mesmerising in its underlying threat.

She felt her pulse quicken, and to her horror, knew
it was more from excitement than fear. What was it
about this man that mixed up her feelings in such an
alien fashion?

"I always let them go," he said softly. "When one
has the power, there is more pleasure in setting them
free."

It snapped the hypnotic spell he had been weaving
with his touch. Leah turned to him in surprise. "Does
that mean you captured me only to let me go? Purely
to feel your power?"

His dark, compelling eyes glittered with triumphant satisfaction, and Leah knew before he replied
that she had been trapped again, drawn into facing
him whether she wanted to or not.

His mouth curled into a cruel little smile. "Your
case is different. The pigeon did no harm to me."

"But I—" She cut off the futile protest. No point
in arguing. To his mind, to every Arab mind, Glen had
done this man an injury, and it was only right that his

family pay the price. Her innocence was totally irrelevant.

"Your brother stole my bride," came the flat indictment.

"No. Samira went with him of her own free will," Leah retorted, denying the false charge of abduction.

"She was promised to me."

"A promise her father made for her."

"She agreed."

"Under family pressure."

"There is no excuse for what was done, Leah Marlow. Your brother took the woman who in all good faith was promised to me. But I shall not go to a cold empty bed tonight. There will be a woman in it. From whom I shall take my pleasure."

He paused, and there was unbending ruthlessness in his eyes when he added, "And that woman will be Glen Marlow's sister."

"No," Leah whispered, unable to believe he would think of taking his revenge so far.

"Yes," he hissed, a deep, deadly anger searing her with its intensity.

"You can't—"

"I shall."

"Have you no decency?" Tears welled into her eyes, grief mixing with a burgeoning rage. "My brother was shot down because of you! Glen and Samira are dead because of you! Isn't that payment enough to soothe your damned pride?"

"Dead?" He gave a harsh laugh. "At this very moment they are probably in each other's arms, making love with all the passion of illicit lovers."

She stared at him in wild confusion, hope taking a soaring leap through every other emotion. "What are you saying? King Rashid announced—"

"The Princess Samira is dead in Qatamah. What else can she be, in the circumstances?" he savagely mocked. "But your brother owns the sky. Isn't that what is said of him by those who aspire to be his peer in the air?"

"Yes. Yes, it is," Leah whispered, hardly daring to believe what the words implied.

"That he goes where no other pilot dares to go. That he and his plane are one. And no-one could catch him. Or shoot him down. He was master of everything sent after him. Even supposedly unbeatable rockets. So it was said in Qatamah. In excuse to me."

"Oh, thank God!" Leah breathed, uncaring of the sheikh's rage or revenge. Glen was alive! Both he and Samira were alive, home free!

"I see you rejoice in your brother's escape. I hope you rejoice in my bed tonight," the sheikh drawled, jolting her out of the sweet elation that had replaced her leaden grief.

"You don't understand," she said impulsively. "Glen and Samira aren't lovers. He's like a big brother to her."

"Her knight in shining armour?" he mocked. "Saving her from the beast?"

Yes, Leah thought, but caution held her tongue in the face of Sharif al Kader's burning fury. Of course, he would not think of himself as a man from whom women had to be rescued. The offence went soul deep. Particularly when he had gone so far as to accept Leah into his household, against his better judgement, for the sake of making his bride as happy as he could.

The humiliation of Samira's rejection was personal as well as public, and Leah sensed that the personal hurt was far greater than the public one. "I'm sorry," she said quietly. "But I swear to you I did not know what they planned, and I played no part in it."

His eyes swept hers in cynical disbelief. "Your brother exchanged one sister for another," he said harshly. "He left you to me. Remember that when you exult over his freedom. Because you will never be free of me, Leah Marlow. Never!"

She suddenly realised his purpose in telling her Glen was alive. "You can't destroy the love I have for my brother," she shot at him.

He laughed. "You think I care what you feel for him?"

"If it's revenge you want, why not let me go on thinking Glen was dead?"

"Perhaps I didn't want a mourning martyr in my bed. A fiery spirit is much more exciting."

Leah flushed under the hot glitter of his eyes. "Glen didn't know what kind of man you are," she said, hating the strong sexuality he exuded, aware that it stirred something in her she did not want to acknowledge.

"What kind of man am I?" he asked with sardonic amusement.

Her eyes hotly challenged the primitive purpose in his. "I guess I'll find out tonight, won't I?"

"Resigned to your fate?"

"I'll fight you every inch of the way," she vowed vehemently.

"I shall enjoy that. Believe me—" his eyes gleamed with unholy anticipation "—I shall enjoy every moment of your surrender to me."

"You can undoubtedly take me by force," Leah fired at him with bitter contempt, "but believe me, Sharif al Kader, *I* shall never surrender to you. Never!"

"We shall see," he said with such arrogant self-assurance Leah wanted to hit out at him with a violence of feeling she had never experienced before. Again she clenched her hands, struggling for the self-control that continued to elude her in his presence.

"You left your tapestry behind in the royal palace at Qatamah. I had it packed for you." His smile taunted her unmercifully. "Perhaps you would like to spend the hours of waiting working on it, since the composition of colour and shape is so much to your liking. I'll have it sent up to you."

He turned and walked away from her.

"I left it behind because it reminded me of you!" she fired after him.

It was a bad mistake.

He paused in his step long enough to cast her a glinting look of satisfaction. "Yes. I thought it would. Until tonight, Leah."

CHAPTER FIVE

LEAH SEETHED over Sharif al Kader's interpretation of the Rubens tapestry. If he had thought she fancied being carried off and ravished by him, he would find out differently tonight.

She remembered his taunt about all the lovers she had tried and found wanting, a taunt she had angrily dismissed at the time, but perhaps she should have positively refuted his insulting insinuation. It might have saved her from this form of revenge.

If she told him she'd never had a serious lover, would it change anything?

He wouldn't believe her, came the swift answer.

And she wasn't about to explain the various events in her life that had shaped her attitudes towards that final act of intimacy.

Besides, to advance another argument about innocence would sound like pleading, and Leah was through with pleading. She would only demean herself in begging his forbearance. His mind was set, and nothing was going to change it. The philosophy of an eye for an eye and a tooth for a tooth was the order of the day. And night.

The heat of anger was banished by the chill of reality. There was no chance of escape for her. Not before tonight. But at least Glen was alive, she consoled herself. He would make inquiries about her, come after her in due course. Her brother would not leave her to rot in a desert fortress. Somehow he would find out where she was and rescue her. She knew he would.

Meanwhile... Her glance skated around the lavishly decorated sitting room, and this time Leah was struck by the sensuality of the furnishings, silks and satins and velvets, gold tassels on the cushions, smoothly polished wood, richly veined marble. This room, the whole apartment, shrieked of one purpose, an indulgence of the senses. And suddenly Leah knew where she was. These were the quarters set aside for a concubine whose duty it was to pleasure the sheikh.

Leah closed her eyes and took a deep breath as a wave of panic churned through her. She knew nothing about pleasuring a man, and she didn't intend to learn, either. She fiercely resolved to be the most unsatisfactory concubine the sheikh of Zubani had ever had. He might let her go once his taste for revenge proved too unpalatable to bother with any more.

A flock of servants interrupted Leah's bitter reverie. They brought a tray of fresh fruit, coffee, a plate of sweet biscuits and her tapestry on its custom-made stand with the accompanying box of wools. The manic impulse to tear the tapestry from its frame and hurl it out one of the barred windows was very strong. Common sense and a spark of proud defiance persuaded her she would very quickly regret such an action.

Firstly, she needed something to occupy her in this sumptuously sexual prison or she would probably go mad. Secondly, why should she let Sharif al Kader's twisted mind spoil her pleasure in an activity she enjoyed? She would mark off a section to do each day, and it would become a secret way of counting the days until Glen came to rescue her. Knowing that, she could laugh at whatever Sharif al Kader made of her interest in the tapestry.

It was a long day for Leah. She tried to block out what she had to face tonight by sleeping through most of the afternoon. It was not a highly successful ploy since fearful dreams chased through her mind. She was woken by a servant who had prepared a bath for her.

The water was scented. Leah momentarily rebelled at the thought of being *prepared* for the sheikh, but some of her muscles were stiff from the long journey in the car, and the idea of a soothing bath was attractive.

She was acutely aware of her body as she lowered herself into the water. She remembered Sharif al Kader undressing her with his eyes. Was it only yesterday? She hated the thought of him seeing her naked. She had spent most of her life covering up her femininity, and having it all bared to *his* eyes would be more a violation than anything else. Maybe she could avoid it. Maybe he would only want to *do that* with her, and it would all be over quickly.

Hope springs eternal, Leah thought with bitter irony. There was probably no hope Sharif al Kader would spare her anything.

It wasn't until she was dressed again and the servants had left that Leah found the knife. She was roaming the sitting room, trying to work off a bad case of nervous agitation when she spotted the ornamental *agal* on a side table. It had a gem-encrusted handle and a wickedly curved blade. She tested the latter for sharpness and realised she had a deadly weapon in her hands.

Her heart thumped madly as her mind leapt through the possibilities.

Could she protect herself with it?

Was she prepared to wound Sharif al Kader . . . kill him?

He had no right to take what he intended to take, yet was what he intended to do a fate worse than death? She would be facing certain death if she attacked the sheikh of Zubani with such a weapon.

Of course, she could always kill herself.

But while there was life, there was hope of being rescued.

Could she escape if the sheikh wasn't around to give orders? Were the cars still in the courtyard? In the dead of night when everyone was asleep, could she creep out and get away? Or were there sentries posted when the sheikh was in residence at the fortress?

So many things she didn't know and had no means of finding out. Unless she asked Sharif al Kader himself. She could pretend curiosity. But he would be suspicious. No, he would simply mock her curiosity, arrogantly confident she could not escape him.

She had to hide the knife.

Not in the sitting room. If she showed it there, he had the strength to overpower her. If it was to be done at all, it could only be done when he was fully distracted by . . . other things. Leah shuddered as she looked at the murderous blade again. Could she do it? If he was doing dreadful things to her, it would be self-defence. At least it gave her a choice. She could use it or not, as circumstances dictated.

She hurried into the bedroom and thrust the knife under the pillows on the bed where he meant to take her. She had to give herself a chance to stop him. He had no right to wreak such a terrible revenge on her. She was innocent of doing him any wrong whatso-ever.

She found that her hands were trembling, and hurried into the sitting room. She went straight to the window where she had stood this morning, curling her fingers tightly around the bars to steady herself. Her mind kept seeing the knife under the pillows. Madness, she thought, yet it took away the helpless feeling that had been eating at her all day.

Beware the claws of this pigeon, Sharif al Kader, she mentally hurled at him, then was startled when a door opened behind her, as though he had come to challenge her menacing thought. She swung around in wild defiance, only to find a stream of servants bringing in a sumptuous feast. Apparently the sheikh was intent on satisfying every appetite tonight.

The lamps were lit. The scene was set. But only one of the players was on stage as yet. The servants cast surreptitious glances at Leah, and she stared right back at them, uncaring what they thought. She wasn't here by her own free will and she would not thank them for following the sheikh's orders.

They no sooner left than their lord and master made his entrance. He was all in white save for the gold-and-

scarlet cord around his headdress. Leah was supposed to be in white, too. The women had laid out a
special robe for her, but she had scorned to wear what
he had designated. She had chosen one of the plain
black robes she had always worn when going outside
the palace at Qatamah. It was as sexless and unfemi-
nine as any robe could be.

She glared at Sharif al Kader, defying his critical
appraisal of her apparel. His mouth quirked into a
mocking smile.

"What are you mourning, Leah? Your lost virtue?"

"I'm not your bride," she retorted, and gave him a
scathing head-to-toe look before adding, "I have
nothing but contempt for the action you're taking."

He laughed and strolled towards her, his dark eyes
sparkling with devilish amusement. "Do you think
you are cheating me of pleasure with that unbecom-
ing garment? Hiding something I shouldn't see?"

He paused at the low central table where his vengeful wedding feast had been set out, picked up a bunch
of grapes, then took a circular route towards her,
around the sofas.

Leah tensed as she realised he would pass right by
the table where the ornamental *agal* had lain. She
watched him step-by-step, fiercely willing him not to
look, not to see the empty space that should not be
empty. His attention seemed to be fixed on the bunch
of grapes, his fingers idly picking through the cluster
as though intent on finding the most perfect speci-
men. She could detect no sideways glance as he passed
the danger area.

Leah almost sagged with relief. She was still collecting her distracted wits when the sheikh came to a halt in front of her.

"Have a grape," he said, holding one up to pop into her mouth. His eyes gleamed a teasing challenge.

Leah kept her lips closed, her eyes deriding the invitation.

"I can't tempt you?" he asked, popping it into his own mouth.

She disdained a reply.

"A hunger strike hurts you, Leah. Not me." He tossed the words at her carelessly, moving to examine the tapestry, which had been set up by the window for her. "Not a stitch done today," he observed. "Too unsettled? Or too excited?"

"I know you'll find this difficult to believe, but the decisions I make do not spin around you," Leah said acidly. "I shall eat when I want to eat, and I shall do as I please regarding everything else."

"Ah, yes!" he drawled. "The proudly independent Miss Marlow who will not bend to anyone's will."

He set the bunch of grapes on the windowsill, gave her a smile that sent danger signals down her spine, then moved on in what seemed to be a continuation of his walk around the room. Leah remained where she was, pretending to ignore his progress, pretending she didn't care where he went or what he did. Yet she was acutely aware of his prowling presence, and every nerve in her body was waiting for him to pounce.

Suddenly she felt fingers grazing down the sides of her face, scooping her hair back, lifting it up. The action happened so quickly, Leah simply froze in shock.

She was totally unprepared for the touch of warm lips on the exposed nape of her neck, the soft, sensual kisses that made her skin tingle with unbearable eroticism. She ducked her head in an instinctive bid to escape the sensation. An arm slid around her waist, pulling her against a hard, unyielding male body, and his lips moved to her ear, arousing such an electric feeling that she jerked her head aside.

"Your head bends to my touch," he murmured.

"Only to get away from it."

"I can feel your body tremble against mine."

"In indignation at being manhandled!"

It was a lie, and she knew it. She was frightened by the havoc he was stirring inside her. She pushed at his restraining arm, but it tightened around her. He trailed his lips down the outstretched curve of her neck, then back to her ear, softly nuzzling the lobe as he whispered, "Your skin is so soft, so fine, I think I shall find pleasure in tasting it all night."

"Stop it, damn you!" Leah cried, shaking her head violently to deter any further kissing. "I don't want this."

The caressing whisper roughened to a rasp. "What do you want? Pleasure or pain? It can be done either way."

"You can't give me pleasure," she declared vehemently.

"You think I don't feel your response to me?" He released her hair and softly stroked it to one side, splaying it over her shoulder. "It's yourself you're fighting, not me. And that's a fool's playground, Leah. Make your choice. Put on a martyr's mask and suffer my desire. Or be honest and let yourself relax and enjoy."

Her mind shied away from whatever truth was in his words. She thought of the knife. But it was too soon. She didn't know the things she needed to know.

"I'd like to eat first," she said. That would give her time to think, defer the moment that was coming and have the immediate effect of stopping him from doing these intensely disturbing things to her.

There was a moment of taut stillness from him, then he relaxed into a low laugh. "By all means, let us eat first." He smoothly spun her around to face him, and while Leah was still off balance, he tilted her chin, compelling her to meet the glittering mockery in his eyes. "Shall we start with an appetiser?"

His mouth closed on hers with a devastating swiftness and sureness. Her body was swept against his, allowing her none of the personal space she had clung to for so long. She felt unbelievably weak and helpless against the power of his invasion. Shields that she had erected against all men were smashed to smithereens. Her whole body was suffused with sensitivity, absorbing the imprint of his.

The wild, reckless passion of his kiss stirred sensations both frightening and fascinating. Frightening because she had no control over the feelings induced by what he was doing to her, fascinating because they weren't unpleasant. Leah was conscious of a desire to know more, a curiosity mixed with a strange yearning for a fulfilment she had never known. He aroused some deep feminine need in her that had never been aroused by any man before, something primitive that

urged her to savour this new inner world of swirling
excitement, to feel all there was to feel in the mating
of a man and a woman. But years of deeply ingrained
inhibitions made her fight against the tantalising
temptation. She could not let herself be dominated by
this rampant sexuality.

She twisted her head and shoulders away from him,
breathing in hard to sober the seductive turbulence
that had shredded her dearly held convictions. She
would not be like her mother. Or her father. Never
would she let the treacherous need for physical satisfaction rule her heart and mind! And that she could
feel such things with a man who intended taking her
in place of his wife was the ultimate in madness!

"You're vile!" she spat, her mouth still throbbing
with the taste of his.

"But you tremble."

"From weakness. I haven't eaten since this morning."

"You have a reason for everything. But is it what
you feel?"

"You're drunk with your own power, Sharif al
Kader."

"I'm intoxicated with the thought of setting you
free."

It snapped her head up. She searched his eyes, not
wanting to be fooled. "You're just playing with me?
You mean to set me free?"

There was a flash of irony. "There are many kinds
of prisons, Leah. Freedom can be a state of mind. If
you mean physically... yes, eventually. After the bride
price has been paid."

Bitterness rose from that swiftly crushed illusion. "You know what you're doing to me will be found out. Your name will be denounced throughout the world."

His eyes hardened. "It will be feared."

"Is that what you want?"

"It is better than being laughed at. I shall command respect. What has to be done to achieve that purpose will be done."

"But it doesn't have to be," Leah argued, trying one last desperate plea. "If you think it's necessary to have it known that I was taken in Samira's place, I don't mind going along with the story."

"And give you the chance to betray my trust, as your brother betrayed King Rashid's?"

"But—"

He placed silencing fingers on her lips. "There is no argument that will change my mind." The grim set of his mouth slowly softened into an indulgent smile. "But I shall feed you first."

Leah was once more stunned by the way his face could be transformed by a smile. What was the power that lit this man's soul, that could make him a figure of dark menace or a man of compelling attraction?

While she was still staring at him in bedevilled confusion, he stooped and swept her off her feet, cradling her against his chest with alarming possessiveness.

"Put me down!" Leah cried in panicky protest.

He grinned at her. "You said you were weak from hunger. If I remove my support you might faint from lack of strength. So being a kind and considerate host, I shall carry you to a sofa.''

"Oh!" Leah gulped, and as he carried out his declared purpose, she found she was mad enough to wonder what it would be like to be married to such a man. And if Samira had been a fool to run away from him.

Which meant things were going from bad to worse, and she had better straighten out her muddled mind and firmly ignore treacherous feelings or she would end up being the spineless victim! And how could she hold her head high after that?

CHAPTER SIX

LEAH WORKED HARD on restoring an appropriate simmer of justifiable hatred for Sharif al Kader's treatment of her. Her whole body burned with it. Or so she sternly told herself. She was certainly considerably heated from the way he held her around her thighs and pressed her to his chest.

He leaned over a chaise longue and as he set Leah down on it he swept the decorative cushions onto the floor. Having seen to her comfort, and with a casual air of pleasing himself, he proceeded to toss every cushion from every sofa onto the floor between Leah and the round table.

It was just as well she hadn't chosen to hide the knife behind them, Leah thought. He would be laughing at her now, his dark eyes mocking her futile attempt to change the course of this night. Despite the reassuring knowledge she still had a card up her sleeve, Leah's heart fluttered nervously as he sank down on the cushions beside her.

"Let me make you more comfortable," he said, and before Leah could guess his intention he deftly slid the light sandals off her feet.

She instantly curled her legs up away from him.

His eyes danced teasingly at her. "Cast aside your fears, Leah. This is a night for loving."

"There's no love involved in what you're doing," Leah retorted hotly.

"What is love?" he countered, raising a quizzical eyebrow.

"It's caring about what the other person feels."

"But I do care what you feel, Leah." He reached out, picked up a dish of perfect melon balls and offered it to her. "Here I am, catering to your needs."

She had to fight the impulse to throw the whole dish in his tauntingly handsome face. Sanity prevailed. She ate some melon and worked on getting her mind straight. She was wasting precious time reacting to him instead of steering her own course.

"How old is this fortress?" she asked, hoping to lead him into answering more pertinent questions.

"It has stood for over a thousand years, protecting the oasis of Shalaan from those who wanted to seize control of the ancient caravan routes from the mountains to the sea."

"The men who brought me here said it was your birthplace and spiritual home."

"It is true. My family has ruled this land for many centuries. This is our ancestral holding."

Leah wondered what it would be like to belong to a family and tradition that had continued unbroken for centuries. She had no sense of roots at all. Glen had been her only mainstay in a life marked by shifting loyalties and relationships. It was one of the things she had admired about the Arab way of life, the security of closely knit family where doubts about one's position were never harboured.

Samira would miss that. The probability was that Samira would feel more lost and lonely than Leah had ever felt, and end up bitterly regretting the choice she had made. It was so easy to overlook what one took for granted until it was no longer there. Did Glen realise the enormity of what he'd done in taking Samira away from all that had been dear and familiar to her? Why had marriage to the sheikh of Zubani been so repugnant to her?

Leah looked searchingly at him as he returned the dish of melon to the table. Handsome, intelligent, powerful. He might not have made the most comfortable of husbands, but if one were to choose a man to have children by, Sharif al Kader was certainly not without many attractive qualities. To all intents and purposes, he had been a very good match for Samira.

Leah was jolted out of her introspection when he offered her a finger bowl to wash away the melon juice. He threw her into more internal turmoil when he made a slow, sensual ceremony of wiping her fingers dry, one at a time, with a soft hand towel. Why did his touch affect her in so many disturbing ways? *I mustn't think about it,* Leah swiftly cautioned herself.

"There can't have been any practical need for this fortress for a long time now," she remarked.

He lifted his head, pausing in his playful task to give her an ironic smile, creating more internal havoc for Leah. "I do find a practical use for it now and then."

"But you don't post guards or anything like that, do you?"

His smile grew wider and he lifted her hand to his lips. "Looking to escape me, Leah?"

She watched in fascination as he slid one of her fingers into his mouth. She felt her stomach clench in some wild anticipation.

Stop it! her mind screamed. She wrenched her gaze up to his, saw a smouldering satisfaction in his eyes and tore her hand out of his grasp before he could entrap her any further with his potent brand of sexuality.

He laughed and turned to the table to select another dish. "The chicken salad looks tasty," he mused. "Would you like to try some?"

"Yes," she said huskily, then swallowed hard to get more self-assertion into her voice. "The gates to the fortress were open when I arrived this morning. Can they still be closed?"

"Of course. We would never let this fortress fall into disrepair. The doors are always closed during a sandstorm."

"At no other time?"

His eyes twinkled amusement as he handed her a small plate of salad. "There is no need," he answered. "I can hold you without sealing the fortress, Leah."

She could not control the flush that swept into her cheeks. "Do you make a habit of locking up your concubines in this apartment?" she shot at him in fiery contempt.

His amusement slid into something far more dangerous and heart twisting. "I have never been tempted that far by a woman. I was satisfied with my first wife.

And I anticipated being satisfied with my second. This apartment was prepared for her pleasure. Not for any concubine.''

No wonder the servants had acted as they had! She was wrong for their sheikh, wrong in every way, since she was not his wife and never would be.

Despite her antagonism towards him, she could not doubt what he said, and it forced her to reevaluate the man. He had looked forward to his new marriage, prepared for it, sought ways to make his bride happy, even to employing Leah against his personal inclination, purely to give Samira a familiar companion. That kind of dedication to making a marriage work evoked respect.

But Sharif al Kader was still a menacing force, Leah reminded herself, and it was sheer stupidity to feel any sympathy or compassion for him. He allowed none for her.

She forced herself to eat the light helping of chicken salad, a mixture of chopped meat and cucumber and celery, blended together with a sweet mayonnaise.

At least now she knew the way out of the fortress was open. If she could keep spinning out the time before he took his satisfaction from her, she might have a chance of getting away.

If she could bring herself to use the knife!

"Why did you accuse me of being a concubine if you don't have them yourself?" she asked resentfully.

He gave her a searing look that completely undermined her hard-won composure. "Perhaps I found you too desirable to imagine anything else."

"Well, you were wrong," she snapped. "And this is wrong."

"On the contrary, never have I felt anything so right."

Leah berated herself for making another useless protest. She thrust her empty plate at him, desperate for more distraction.

He supplied her with a variety of delicacies, infinitely patient in pleasing her appetite yet subtly making her more and more aware of what was coming. He idly stroked the soles of her feet, caressed her hair away from her face, wiped a pastry crumb from her lips, a light, gentle, seductive, touching, relentless in arousing a constant and acute sensitivity. If she pulled away, he simply moved his hand to somewhere else, to touch again where she least expected it. And always the predatory look in his eyes, waiting, watching her resistance dwindle into helplessness.

What could she do?

There was no evading him.

He had a countermove to any move she made.

If she tried to fight him, he would revel in subduing her with his superior physical strength. She knew he would. And she hated the thought of letting him feel that kind of power over her. Yet was submission to his insidious touching any better? It was more dignified, she argued to herself. And it lulled him into being off guard. She still had the knife to stop him from taking his ultimate revenge.

But could she do it?

And where would it lead?

Leah found it harder and harder to keep any train of thought in her mind. The sense of there being no escape from Sharif al Kader, no matter what she did, became more and more pervasive. Eating became a mechanical exercise, purely defensive. She tried asking questions to promote conversation, but somehow words became meaningless. She drank what he gave her to drink, and he sipped from the same golden goblet, making an intimate ceremony of it, his lips replacing hers, his eyes compelling her to watch, to feel the bond he was forging with everything he did.

She felt she was drowning in his eyes. When he leaned over and kissed her she did nothing to stop him, even though he did not storm her mouth as he had before. It was the gentlest of pressures, his lips grazing softly over hers, slowly, hypnotically, drawing her into a response. Her lips moved, clung to his, parted, and then she was whirling into an ever-increasing spiral of sensation, lost to any outside reality.

She felt strangely weightless when he lifted her from the chaise longue. As he carried her in the protective warmth of his arms, her whole body seemed to pulse to the beat of his movements, a drumming of inevitability that could not be turned aside. It was only when he set her on her feet and disrobed her that a frisson of horror ran through Leah, yet it did not have the power to drive any resolution into her mind. Her hands fumbled in agitated protest as he removed her underclothes, but before the chill of her nakedness could permeate the swirling chaos inside her, he was naked, as well, and pressing her to his warmth again.

The shock of feeling his flesh against hers was intense. Her thighs quivered against the hard strength of his. Her stomach contracted, shrinking from the threat of his fully aroused virility, yet clenching with excitement at the same time. Darts of piercing sensitivity exploded through her breasts. His mouth ravished hers with a sweet violence as his hands roamed her back, caressing, moulding her softness with a possessive desire to have and to hold all that she was.

Her hands moved, drawn by a need that could no longer be denied, sliding up the powerful muscles of his thighs, over the taut mound of his buttocks, discovering the pit of his back and travelling on in their blind quest of fascination with his maleness.

He swung her onto the bed and rolled with her, their bodies entangled in a mesh of limbs, his face buried in the silky flow of her hair, her hands finding the fascination of soft curls at the back of his neck. He trailed burning kisses over her shoulder, moving with devastating passion to the swell of her breasts. Leah arched in a paroxysm of wild feeling as he kissed them, sucked on them, swirled his tongue around nipples hardened to fierce arousal.

Her body was a mass of writhing nerves when he moved lower. She clutched at his head but was hopelessly distracted by the stirring caress on her inner thighs. It drove her beyond control. She didn't know what was happening to her. It was frightening, as though she was undergoing some metamorphosis, everything inside her breaking down and flowing into some other form. She ached for it to be finished.

She was barely aware of the movement that at last provided focus for the torment inside her—Sharif's arms under her, lifting her, and the welcome pressure of his body entering hers, a solidity that she craved. She was totally uncaring of the tearing pain of his penetration. A sigh of relief whispered from her lips as her body found form again, convulsing in exquisite pleasure around a firmness that was wonderful. She cried out in anguished protest when he started to withdraw what he had given her, then moaned with satisfaction when he surged more deeply to fulfil her need again.

Slowly her body began to hum to the rhythm of his movement, to sing exultantly to each inward beat, to soar with wild elation then swoop to throbbing antic-ipation, only to soar higher and higher with every sweet thrust of his possession. She felt herself melting around him, a strange, warm flooding on which she floated into blissful contentment. And the movement stopped, as though their togetherness was sealed for-ever.

She was vaguely aware of Sharif carrying her with him as he rolled onto his side. She could hear his heart thumping madly and idly wondered why. Her heart was at peace. Everything had slowed down. Her limbs felt limp and heavy, although tingling in the after-math of such extreme turbulence. It felt good when Sharif began to stroke her back, softly soothing. She shivered with pleasure, her skin still alive with sensi-tivity.

"Leah..." There was a strained note in his voice, as though it pained him to say her name. His arms came around her in an enveloping sweep, holding her more firmly to him. She felt his chest rise and fall in a deep sigh. Then, in flat murmur, he said, "It is done."

It is done.

The words echoed in Leah's emptied mind, gathering a force that shattered her peace. Her heart hammered an agonised protest at what he meant, but there was no denying the truth of those pitiless words. He had done what he had set out to do, avenging the wrong that had been done to him. That was all this meant to him.

Revenge!

And she had shamed herself in letting him have it, becoming a willing party, an avid, completely wanton party to the lovemaking that had nothing to do with making love. Humiliation swept through her from head to toe. She had let herself be seduced and deceived by a sexual expertise he had wielded like a weapon against her, totally careless of what wounds it left. If he had knifed her heart it couldn't be worse.

The knife!

A surge of bitter hatred fired her blood. She pushed out of his arms, scrabbled under the pillows for the *agal* she had hidden there. Her fingers found the gem-encrusted handle, curled around it. A savage satisfaction gripped her. She could deliver vengeance as ruthlessly as he.

He had turned on his side, was looming over her, dark and menacing again. No more, she thought in violent mutiny. The knife did not even clear the pillow. She knocked the obstruction aside as her hand swept up and stabbed down.

A rock-hard palm stopped the killing arc, jarring the bones of her arm. Steel fingers closed around her wrist like a vise.

"Let me go!" she screamed at him.

He pried her fingers from the handle and flung the *agal* across the room. She flailed at him with her free hand, wanting to punch and claw and bite in her furious frustration. He captured it, pinning it down with the same viselike grip as he moved his body over hers, defeating her fierce struggle against him with his superior weight. She lay helplessly beneath him, heaving her rebellion until the last shred of mad strength drained away.

"Even now, after what we shared, I cannot trust you."

He breathed the words with harsh feeling, and to Leah's ears the accusation held the most bitter irony. "From the moment I first set eyes on you, I knew you couldn't be trusted," she spat at him.

"Yet there was one thing you did tell the truth about," he acknowledged. "You have never been with another man."

She glared at him, hating all his judgements of her, hating all he had made her feel. Everything false! "You were the first. And as God is my witness, you'll also be the last!"

He shook his head. "Why are you so embittered?"

"Because people tell you that they love you, but they don't care about you. It's all lies!"

"And if you were to find someone with whom it could be different?" he asked with insidious softness.

"I wouldn't believe it," she retorted with vehement passion.

"Who hurt you so badly, Leah?"

She couldn't say her mother or her father. In the Arab culture that would be unthinkable. "People like you who only care for what they want."

"Is that all you have known?"

No, there was Glen. Glen had always cared. But he had left her to this man, left her to be taken and... Tears welled into her eyes.

"Leave me. Let me go," she choked out, her throat thickening with an uncontrollable swell of painful emotion. "You've had your revenge."

But he did not let her go or leave her. He moved to one side and gathered her into his arms, holding her tightly to him as she wept out her grief for all the faith and trust and love that had been taken away from her.

CHAPTER SEVEN

LEAH AWOKE SLUGGISHLY. Her eyelids felt too heavy to open. Better to go back to sleep, her mind said. She moved to settle her head more comfortably on the pillow and instantly felt the alien sense of nakedness. She froze as the memory of last night burst into full consciousness.

Was he still in the bed with her?

She held her breath and listened.

No detectable sound.

Her nerves screaming caution, she slowly raised her eyelids.

The dark eyes of Sharif al Kader looked down at her with indulgence. He was propped on his side, and a long tress of her hair was woven through his fingers. He smiled. "You slept long and well."

Leah's heart clenched. She closed her eyes and fiercely wished she had never woken. She didn't want to face another day with him in it. He did things to her that she had no answer to.

What manner of man was he?

He should have spurned her after she had struck at him with the knife. If he had called up his guards and had her dragged off to some vile dungeon, that would have been in keeping with what she had thought him to be.

Why had he held onto her? And the gentleness with which he had settled her for sleep when she had exhausted herself with weeping, the tender way he'd stroked her hair as though she was a troubled child, comforting, soothing... It didn't fit the other things he'd done.

Although it did, in a way. He hadn't taken her roughly, as she had dreaded he might. But that only made it worse in the end. A spasm of anguish twisted through her at the memory of what she had felt, lifted to incredible heights of ecstasy, then crushed by the horror of knowing all the wonderful intimacy was a lie.

Some of her feeling must have shown on her face. He tenderly cupped her cheek and asked, "Do you hurt, Leah?"

She glared at him, rejecting his concern, which only disturbed her further. "I don't want you here."

"As you wish," he said surprisingly, and bent to brush his lips over hers, leaving them tingling.

She watched him roll away from her, then stride around the bed to where their clothes had been dropped on the floor. She could not help thinking he was beautifully made, his body sleekly muscled, firmly fleshed and perfectly proportioned. He moved with the grace and assurance of an athlete who knew precisely what his body could do.

He walked past the clothes, and Leah shuddered with revulsion when she saw him pick up the *agal*. Whatever her fate with Sharif al Kader, she was glad his reflexes had been quick enough to check that utterly crazed attack.

She tensed as he straightened, expecting him to make some critical comment on her extreme action. He gave her a sardonic look. "It was a good stroke. Straight at the heart."

Leah stared at him in helpless confusion. Could he shrug off a threat to his life so easily? Was he without fear?

He moved to the heap of clothes and scooped them over his arm, including her black robe.

"That's mine," she said.

"Yes, I know." His eyes glittered some deep satisfaction at her. Then he crossed to the ornately carved wardrobe, opened the door, found her other black robe and threw it over his arm, as well. "I do not want you to wear black," he said.

"Why? Because it would make you feel guilty?" she shot at him.

He raised a mocking eyebrow at her. "Of what should I feel guilty, Leah?"

She flushed, painfully aware that her vengeance had been far more grievous than his. But he had driven her to it.

His eyes burned into hers. "It was right, Leah. Never have I felt it so right. No matter the reason it was done, or why you are the way you are, you cannot say you did not feel it was right between us. And I will not let you devalue what we felt together."

The arrogance of certain knowledge was stamped on his face, and Leah's denial stuck in her throat. No other man had even come close to stirring her into the responses he had drawn. Would there ever be another man who could? And Sharif had felt the same.

She stared wonderingly at him as he walked to the door to the sitting room. Was that why he had forgiven her the knife? Had he understood what she felt because he also had felt something beyond his experience?

He opened the door and paused to look at her. "Will you be ready for breakfast in half an hour?"

"Yes." A cup of coffee was precisely what she needed.

"I'll join you in the sitting room and we shall have it together."

Leah frowned, not having expected another session of togetherness so soon.

"Did you really think I would leave you alone, Leah?" he asked softly.

"Why not?" she flashed at him. "Isn't your revenge complete?"

His smile mocked her reasoning. "Have you forgotten that a month was scheduled for wedding celebrations?" His eyes gleamed with determined purpose. "I think I shall find it a very interesting month with you."

He left her with that thought, and to Leah's intense displeasure with herself, her sense of outrage was considerably depleted by a treacherous feeling of lively anticipation. She couldn't *want* to spend a month with him.

But he was the most intriguing person she had ever met.

That didn't mean she wanted to stay with him. Not at all. It simply meant that since she didn't have any apparent choice about it, she might as well spend her captivity trying to satisfy the curiosity Sharif al Kader aroused in her.

She needed something to lift her mind off the terrible storm of sexuality he had the power to invoke. And she would certainly fight that next time. She had to. It could never be right to her. Not in these circumstances.

She was not going to succumb to such dreadful mindlessness again. He might force a surrender of her body until such time as she *could* get away from him, but she would never let herself forget she was here to satisfy his sense of revenge. Whatever other satisfactions he got from her were incidental to that. She would not let him delude her into thinking there was something *right* in anything they shared together.

Half an hour later Leah was washed, groomed and dressed in blue. Her captor might have prevented her from wearing black again, but be damned if she would wear white for him!

When she entered the sitting room, the remnants of last night's feast had been cleared away and the cushions replaced. As she wondered when the cleaning up had been done, servants started bringing in the breakfast their sheikh had ordered. The sound of an approaching helicopter caused them to pause in their work. They looked at Leah, as though it had to be connected to her.

Leah wished it was, but knew it was far too soon for Glen to know of her predicament, and there was no-

one else who cared enough to rescue her. Nevertheless, she soon realised that the arrival of the helicopter carried some import. The servants left, several
minutes ticked by, and the sheikh of Zubani did not
make an appearance.

Since it was unlike him not to do what he said he
was going to do, Leah could only conclude he had
been unavoidably delayed by matters that demanded
his urgent attention. She decided there was no point in
letting the hot croissants get cold. She poured herself
a cup of coffee and sat down to eat, telling herself
what she felt at being left alone was definitely relief,
not disappointment.

She had finished her breakfast when he made his
entrance, perversely enough wearing a plain black
robe and a black cord around his white headdress. His
dark eyes glittered with some private satisfaction as he
appraised her appearance, but he made no comment
on it.

"You did not wait?"

"No. Why should I? You made the appointed
time," she reminded him tersely, more from the tension his presence brought than from any offence at his
tardiness.

"Forgive me," he said, a smile twitching his lips.
"A visitor arrived."

"Someone important?" she asked curiously.

"It should be interesting."

Again that glittering look of satisfaction.

Leah didn't know what to make of it, but she knew
intuitively he was not about to elaborate.

He poured himself a cup of coffee and sat down on the sofa opposite her. He wore an air of preoccupation as he ate a light breakfast. Occasionally he cast a speculative glance at Leah but he made no attempt at conversation. She did not know why he was bothering to pass the time with her.

Pride forbade her to show any inclination for a more companionable effort from him. Having borne his silence for far longer than any normal politeness demanded, Leah stood up and walked over to her tapestry. Her sense of independence dictated that she pay him even less attention than he was paying her. She opened the box of wools and selected the colours required for the section she would do today.

"Blue becomes you."

Leah ignored the appreciative remark. She concentrated on threading a needle, which was difficult. She could feel the full force of his attention burning into her.

"Leave that, Leah," he softly commanded. "We are about to take a little walk. I want you with me."

The lure of the open air was enough to convince Leah that any rebellious stance was self-defeating. Besides, it might be to her advantage to learn everything she could about the fortress and its environs. Who knew what loophole she might find for escape in the month ahead?

She put down the needle and swung around. He was on his feet, turned towards her, the light from the window shining directly on his face. Leah was instantly reminded of her first sight of him. The aura of indomitable power forged to his will, his way, his destiny, was so strong, Leah was once more swept by a weird fluttery sensation. Like the pigeon caught in his hands, she thought, with a little stab of fear.

"Where are you taking me?" she asked, a brittle edge to her voice. *The walk* suddenly had dark menace behind it.

"To the room where I usually hold *majlis* when I am in residence."

"I thought that was for men only."

"You shall be the exception today."

"Why?"

His mouth curled into a cruel little smile. "Because a nail is driven home most effectively with a hammer." He gestured towards the door. "Come. It has been a long enough wait."

Leah could make no sense of his enigmatic words, but it was crystal clear he was in no mood to brook any disobedience to his command. She took the course of dignified compliance, but her mind warred between fear and curiosity. Something was afoot, and Leah had the sinking feeling that her part in it was not as an onlooker.

They did not go outside. He led her into a corridor that took them to a wide staircase. At the foot of this was a spacious foyer, decorated with murals made of tiny ceramic tiles. Guards stood on either side of the arched entrance to the courtyard. Another set of guards stood at the double doors at the far end of the foyer. As their sheikh and Leah approached these doors, the guards moved into place to open them at his command.

Sharif al Kader paused in front of them. He took Leah's hand and placed it on his arm, holding it there with his other hand. "So, my little captive," he said with sardonic amusement. "We shall see how the crimes are to be appeased."

Leah knew his fingers would tighten around hers like steel bands if she tried to remove her hand. She could feel the latent power there, ready to take action. Did he intend to flaunt his possession of her in front of his people? Was this the next step in his revenge?

He nodded to the guards and the doors were flung open. Leah called on all her inner resources to detach herself from whatever was planned. It had no meaning to her. A month, at most, and she would be away from here. Yet as they entered the reception room, Leah's resolve to cocoon herself against the reaction of a crowd of men was totally shattered.

There was only one man waiting for them. He rose from his chair, a startled sound breaking from his lips as he stared at Leah. His gaze jerked to Sharif al Kader, down to the hand clasp on the sheik's arm, then back to Leah. His expression changed from shock to anguished dismay as he saw the flush of shame and humiliation burn into Leah's cheeks. Her legs would have faltered if she had not had the enforced support of the man who held her captive.

Over the years of his close friendship with her brother, Prince Youssef of Qatamah had always treated Leah with the respect he gave to his own sisters, the kind of respect Sharif al Kader had ruthlessly violated. Youssef knew—it was too obvious for him not to know—why she was being paraded in front of him.

Nevertheless, it was imperative that all personal feelings about this situation be set aside. He had undoubtedly been sent by his father, King Rashid, to perform a highly delicate political mission, and that could not be jeopardised. He made a valiant attempt to recover before the sheikh of Zubani came to a halt in front of him.

Formal greetings were made and returned.

The sheikh escorted Leah to a chair that had been set beside his. He released her long enough for her to sit down, then as he settled himself he took her hand again and held it under his on the armrest of his chair.

The action was pointed enough to draw Youssef's attention. Leah saw the struggle on his face, saw it harden into resolution. He lifted his gaze to hers, silently promising all the support he could give, then with an air of proud integrity, he turned to the man he had to challenge.

"Forgive me, Your Excellency, this is not what I have come to say, but may I put to you that you have an innocent hostage in Miss Marlow."

"You surprise me, Your Royal Highness," Sharif al Kader drawled. "Believe me, Miss Marlow is not a hostage. She remains with me at my pleasure."

The deliberate emphasis on Leah's fate made Youssef flinch. Leah felt an intensely bitter hatred towards the man who held her forcibly at his side. He was sparing her nothing in his quest for revenge.

Youssef gathered himself and tried again, his voice terse with barely restrained anger on her behalf. "I knew Glen Marlow for a long time. He would never involve his sister in anything he considered dangerous. She was not directly involved, Your Excellency.''

"Glen Marlow endangered his sister by abducting your sister," the sheikh pointed out with unarguable logic. "Abducting my promised bride," he added with more bite.

"No." Youssef grimaced. "As much as it pains me to say it, my father chooses to believe that, but it is not so. My sister Samira went with Glen Marlow of her own free will. I have no doubt in my mind it was also at her request. Glen would never have tried to persuade her against fulfilling a duty of state.''

"But he did take her."

"Yes."

"The woman who was promised as a wife to me."

"Yes," Youssef agreed on a despairing note.

"And he left his sister."

"To be expelled from Qatama, as he had clearly anticipated, Your Excellency."

The plea was futile. Leah knew it, and Youssef must have realised it, too. She was grateful to him for trying, but her present situation did not hang on her innocence. The sheikh proceeded to clear Youssef's mind of all concern on that score.

"The balance of justice had to be redressed, Your Royal Highness. Forgive me, but I thought your father, King Rashid, left much to be desired." He paused, then drove in the point. "At my cost."

"My father appreciates that very keenly, Your Excellency, which is why I have come to bring you the offer he now makes to you. And since it is a matter of some delicacy, I would like to speak to you alone."

"Oh, I do not think Miss Marlow will divulge my private affairs," the sheikh drawled. He turned to Leah with an air of indulgent consideration. "I'm sure you would like to hear what is offered to me from the royal family of Qatama. With whom you have been so intimately associated."

Her eyes spit blue fire at him. She hated him all the more for so callously using her as a political pawn. "I am not interested in your affairs. I would rather go."

His hand tightened around hers. "No, no, there is no need for you to be tactful. You must stay. I want you to."

He turned to Youssef. "Miss Marlow stayed in the throne room at Qatamah to hear the end of the alliance that had been agreed upon by your family, Your Royal Highness," he said with silky venom. "I think it only fitting that she hear what you have to offer in its place."

Youssef's face tightened as he comprehended the depth of the offence given to the sheikh of Zubani. Leah looked away. She was painfully acquainted with humiliation. She had suffered it at the hands of her father. She had suffered it at the hands of her mother. She had suffered it at the hands of Sharif al Kader. She did not want to watch the effect on Youssef while the sheikh made mincemeat of him.

"As you will, Your Excellency," Youssef said in grim resignation.

"You have my attention, Your Royal Highness."

"My father has many daughters. The Princess Fatima is of marriageable age."

A wave of repugnance swept through Leah. Fatima was only sixteen, and no match for the man beside her. The thought of his taking Fatima as his wife, making love with her, doing all that he had done to Leah last night... It wasn't right. Couldn't be right. To Leah's mind it was obscene. Callous, she reminded herself savagely.

A shudder ran up her arm as she felt Sharif's fingers moving caressingly over hers. Only then did she realise her own had curled up, her fingernails digging into the wood of the armrest. She instantly straightened them and took a deep breath to steady her reaction to what Youssef was offering.

He was listing Fatima's attributes, painting the image of a beautiful and dutiful young woman who would quickly fit into the role of the *sheikha* of Zubani and be all the sheikh could want in his wife. He spoke with eloquent persuasion and finished by assuring the sheikh that his every requirement would be conscientiously fulfilled with this new alliance.

"It is to our mutual benefit that we conclude this affair in harmonious accord," Youssef finished on a pertinently political note.

Why should she care if Sharif al Kader married Fatima, Leah fiercely argued to herself. It was a way out for her, wasn't it? And undoubtedly Fatima would accept her fate placidly. Fatima had a placid nature. Let him agree to the marriage. Then he would have to release her.

"More," the sheikh said icily. "I want more."

Of course, Leah thought cynically. He already had a woman to warm his bed. She was the hammer to drive that nail home. Qatamah had to offer more than a wife.

Youssef stiffened. "The border village of Reza, which has been a source of dispute for over a century, and which you now control. We will cede all claims on it."

"More," said the sheikh.

"Reparation of a hundred million dollars will be paid to your state."

"More."

"I am not authorised to offer more."

This statement was greeted by stony silence.

"Your Excellency—" Youssef took a deep breath. "Whatever safeguards you require to be assured of a happy conclusion—"

The opening of the doors behind him was a distraction that could not be ignored in the middle of such an important meeting. Youssef turned to frown at the unwelcome intrusion.

The woman in the doorway galvanised all eyes. She was dressed in a striking robe of brilliantly swirling violet and turquoise. A matching turban was wound around her head. She moved with a majesty that was unique, and as she advanced down the room, the swaying grace of her walk added its mesmerising wonder to the Ethiopian's magnificent beauty.

The doors were closed behind her.

Tayi had made her entrance.

CHAPTER EIGHT

ALTHOUGH TAYI WAS visibly jolted at her first sight of
Leah sitting beside the sheikh, the crack in her composure was swiftly attended to. Her large velvety eyes
focussed on the man beside Leah with deep intensity
as she walked forward.

Leah wondered why a nanny would be allowed to
interrupt a meeting concerning critical matters of
state. But she sensed no alarm in the man at her side.
No tension at all. He was not disturbed by Tayi's admission to this room.

It was Youssef who reacted. He rose from his chair,
his gaze riveted on the woman who approached.
Whether this was an unexpected interruption or some
prearranged ploy by the sheikh, Leah did not know.
Perhaps it was the regality of Tayi's bearing that
prompted Youssef to stand, but it was more likely he
had risen in offence that a woman whose antecedents
had surely been slaves was now to be given attention
ahead of his mission.

Youssef's movement diverted Tayi's attention from
the sheikh. Her feet stopped moving. There was a
flicker of disquiet in her expression as she stared at the
handsome nobility of Youssef's face. At that moment
he was very much the son of his father. Youssef's body

stiffened with proud dignity. Tayi quickly turned her head to the sheikh, perhaps realising she had blundered in coming into this room. Nevertheless, she resumed her approach as though it had never been broken.

"What brings you here, Tayi?" he asked when she stopped in front of him. "This is a very important meeting."

"There is one more important thing," she answered in soft, melodious tones.

It was the first time Leah had heard Tayi speak. Her voice had a velvety quality that somehow matched her eyes.

"What is it?" Sharif asked sharply.

"Jazmin is sick and calls for you."

"I will come immediately."

This reaction surprised Leah. She cynically wondered if his concern for his daughter was really so urgent, or if he simply chose to end the meeting with Youssef. She remembered the death of his first wife and what had followed from that. Perhaps the welfare of his children was of prime importance to him.

Tayi did not appear surprised by his decision. She turned and looked straight through Youssef as though he weren't there, her head tilted high in disdain of his status and his mission. She had shown that her power over the sheikh's attention was much higher than his. She made her exit with the same supreme dignity with which she had made her entrance.

The sheikh rose from his chair, drawing Leah to her feet with him, her hand firmly clasped on his arm.

"Who is that woman?" Youssef demanded.

"That is Tayi, the minder of my children."

"She is very striking," Youssef remarked, frowning over Tayi's relatively low status in the sheikh's household.

"Yes. One day I hope to marry her off advantageously to her position," Sharif said dismissively. "But we digress. And I must leave you. Tell your father I will reflect on his offer. Perhaps we shall talk more anon."

There were no formal farewells. He swept Leah from the room, leaving Youssef to make his own departure. Tayi was waiting in the arched entrance to the foyer. As soon as she saw them, she went ahead, walking along the arcade in the opposite direction to the way Leah had been taken yesterday.

This was one time Leah didn't mind being swept along with the sheikh. It gave her the opportunity to check out the courtyard. The scene with Youssef had convinced her she must do her utmost to escape from this dreadful situation.

She felt both used and abused by Sharif al Kader. Having been offered such handsome reparation by King Rashid, he had no justification in continuing his revenge. For Leah to be taken *at his pleasure* while a marriage with Fatima was being negotiated was the ultimate in degradation. Clearly he could have no feeling for her whatsoever, and she could not bear to be a victim of his powerful personality again. She had to escape!

Leah counted ten cars parked against the walls on either side of the great iron gates. Whether keys were hanging ready in ignitions she had no way of knowing. Besides, there were men everywhere, around the ancient well, next to the gates, sitting in the shade of the arcade. Some were armed with guns, some not. The sheikh's entourage was formidable. If the guards had been issued with orders to prevent her from leaving, she saw no ready way past them.

Depression weighed heavily on her heart as they mounted the staircase to what was presumably the children's quarters. If there was no way out of this fortress, what was to become of her? How could Glen stage a rescue under these conditions? It was hopeless. Hopeless!

A servant opened a door for them, and Tayi ushered them into what was obviously Jazmin's bedroom. The little girl was propped up on pillows, her face pale and tear-streaked and woebegone, although her older sister, Nadia, was sitting on the bed trying to interest her with a selection of dolls.

Both children instantly brightened at seeing their father. "Papa, Jazmin has tonsillitis again," Nadia informed him.

"Ah, yes, I can see it hurting, my poor brave little one," he said with loving sympathy. He sat on the bed and felt her forehead. "What did the doctor say?"

"That it wasn't bad, but she's got to take medicine," Nadia answered him.

"Then we will soon make it better, Jazmin," he assured her, and bent to kiss her nose. "Now, what would you like your papa to do for you?"

"You brought the lady with the golden hair," Jazmin said in a husky whisper, her eyes turning to Leah in wonderment.

"Yes. Do you remember her name?"

"Miss Marlow," Nadia said triumphantly.

"Can I talk to her, Papa?" Jazmin asked.

Sharif al Kader turned commanding eyes to Leah. It was on the tip of her tongue to refuse, to say she would have nothing to do with his daughters under the obscene terms of her captivity. But then the thought struck her that his daughters might provide a means of getting away from here. Surely they were not kept within the walls of the fortress day in and day out. If they should become eager for her company, and want her to go with them on their outings, this was a chance she would be foolish to ignore.

She smiled at the sick little girl and went to sit beside her on the opposite side of the bed to her father. "Would you like me to tell you a story, Jazmin?"

For the next hour Leah had both girls entranced with fairy stories. Their father's dark eyes sparkled amusement and approval and warm pleasure at her, as though the public flaunting of his revenge was of no consequence whatsoever. Leah silently but fiercely promised herself she was not about to forget it at *his* convenience.

Jazmin's eyelids gradually drooped lower and lower. By the time she drifted into sleep, Leah was satisfied she had achieved her purpose. Both little girls would certainly be asking to see her again. She had made allies of Sharif al Kader's daughters, but as she left the room, Leah found she had made one enemy. Tayi stood by the door to see them out. She said nothing, but her large, expressive eyes spoke volumes to Leah, and none of it good.

Jealousy? Leah wondered. But jealous of what? The liking of the children, or the way the sheikh of Zubani had reacted to her? She remembered the initial jolt of shock on Tayi's face when she had seen Leah seated beside the sheikh at the meeting with Youssef. Was there more than loyalty in Tayi's heart for her employer?

Leah shook her head. That was no concern of hers. Her major concern was to get out of this place and way beyond Sharif al Kader's reach. Unfortunately that seemed beyond the realms of possibility today.

He escorted her back to the sitting room in the tower and had the crass insensitivity to swing her straight into his embrace. "You were very good with my daughters," he said, his eyes simmering with a desire that had nothing to do with her ability to relate easily to children. "I think I shall have to make love to you."

"No!" Leah cried vehemently, curling her hands into fists against his chest.

"Why not?"

"If you're going to marry Fatima..."

"No commitment has been made. I am a free man. And I want you, Leah Marlow." A teasing smile hovered on his lips as he raised a mocking eyebrow at her persistent resistance to his embrace. "Did I not demonstrate this morning how highly I value you?"

"By humiliating me in front of Prince Youssef?" she raged.

"By refusing all he offered me. I would not exchange you for his sister, not even for the further inducement of undisputed control over Reza and a hundred million dollars. Does it not warm your heart to know I am so deeply in your power that I prefer to have you to—"

"Don't think you can fool me, Sharif al Kader!" Leah snapped. "You're holding out for more."

He laughed. "Perhaps I am. More of you. More of this . . ."

His mouth claimed hers with passion, and Leah's resistance fought a losing battle against the overwhelming power of his will. He gave her no time to erect defences. The blows she struck were like water off a duck's back to him while he skilfully fed the temptation to feel again what he had made her feel last night. In the end, her struggle against the inevitable only seemed to heighten the excitement of the physical intimacy he forced upon her, and the only battle she fought was to incite him out of his damnable control so she had the satisfaction of drawing a wild response from him.

"The earth moved," he murmured afterwards, giving Leah a smile that seemed to make the earth move for her.

But she would not admit it. She would not be beguiled or seduced or deceived into conceding anything more than some mad sexual compatability with him. Which was inexplicable. But undeniable. Sharif al Kader had stripped her of any choice about it, but Leah told herself if she was ever free to choose, she would never be held or swayed by such purely physical feelings. It was a trap that blinded people to the more important values of real loving and caring.

In the days that followed, Leah was invariably defeated by Sharif al Kader's will, no matter what she said or did. He not only spent every night with her, but frequently took her to bed during the day, as well. As a lover, he was overwhelming and apparently insatiable, and Leah was both shamed and exhilarated by the response he always drew from her. She railed at herself with heated disgust. She was no better than her mother, revelling in sexual pleasure, but Sharif had only to look at her with desire and a treacherous excitement seized her.

It was not all sex. Sharif would talk to her about the programs he had set up for the welfare and education of the women and children of Zubani. He would ask her opinion and draw her into a discussion on plans for the future. Leah's attempts to maintain disinterest in his affairs usually crumbled under his persuasive persistence. Besides, she enjoyed challenging his point of view, and she told herself that conversation staved off the more insidious form of intimacy.

He was only too happy for her to visit his children in their quarters, but he always came with her and stayed the whole time, as though they were playing at being a family. Jazmin was soon well again, and the little girls did have outings, but only with Tayi. Leah was never given a chance to get beyond the fortress walls.

Time started to become meaningless, the days flowing into one another, each one barely distinguishable from the last and the next. Leah clung to doing a section of her tapestry every day to mark some difference. She had bursts of rebellion, demanding to know if Sharif had made any decision about the negotiations with Qatama, but he always dismissed that issue by kissing her senseless and telling her he preferred the reparation he had chosen for himself, implying *she* satisfied him.

Leah knew this couldn't be true. The revenge he had taken might earn a fearful respect, but it did not settle the political impasse between Qatama and Zubani. Sooner or later some resolution had to be found. Alliances could be of critical importance in the Middle East. Youssef had not been speaking lightly when he said it was of mutual benefit for the two states to be in harmonious accord.

A week slid by. Two. Glen had to know she was being held by now. Was he doing anything to effect her freedom? Youssef knew where she was. Surely he would tell Glen. Or was the political situation too delicate for it to be known he had revealed her whereabouts?

There was nothing Leah could do to break her imprisonment. If Sharif wasn't with her, there was always a woman sitting outside her door. All her movements were observed. If Glen didn't come to rescue her, would Sharif let her go when the month was over? Or would she be held here at his pleasure until he no longer found pleasure in her?

Despair hung heavily on her heart at times. Sharif's pleasure in her was certainly not waning in any way whatsoever. What if he intended to keep her on as his concubine after he married Fatima? Leah couldn't bear that thought.

On the afternoon of the eighteenth day of her captivity Sharif announced that matters of state required him to he be at his palace for a day or so, but he would come back to her as soon as he could. He flew off in his helicopter.

Leah wondered if King Rashid himself had come to negotiate a settlement this time. One thing was certain. Whatever was agreed between the rulers of Qatama and Zubani, Sharif was not yet prepared to let her go.

Leah spent a miserable night alone in her bed. Sharif's absence brought home to her how very deeply enmeshed she had become in the relationship he had forced upon her, depending on him for company and the sense of intimate togetherness they shared in bed. It could only get worse, she thought, despairing of ever being free of him even if he did let her go.

The next morning, she was sitting listlessly in front of her tapestry, forcing herself to get on with it, when she received a surprise visitor. Leah had no reason to think Tayi cared about her loneliness, and she was amazed to see the nanny enter the sitting room. Tayi was carrying a basket, and Leah was even more astonished to see her draw from it the money belt that had been left on the floor in the throne room at Qatamah.

"How did you get that?" she asked.

Tayi did not reply. She walked forward to hand Leah the belt. "Put it on under your robe," she commanded.

"I don't understand." Leah rose from her chair. Despite the fact it was Glen's, she felt reluctant to take the belt. Was this some trick to get her into trouble with the sheikh? "Why are you giving it to me?"

"Do you want to stay here or go free?" Tayi demanded, her large, velvety eyes firing a hostile challenge at Leah.

"I must get away," Leah said vehemently.

"Then there is no time to waste. Do as I say."

"Why are you helping me?"

Tayi disdained a reply to that question. "Put the belt on now."

Leah took the belt, and as she hitched up her robe to fasten it around her waist, Tayi went to the central table and deliberately knocked a bowl of fruit over. Then she walked to the door and waited for Leah to join her.

As usual, a woman servant was sitting in the corridor just beyond the door. Tayi ordered her to clean up the spilled fruit in the sitting room, then swept off down the corridor with Leah fast on her heels. The moment the servant was safely out of sight, Tayi drew a black cloak and *abba* from her basket and handed them to Leah.

"Cover yourself," she commanded.

Leah made sure there was only a slit for some eyesight left uncovered as they hurried down the staircase. No-one challenged them as Tayi led the way across the courtyard to a car by the gateway.

"Get in the passenger side," she directed.

Leah did not hesitate. Why Tayi was risking the sheikh's displeasure in doing this, she did not know, but she was not about to do anything to jeopardise this chance at escape.

None of the sentries made any attempt to stop them or question where they were going as Tayi drove the

car out of the courtyard. Few women drove cars in
Arab countries, but apparently Tayi had the privilege
of complete freedom of movement, going wherever
she pleased. Again Leah wondered if the Ethiopian
woman was a simple minder of children. She had an
air of authority that seemed to go much higher than
that.

"Who are you?" she asked impulsively, as they
travelled towards the village.

Predictably enough, Tayi made no reply.

It didn't matter, Leah told herself. If this escape
worked, she would soon be out of Zubani, and Tayi
and Sharif al Kader would play no further part in her
life. The sudden wrench on her heart at that thought
was proof enough that this opportunity had come
none too soon.

"Can you drive?" Tayi asked abruptly.

"Yes."

They went through the village and stopped at the
outskirts on the other side. Tayi turned to Leah, the
light of a mission accomplished in her eyes. "The car
is yours. Go. And never come back."

"Why did you do this?" Leah asked, still not sure
it wasn't a trap of some kind. "You don't care about
me."

Again there was no reply. Tayi alighted from the car
and walked away, a majestic figure who feared nothing and no-one. Unforgettable, Leah thought, as she
quickly rounded the car to take the driver's seat.
Whether it was a trap or not, freedom beckoned.

Leah put her foot down on the accelerator and
drove as fast as she deemed safe. If she was caught, the

sheikh's revenge did not bear thinking about. She
breathed a sigh of relief when at last the road joined
the four-lane highway. Not far now, she told herself,
anxious to have the most dangerous part of this journey over and done with. She was fifty miles short of
the border when she heard the helicopter overhead.

It couldn't be him, she told herself, but her whole
body churned with turbulent emotion at the thought
that he had come after her and would not let her go.
The helicopter seemed to hover above her for long,
interminable minutes, then she saw it swooping ahead
of her. Yet there was the sound of one behind her, as
well.

The highway was dead straight for miles. Two hel-
icopters, clearly belonging to the military, landed in
unison, one in front of her, one behind, effectively
blocking the road with her car neatly trapped between them. Armed men poured out of both and
spread out in a line. There was no way past them.

Leah slowed her car to a halt, turned off the igni-
tion and sat waiting, knowing she was captured but
feeling strangely numb about it now that it was done.
Two men broke from the line ahead of her and came
forward to the car. One opened her door and motioned her out. Leah complied. She was asked to remove her *abba*. It made identification easy enough,
she realised. The two men stared at her long, pale gold
hair for several moments before one of them spoke.

"Come," was all he said.

There was no point in trying to disobey. Her bid for
escape was comprehensively crushed. As she was escorted towards the helicopter, Leah again wondered if

it had been a trap all along. Would Tayi be rewarded or punished for what she had done? Whatever the outcome for the other woman, Leah knew she was about to feel the weight of the sheikh of Zubani's displeasure. Yet what greater price could be asked than that already paid?

She was motioned towards a seat in the helicopter and strapped in. As the vehicle took off, Leah felt absolute despair. Undoubtedly she would be taken back to the desert fortress from where she'd come. No-one could save her. No-one could rescue her. As far as she was aware, she could spend the rest of her life as the sheikh's captive, giving him whatever pleasure he desired.

CHAPTER NINE

LEAH SUFFERED THE TRIP in total disinterest. When they landed she submitted to being helped out of the aircraft with dull resignation. Only then did she realise they were not in the desert. They had landed on a helipad within the grounds of what had to be the palace of Zubani.

While Leah was in no mood to appreciate the elegant architecture of the impressive white palace, she had to admit it looked a whole lot better to her than the fortress outside the oasis of Shalaan. It had obviously been built in recent years to reflect the new wealth and importance of the country, and the windows she could see were not barred.

It was also an unexpected pleasure to see grass, flowering shrubs and stately date palms. She had sorely missed her private garden in Qatama. Not that she expected to be allowed to roam free here. It was simply a relief to have some other view than desert and distant mountains.

She was not given much time to enjoy it. The guards marched her straight inside the palace. There she was passed to another set of guards who were apparently waiting to escort her directly to the sheikh. They crossed the huge domed foyer and entered a wide

arched hallway. At the end of this was a set of double
doors, which were ceremoniously opened for her.

Leah walked into a fabulous art gallery. Paintings
from the Renaissance, impressionists and Fauvists
virtually leapt at her from the walls, masterpieces from
some of the greatest artists the world had known. No
wonder Sharif was familiar with Rubens and Leonardo da Vinci if this was his private collection, Leah
thought. But she had no time for more than a cursory
glance at the paintings. The sheikh of Zubani com-
pelled her full attention as he rose from the bench that
ran down the centre of the room.

Whether she liked it or not, Leah felt linked to him
in some unfathomable way, and she realised with a
considerable jolt that it was curiously comforting to
see him again, as though he added a vibrancy to her
life that would be forever lost without him. The dull
sense of resignation was dispersed the moment her
eyes clashed with his. Her whole body was poised in a
high state of awareness, ready to meet the challenge of
his reaction to her flight for freedom.

"Ah! You have arrived," he said with satisfaction.

Leah waited, expecting an angry outburst for putting him to so much trouble in foiling her attempt at
escape.

He frowned as he walked towards her. "Did I not
say you weren't to wear black?"

Leah stared at him in disbelief. To pick on such an
irrelevant detail as his first reprimand seemed totally
out of keeping with the situation.

He reached her, unfastened the cloak, whipped it
off her and tossed it away. His eyes glittered over the

blue caftan she had put on that morning. "That is much better."

Leah was relieved he could be pleased about something, but she suspected this was the calm before the storm.

His hands started to slide around her waist, abruptly stopping when he felt the money belt. "What is this?" he demanded, his dark eyes searing hers with distinct displeasure.

Leah winced. "My brother's money belt."

He frowned in disapproval. "So! You accepted it after all."

"A matter of necessity, under the circumstances," she defended.

"Take it off. Now!" he commanded, then turned and paced halfway up the gallery while Leah removed the belt.

She placed it on top of the despised black cloak and composed herself as best she could for the diatribe that had to come.

Sharif swung around and shook an accusing finger at her. "This escape of yours. It was gratuitous ill-mannered misbehaviour. I don't find it at all becoming in you."

"I'm sorry," she said, wary of giving him more offence.

"So you should be. Have I not done everything I can to please you? Do you not yet know that we are right together? It is foolish for you to want to leave me," he declared with passion, his eyes searing hers, compelling her to feel the same desire for him as he felt for her.

Leah took a deep breath, defying the power of his undeniable charisma. "I don't like being a prisoner," she stated, her eyes flashing their accusation at him.

He gestured dismissively. "That is your own fault."

"*My* fault?" Leah echoed incredulously.

His challenge was instant and unequivocal. "How can I trust you to stay with me?"

"I want to be free, Sharif. You can hardly blame me for trying to attain what you deny me," Leah argued.

He heaved an exasperated sigh. "Well, if you must try escaping again, do me the honour of being more clever next time."

While Leah was still swallowing her astonishment at such a perverse piece of counselling, his eyes flashed sparkling admiration at her. "Now the knife," he said with relish. "*That* was worthy of you. But this plan—" He made a contemptuous sound. "Too predictable!"

"It wasn't my plan," Leah heard herself say, as though needing to defend her lack of cleverness.

He grimaced. "Tayi means well. She simply does not comprehend the situation. She sees, yet does not see."

So it hadn't been a trap, Leah thought. Tayi had acted on her own. Which made her remarkable in character, as well as in person.

"What will you do to Tayi?" she asked in concern for the other woman.

He looked surprised. "Nothing! Why on earth should I do anything to Tayi? She acted in good faith."

The machinations that were going on here made Machiavelli look like a schoolboy, Leah thought. Sharif al Kader was certainly the most *unpredictable* man she had ever met! He was not only dismissing her attempt at escape as inconsequential, he was shrugging off Tayi's part in it, as well.

"Maybe I don't see either, Sharif," she said with feeling. "Why am I here? What do you intend to do with me now?"

He frowned and kept on frowning as he paced around the far end of the bench and halfway up the other side of the room. Then he paused and shot her a hard, measuring look. "Things have changed. I shall take you into my confidence."

"Thank you. I'd like that," Leah said, quick to encourage any offer of information.

"Representations have been made on your behalf," he said, as though deeply vexed by this development. "The situation is extremely delicate, to say the least."

Glen had come forward, was Leah's immediate and exultant thought. But surely it was terribly dangerous for her brother to confront the man who had every reason to do him long and lasting damage. Perhaps Glen had contacted the Australian embassy, informing them that one of their nationals was missing and it was rumoured she was with the sheikh of Zubani. In the end, it could only be her brother prompting action on her behalf.

Rather than increase Sharif's vexation with the situation, Leah held her tongue, hoping to hear precisely who was inquiring after her and how Sharif meant to deal with it.

He glowered reproof at her as he continued. "You gave me to understand that you were unloved by any family other than your brother, who has had you under his protection for the last eight years."

"That's correct," she said, wondering why he should question it.

"No. It is not."

The emphatic rebuff startled Leah into asking, "Has the government made inquiries about me?"

"No. It is the person who it should be. Your father."

Leah could hardly believe her ears. "Why did he bother coming?" It made no sense to her. Her father had abandoned her sixteen years ago, devoting himself to his second marriage and the stepchildren who came with it.

"It is his duty," Sharif answered, too imbued in his Arab culture to comprehend a father who felt no paternal duty to his daughter. "He wishes to see you and be certain that you have been well looked after. Which you have. And to pay whatever price I ask to set you free."

"My father?" Leah felt completely bewildered.

"Of course. You are his daughter. Naturally he is concerned for you. He will pay handsomely for your release."

For several moments all the stored-up bitterness was infiltrated by sweet memories of her childhood, her father coming home from his overseas flights and swinging her up in his arms, loving her and teasing her about the doll she knew he would have for her in his suitcase. He had bought her a wonderful collection of dolls, all in national dress from the countries he had flown to in his job as a Qantas pilot. But that was before...

She looked at Sharif with pained uncertainty. "My father really has come for me? You're not just saying this?"

His eyes probed hers with sharp intensity, wanting to understand. "Why should he not, Leah?" he asked quietly.

A thousand reasons why not, she thought sadly, but gave a dismissive shrug. "It doesn't matter."

"I think it does. It was he who hurt you?"

"Things happen," she said flatly. "My parents were divorced when I was ten. My father has another family now."

"But you are still very dear to him."

She gave a rueful smile. "It seems that way. Are you going to let me see my father, Sharif?"

He slowly nodded. "Yes. There is a need." He walked up to her and drew her gently into his arms. Leah did not resist. She felt too confused by what he had told her and by the way he was acting towards her, as though he cared that she had been hurt and wanted to make things better for her.

He returned her rueful smile. "I cannot deny a father his daughter. And you will feel more free with seeing him and talking to him."

"When do I get to do that?" she pressed, as his head bent to hers. "Where is he staying?"

His lips brushed a tantalising kiss. "He is staying here in the palace." Another more sensual kiss. "And you will meet him tomorrow." A kiss that simmered with passion. "After we have made love many times."

More than that he would not say. He conducted her to a suite of rooms that guaranteed them privacy, and although it was weak of her to submit without at least some token protest, the urge to know if there would be some different quality in Sharif's lovemaking overrode every other consideration. It was crazy to wonder if there could be some lasting future with him, yet she could not stop herself from dreaming foolish dreams as he comprehensively demonstrated that his pleasure was also hers.

At first he made love to her with a fierce possessiveness, perhaps prompted by her trying to leave him, a deeply primitive male need to affirm that she belonged to him. Then there came a tender loving, as though she was truly precious to him and he cherished all she was. Leah found it utterly impossible not to respond to him. There was a side of her that craved for this intimacy to go on forever, another side that wanted to hoard the memory of it because sooner or later it had to come to an end, no matter how *right* it felt with him.

As she lay in the seductive warmth of his arms, she had to remind herself that the sense of fulfilment he gave her was only transient. To her, Sharif was a totally confusing mixture of a man, hard and ruthless in going after what he deemed would best serve him, yet there was kindness and caring and a fine understanding in much of what he did.

His plans for his people and the progress of his country were far-thinking and admirably idealistic. She wished she could stay with him and share in them, to see worthwhile goals coming to fruition. But that wasn't what Sharif wanted her for, and Leah knew she could never be happy in the role of a concubine.

For the welfare of Zubani, Sharif would have to terminate what he shared with her. It was probably that very knowledge driving him to take all he could of her now, while it was still possible, without adverse consequences to his political position.

His judgement over the issue with her father had undoubtedly been swayed by his love for his own daughters, but perhaps there had also been representations from Qatama within the past twenty-four hours. If his revenge on Leah had served its purpose, Sharif could possibly be seeing her father as an appropriate way to let her go.

She remembered him saying, "Things have changed." How much? she wondered. Was he beginning to care about her feelings, or was he simply referring to the political situation?

"Will you let me go home with my father, Sharif?" she asked, wanting some hint of what was on his mind.

He turned her onto her back and propped himself up on one elbow, eyeing her sternly as though she had earned his disfavour with that question. "What is this home you speak of?" he demanded. "Your father has another family. You said so yourself."

"I meant home to Australia," Leah swiftly corrected.

"You left it behind long ago," came the terse dismissal. "Have you not made your home amongst people like mine for the last eight years? Of your own choice?"

"I was happy in Qatama," she conceded. "But I did have my brother there, Sharif."

"And now you have me to make you happy," he argued. "You like being with me. We are right together. Do not deny it."

Leah heaved a deep sigh. She was hardly in a position to deny it right now. "You said my father would pay the price for my release," she reminded him.

"He made the offer. Which shows he cares for you. As he should."

"And what did you say to him?"

"I said *more*."

"My father isn't a rich man."

"That is irrelevant." The dark brooding disintegrated into a slow, satisfied smile that squeezed her heart. "I am thinking there is no price that could buy your release. I know that you do not want to leave me."

"I tried to leave you today," Leah said dryly.

"That was untimely. And not your plan. Tayi did not understand."

"Sharif, you must know this revenge of yours can't go on forever. The month will soon be over, and you'll have to make some settlement with Qatama. I'll only be in the way then."

"We shall see," he said, and would not be drawn any further on the matter.

But throughout the many ways and many times he made love to her, Leah kept wondering what was *timely* in Sharif's mind. Was tomorrow the day of decision? Or did he really mean there was no price that could buy her away from him?

CHAPTER TEN

IT WAS ALMOST NOON the next day when Leah received the sheikh's summons to a meeting with her father. All her belongings had been brought from the desert fortress, and she had been established in a light, airy apartment in the women's quarters of the palace. Despite the lift in her spirits from feeling less of a prisoner, she had been tense all morning, waiting for this moment, not knowing quite what to expect.

As she was led through seemingly interminable hallways, a host of inhibitions crawled around her heart. It had been too long an estrangement, with far too much water under the bridge for her to feel close to her father. He had let her down in so many hurtful ways, she could not bring herself to believe he would not do it again in front of Sharif. Which would be intensely humiliating.

It was stupid, really, to have dressed as attractively as she could. What difference would it make? None to a father who had left his daughter behind in favour of making a new life for himself. It was pride, she supposed, pride in herself that had made her select the embroidered and beaded turquoise robe that was her favourite.

Sharif would appreciate it, she thought, which was probably why her eyes went straight to him when she was ushered into the formal reception room where he and her father were seated. Both men rose to their feet at her entrance. The flash of admiration in Sharif's dark eyes, the look of pride in her that shone from his wonderfully autocratic face was precisely what Leah needed.

Her head tilted slightly higher. She didn't stop to think how strange it was for her to gather strength and self-assurance from the powerful charisma of her captor. He looked very much the sheikh of Zubani this morning, as she had first seen him in her garden at Qatama, but he no longer struck fear in her. His re-action to her escape yesterday had dissipated all fear of him. In his way he treated her well, within the framework of his revenge.

Her gaze slowly shifted to the man who had come for her, Captain Robert Ian Marlow, at her service. Glen took after him in looks, big, blond, skin that took a golden tan, handsome in the clean-cut way that invited trust. But there was uncertainty in the blue eyes that fastened on Leah's, a look of appeal that had lit-tle hope in it.

"As you can see, Captain Marlow, your daughter is in fine health," Sharif said matter-of-factly, then very personally to Leah, "and very beautiful."

"Yes. Thank you, Your Excellency." Her father's voice did not quite attain a similar aplomb. He of-fered her a tentative smile. "It's good to see you, Leah."

He stood stiffly, not expecting her to fly into his arms as she would have done a long time ago. Leah came to a halt several arm's lengths away from him, her mind too cluttered with question marks to think of smiling.

"It was kind of you to come," she said, her eyes searching his for the reason behind this extraordinary gesture. What did his wife think about it? His stepchildren?

"I had to," he answered simply, and there was a look of painful regret in his eyes. "I won't let you down this time, Leah."

A sudden well of emotion choked any possible reply. As though sensing her distress, Sharif seized the moment to take her hand and lead her to an armchair. "Be seated, Captain Marlow," he said to cover any awkwardness, then proceeded to seat himself where he had Leah to his right and her father to his left. Clearly he had no intention of leaving the two of them alone together.

Leah desperately cast around for something to say to her father. "Have you seen Glen?" she blurted out.

"He came straight to me." Said in a firmer voice. "He asked if I would fly the plane he had taken back to Qatama."

A wry little smile flitted over Leah's lips. Glen had always stayed close to their father. Of course, he had been much older than she at the time of the divorce, sixteen to her ten, and he had bitterly blamed their mother for the marriage break-up. Apart from which, Glen had always wanted to be a pilot, and he shared that interest with their father.

"I'm glad to hear that he's safe. Until Sharif told me otherwise, I thought he had been shot down," Leah said ruefully.

Robert Marlow frowned, his gaze flicking sharply from her to the sheikh and back again. "We waited to hear from you, Leah. Glen anticipated that you would be expelled. When there was no word, I flew the plane to Qatama and sought an audience with King Rashid."

Leah looked at him in surprise. "He saw you?"

"No. But Prince Youssef did."

"And he told you where I was?" It was a monumental indiscretion on his part with regard to such a delicate political situation between the two states.

"No. He was deeply concerned for his sister. I was able to assure him she was safe and very shortly to be married to my son."

"Married! Glen and Samira?" Leah shook her head in bewilderment. "I thought—" She shot a probing look at Sharif, but he did not appear the least bit concerned by this information, let alone offended by it. Perhaps he had already drawn these facts from her father. She turned back to him. "I didn't know...had no idea they felt like that."

"As it was told to me, Glen and Samira have loved each other for a long time," he replied quietly, "but neither had ever spoken of it. Both of them had obligations and responsibilities that precluded any expression or pursuit of what was in their hearts. It was only on the eve of her wedding that Samira broke down and told Glen how she felt, that she'd rather have any kind of life with him than without him."

There was a pained apology in his eyes as he continued. "Glen had very little time to get Samira out of Qatama, Leah. She masqueraded as you so she could leave the palace with Glen without any questions being raised. There was no other way it could be done. Glen had to ask you to remain out of sight. And leave you behind."

So that was how it happened, Leah thought in bemusement, remembering the turbulent feelings emanating from Glen that fateful afternoon. Not only worry for her, but the hidden love for Samira coursing wildly, hopefully, fearfully through him. Little things came back to her, the softening of Glen's voice when he spoke of Samira, the way Samira looked at him. Not hero-worship. Something far deeper. And desperate enough to tear asunder the long-woven fabric of both their lives.

"Glen didn't want to leave you, Leah. He had to make a choice. He did the best he could for you at the time."

The strained plea in her father's voice drew her gaze to his. Did he think she blamed Glen for what had happened to her? It was impossible for her brother to have foreseen the sheikh of Zubani's revenge. Not in the heat of the moment, anyway, not when fast and dangerous action had been called for. She didn't begrudge Glen and Samira their chance at happiness together.

"I understand, Dad," she said softly, dismissing the recriminations he thought she might be harbouring.

"Do you, Leah?" His eyes searched hers uncertainly. "You can forgive your brother?"

She flushed as she realised the question was a reflection of what he felt himself, that she had never
forgiven him for the choice he had made in leaving her
behind. But that was different. A whole lot different,
in Leah's book.

Was it the best he could do for her to leave her with
a mother who put anything her new husband wanted
ahead of everything else? And what attention had her
father ever given her on the visits she was allowed?
Nothing special. Nothing just for her. She had had to
share him with his stepchildren, and they always got
the lion's share of his attention. His priority had been
the same as her mother's. Pleasing his new partner.
Leah was only in the way to her parents after their divorce.

"I don't understand why you came here," she said
flatly. "You never put yourself out for me when I
needed you before."

"Leah..." A spasm of guilty anguish crossed his
face. "It was a chance for me to say I'm sorry. And,
perhaps, for you to believe me."

"No." She shook her head, unable to accept that.
"You did it for Glen. Not for me. My brother asked
you to come in his place, didn't he?"

He sighed. "Yes. But I wanted to, Leah."

She blocked her heart to that assertion. "How did
Glen find out where I was?"

Robert Marlow threw a wary look at Sharif.
"Through contacts he has. As you know, Glen was
well-liked and respected by many people here."

Leah felt a surge of pride in her brother. He would
have tried everything in his power, and never stopped

trying until he found her. "Tell him not to worry about me anymore," she said impulsively. "And please thank him for me for offering a ransom. I appreciate the—"

"I offered the ransom, Leah."

The flat statement shook Leah's perception of her father. She stared at him uncertainly. There was grim resignation on his face, but he met her gaze with a look of hard pride.

"I'm aware that I haven't done much right by you, Leah. I'm sorry you were short-changed in the choices I felt I had to make. It wasn't that I loved you any less. But after the kind of marriage I had with your mother, I needed Helen in my life. And I truly believed it was best for you to stay with your mother."

Best for you, you mean, was the bitter thought that ran through Leah's mind, but she didn't voice it. Maybe he did regret the way he had let her become the leftover baggage from a marriage he wanted to put behind him.

"What does Helen think of this offer you've made for me? Or doesn't she know about it?" Leah asked, scepticism creeping into her tone as she added, "Won't it disadvantage her and her children?"

His gaze dropped, then slowly lifted to hers again with heartbreaking sadness. "I do care about you, Leah. Very much. And Helen understands that I couldn't live with myself if I didn't do all I could for you now. However too little it is, and however too late."

The protective shell she had clung to for so long cracked open, and the bitterly repressed love for her father welled up and pricked her eyes with tears.

"I don't suppose..." Her voice failed her. She took a deep breath, offered him a wobbly little smile and tried once more. "I don't suppose you brought me a doll."

"No. I didn't think of it. I wish I had," he replied gruffly, a sheen of moisture in his eyes as they both remembered shared happier times.

"Captain Marlow," Sharif suddenly interjected, compelling their attention. "I respect your offer," he declared, giving a nod of approval. "It is worthy of your daughter."

"Does that mean you're accepting it, Your Excellency?"

Leah was instantly plunged into emotional confusion, knowing she should be feeling the same eagerness for her release from captivity that her father was expressing, yet torn by a sharp sense of loss at the thought of never being with Sharif again.

"Let it be understood, Captain Marlow, that it is not a case of too little. You have spoken well. I am impressed by your sincerity. Because of this, I shall grant you time alone with your daughter."

He rose from his chair and smiled approvingly at Leah, his dark eyes caressing her with warm respect. "The strength of your mind is matched by a heart that is good. I did not think otherwise. I shall order lunch to be served here for you and your father. You may walk in the palace grounds afterwards, if you so desire."

"Your Excellency," her father pressed. "How can I persuade you to release my daughter to me?"

Sharif turned to him, his demeanour arrogantly resolute but not unkind. "You cannot, Captain Marlow. I recommend that you do not waste your time with plots and plans. Your daughter will remain with me. Make your peace with her."

He strode towards the doors, half turning when he reached them to deliver an afterthought. Or perhaps it was a well-calculated punch line. "Captain Marlow..."

"Yes, Your Excellency?"

"Tell your son I want him here. It is his duty to come. It is not seemly that the men of Leah's family do not do right by her. That is the way of my people, and that is what I expect, Captain Marlow."

CHAPTER ELEVEN

SHE SHOULD HAVE KNOWN, Leah thought despairingly, that Sharif would exact the full price of revenge—her for the bride stolen from him. Glen for the loss of face he had suffered politically. Her brother was, of course, the coup de grâce to deliver to Qatama, the man *they* had been unable to prevent from going free with their royal princess. And Samira would pay by being deprived of the man for whom she had publicly rejected the sheikh of Zubani.

What a fool she had been to think for one moment that Sharif had begun to care for her! It shamed Leah further to remember the dreams she had indulged in last night, dreams that could never come true. All she was to Sharif al Kader was a tool in his grand plan for revenge. With the additional advantage of her service as a woman in his bed!

She turned to her father. His face was drained of all colour. He looked at her with tortured eyes. "Must I lose my son to regain my daughter?" he asked, but it was not so much a question as a cry torn from a soul that had borne too many painful choices.

"No, Dad," Leah answered, her heart torn by the love he had shown her. Words spilled from her lips in a stream of reassurance. "Glen doesn't have to come for me. I don't want him to. I'd rather stay here. Tell him I wish him and Samira every happiness, and he's not to worry about me. I'm fine. I don't have any plans for the future, anyway. It doesn't matter for me."

"Oh, Leah!" Tears swam into his eyes. He swallowed convulsively, shook his head, but he fought a losing battle against the emotion that racked him. He lifted his hands in a gesture of helplessness. "How can I let you be the one to lose out again?"

Leah moved instinctively to comfort, to close the cold distance that could no longer be upheld. She threw her arms around him in a tight hug and felt his arms enfold her with anguished tenderness. "Leah," he murmured gruffly, and slowly rubbed his cheek over her hair.

Tears filled her eyes, as well. To be held like this by her father again, knowing he cared for her, really cared, meant more than she could say. Especially with the disillusionment Sharif had just dealt her fretting through her mind.

She now knew she had been wrong to judge her father so bitterly, that the betrayal she had felt so deeply was not quite as black and white as it had seemed to her at the time. But the fact remained he did have a family to go back to, and she did not belong to it.

"It's all right, Dad," she assured him huskily. "I'm glad you came for me, but I've learnt to live with myself. And Sharif is good to me. In his own way. Besides which, he'll let me go eventually. Neither you nor Glen have to do anything."

She felt his chest rise and fall in a deep, shuddering sigh. "No, Leah. You will not be sacrificed for my happiness, or Glen's," he said heavily. "I shall ask the sheikh to take me in place of my children. Whatever penalty is to be paid in order that you and Glen go free, I will pay it."

"No. It won't work, Dad," Leah protested, her eyes lifting anxiously to his.

"It must!" he replied with desperate conviction. "I'm your father. Glen's father. If the sheikh of Zubani wants blood, let it be mine. Surely to God he'll see the justice in that!"

"Please listen to me, Dad. It's not as bad as you think."

"Leah, Glen and Samira were married the day before yesterday. Their love for each other is something I never expected to see. I thought Glen had been turned off everything to do with marriage. And you—" he gently stroked her cheek "—as the sheikh said, you are very beautiful. And you deserve to find love, too, instead of leading this...this stifled half-life in rejection of so much of what your mother and I did. The least I can do now is give my children the opportunity to fulfil their lives."

"But there's Helen," Leah argued. "And your other children."

His face tightened. "I've done my best by them for sixteen years. At your cost. And Glen's. It's time the scales were balanced, Leah."

She saw the grim determination on his face and knew there was only one way to break it. Besides, it gave her a savage satisfaction to use Sharif's revenge on her to put a stop to the rest of his grand plan. She would not let him draw Glen or Samira into his vengeful net. She would not let him use this insidious emotional pressure to get at the rest of her family.

She pasted a smile on her face and spoke with loving indulgence. "You don't understand, Dad. It's not a half-life anymore, and I don't want to leave it. I want to stay with Sharif al Kader. I love him. And I know I couldn't love any other man as I love him."

Her father's hands moved to grip her upper arms in an agitated denial of her allegiance to the man who had taken her by force. "Don't, Leah!" he begged. "You're only saying that to—"

"It's true." Her eyes held his in a steady blaze of conviction. "You forget that I've made this life mine. I don't want to go back to Australia. Sharif is the man I want. So let it be."

"Leah, you've been his prisoner for three weeks…"

"He's also made love to me for most of those three weeks," Leah countered, pouring as much warmth as she could into her voice. "Sharif is a wonderful lover."

Her father looked intensely disturbed. "He took you in place of Samira?"

"It more or less started that way," Leah said, "but things have developed between us since then. In any event, I want to see where it leads, so I'm not going to leave him until he wants me to. There's no point in either you or Glen making any sacrifice on my account. I'm perfectly happy here."

"You love your brother more than yourself," her father said gravely. "And you'd do anything, say anything, to safeguard his happiness. And his marriage. But you're not to worry about it, Leah. We will find a way."

"Dad, just let it be," she pleaded.

"No more, Leah. We will talk of other things. Come sit with me now, and tell me the happiest things that have happened in your life. I would like very much to hear them."

She wanted to argue, wanted to resolve the situation along the lines least harmful to all their lives. What did it really matter if she remained Sharif's concubine for as long as he wanted her? It wasn't as though she found him unbearably loathsome or anything like that. And she wanted, from the most primitive depths of her soul, to turn the tables on the single-minded and totally ruthless sheikh of Zubani. He would find her a worthy opponent, all right! To the death, if necessary!

But she saw that to persist with the argument of her love for him would only disturb her father more deeply. There was a need in his eyes begging the kind of response she had once given naturally to the father she had adored. She forced her mind back to the past and smiled to show her lack of concern about the present.

"The happiest times for me were when you came home from your flights, and you'd play with me, cuddle me..."

"And tease you before giving you the doll. Yes. They were happy times." He returned her smile and drew her onto a sofa with him, holding her hand as though desperately wanting to reforge the link between them. "Your mother needed a man at her side,

Leah," he said quietly. "I wouldn't give up flying.
Don't blame her too much. Our marriage was a mistaken love."

His eyes pleaded for understanding and forgive-
ness. "But you were a joy to me, Leah. The only
beautiful light in some very dark years. Please believe
that."

She gave his hand a reassuring squeeze. "It's okay,
Dad. Remember when . . ."

The hours passed all too quickly, bittersweet hours
filled with love and sadness as both of them reached
across the chasm of years and became father and
daughter again. When it came time for them to part,
Leah hoped she had said enough to undermine his
resolution to put himself in jeopardy for her sake and
Glen's. She planted a loving kiss on his cheek and
smiled at him with warm confidence.

"Give Glen and Samira my love. And tell Helen
thank you for letting me have my father back. And no-
one is to worry about me. I'm fine here. Truly I am."

Her father said nothing. He hugged her tightly.
Then after one last long look at her, as though imprinting all that she was on his mind, he surrendered
himself to the escort that had arrived to take him away.

Leah also had an escort, back to her apartment in
the women's quarters. She found her tapestry set up
for her by a window in the sitting room. Despondent
from saying goodbye to her father, goodbye to a lot of
things, she walked to the frame and slowly ran her
fingers over each section of tapestry she had worked
while waiting for Glen to come.

He wouldn't come now.

She didn't want him to.

As for the tapestry, well, she might as well keep doing it, something to fill in her time until Sharif came to a decision about her. She sat down, threaded a needle, but the stitches her fingers could work so nimbly came at long intervals. Her mind kept filling with the wonder of Glen and Samira and all the other things her father had told her.

It changed her perception of so much, forcing her to rethink her life, her reactions, her responses. Perhaps if she had been different, less defensive, less critical, less prickly, not so quick to judge bitterly and hatefully, her life may well have taken a far different course. Yet regrets were pointless. Better to learn from her mistakes and move on. If that became possible.

An intense loneliness seeped through her. She told herself she was glad that Glen and Samira had each other, glad that her father had Helen and her children, even glad that her mother had found whatever contentment she craved with her second husband. It was just that she had no-one special to herself anymore, now that Glen had gone. She was going to miss her big brother. Terribly.

The slamming of a door snapped Leah out of her reverie. The accompanying swirl of tension warned her that Sharif had entered the room, yet she felt reluctant to face him right at this moment. The hours with her father had left her feeling drained and empty. Defenceless. She moved her fingers, pressing the needle through the tapestry, pretending that she was not affected by the power of his presence.

"How can you sit there, so calm and serene, when you create so much continuing trouble for me!" he hurled at her accusingly.

Leah was so stunned by this incredible statement that surprise made her turn to look at him.

Satisfied that he had her full attention, Sharif stalked around the room, glowering with discontent. "You have brought chaos into my life ever since you walked into it!" he declared.

Leah rose from her chair, spurred by the outrageousness of his claims. "It was you who walked into my life, Sharif al Kader. I had nothing to do with it. I was sitting alone in my private garden, minding my own business..."

"Doing that tapestry that made me think things I should not have thought," he shot at her.

"I did my best to correct you," she retorted hotly.

"Which made everything worse! Arousing my interest. Defying me. Challenging me. Why pretend you are meek and mild when you are patently not? Never has any other woman looked at me as you did!"

"And just what do you mean by that? It was you who undressed me with your eyes, making me feel..."

"Huh!" His finger went up in triumph. "You admit it then."

"Admit what?"

"You wanted to know what it would be like with me. So now you know. It is therefore totally capricious of you to complain about it to your father."

"I did not complain about it to my father!" Leah cried indignantly. "Quite the opposite, in fact."

"What opposite?" Sharif demanded.

"I told him I loved you. That you were a wonderful lover. And that he should go home and not worry about me because I was perfectly happy to stay here with you." Her blue eyes blazed absolute fury at him as his whole demeanour was transformed by beaming delight. "I only said that—"

"Because it was the truth," he cut in with relish.

"To stop him and Glen from doing something stupid, like putting themselves in your power for my sake," she finished in vengeful triumph.

"I knew you would come to love me," he said, arrogantly ignoring her disclaimer and apparently uncaring that she had done her best to torpedo his grand revenge. "It is good that you can now admit it to yourself."

"I do *not!*" Leah fumed at him.

"It had to be in your mind and heart, or you would not have said the words."

She stamped her foot in frustration. "Sharif, will you listen to me? I do *not* love you! How on earth could I love you when you've done what you've done to me?"

His dark eyes sparkled with amusement at her protests. "What is it I've done that you did not truly want?"

"You kidnapped me, for a start," she flung at him scornfully.

He raised a mocking eyebrow. "Did you not challenge me to do precisely that when you looked at me in the throne room at Qatama?"

"Of course not!"

"Yes, you did, Leah. You deliberately challenged me. And you would never respect a man who did not meet your strength with more strength."

His eyes burned knowingly into hers as he moved to sweep her into his embrace. Leah curled her hands against his chest, a small, instinctive rebellion that was totally ineffective in preventing his power to arouse responses in her that she could not control.

"You wanted to know me," he declared with searing certainty. "It is merely your contrary pride that denies it. And the sense of your power as a woman. You do not like to concede anything too easily."

Leah was flooded with confusion as Sharif gathered her closer to him. Was there any truth in what he said? Had she put other faces on her reactions and responses because they didn't suit her perception of herself? Everything seemed to be changing today. First her father, making her see the past in a different light. Now Sharif, making her feel . . . What did she feel? It was all so complicated and messed around with other considerations.

His lips grazed softly over hers. "Say you love me. I want to taste the words," he murmured.

"I'm still your prisoner," Leah forced out, fighting the insidious rush of warmth through her body. She would not surrender to his will. Not while his mind was still bent on revenge. But was it? He no longer seemed to care about it.

"Say you love me and I will give you more freedom," he promised, kissing her with sensual seduction.

"Without freedom, how can I know what I feel?" she argued.

He lifted his mouth from hers and heaved a rueful sigh. "Why do you make difficulties when the obvious is looking you in the face?"

Leah suddenly recollected what had brought this whole subject up in the first place. "Why were you so angry about my father?"

He shrugged dismissively. "It does not matter. All is explained. It is only natural your father should take offence. He is very stubborn. Like his daughter."

"Why do you say that? What did he do?" Then more fearfully, "What did you do?"

He grimaced. "I thought you had ruined all my good work in affecting a reconciliation between you. Which would have been very ungrateful of you, Leah. As it is, your father has made difficulties where there should have been none. I have now made sure he is on his way home."

"Unharmed?" Leah asked anxiously.

Sharif frowned. "Of course, unharmed. I do not want his life."

Leah's heart sank. Her father had clearly gone back to Sharif and tried to bargain with his own life. She desperately hoped he would give more credence to what she had told him and not upset Glen and Samira with his disbelief in her happiness with Sharif.

"While I respect his sense of paternal responsibility," Sharif continued in a somewhat vexed tone, "he must respect the reality that I also have responsibilities. The welfare of Zubani has to be considered. I cannot always do what I want, when I want. The proper steps must be taken.''

Leah's heart sank lower. She did not ask herself why the warmth Sharif had aroused suddenly chilled into misery. "You mean you must marry Fatima," she said dully.

"I have no intention whatsoever of contracting a marriage with her or any princess from Qatama," Sharif declared, sounding even more vexed. "Why should you think it?" he demanded.

She looked at him in bewilderment. "For the welfare of Zubani. Wasn't that what you meant?"

He made a contemptuous sound. "You think I would accept the terms offered by King Rashid?" His eyes glittered with vengeful pride. "No, my beautiful Leah, *they* will come to *my* negotiating table and accept *my* terms. Qatama must be humbled to Zubani's will. I shall not have it any other way."

Thus spoke Sharif al Kader, Leah thought with a wild lilt of exhilaration, hunter, warrior, zealot determined to conquer whatever needed to be conquered in forging the destiny of his choice. It was certifiable madness to think he meant to forge a future with her, but suddenly there was a smile on her lips, a gush of pleasure streaming through her veins, and her hands uncurled and slid around his neck.

"Perhaps I did want to know you, Sharif," she conceded.

Desire instantly blazed over pride. "So now you will say you love me."

"There's a little matter of my freedom."

"Can I trust you not to cause more trouble for me?" he countered, lowering his eyebrows sternly.

"Hmm...we shall see." She enjoyed using his own words back at him.

He laughed, a joyous ripple of laughter that jiggled her heart and took her breath away. His eyes danced intense pleasure in her, and Leah knew—there was no questioning it—she wanted this man to be hers. Perhaps it was the loneliness inside her prompting the need or desire, but she wanted to belong to Sharif al-Kader, and she wanted him to belong to her. No matter what it led to in the future.

A knock on the door demanded attention.

Sharif's laughter faded into a sigh as he reluctantly released Leah. "There are times when it is inconvenient to be a father, but a promise is a promise. My daughters are eager to see you again. I had them flown up from Shalaan."

He opened the door, and the two little girls rushed in to greet Leah, hurtling past their father in excited anticipation.

"Miss Marlow..."

"Miss Marlow..."

"Will you tell us another story?"

"And Papa said you will teach us to speak English."

"But a story first," Jazmin appealed. "Can I sit in your lap?"

"It's my turn, Jazmin," Nadia reproved.

Sharif swooped on them and lifted them up, one daughter in each arm. "What is this? You do not even greet your father?" he chided.

"But we've already seen you today, Papa," Nadia said.

"And we've been waiting and waiting to see Miss Marlow," Jazmin complained.

"Then I will pardon you this once. But you are to remember your manners with Miss Marlow, who may tell you a story if you ask her nicely. And may teach you to speak English if you are very good girls."

"Yes, Papa," they chorused fervently.

In the hour that followed, Leah felt very much included in a family circle of love. Surely Sharif would not encourage such a situation if he did not mean it to continue indefinitely. How he intended to resolve the political problem with Qatama Leah had no idea, but she resolved to stop worrying about the future. One way or another, Sharif al Kader would take care of it.

Two things were certain.

He was not going to marry Fatima.

And Leah did not feel lonely anymore.

CHAPTER TWELVE

SHARIF HAD NO SOONER left Leah the next morning than Tayi arrived. The two women faced each other across the sitting room, the memory of their mutual failure to effect Leah's escape weighing heavily between them. Tayi's dignified bearing did not invite any closing of the distance she maintained, but her dark, velvety eyes were no longer hostile. Leah felt she was being assessed in some enigmatic way that would have meaning only to Tayi.

"I did not think we would meet again," she offered, wanting to reach out to the woman.

The comment was ignored.

"I wish to ask your advice," Tayi said.

Leah had the impression this must be a first in Tayi's life. She had always gone her own way. Even now, in making her request, she projected an air of personal decisiveness that denied any dependency on whatever Leah replied.

Before she could stop herself, Leah asked. "Why? What do you care about how I think?"

Tayi eyed her with wary reserve. When she finally replied, her melodious voice came in short, lilting cadences, giving a hypnotic power to her speech. "You do nothing. Yet the world changes around you. You create a storm. I've watched you. Now I, too, wish to create a storm. I ask you how you do it.''

Leah was nonplussed. It was clear that to Tayi the words had momentous import, but to Leah they made no sense at all. A series of contradictions. Although there was one correct observation amongst them. It was true that Leah had done nothing. Everything lately had been done to her! As for creating a storm or the world changing around her, Leah had no knowledge of either. Tayi could hardly be referring to the chaos Sharif declared she had brought into his life. That was undoubtedly a personal exaggeration.

''You will not answer?''

Leah shook her head in helpless confusion. What could she say? ''I don't know how to answer,'' she blurted out.

The ensuing silence vibrated with tension. With the swaying grace that gave her so much regal dignity, Tayi walked to the window closest to where Leah stood. She looked out with a fixed gaze that suggested to Leah she saw nothing but her inner thoughts. Slowly her head turned, the large, dark eyes focussing directly on Leah's, searching for truth.

''Or you have decided not to answer?'' she asked. ''Not to help me?'' There was a pained look of rejection as though she had laid herself open in a way she never did, and didn't know how to handle it.

Leah stepped forward, her hand lifting in instinctive appeal, touching Tayi's arm in a gesture of reassurance. ''What is it that you want, Tayi?'' she asked, trying her utmost to project sympathetic encouragement. ''Tell me specifically.''

Tayi instantly withdrew, guarding the reserve she kept around her. "I cannot give myself over to an enemy," she said, watching Leah with heightened intensity. "It would give you the power to destroy me."

"You're not my enemy. Nor would I ever destroy anyone."

The reply spilled naturally from Leah's lips, and Tayi slowly accepted it. "Then you will tell me how it is done. How you did it."

"Yes. Everything I can," Leah affirmed, although she still had no idea what the other woman was talking about or what was required of her. That had lost any importance. It was the reaching out and acceptance that was most needed here and now.

Tayi's tension eased. The music of her voice softened to a warmer tone. "The sheikh has always promised he will arrange a marriage for me that is advantageous to my position."

Leah's mind leapt through a range of logical possibilities, desperately trying to pick on Tayi's obscure train of thought. "You've fallen in love?" she asked.

A faraway look crept into her eyes. "I have seen a man who stands above all others."

Leah felt a sense of triumph at having finally hit on the right wavelength for this strange conversation. She wondered who had found favour with this majestic woman. A soldier? One of the sheikh's attendants? It would surely have to be someone attached to the household.

"Who is he, Tayi?" Leah asked with keen interest.

She smiled with all the magical mystique of a woman fathoms deep in love. "Prince Youssef of Qatama."

Leah's heart turned over with painful compassion. It was an impossible match. Surely Tayi had to understand that. Yet the dream in the dark velvety eyes denied any recognition of reality. Leah swallowed her shock and tentatively tried to spell out the indisputable facts.

"You realise, of course, that such a love, such an ambition, would one day lead . . ."

"Yes. I would be Queen of Qatama. But it is not for that reason I asked for your advice. He looked at me. I felt it. Drawing me to look at him. And it was written into my destiny."

The blissful conviction in Tayi's voice made Leah feel helpless. Her mind slowly grasped the parallel that must have worked through Tayi's mind. If a minder of children could captivate the sheikh, why should not a minder of children captivate a prince? Leah had no sooner worked this out than Tayi pressed the question.

"You will tell me how it's done. What herbs to put in his drink."

"This cannot be done with herbs," Leah said hopelessly.

"But you will help me," Tayi pressed with artless appeal. "The sheikh is angry with Qatama. You have made him happy. Happier than he has been since his wife died. If you were to suggest the marriage . . ."

Leah simply could not bring herself to erase the wondrous glow of anticipation in the other woman's eyes. "For what little it is worth, I will do everything in my power to help you, Tayi."

"You will not betray my secret?"

"Never."

Her beautifully sculptured lips curved into a satisfied little smile. She turned her head to the window, her long, graceful neck arching as she looked out to some distant horizon. "The winds of change howl through the desert. Nothing will ever be the same again," she said in the dreamy tone of a mystic soothsayer.

"Is that good or bad?" Leah was drawn to ask.

"Both. But change is inevitable." She slowly swung her gaze to Leah, and there was the light of sure destiny in her eyes. "I will be part of it."

Content that Leah understood and empathised with her position, Tayi departed, completely unaware of the storm of confusion and despair she left behind. Everything she had said kept revolving around Leah's mind for hours afterwards.

Why had Tayi considered her an enemy? Was it because of the children's ready affection for her? Because of Sharif's desire for her? Had she seen her world changing because of Leah, the sheikh placing her at his side where his wife had once been?

Perhaps Tayi had leapt to the conclusion the sheikh intended to marry Leah because he would not let her go. A most unlikely outcome, Leah thought with painful irony. But that idea might have seeded Tayi's unrealistic hope for a marriage with the crown prince of Qatama.

Could a single look at a man strike a woman's heart so deeply? Leah wondered. Was that how it had been for her that afternoon in the garden at Qatama, looking at Sharif and feeling the sense of destiny? She shook her head. So difficult to sort out how she felt when he held her a prisoner of his will. But Tayi and Youssef...

Youssef had definitely been struck by Tayi. He had said as much. But on being told her status in Sharif's household, he would have known a pursuit of interest was pointless. A crown prince did not marry a simple minder of children. The winds of change did not howl that fast through the desert.

Her promise of help was futile. Leah knew it in her heart, and empathised deeply with the disappointment and loss Tayi must inevitably feel. Nevertheless, when the opportunity arose to bring up Tayi's cause with the sheikh, she would do so. A promise was a promise.

As it turned out she did not see Sharif until late that evening. Nadia and Jazmin were brought to her for an English lesson that extended into the lunch hour, making the meal a lot of happy fun together. Then, to Leah's surprise, she was taken on a tour of a girls' school in the city, and had the system of education explained to her by the headmistress.

When Sharif came to her apartment after dinner, he wanted Leah to give him a critical appraisal of all she had seen and heard at the school, relating it to her Australian education. He listened, questioned, discussed possible improvements with her and smiled his pleasure and approval at her willingness to express her opinions.

"You care about my people," he declared with satisfaction.

"I care that girls be given as much opportunity to develop their capabilities as are boys," she corrected with some asperity. "And what's more, Sharif, you're going to need them to help run this country of yours, if you don't want to depend on the expertise of foreigners forever and a day."

His eyes sparkled with triumph. "You care."

"I care about a lot of things."

"Tomorrow I have arranged for you to visit the women's health centre. It will be of interest to you." He rose from his chair and drew Leah from hers, gathering her into his embrace. "You are right. It is good for you to have more freedom. I want you to be happy with me."

Her eyes ruefully mocked his idea of freedom. "I'm not exactly being given a choice, am I?"

He raised his eyebrows. "You do not want to go to the women's centre? There is also the museum to visit, and the..."

Leah sighed at the futility of arguing over the essence of freedom. "The centre is fine," she said, grateful for small mercies.

"Ah! You surrender to me."

"No, I don't," Leah flashed at him. "I will never surrender to any man. I simply decided on the centre."

His eyes challenged hers with simmering desire. "Then I shall have to take you to bed and make you love me."

Leah didn't have much choice about that, either, but she did privately concede Sharif was a wonderful lover. Which he proved once again.

It was while she was lying in his arms after being very thoroughly made love to that she was reminded of her promise to Tayi. With Sharif's heart beating with slow contentment in the fulfilment of his desire for her, Leah decided this had to be the best possible time to approach the delicate subject of Tayi's desire.

"Remember when Prince Youssef came to the fortress, Sharif?" she started.

"Mmm..." It was a noncommittal sound. He was weaving her long hair through his fingers, as he often did after making love.

"And Tayi interrupted the meeting?"

"Mmm."

"You said you would arrange an advantageous marriage for her."

"It is being done."

Leah jerked her head up, causing the long, silky tress he had been weaving to slide through his fingers. He smiled, enjoying the sensation.

"You're arranging a marriage for her right now?" Leah asked, demanding his full attention.

"It is a matter of negotiation." A gleam of steely purpose speared through the hazy contentment in his eyes. "I shall have my way."

"But what about Tayi?" Leah asked in alarm. "What if she doesn't love the man you've chosen?"

"I have Tayi's best interests at heart."

"Have you talked to her? Does she know?"

"There is no need. Tayi will be happy with my choice."

"How can you know that?" Leah cried despairingly. "What if she wants to choose for herself?"

Sharif frowned at her. "Why do you question it? I have made my judgement. It will stand."

"Like King Rashid's judgement with Samira?" Leah snapped in frustration.

There was a blaze of something very dangerous in his eyes. "You dare to throw that in my face, Leah?"

"Yes, I do!" she retorted recklessly. "What if Tayi loves another man? You could at least try asking her, instead of treating her as though she had no mind and heart of her own."

"Did I not know your heart and mind better than you did yourself?" he demanded.

"That's very much open to question," Leah insisted vehemently.

"The winds of change might be howling through the desert, Leah Marlow, but I shall do what I believe is right. For you. For me. For Tayi. For Zubani. Let there be no more question about it!"

And that was that, in Sharif's mind. Leah realised she was going to have an uphill battle trying to change it in any way whatsoever. Arguing was utterly useless. Maybe if she worked hard at making Sharif happy, she might bend him more to her way of thinking. Tayi apparently believed she had the power to do it.

If she created a storm by doing nothing, what could she do if she really tried?

CHAPTER THIRTEEN

LEAH DID NOT find it difficult to make Sharif absolutely delighted with her over the next few days. The places he sent her to visit were of interest to her anyway, and she applied herself to finding out all she could about them, the programs being followed and what could be initiated to improve what was already being done for his people.

She could see the difficulties in assimilating the huge technological leap the country was making, the reluctance of the older people to accept change, the fear of the unknown. She developed a new appreciation of too much, too soon. Yet the eagerness in the younger people to broaden their lives captured her imagination and lent zeal to her voice when she talked all these matters over with Sharif.

Oddly enough, in working to make Sharif happy, Leah found a happy purpose in her own life that was immensely satisfying. It was easy to forget she was a prisoner most of the time. And Sharif listened to her more and more.

When Tayi approached her after one of the children's English lessons and inquired in her shy, obscure way if Leah had spoken to the sheikh, Leah could say with considerable confidence that she was

working on it. Nevertheless, the resulting glow in
Tayi's eyes did give Leah a twinge of guilt. It was all
very well for her to want Tayi's love answered, but
what of Youssef? Was it remotely possible that a man
of his status would accept Tayi as his wife?

Perhaps it was a fool's dream. Yet somehow Leah
could not give up hope of making it come true, however unlikely it was. Soon, she promised herself, she
would bring it up with Sharif again, at least make him
see he was wrong not to consider Tayi's feelings.

In the fervour of all her planning and the pleasure
of Sharif's happy response to her more positive attitudes, Leah forgot that her month with him was coming to an end. She also forgot the deep, blinding
compulsion for revenge. When she least expected its
reemergence, Sharif totally devastated her with a dis-
play of feeling that rocked her world again.

He swept into her apartment on the heels of her return from visiting a baby health clinic. He exuded an
aura of highly fired energy. Leah had never seen his
face so animated, his eyes so brilliant, and his voice
vibrated with exultant power.

"I have them. At last. Finally."

He laughed from sheer elation as he paced to one of
the windows, looking out with the distinctive air of
being lord and master of all he surveyed. He breathed
in as though the air held the scent of the sweetest nec-
tar. "What a glorious, wonderful day to be alive!"

Then he swung around to face Leah again, emanating total exhilaration as he lifted his arms in an open-
handed gesture. "They're in my hands. The instruments of power." His fingers curled into fists. "And

they shall beat to my drum!" he declared with intense relish.

Leah snapped out of her bemusement with him and fired an appeal. "If you'll tell me what you're talking about, I might be able to appreciate it, Sharif. What instruments?"

His smile glittered with triumph. "The Princess Samira and your brother!"

Shock splintered into fear. "What's happened? Have you had them abducted, too?"

His lips curled in mocking indulgence of her lack of understanding. "No. It was far simpler and more subtle than that. They have come to offer themselves as hostages, malefactors, in order to secure your release."

Leah barely stifled a groan of despair. Her father had not delivered the messages she had asked of him. Her revelation that she and Sharif were lovers must have made things worse, not better. "How could they be so stupid!" she cried in bitter frustration.

"Their sense of honour outweighed their self-interest," Sharif replied with intense satisfaction. "I expected it of your brother, Leah. He would not be a man if he had not come for you. But the Princess Samira... She is a bonus. The anvil to my hammer."

The dark, vengeful note in his voice struck more fear. "You won't hurt them, Sharif," Leah pleaded. "You can't."

"I shall pass the sentence of the law upon them."

The light of a zealot was in his eyes, and his face wore the hard, immutable look of a relentless and vengeful judge. Leah could feel herself shrinking from it as the pain of disillusionment withered the liking and loving he had drawn from her. Revenge had been his mission all along, the one he had nursed in his heart and soul.

She had fooled herself again. Taking her, having her, had only been incidental to the main thrust of his purpose. Perhaps an amusing little challenge on the side. A charge to his ego to get her to love him. Or better still, to surrender to him.

And she almost had.

"You've used me as a lure," she accused in her need to lash out at him.

His eyes danced with unholy amusement. "You fulfil my purpose."

Her eyes blazed with fury. "If you so much as touch a hair of their heads..."

"You will use the *agal?*"

He laughed, a joyous shout of laughter that rang around Leah's mind, inflaming her to a rage of monumental intensity. She flew at him, wanting to rake his eyes out and pummel his chest with her fists until his deceiving heart stopped beating.

"I hate you, I hate you," she cried as she rained blows at him. "You're the vilest, most despicable man I've ever come across. You are without shame. You bring dishonour upon yourself, your family, your country..."

"Stop this foolishness!" He caught her wrists and forcibly held her back from him.

Leah's eyes fiercely challenged any force he could bring to bear on her. "I will never stop!" she said with heated venom.

A wild exultation leapt into his eyes. Before Leah could catch her breath he swooped to pick her up and hoist her high in his arms. She kicked and hit out at him as he marched into her bedroom, but he might have been a rock for all the effect her blows had on him. He tossed her on the bed and stood, arms akimbo, glowering at her.

"I can have you any time I like," he declared with all the arrogance of his superior male strength.

Leah hurled herself off the other side of the bed and faced him across it, her arms planted on her hips in matching aggression. "I'd rather die than ever let you touch me again," she flung at him. "I won't talk to you. I won't eat with you. I won't sleep with you, and if you try anything I'll spit in your face."

He raised his eyebrows in haughty disdain of her threats. "I will not stay with you when you are in such an unreasonable mood."

He turned his back on her and headed for the door, denying her any more expression of the fury aroused by his perfidy. Leah would not let him get away with it. She whirled over to a side table, seized a vase of flowers and hurled it after him. It smashed against the door jamb at head level. He did not so much as pause or flinch. He passed through to the sitting room with arrogant dignity intact.

"You hurt Glen and Samira, and see what you get!" Leah yelled at his retreating back.

He strode on.

Leah charged into the sitting room, picking up and hurling whatever objects came to hand, but her moving target continued to ignore the missiles thrown at him. Her aim was frustratingly awry. As he opened the door that led out of her apartment, she only just missed him with a dish that flew over his shoulder and smashed somewhere in the corridor beyond him.

"You think I've brought chaos into your life, Sharif al Kader?" she shouted. "I'll give you chaos like you've never seen chaos before! I'm warning you!"

She groped for something more to throw and was forced to look down when nothing came to hand. When she looked back, Sharif was gone and Tayi was standing in the doorway. The woman had a look of intense interest on her face. Her eyes shone with admiration.

"I now understand the storm," she lilted.

With a sigh of deflation Leah lowered the little brass bell she had picked up. "Your sheikh is impossible, Tayi," she replied bitterly.

"He will come back," Tayi said with unshaken confidence in Leah's ability to draw him back.

"He'd better not," Leah seethed. "Unless he changes his mind."

"So, you have asked him and he has refused?"

It took Leah a moment to rearrange her mind to Tayi's wavelength. She had obviously come about Youssef again. "I'm sorry, Tayi. I tried. But he wouldn't listen."

The other woman nodded sagely. "What you have done is good. You are on my side."

"What I need is an *agal*," Leah said, more to herself than to Tayi.

"Do I need an *agal*, too?" came the serious inquiry.

Leah's eyes flared with righteous fury. "All women need *agals* against men like him!"

Tayi turned aside from the doorway and clapped her hands. Two women servants arrived in a flurry. "Go and get two *agals* and bring them to me," she commanded. "I shall be with Miss Marlow."

Leah stared in astonishment as the servants hurried off to obey. Then, with a majestic air of authority, Tayi stepped inside the sitting room and closed the door behind her. Leah couldn't help thinking Tayi was certainly made in the mould of a stately queen, and there were many questions about her that Leah wanted answered.

"I have much to learn from you," Tayi declared, a burning light of mission in her beautiful dark eyes. "It is with power that you deal with power. I am beginning to see."

"Who are you, Tayi?" Leah demanded, deciding it was well past time she had all the information she could get. "You go where you like, when you like. You give orders as though you were born to it. Everyone makes way for you."

Tayi looked surprised at Leah's ignorance. "I am of the ruling family. There is no question that I should be obeyed."

"You're part of Sharif's family?" Leah could hardly contain her shock. That was the last thing she had expected.

"I am his closest cousin," Tayi said with great dignity. "My father was the sheikh who stood aside. He had three wives. I am the daughter of the youngest wife, Shasti. My mother was of the ruling family of

Omala, but she married beneath her status, and the children of a sheikh take their status from him," Tayi explained with regal pride.

This accounted for the majestic image Tayi had invariably painted in Leah's mind, and it was more than enough to stir her simmering rage into another wild ferment. How dare Sharif call Tayi a simple minder of children! And not to consider his closest cousin's feelings on the matter of her marriage partner was totally abominable male chauvinism! He deserved to be hanged, drawn and quartered. And not only on Tayi's behalf. If he intended to harm Glen or Samira . . .

"I'll kill him," Leah muttered with venom.

Tayi looked at her in bewilderment. "How will that help?. Will it solve the problem?"

"He has to know we are very serious in what we say. What we want. We have to make him see that there is a price to pay if he doesn't do as we ask."

"Ah!" The large, dark eyes glistened with approval. "That I understand. It is a good plan."

Leah wondered if a strong sense of revenge ran in the family. If so, it was far better to have Tayi on her side than against her. Which meant it was imperative to tackle the Youssef problem head-on.

A knock on the door heralded the return of the servants who had been sent to do Tayi's bidding. They handed over the two *agals* to their mistress. As though it was perfectly natural for her to carry such a weapon, Tayi slid one of the *agals* into the folds of her turban. The other she presented to Leah.

"There is not much time," she advised. "King Rashid of Qatama has been summoned. Perhaps

Prince Youssef will accompany his father. That will be a very positive sign. Do you not think?''

"Yes. Youssef will come," Leah said with certainty. For his sister's sake, if not for Glen's. It could be the last time they would ever see each other. "If my brother and the Princess Samira are to be judged by the law, Youssef will undoubtedly accompany his father."

"There is to be a special *majlis* tomorrow morning. You think Prince Youssef will attend?''

Leah was intensely grateful to Tayi for this information. "Yes. And we must attend, as well."

"It is forbidden. The *majlis* is only for men."

Leah eyed her sternly. "We have to attend that *majlis*, Tayi. It is your only chance to fight for what you want. The sheikh has to know you are very serious about your desire to marry Prince Youssef."

It might also be Leah's only chance to influence the judgement made on Glen and Samira. Or, failing any mercy granted, to take her revenge on the sheikh of Zubani.

"The sheikh will not like it," Tayi warned.

"Let the winds of change howl tomorrow morning!" Leah quoted at her. "You said you would be part of it, Tayi. If you want Prince Youssef of Qatama as your husband, the time for change has come."

Tayi seemed to grow immeasurably taller as conviction blazed in her eyes. "I will be part of it. I will do it," she affirmed. "I thank you for your advice. Tomorrow I shall create a storm."

So take that, Sharif al Kader! Leah thought with intense satisfaction as Tayi made her queenly way out of the apartment.

Revenge would certainly be taken tomorrow.

Chaos would reign.

CHAPTER FOURTEEN

LEAH SPENT a very restless and disturbed night alone. It spurred her determination to break in on the morning *majlis* and make her presence felt, one way or another. Sharif al Kader would find out she could not be overlooked or ignored.

It gave her a perverse pleasure to dress in white on this day of ultimate decision. She strapped the *agal* to the inner side of her left arm, carefully testing that the long sleeve of her robe completely covered it. As usual, breakfast was served in her sitting room, and she tried to eat some of it in order to settle her stomach. She was nibbling at a croissant when Sharif suddenly stepped inside her apartment.

He stood by the doorway, eyeing her balefully. "I trust you have recovered your temper this morning."

Leah's eyes flashed scorn at him. "No," she snapped. "I doubt I ever will."

His face looked drawn and tired, as though he also had spent a restless night. His dark eyes brooded over her in turbulent discontent. "What is it that you want from me?" he demanded. Then, as she was about to answer, he gruffly added, "Apart from releasing the Princess Samira and your brother."

Leah glowered her discontent right back at him. "I want to be free. I want to go to the *majlis* today. I want—"

"It is forbidden for a woman."

"I don't care if it's forbidden or not. You're the sheikh of Zubani. You make the rules. You can change them." A spark of inspiration added the silky taunt, "I would find that very becoming in you."

He frowned. "If you come to the *majlis*, it will be seen as insulting to King Rashid and Prince Youssef."

Leah disdained any reply to that excuse. She simply stared at him with steely resolve in her eyes.

An air of decision slowly gathered and stamped itself on the sheikh's face. The powerful charisma of a man of destiny shone once more. "It shall be as you wish. You may come to the *majlis*. I will send an escort for you when it is time."

He left Leah to savour her sense of triumph alone. She could hardly believe he had actually bent to her will. What did it mean? Had she become more important to him than his revenge? Had he reconsidered his judgement on Glen and Samira? Or was that hoping for too much? *Apart from their release,* Sharif had said.

But at least she now had entry to the *majlis*. She could afford to play a waiting game to see what Sharif had in mind. If his judgement did not meet her approval, she would take whatever action was warranted in the circumstances.

Having sorted this through in her mind, Leah summoned one of the servants to send a message to Tayi. Her new friend and ally had to be informed that the

sheikh was allowing Leah to be present at the *majlis*.
This exception to the men-only rule would undoubtedly bolster Tayi's resolution to break it. Leah had no
scruples whatsoever about having encouraged Tayi to
go after what she wanted. It was, after all, what Tayi's
closest cousin invariably did as though it was his divine right.

Other people had rights, as well, whether they were
divine or not, and it was about time the sheikh of
Zubani started respecting them, Leah thought with
burning conviction. And what's more, if he didn't do
that, no way was Leah going to remain at his side!

She fretted through two long hours before the escort came for her. It gave her a deep appreciation of
what Glen and Samira must be going through, not
knowing what their fate was to be but fearing the
worst at the hands of the sheikh of Zubani.

When she was ushered into the official room for the
majlis, the scene was almost an exact replica of what
she had experienced at Qatama a month ago. A line of
men seated along the side walls, their murmurs to each
other halting as Leah was brought in by two armed
guards. Facing her at the far end were the sheikh of
Zubani and King Rashid of Qatama, seated side by
side on elaborately carved, high-backed chairs that
denoted their status. To the left of King Rashid, and
at an angle to him, sat Prince Youssef. A chair simi-
larly placed to the right of the sheikh was empty.

A tense silence accompanied Leah's long walk down
the avenue of men. Leah sensed that whatever negotiations had been discussed prior to her arrival had not
gone well. Both the sheikh and the king were stern-

faced. There was certainly no air of amity between them. The atmosphere in the room bristled with discord. It did not bode well for Glen and Samira, Leah thought, her heart torn between fear and a fierce, desperate courage.

She kept her head high, defying the right of both king and sheikh to have any power over her and denying them the obeisance of a bow. Her eyes clashed momentarily with Sharif's. An electric challenge vibrated between them for several long seconds. Then he gave a slight nod, and she was led to the vacant chair to his right.

Leah sat with her hands folded in her lap, surreptitiously feeling for the handle of the *agal* under her sleeve, anxious that it be easily accessible to her. Her heart was pounding so hard it seemed to be ringing in her ears. She looked across at Youssef. His eyes met hers but expressed nothing. His face was tightly closed against showing any feeling.

It's going to be bad, Leah thought in sickening panic. If Sharif had not won what he wanted from King Rashid, there would be no room for mercy in the judgement on Glen and Samira. Leah turned her head to the king. His gaze was directed at the entrance doors, but his eyes had a fixed, unseeing look that suggested to Leah he would not allow the sight of his daughter to make any impression on him. He had declared the Princess Samira dead, and dead she would remain to her father.

The doors began to open.

Leah sucked in a deep breath.

But the doors were not opening for Glen and Samira. It was Tayi who stepped into the room, Tayi in all her magnificence, robed in shimmering scarlet and gold, a matching turban wound around her head and an *agal* prominently displayed in her hand.

There was a rustle of movement amongst the men seated along the walls, murmurs of disquiet. Tayi swept a commanding gaze around them, regally defying anyone to stop her from doing as she willed. The sheikh raised his hand in a motion for everyone to be still. Tayi gave a little nod of acknowledgement to Leah, then looked directly at Prince Youssef. The dark, velvety eyes glowed with a luminous love that seemed to transfix the crown prince of Qatama.

"Who is this woman?" King Rashid demanded.

"My closest cousin, Tayi al Kader," the sheikh replied with strong emphasis on her status.

Youssef rose from his chair, as though drawn hypnotically to his feet by the power of the feeling flowing from Tayi to him.

Perhaps it was the signal Tayi had been waiting for. She started forward, moving with a slow, swaying grace that held even the king of Qatama mesmerised with her approach. She came to a halt at a respectful distance from the sheikh and the king. Her gaze fastened purposefully on her cousin's.

"I have come to speak my heart," she announced with grave dignity.

"Does that require an *agal* in your hand, Tayi?" Sharif asked with equal gravity.

"It is to show that I am serious."

Sharif flicked a hard look at Leah, who returned it with interest. He addressed Tayi in a sterner voice. "It is not seemly in this company."

The advice had no effect on Tayi. She emanated fixed and unshakeable purpose. "You will listen," she demanded.

The sheikh apparently decided he was not averse to a diversion at this point. "Speak as you will, Tayi," he said with good grace.

"It concerns the arrangement of my marriage."

"It is still to be fully negotiated."

Her gaze swung to Prince Youssef. "There is one man who stands above all others."

"I have made other plans for you," Sharif said, frowning over this new complexity in the situation.

"I shall have no other man," Tayi declared, still looking straight at Youssef, leaving no-one in any doubt as to her choice of husband.

Youssef stepped towards her, and there was certainly no lack of expression on his face now. He was utterly captivated by the woman who was openly declaring her love and desire for him.

"Completely out of the question," King Rashid snapped, glaring furious disapproval at Youssef. "I wish to marry off my daughters, not my son. I won't countenance such an alliance. It does not have my approval."

Youssef wrenched his gaze from Tayi's to shoot a glowering frown at his father. Rebellion was in the air, and Tayi was well on the way to creating the storm that would change her life. Leah watched Sharif, willing him to respond to his cousin's initiative. She saw the slight curve of his mouth as his mind grasped the possibilities of exploiting what was happening in front of him. A gleam of animal cunning brightened his eyes.

"Such a marriage has certain advantages," he said, as though musing over the idea. He turned to King Rashid with an air of weighing important factors. "It would cement the alliance between our two countries." He paused, then ruefully added, "But I had planned to marry my cousin to King Ahmed of Isha."

Tayi's head swivelled instantly to the sheikh. Her whole body arched in protest. "King Ahmed of Isha is seventy-five years old."

"I did not expect the happiness of the marriage to last forever," Sharif said dryly. "You will understand that Prince Youssef is of much lower status than King Ahmed, Tayi. Such a marriage would be quite unacceptable in comparison unless adequate compensation were to be offered."

King Rashid's long, noble face took on a grimmer expression at the sting to his pride. "A mere cousin," he began, clearly about to voice rejection of the idea.

"Father," Youssef cut in with urgent intent. "Think of the advantages. It will redress the problems caused by the desertion of duty by Samira."

The king looked at him in disgust. "The Princess Samira is dead."

Leah saw her chance to break the king's intransigence and strike a blow against any harsh judgement on Glen and Samira. "If your daughter is dead, Your Majesty," she said, her voice raised for all to hear, "then the sentence of the law cannot be passed against her."

A murmur ran around the room as that inarguable piece of logic sank in.

"A debating point," the king scorned.

"We need some clear thinking," Sharif declared with ponderous gravity. But there was a sparkle of appreciation in the glance he flashed at Leah.

"Perhaps we could bring her back to life," Tayi suggested, her melodious voice lilting with sweet reason as she added, "if she is to be my sister-in-law, I do not want her dead."

"Neither do I," Youssef pressed in fervent support. His eyes glowed pure adoration at Tayi. "You are a woman who stands above all other women."

"There is no dignity in being stoned to death in the marketplace," Tayi said. "The time for change has come."

"I couldn't agree more," Youssef said strongly. He reached out and took the *agal* Tayi held, then slowly enfolded her hand in his. "You speak my heart, as well."

The sheikh cleared his throat in a rumbling demand for their attention. "In the interests of amity and friendship..."

"You call this amity and friendship?" King Rashid thundered in towering disapproval.

Sharif turned to him with a greater measure of towering disapproval, his dark eyes as cutting as lasers. "Do you forget the humiliation Zubani has suffered because you did not listen to your daughter's heart? Your son speaks well. I am favourably impressed."

The king flushed, highly discomfited by the reminder of Qatama's shame at not delivering what had been promised. "Very well. We shall call this amity and friendship," he conceded tersely.

"In view of the fact that my cousin wishes this marriage," Sharif continued with unrelenting purpose, "I am willing to forgo some of the compensation that should be given for the lowering of her status."

There was a look of black fury from the king at the repeated slight to his son's status.

"But such matters as need to be negotiated can be worked out at a later time," Sharif allowed with a show of benevolence. "Are we agreed on this marriage?"

The king's mouth tightened, resisting to the bitter end.

"Father, I ask your consent." It was more a command from Youssef than an appeal. Although he was as tall as Tayi, he seemed to have gained in stature simply by having her at his side.

For a few tense moments the king's eyes warred with his son's. Then his gaze moved to Tayi in all her regal glory, and a flicker of wonderment softened his expression. It was not difficult for Leah to read the king's mind. Tayi would certainly cut an impressive figure as queen of Qatama. Besides which, he could not afford the scandal of a second runaway couple from his royal household.

"We are agreed on the marriage," he said, making it a clear and firm announcement.

Tayi smiled with happiness at Leah, her eyes glowing with gratitude for the plan that had won her heart's desire. Leah smiled back, then turned challenging eyes to Sharif al Kader, who was observing this side play with acute interest. An amused little smile twitched at his lips as he shifted his attention to Tayi again.

"You have your wish," he said with familial benevolence.

It was a dismissal, but Tayi was having none of it. "I shall sit with Prince Youssef and attend the *majlis*. It is of concern to both of us," she announced with conviction.

Youssef instantly led her to his chair, taking it upon himself to bypass any rebuff from the sheikh or the king on the matter of Tayi's right to stay. He stood at her side, ready to defy any criticism.

The king looked decidedly ruffled by this further erosion of tradition. He shot Sharif a beetling look that clearly said his patience was being sorely tried. The sheikh's shoulders lifted a fraction, then dropped in imperturbable acceptance of the changes being wrought in front of his eyes. Not a word of protest was raised by the men in the room, but after a few mumbles amongst themselves, they looked at the sheikh with an air of expectation.

"Bring in the prisoners," he commanded.

Leah tensed, her pleasure for Tayi withering as fear clutched her heart. The doors were flung wide. An escort of four armed guards marched in with Glen and Samira between them. Relief surged through Leah as she saw that no apparent injury had been done to either of them. Their hands were linked in a tight clasp, but apart from that statement of togetherness, they showed no fear of what was to come, walking with their heads high in disdain for any judgement of what they had done.

Leah couldn't help thinking they made a striking couple. Her brother's tall and muscular physique was always impressive, but it was the strong character lines of his handsome face that drew most attention. His sun-streaked hair and golden tan emphasised the azure blue of his eyes, his expression hard and unwavering with the determination to fight whatever needed to be fought to protect his sister and his wife.

Beside him, Samira looked small and exquisitely feminine, her beautiful face framed by a shiny cascade of black curls. But there was nothing weak in her slighter stature. There was no quiver to her sweetly curved mouth, no dropping of her lustrous dark eyes, no lowering of her delicately rounded chin. She walked with her man, proud to be at his side.

Glen's eyes fastened on Leah's in a clear promise that he was ready and willing to pay the price for her freedom. But she didn't want him to. She desperately didn't want him to. She looked at Samira. Her gaze was fixed on her father, perhaps pleading for his pardon before she paid for loving a man who was not her father's choice.

Was Sharif thinking this woman should have been his bride? Leah darted an anxious look at him as the prisoners were halted halfway down the room. He was not looking at Samira. He was eyeing Glen in the measuring way that one strong man looked at another.

Leah glanced at her brother and found him eyeing the sheikh with belligerent anger for what had been done to his sister. No, Leah thought helplessly. It didn't matter. Yet she felt a deep sense of pride that her brother had come to challenge Sharif al Kader over his treatment of her. It was obvious that Glen was simmering with the need to speak out and deliver his own condemnation.

Which would only make everything worse, Leah thought despairingly. Somehow she had to stop this before it got started and irrevocable things were said. As she was searching her mind for a way to intervene effectively, Youssef stepped forward with a passionate outburst against any proceeding.

"If we're all agreed Samira is dead, the sentence of the law cannot be passed upon her, Your Excellency."

"I thank you for your caring, Youssef," Samira said with loving pride. "But if my husband is to die, I wish to die with him."

"No!" Leah cried, rising to her feet and shooting a pleading look at Sharif.

"Has not the price been paid?" Tayi said, gesturing her support for Leah and giving the sheikh a knowing look.

Sharif frowned, considering the storm that could very well break out on both sides of him.

Leah seized the initiative before it was too late. "I respectfully request a private audience with you, Your Excellency. If you would call a short recess..."

Sharif was not slow in coming to a decision. He rose to his feet. "I declare a recess," he announced. "The prisoners are to be seated until I return."

He turned to bow to King Rashid. "You will excuse me, Your Majesty. With due weight to be given to the cementing of this new alliance, there are grave matters to be taken into consideration."

The king nodded his acquiescence.

Sharif swung around and gestured for Leah to accompany him. He led the way to a side door that opened to a private office. No sooner was the door shut behind them than he grasped Leah's left arm and pulled her towards him, his eyes glittering with knowing mockery.

"First the *agal*. I do not care to be stabbed in the back by a woman to whom I have granted many favours. One *agal* a day is quite enough for me to cope with."

Leah surrendered her weapon with a rueful sigh of resignation. "You can't say it didn't work for Tayi."

"It worked because I let it work," he said in arrogant dismissal, tossing the knife on the large desk at the other end of the room. "Now what's on your mind, Leah?"

She took a deep breath and searched his eyes in desperate appeal. "Do I mean anything to you, Sharif? I mean personally, not as an instrument of revenge."

His mouth twisted with irony. "You mean more to me than I care to admit. Why do you think we are here, Leah? Do I not try to give you everything you ask?"

Relief flooded through her, untangling the knots of pain and fear and bitter turmoil. "Then please listen to me, Sharif," she begged. "Since Princess Samira is dead in her own country, you should take her under your protection for the advantages it will give you."

He frowned. "What advantages?"

"Prince Youssef's gratitude. He loves his sister. Surely that is clear to you?"

"Yes."

"And if you have Samira under your wing, you get my brother, as well. If Prince Youssef changes his mind about marrying Tayi and flies off in his airplane, you need Glen on your side to shoot him down. Everyone knows that no-one can handle a plane as well as Glen."

"What other advantages?" he asked with a calculating air.

"You could take Glen on as your personal pilot. That's one in the eye for King Rashid, as well," she argued. "I think this amity and friendship thing can be a bit overdone. His manner to you was quite insulting, Sharif. But if you end up with his daughter, his pilot *and* your cousin married to the prince who will make her queen of Qatama, you'll definitely be seen as the winner."

His smile caressed her with warm appreciation. "I agree. I like the way your mind thinks. I shall take your brother as my personal pilot. That will be part of the sentence I will impose. Will that please you and give me credit in your eyes?"

"Yes. Oh, yes, Sharif." She threw her arms around his neck in an exultant hug. "And you'll find him the best pilot in the world. Truly you will," she cried, her eyes shining with the love that had burst free of the constrictions forced upon it by his earlier thirst for revenge.

His arms swept around her in a fiercely possessive embrace, and he kissed her with all the hunger of a man who deeply felt the deprivation of the intimacy they had shared. "Leah," he groaned as he moved his lips to cover her face with kisses. "Do you really want to be free of me?"

"I can never be free of you, Sharif," she whispered, blissfully turning her face to the warm fervour of his desire for her. "You've become part of me, whether I want it or not."

"I want you to choose freely." He drew back a little, his eyes seeking hers, searing them with his need. "Will you marry me, Leah? Share my life with me? Be my *sheikha* who cares for my people? Or would you rather leave me?"

Leah's heart turned over. She had never once dreamed that Sharif would want her as his wife. While she was still stunned by his unexpected proposal, he quickly added another persuasion.

"It gives me good reason in the eyes of my people to pardon my brother-in-law."

"You really want to marry me?" Leah asked breathlessly, her eyes sparkling with incredulous hope and happiness.

"Yes. Very much. Say you love me, Leah," he pleaded gruffly.

"I love you, Sharif. And I'll be anything you want. Everything," she promised, and she carried the promise to his lips, to seal it there forever.

Elation sang through her mind at the wonderful future Sharif was offering. He smiled his delight in her. "This is the way marriages should be arranged.

Emotion must not be allowed to get in the way," he said, then completely disproved his argument by kissing her with more and more emotional passion.

Leah eventually became aware that a considerable amount of time had passed. "We should go back and tell the others," she murmured reluctantly.

"They can wait a little longer," Sharif said with firm authority.

And they did.

CHAPTER FIFTEEN

"YOU REALLY WANT to marry him, Leah?" Glen asked for the umpteenth time, unable to shake his concern that she was sacrificing herself for his sake and Samira's.

Leah laughed at him, her eyes happily teasing. "You think you're the only one who can fall madly in love? Let me tell you it was lucky Samira didn't have Sharif to compare with you, or you might have lost out."

"No. Never," Samira said with an adoring look at Glen. "There is no-one to compare with my husband."

"Well, Tayi thinks the same of Youssef, so I guess everyone sees from the heart," Leah said with warm pleasure in how everything had turned out.

They were sitting in the reception room where Leah had met with her father. The *majlis* was long since over, but Sharif was still closeted with King Rashid and Prince Youssef, negotiating the details of the compensation between Zubani and Qatama. Leah and Glen had been granted permission to call their father and assure him that all was well and he would be welcomed to the palace at any time he cared to visit.

"Tell me about Tayi," Samira pressed with eager curiosity. "And how did it happen that she is to marry Youssef?"

Leah related the sequence of events that culminated in the agreement made at the *majlis*. Samira was still expressing her admiration for her future sister-in-law when Sharif swept in on a wave of exuberant good humour, his eyes brilliant with the wild elation of success. They automatically rose to their feet in deference to his commanding presence.

"It is done!" he declared. "The royal family of Qatama are to be summoned to honour the celebration of our marriage, Leah. As you say, one in the eye for King Rashid!"

She laughed and giddily hurled herself into his embrace. "You are the cleverest negotiator in the world, Sharif!"

"It is merely that I have a fine appreciation for what happens around me," he said with a hopeless attempt at humility. He grinned at Glen. "I think I should thank you for your example."

"What example is that, Your Excellency?" Glen asked in puzzlement.

"Sometimes there is only one chance to have what one wants. You did well to take Princess Samira. It left me free to take Leah. So we are all happy, are we not?"

"Well, that's one way of looking at it," Glen conceded ruefully.

"I have been thinking," Sharif said with more seriousness. "As my wife's brother, you need more status than that of my personal pilot. You should be head of the air force in Zubani. Are you agreed?"

"It's a very generous offer, Your Excellency."

"Family is family. You have proved yourself a worthy brother to your sister. Who is an exceptional woman. I have no doubt you will serve me and my people well."

"Thank you. I appreciate your confidence," Glen said in some bemusement at his change of fortune.

Sharif directed a sympathetic smile at Samira. "I regret to say your father is proving obdurate over your status in Qatama. However, I leave that problem in the hands of your brother Prince Youssef and my cousin, Tayi, who together will be a formidable lobby in your cause."

"My father would never have listened to me as you listened to Tayi," Samira said with a mixture of apology and admiration.

"Acceptance of change sometimes comes slowly," Sharif said, his arm tightening possessively around Leah. "However, with the new alliance between our countries, you will undoubtedly have ample opportunity for visits from your family."

"Thank you, Your Excellency," Samira said with warm sincerity. "You are most kind."

His eyes twinkled. "Your family will be here for a month. There is not only my marriage to celebrate, but the marriage of Youssef and Tayi, which will take place on the same day."

A month for a month, Leah thought, imagining Sharif's relish in stipulating that length of time. There could be no doubt he had enjoyed the negotiations immensely, once she and Tayi had put him on the right track. Although, of course, she would never point that out to him. It was to his everlasting credit that Sharif al Kader had accepted change with admirable speed and aplomb.

Tayi came in, no less exuberantly triumphant than Sharif, but retaining her dignity, as always. She addressed the sheikh first. "I thank you for all you have done for me today. Have you sent messages to King Ahmed of Isha calling off the negotiation of the intended marriage to him?"

"Yes, I have. And expressed my concern that if the intended marriage with you had gone through, it would have endangered not only his heart, but also his life," Sharif said dryly. "I've also asked for compensation because he suggested the marriage in the first place, and quite clearly he is out of tune with the times. In retrospect, I find the offer provocative and insulting."

Tayi turned her shining gaze to Leah. "I have learnt much from you. I shall make Youssef very happy."

"I'm sure you will," Leah said warmly, although she couldn't help wondering how Youssef would weather the storms ahead. Tayi was extremely single-minded once she had a purpose dear to her heart. However, since Youssef's happiness was now her prime concern, Leah had no doubt nothing would be allowed to get in the way of achieving precisely that. She had a vision of the winds of change howling around King Rashid's head. Qatama was never going to be the same again.

Tayi smiled at Glen and Samira. "I have come to show you to your apartment in the palace. All has been arranged for your comfort and convenience."

"Thank you, Tayi," Samira said with glowing admiration for this remarkable woman who had given Samira entry into her family again.

Glen moved forward to offer his hand to the sheikh. "We have much to thank you for, Your Excellency. But above all else, I am glad that you care for my sister's happiness. Leah is very dear to me."

Sharif gripped Glen's hand with both of his. "And to me. We shall be good friends, you and I." His eyes sparkled at Leah. "Your sister will tell you that I listen."

"Then does what he wants," Leah said dryly.

"With due regard to your happiness," he retorted.

Leah laughed. "All right, Sharif. I surrender."

"Ah!" he said with intense satisfaction. He released Glen's hand and waved towards the door. "We shall talk more tomorrow. Be at ease in your new home."

The moment they were gone he drew Leah into his arms. "I think I need to taste this surrender of yours and make sure it is true."

"I agree. It might only be a passing surrender."

"Then there is no time to waste."

Leah gave him an inviting kiss. "I missed you last night, Sharif."

He took full advantage of the invitation. "Not as much as I missed you. Which I shall prove. Now."

The rest of the afternoon was spent in Leah's apartment. Strict orders were given that they were not to be disturbed.

"Soon I shall be your wife," Leah said dreamily as the light began to fade.

"You have been my wife from our first night together," Sharif said smugly. "I was merely waiting for your surrender to the fact."

She levered herself up from the pillows to challenge him. "You can't really mean that."

His eyes glowed with the light of destiny. "It was meant, Leah. We are right together. It could be no other way."

She smiled, knowing it was true. For Sharif al Kader, his choice was the way, and always would be, and he had made it her destiny, as well. Leah was more than content for it to be so. In surrendering to him she had found a freedom of the heart that was above all other freedoms. To share her life with the man she loved above all others was the only freedom she wanted.

Jacqueline Baird loves travelling and worked her way around the world from Europe to the Americas and Australia, returning to marry her teenage sweetheart.

She lives in Ponteland, Northumbria, the county of her birth, and has two teenage sons. She enjoys playing badminton, and spends most weekends with husband Jim, sailing their Gp.14 around Derwent Reservoir.

Jacqueline began writing as a hobby when her family objected to the smell of her oil painting, and immediately became hooked on the romantic genre. She has now been writing for Mills & Boon® for ten years and has sold nearly six million copies of her books worldwide.

GAMBLE ON PASSION
by
JACQUELINE BAIRD

CHAPTER ONE

'QUIET, everyone.' Replacing the telephone receiver, Liz glared threateningly around the crowded lounge of her apartment. 'Ssh. That was the porter. Tom is on his way up.' Her glance rested on the attractive blonde standing by the door. 'Dim the lights, quick,' she commanded, pushing her way through the crush of people to join her friend.

Jacy switched off the light and glanced down at her hostess for the evening. 'Stand by for action,' she prompted reassuringly. Liz was petite, with short black curly hair and sparkling blue eyes, but tonight she looked decidedly nervous.

'Do you think he will be pleased at a surprise fortieth birthday party?'

'Liz, your husband worships you and the terrible twins; anything you do is great with him and you know it!'

'Yes, you're right—I hope... But what about our bet—are you still game?'

Jacy glanced around the crowd of partygoers assembled in the large, comfortable room, all friends of Liz and Tom. 'Of course I am.' She grinned. 'But in all fairness to you I should point out that, as all the guests have arrived and all the single men here are my friends, it's no contest. The first one to walk through this door will be the one I date for a month. I'm bound to win.'

Liz smiled mischievously. 'I don't mind. I'll take the chance if you will.'

'Shake on it, partner.' Jacy grasped her friend's hand, shaking it vigorously, and couldn't resist adding, smugly, 'The *netsuke* is as good as mine.'

The door swung open and Tom, a tall blond-haired man, strode into the room. 'What the hell——?'

The room erupted to the strains of 'Happy Birthday to You' as Jacy clicked the light back on, and she stopped singing in mid-note, her eyes widening in horror at the black-haired, dark-eyed man who walked in behind Tom. Oh, no, she groaned inwardly, it couldn't be... She tried to sidle backwards into the crush of people surrounding the birthday-boy, but in the enthusiasm of the moment, to her horror, she was pushed slap-up against the tall dark man she was hoping to avoid.

A strong arm curved around her waist, and dark brown eyes glittered knowingly down into hers. 'Hello, Jacy, you're looking good.' A cynical smile twisted the hard mouth. 'But I admit I didn't think your sort would be a friend of Tom and Liz.'

Jacy, numb with shock, managed to reply icily, 'I could say the same about you,' while registering the fact that the black eyes burning into hers did not look in the least surprised to see her here. She dismissed the thought as fanciful and pushed past him and out into the hall.

She closed the door of the dining-room behind her and fell back against it. Her legs were trembling and the beating of her heart sounded unnaturally loud in the quiet of the room. Her glance slid across the dining-table, groaning under the weight of all the food she had helped prepare earlier and had been looking forward to eating. Now she had no appetite at all.

Damn! she swore under her breath. What was Leo Kozakis doing here? The internationally known Greek tycoon, at Tom's party? A family birthday party was hardly his scene, she thought bitterly. She hadn't realised Tom even knew the man.

Briefly she closed her eyes and ten years of her life were swept away. She swallowed hard on the lump that rose in her throat, feeling once again all the old pain and heartache of her much younger self. At eighteen Leo Kozakis had almost destroyed her, and now once again he had appeared in her life. The last man on earth she wanted to meet.

Taking a deep breath, she straightened and crossed to the table. She was over-reacting, she told herself. So what if Leo was at the party? It didn't make any difference to her. She was no longer a naïve teenager but a mature, successful career-woman of twenty-eight. Tom and Liz were her friends, and there was no way she was going to allow the unexpected appearance of Leo to frighten her into walking out on their celebration.

An ironic smile twisted her wide mouth as she realised Kozakis had been the first unattached male to walk through the door. Well, that was it! She had lost the bet… There was no way she could date him for a month, or would even want to. It had been a stupid bet, but there was no escaping the fact—Liz had won. Jacy was going to have to spend eight weekends looking after Liz's twin five-year-old boys. Still, it was her own fault, and she didn't mind: she loved the two boys, and her social life wasn't that exciting anyway.

It had all started earlier that afternoon. Jacy had promised to arrive at three to help prepare the food for the party. Liz hadn't wanted to use caterers, saying it seemed wrong to throw a surprise party for her husband and then stick him with a huge bill. Planning on leaving the office early, Jacy had been delayed by her office junior, Barbara, crying her heart out. The man from the assessors' department whom the girl had dated since the office Christmas party three months ago had finally talked her into bed. Unfortunately Barbara had been dreaming of wedding-bells until today. At lunchtime the

poor soul had walked into the local pub in time to hear
two of the male members of the staff talking to her boy-
friend, and money changing hands. Seemingly, the man
had only taken her out for a bet. They had laid odds on
how many weeks it would take to get her into bed.

Jacy had arrived at Liz's two hours late, fuming over
what swine men were, and declaring that just *once* she
would like to do the same to one of them. Plus, in a
way, she blamed herself, as it had been she who had
persuaded the girl to go to the office Christmas party,
and encouraged her to mix socially with the rest of the
staff. She had felt sorry for Barbara, fresh from the north
of England and in her first job in London.

Liz had listened to Jacy's angry tirade and then said,
'Well, why don't you?'

Jacy would never have bet money, but Liz had been
clever; she had known the one thing that would tempt
her. Six years ago the two women had met for the first
time at a country house auction. They had both been
bidding for the same lot: a delightful ivory *netsuke* with
unusual jade eyes. Jacy had a modest collection of the
tiny figures and had set her heart on the tiny Buddha.
But Liz had outbid her. After the sale Jacy had congratulated Liz, and the two girls had got talking. It was
an unlikely friendship. Liz had never worked since her
marriage a year earlier and was heavily pregnant with
the twins, while Jacy was quickly climbing the career
ladder as a loss adjuster with a large insurance firm.

The sudden upsurge in the music and laughter brought
Jacy back to the present with a jolt. The party had spread
to the hall, and in only moments she would be forced
to face the crowd again and Leo Kozakis… She couldn't
do it. Her stomach churned sickeningly, and it was only
with the greatest effort of will that she managed to
straighten her shoulders and pin a smile on her face as

the dining-room door swung open. She relaxed slightly when she saw who it was.

'There you are, Jacy. I wondered where you had got to.' Liz, a smug smile on her pixie face, added, 'You lucky lady, did you see that Leo Kozakis? Aren't you glad you made the bet?'

'No! And you win. Just tell me which weekends you want me to babysit.'

Liz stood in front of her, her blue eyes narrowed on Jacy's sombre face. 'Come on, love, you can't chicken out now. In the six years I've known you you have never gone out with the same man more than a couple of times. What is it? Are you afraid you might discover you like men?'

'No, of course not, but...' How could she explain how she felt? Liz would never understand. She was a happily married woman with a loving husband who had a good position as the director of a merchant bank. They owned a house in Surrey, and this apartment in town. They adored each other, and their twin boys were icing on the cake. Whereas Jacy had been deeply hurt as a teenager and had vowed never again to get involved with a man. She had a good job and was thoroughly independent, and that was the way she liked it.

'I never had you down as a coward, Jacy,' Liz said bluntly. 'Let me introduce you to Leo; he really is a great guy. Tom brought him down to Surrey last weekend and I thought straight away that he was perfect for you.'

Jacy eyed Liz with growing suspicion. 'Wait a minute... Tom rang to say he was on his way up,' she murmured, and watched the elfin features of her friend colour a delicate red. 'You knew... You *knew* he was bringing that man when we shook on the bet.'

'*Mea culpa*,' Liz admitted unashamedly. 'But a bet is a bet, and he is gorgeous!'

'It's no good, Liz, you're wasting your time, for the simple reason that the man would never ask me out in a million years!' Jacy knew it was true, but she had no intention of telling Liz how she knew. Some things were too painful to discuss even with her best friend.

'Now you *are* being ridiculous.' Liz stepped back and surveyed Jacy from head to toe. 'You're drop-dead gorgeous, five foot five, gold hair, gold eyes, and that slip of a red sheath you're wearing clings to every luscious curve. Who are you trying to kid, pal? One flutter from those incredibly long eyelashes and the man will be kneeling at your feet. Your trouble is, you can't accept how attractive you are. Even my Tom said that when you walk across a room you're like a magnet, attracting every male eye in the place.'

'Flattery will get you nowhere, friend. Take it from me, Mr Kozakis will not ask me out, even if I were to strip naked in front of him.' Jacy was not aware of the bitterness edging her tone, or the questioning look the other girl gave her, as she continued, 'I may be a liberated female, but when we made the bet you did agree that I don't have to ask the man. He has to ask me, and in this case it will never happen. So tell me when you want your first free weekend, hmm?'

'Think of the *netsuke*, the exquisite Buddha, the jade eyes,' Liz tempted teasingly. 'A month dating Leo the Hunk wouldn't kill you, and I expect you to at least try and honour the spirit of the bet.'

Jacy never had a chance to answer, as a voice broke into their lively exchange.

'The two most beautiful women in the place.' Tom appeared beside his wife, curving an arm around her shoulders. 'But I should be angry with you, Liz; now everyone knows just what an old married man I am.' His blond head swept down, and he kissed his wife firmly before adding, 'Poor Leo here thought he was going to collect some papers and go.' Tom turned his sparkling blue eyes on Jacy. 'Jacy, let me introduce you to Leo, a business friend of mine. I want you to look after him and make sure he gets fed, while *I* deal with my scatty wife.'

Jacy forced a smile to her stiff lips. 'Happy birthday, Tom.' And, leaning forward, she kissed him lightly on the cheek, studiously ignoring the man at her side.

There was no way on God's earth she wanted anything to do with the arrogant Greek. But Leo had a different idea. Stepping in front of his host, he quite deliberately caught Jacy's hand in his before she could object and, moving closer, he flicked his dark eyes coldly over her flushed face.

'There's no need for introductions, Tom; Jacy and I are old friends. We met when she was a budding reporter.' Dropping her hand, he deliberately turned his back on her to speak directly to Tom. 'Though given the sensitive nature of some of your work I was surprised when you mentioned that Jacy, a journalist, was a family friend of yours...'

Tom threw his blond head back and burst out laughing, while Liz's inquisitive blue eyes darted from the Greek to Jacy and back again.

'Jacy, a reporter?' She grinned. 'You must have the wrong girl. Jacy is a very valued member of the Mutual Save and Trust Company. In fact, she's their top loss adjuster. She can smell a fraud a mile off.'

As far as Jacy was concerned, Leo Kozakis was the biggest fraud alive, she thought angrily; and what did he mean? He'd said, 'was a friend'. Had he known she would be here tonight? No, it was impossible; and at that moment her attention was caught by someone calling her name.

'Jacy, darling, I've been looking all over for you. I've got your G and T.'

Thank God for Simon, she thought gratefully, and
with a mumbled, 'Excuse me,' she walked across to join
the laughing crowd that had entered the dining-room.

'Thank you, Simon.' She took the proffered glass from
the hand of the tall ginger-haired fresh-faced young man,
and urged him back out into the hall towards the lounge.
'Let's find a seat and gossip,' she encouraged, shooting
him a brilliant smile. She could have hugged him for
getting her out of an intolerable situation, but she
doubted it would be appreciated, as she was one of the
very few people who knew that Simon's taste ran to
members of his own sex rather than females.

They found a vacant armchair and Jacy sank down
into it with a sigh of relief, and took a long swallow of
her drink. 'You've no idea how much I needed that.' She
turned her face up to look at Simon who was perched
on the arm of her chair, with a glass of whisky in one
hand and his other arm resting lightly along the back of
the chair.

'I don't believe it. Jacy the ice-maiden actually ruffled;
and by a man, if I'm not mistaken.' And, lowering his
head, he whispered in her ear, 'You can tell *me* about
it, Jacy; your secret is as safe with me as I know mine
is with you.'

'Simon, don't ask me to explain, just stay with me for
the rest of the evening.' She turned sombre golden eyes
up to his. 'Pretend we're good friends.'

'I don't need to pretend, we *are* good friends; and
don't worry, I'll shield you from the Greek.'

Her eyes widened in shock. 'How . . . ?' She stopped
herself, but it was too late.

'It doesn't take a genius to work it out. He's the only
new male in this crowd, and gorgeous with it. I watched
him myself when he walked in, but I could tell instantly
that he's not for me, more's the pity.'

Jacy burst out laughing; she couldn't help it. The idea of Simon seducing Leo: now that really did appeal. Draining her glass, she settled back in the chair and prepared to be entertained by Simon's outrageous stories for the rest of the evening. But some inner radar told her the instant Leo Kozakis walked into the room. She couldn't actually see him from the depths of her chair, but she had the uncanny feeling he was watching her.

Someone put the stereo on and the centre of the room gradually filled with swaying bodies, and then she saw him; he was dancing with a tall blonde. Dancing wasn't the word, she thought disgustedly. The woman had her arms around his neck, and Leo's hands were settled intimately over the blonde's buttocks. Ten years hadn't changed him at all. He was still the lecherous swine he had always been.

He looked over his partner's shoulder, his dark eyes catching Jacy watching him; and to her chagrin his lips curved in a knowing smile. She felt the blood surge in her cheeks and quickly looked away. Years ago she had thought herself in love with Leo Kozakis. A few magical weeks on the island of Corfu; the sun, the sea and the sand; a vibrant, tanned male body...

Jacy drained her glass in one gulp, dismissing the memory from her mind. Of course it had only been a childish crush, and she had quickly recovered; but the hurt and humiliation still lingered. Abruptly getting to her feet, she caught Simon's hand in hers. 'Come on, Simon, let's find the bar and have another drink. Tonight I think I'm going to need it,' she concluded as with Simon's arm around her shoulder they circumvented the dancing couples to arrive at the makeshift bar set up in one corner of the lounge.

Grasping her second gin and tonic, Jacy deliberately kept her back to the room and drank the potent spirit much too fast. But she had the uncanny feeling that Leo

Kozakis's dark eyes were watching her, and that he was laughing.

'Take it easy, Jacy,' Simon remonstrated as she held out her empty glass for a refill. 'An hour or so and I'll take you home.'

'Get lost, Simon. I want to talk to my friend,' Liz's laughing voice interrupted.

Jacy sighed, and sipped her drink, eyeing Liz over the top of her glass. 'Lovely party, Liz,' she said politely, the warning in her dark golden eyes telling her friend more plainly than words that she was not going to discuss Mr Kozakis.

'Don't try and intimidate me with your best "claim refused" frown. I want some answers. A: when were you ever a reporter? and B: how did you meet Leo? And the biggy: were you an item? That will do for starters.'

Jacy's first thought was to refuse to answer. Then, whether it was the drink or because she had finally regained her self-control, she thought, Why the hell not? Liz was her friend and Leo Kozakis meant nothing to her.

'I was never a reporter: that was a particular misconception of Mr Kozakis'; something he is prone to. As for how I know him, I met him when I was eighteen and on holiday in Corfu for the summer. As for being an item, as you so crudely put it, Liz: what do *you* think?' she drawled scornfully, her glance slanting over the delicate features of her friend's face. Without noticing the warning look in her sparkling eyes, Jacy continued, 'Give me some credit! The man's affairs are legion and very well documented by the Press; the swine's reputation is as black as his hair.'

'Does that mean that now I'm going grey my reputation will improve accordingly?' a deep mocking voice drawled in Jacy's ear.

She swung around, the glass slipping from her hand, and with lightning reflexes it was caught by the man standing in front of her, only a few drops splashing on his immaculate business suit.

'I did try to warn you,' Liz murmured as she faded away into the crowd.

Jacy stood as though turned to stone, the colour flooding into her pale cheeks.

'No answer, Jacy; but then you always had the ability to remain mute when it suited you, I seem to remember,' he declared hardly. His dark eyes blatantly surveyed her, from the top of her head, where her long golden blonde hair was swept up into a coronet of curls, down over the swan-like arch of her neck to her bare shoulders. They lingered on the soft curve of her breasts, lovingly cupped by the smooth red velvet strapless bodice of her dress, and continued down to her narrow waist, the round curve of her hips, and the long length of her legs, exaggerated by the spike-heeled red evening sandals. 'I must admit,' he confessed, his dark glance flicking back to her flushed face, 'my memory of your delightful body does you an injustice. You have certainly matured into a stunning woman, Jacy.'

Recovering from her initial dismay at his intervention into the conversation, Jacy was doing some appraising of her own. She had forgotten just how shockingly masculine he was. His navy pin-striped jacket fitted perfectly over his wide shoulders, and the matching trousers, belted low on his waist, clung to his muscular thighs. Slowly she raised her head to look up into his handsome face. His pale blue silk shirt contrasted sharply with the bronzed skin. His mouth, the bottom lip fuller than the top, curled back over perfect white teeth in a mocking smile that as she tilted her head further she realised didn't reach the dark brown, almost black eyes. His black hair *was* going grey, she realised in surprise; in fact, two silver

wings brushed back from his temples. The shock of black
curls that she remembered falling over his broad forehead
were now cut fashionably short and were also liberally
sprinkled with grey. But then he must be almost forty.
When she'd first met him he'd been twenty-nine. Ten
years! It didn't seem possible.

'Sorry I'm not dressed for dinner, but will I pass?'
Leo demanded mockingly.

Pass? He knew damn well he would, Jacy thought bitterly. But it didn't stop her too-fair skin from betraying
her now as it had when she was a teenager. The blush
that had started on her pale cheeks suffused the whole
of her body. 'You can pass me by any time. In fact, I
would prefer it,' she managed to respond cuttingly, proud
of the cold tone in her usually husky voice.

'Now, is that any way to greet an old friend? A dance
would be *much* more acceptable.' And, before she could
protest, his strong arm had encircled her waist and his
other hand had put the glass back on the bar and caught
Jacy's slender hand to his broad chest.

A shudder skittered down her spine, and she stiffened.
'I do not *want* to dance,' she snapped; his arm around
her waist was like a ring of steel.

'You must, they're playing your tune, Jacy,' Leo
prompted, holding her away from him, his mocking
glance sweeping down her body and back to her flushed
face before pulling her into intimate contact with his virile
form.

The lively music had given way to 'Lady in Red', she
realised angrily; but unless she wanted to make a scene
in front of her hosts and all their friends she knew she
would have to endure dancing with the man.

Shakily she moved where he led, trying to still the insistent tremors inside her. What was happening to her?
Jacy thought wildly. She despised Leo Kozakis but, held
close to his hard body, with his strong hand holding hers

firmly to his chest, she felt an incredible urge to close her eyes and relax into him. Until he spoke.

'So, when did you give up the reporting?'

Jacy clenched her teeth and swallowed hard. She would not let him bait her, she vowed. She had never *been* a reporter; had never really seriously considered the idea. But her father had been an editor of an American tabloid, and that had been enough for the younger Leo Kozakis...

'What happened? Couldn't you compete with your father?'

'My father is dead,' she said flatly, persuading herself that the shiver from her hand in his to her arm and right through her body was pure anger.

'I'm sorry, I didn't know.'

Jacy tilted her head back the better to look into his dark face. Her strange golden eyes flashed angrily as they clashed with black. 'You're not sorry, you liar. You despised him.' She spat the word out, trying to ease herself away from the closeness of his overpowering male form; but he strengthened his grip on her hand, his arm around her back holding her tighter.

'I never lie. I *am* sorry for the death of any living being.' His dark eyes burnt into Jacy's. 'I didn't despise your father, only the rag he worked for. How could I hate him? I didn't know him personally.' His firm mouth relaxed into a smile. 'But you—*you*, Jacy, I did know very personally; or so I thought at the time.'

Jacy stiffened in his arms. 'Well, you thought wrong; you didn't know me at all,' she said icily, ignoring the sensual knowledge in his smile.

'Then perhaps we can rectify that. Have dinner with me tomorrow night.'

'Huh!' A surprised gasp escaped her. The conceit of the man was unbelievable. To casually ask her out to dinner when the last time they had met he'd called her

worse than a whore! The words were indelibly carved
into her brain. She could hear them again in her mind,
his voice icy with contempt as he told her, 'At least a
whore has the basic honesty to state a price. But women
like you turn my stomach. Your type bleed a man dry
before the poor sod even knows he's paying for it.'

Jacy hadn't responded to him then, and she didn't
now. A chilling coldness took possession of her body;
her golden eyes, strangely blank, stared up into his darkly
attractive face. 'No, thank you,' she said politely.
Conveniently for Jacy, the music stopped, and, pulling
her hand from his, she stepped out of his hold, adding,
'Thank you for the dance.'

'Wait!' His large hand once again closed over her arm
as she turned to walk away. 'Why not?' The question
brushed past her ear. 'I'm in town for a month, we could
have some fun.'

Jacy looked down at the long brown fingers encircling
her white flesh and had to fight down a shudder of distaste. She raised her head and Leo moved in front of
her, blocking her escape.

'After all, Jacy, you're no longer a teenager but a
mature woman. Better still, you're not a reporter as I
thought. I can see no problem with our getting together
again for a while.'

The amazing thing was, Jacy realised, the man actually believed what he was saying. Her glance slid up
over his handsome face. It was all there: the sensual anticipation in his dark eyes, the self-satisfied smile curving
his generous mouth. He moved closer, his warm breath
touching her cheek.

'Liz told me that you're unattached at the moment,
so how about it?' He murmured the words against her
temple, his lips brushing her skin like softest silk. 'I can
still remember how great we were in bed together,' he
breathed throatily.

Later, Jacy was to ask herself again and again why she did it. Was it Liz's bet? Or was it the red haze of fury that engulfed her when Leo reminded her of their past intimate relationship?

CHAPTER TWO

LEO KOZAKIS was without doubt the most arrogant, insensitive male chauvinist pig it had ever been her misfortune to meet, Jacy thought furiously, rage bubbling inside her like a volcano about to erupt. She clenched her teeth and counted to ten under her breath before even trusting herself to speak to the man. How dared he remind her of the passion they had shared? And to assume that he could take up again where they had left off years ago, simply because he had a few weeks in town and she was no longer a threat as a would-be reporter...

How many women over the years had he used in such a cavalier fashion? Hundreds, if the newspaper stories about him were even half true. She thought of the poor young girl, Barbara, whom she'd spent over an hour trying to comfort that very afternoon. The girl had reminded her very much of herself at that age, and she wouldn't mind betting that Barbara's ex-lover was a carbon copy of Leo Kozakis, but without the incredible wealth.

Betting. The bet... Jacy pinned a smile on her lovely face and, tilting her head to one side, glanced up through her long lashes at the man in front of her. 'You want to take me out to dinner?' she asked coyly, and almost laughed out loud at the gleam of triumph that flashed in Leo's eyes.

'That and more, my sweet.' His lips brushed her brow, and she had to clench her fist to prevent herself from wiping his touch from her forehead. 'Name the time and the place, Jacy, and I'll call for you.'

'As it happens, I have a free evening on Saturday.' She didn't want to appear too eager, and a three-day wait would do the man good. Jacy had never considered herself a vengeful person, but the reappearance of Leo had awakened a lot of bitter memories and these, added to the bet she'd made with Liz, meant that she couldn't resist the temptation to try and deflate the overwhelming ego of the man. She vowed to herself that she'd date the swine for a month, win the bet, and Leo Kozakis would learn a lesson in patience and self-denial that he would never forget...

'Enjoying yourselves?' Liz appeared from behind Leo. 'I hope Jacy is taking care of you, Leo.' The petite woman's blue eyes sparkled happily as she stood between the tall, handsome man and her best friend.

Jacy watched as Leo, ever the charmer, turned his brown velvet eyes on his hostess; the man oozed charm from every pore. 'This is quite the best party I have ever attended, Liz; Tom is a very fortunate man, and yes, Jacy is looking after me beautifully. In fact she's just agreed to dine with me on Saturday night.' His glance slid back to where Jacy stood, his eyes gleaming with pure male satisfaction and something more... 'I couldn't be happier.'

A shiver of unease trickled down Jacy's spine: the challenge in his gaze as it rested on her face then slid provocatively down to her toes and back up again was unmistakable. He reminded her of some predatory jungle cat toying with its prey before finally devouring it completely.

'Yes, well——' she burst into speech, unconsciously taking a step away from Leo and nearer to Liz '—it's a lovely party, Liz, but if you don't mind I'll say goodnight.'

'But it's early, you c——'

'No, I must go,' Jacy cut in. She couldn't keep up the
pretence much longer; suddenly she felt disgusted with
herself, and even more so with Leo Kozakis. She could
feel the onset of a tension headache and all she wanted
to do was get home and forget tonight had ever happened. As for the dinner-date, it had been a stupid idea
to look for revenge—especially with a man like Leo.
'Unlike you, Liz, I'm a working girl, and I have a busy
day ahead of me tomorrow, so if you'll excuse me I'll
call a cab...'

'That won't be necessary: I'll take you home,' Leo
offered smoothly.

'What a great idea!' Liz beamed. 'I hate the thought
of my best friend travelling around London on her own
at night.'

Jacy could have quite happily flattened Liz, and she
deliberately ignored her friend's wink and thumb in the
air, out of sight of Leo.

'No, please... Leo must stay. I'll be OK.'

Ten minutes later, sitting in the passenger seat of a
sleek black Jaguar car with Leo Kozakis at the driving-
wheel, she heard herself giving him her address in
Pimlico.

'Why do I get the feeling you were somewhat reluctant to let me drive you home?' Leo cast her a sidelong
glance before returning his attention to the road. 'Odd,
when you've agreed to dine with me.'

Jacy frowned, her golden eyes flicking to his dark
profile and away again. Did he suspect that she'd been
less than genuine in accepting his invitation? Did it
matter? she thought drily. She no longer had any intention of going out with him; it had been a foolish plan,
formed in the heat of the moment. No—she would
wait until she reached home and then tell him a
firm goodbye...

She wasn't a complete fool. Leo was a devastatingly attractive male, wealthy and powerful, but she knew from experience how ruthless he could be.

'No response, Jacy? But then you always were a quiet girl, as I recall. It was one of the things I liked about you—that and your luscious body...' he drawled huskily.

Liar—he had never liked her at all. He'd made that abundantly clear when they'd parted, she thought, the old bitterness rising like gall in her throat. He had used her *luscious body* and he actually imagined that he was going to do the same again. As quickly as she'd dismissed the notion of revenge, angry pride had her reversing her decision. She would show him that the mature, adult Jacy Carter was more than a match for a lecherous snake like Leo Kozakis!

She recalled Liz's admonishment as she'd followed Jacy into the bedroom while she collected her coat to leave. 'Now don't blow it, Jacy. You only have to date him, not go to bed with him, and the Buddha is yours. But personally if I didn't have Tom I'd rather have Kozakis in my bed than a *netsuke* any day; the man positively smoulders.'

Jacy's lips twisted in a mockery of a smile. Liz was right about one thing: if she, Jacy, had *her* way, she would make damn sure that the man got burned. But how she was going to do it, she wasn't sure. She glanced out of the window, hoping for inspiration. They were driving along her street and in seconds she would be home. Gathering all her courage, she said, 'Stop here.'

The car slowed to a halt and she deliberately reached across the central console and laid a slender hand on Leo's thigh as he made to get out of the car. Jacy could feel the muscle tense beneath the fine fabric of his trousers, and she glanced up into his dark face to catch a flickering puzzlement in his brown eyes. 'You were mistaken, Leo. I had no objection to your driving me

home, but I didn't want to drag you away from the
party,' she explained throatily, amazed at her own acting
ability. 'Promise me you will go back straight away, and
I'll see you on Saturday at seven-thirty.' She had no intention of inviting him in for coffee, she wasn't yet confident enough; and, slowly gliding her hand from his
thigh, she found the door-handle with her other hand.
'I live here—number twenty-seven—there's no need . . .'

'I'll see you to the door,' Leo cut in. 'And I *am* going
back to Tom's. We still have business to discuss,' he offered with a quick smile.

Before she could get out, Leo, with a speed she
wouldn't have thought him capable of, was around the
front of the car and holding the passenger-door open
for her.

He walked by her side up the stone steps that led to
the entrance door of the small mews house that Jacy was
lucky enough to own, thanks to an inheritance from her
late father. She quickly delved into her handbag and
found the door-key before raising her head and facing
Leo. 'Thank you.'

'Till Saturday, Jacy.' His brown eyes, gleaming with
satisfaction, captured hers. 'I'll be counting the hours.'

Before Jacy knew what was happening, his dark head
bent and his lips brushed hers in the softest of kisses.
Too surprised to resist, she made no comment as he deftly
took the key from her hand, opened the door, and with
one large hand in the middle of her back urged her inside.
She turned and Leo pressed the key back into her hand.

'I won't come in now, but be ready, wanting and
waiting for me on Saturday, sweetheart.'

Jacy shut the door with unnecessary force, the sound
of his masculine laughter ringing in her ears and the
image in her brain of his handsome, almost boyish, grin
as he had turned to wave before leaping into his car. For
a moment the years had rolled back and Leo had looked

like the laughing, carefree fisherman she had first met in Corfu, and her heart had leapt in the same way as it had then. Angry with herself and furious with Leo Kozakis, Jacy strode across the hall and opened the door leading to her small living-room.

In the safety of her own private sanctum, she kicked off her shoes and shrugged out of her jacket, dropping it on to the arm of the large, soft-cushioned sofa before walking into her cosy kitchen. The familiar golden pine units, the bright blue gingham curtains at the small bay-window, and the row of flowering plants that she tended so carefully, all gave her a brief glow of satisfaction before she turned to the prettily tiled worktop and switched on the kettle. She needed a coffee, and to think... She rubbed her hands up over her eyes and into her hair, sighing as she did so. What had she let herself in for?

Five minutes later, with the coffee-cup in her hand, she returned to the living-room and sank into the comfortable sofa, curling her feet up beneath her. She slowly sipped the reviving brew then placed the empty cup on the low occasional-table in front of her. Her head dropped back against the large cushion and she closed her eyes.

Leo Kozakis, back in her life! Never in her worst nightmares had she expected to see the man again, and the adrenalin that had kept her reasonably in control for the past few hours suddenly deserted her.

Her golden eyes roamed around the room, her private haven. The muted green and rose of the Laura Ashley drapes at the window was continued in the loose covers of the sofa and two comfortable armchairs. The table between them, a lovingly polished mahogany, gleamed with a soft cinnamon hue that only years of loving care could develop. It had been in her mother's family for generations. She thought of her mother, killed in a car accident not long after the divorce, and for the first time in a decade wished she had a mother beside her to confide in.

A wry smile twisted Jacy's full lips; she had never confided in her mother at eighteen, and it was a bit late to regret it now. God, but it hurt! Seeing Leo tonight had brought it all back—the traumatic events of her nineteenth year. The pain, the disillusion, and the loneliness ...

As a teenager Jacy had considered that she led a pretty normal, happy life. Her parents adored her and she lived in a nice house in Kent, not far from London. Her mother wrote children's books and her father was a journalist who, when she was thirteen, had taken an editor's job with a large American newspaper. Jacy had seen nothing unusual in her father's working in America and returning home several times a year: lots of her friends had fathers who worked abroad in the Middle East or in the Forces.

She and her mother had spent a couple of holidays in California, at the apartment that her father rented in Los Angeles; but the year Jacy completed her A levels it was decided she should have a year out before taking up her place at university where she intended reading politics, economics and philosophy. With two other girls she had travelled across Europe to Greece, and in the July they'd rented an apartment on the island of Corfu for a month. In that one month Jacy's life had changed completely; she had grown up with a vengeance ...

A deep sigh tore from the depths of her heart. Jacy lifted her hand to her cheek and felt the dampness of cold tears. Jumping to her feet, she quickly walked out of the room and up the stairs to the bathroom. She hadn't cried in years and she wasn't about to start now, she told herself firmly. Stripping off her clothes, she turned on the shower and stepped beneath the warming spray.

But it was no good. Dried and dressed in pale blue silk pyjamas, she walked across the hall to her bedroom and crawled into bed, crushed by the weight of memories she had thought long forgotten. She tossed and turned for almost an hour, doing complicated maths in her head, deliberately recalling all the more difficult cases she had solved in her job, anything to try and block out the knowledge that Leo Kozakis had reappeared in her life.

Finally, as she listened to the clock on a nearby church peal out the stroke of two, she gave up and let her mind go back to the island of Corfu and her first meeting with Leo. Perhaps after so many years it would be a cleansing experience, she consoled herself. She could lay the unpleasant memories to rest once and for all, and go forward into the future with no baggage from the past to affect her life. For the first time, Jacy consciously admitted to herself that the affair with Leo Kozakis had coloured the way she saw all men.

Jacy sat on a smooth stone at the edge of the pebble beach, her golden eyes glued to the strange contraption fixed only about four feet from the water line. A large cage was resting in the shallow water; made of wire mesh but with a wood plank top, it was attached to the shore by a few strong ropes. But it was the contents that held her attention—struggling around inside the cage were about a dozen huge lobsters. Some fisherman's catch for the day, she knew, and she was torn between her undeniable liking for eating lobster and the idealism of a teenager that told her all living things should be free. A small chuckle escaped her; she could just imagine what would happen if she did free the poor lobsters! She would probably end up in a Greek jail...

A frown marred her smooth, lightly tanned brow. Would anyone care if she did? She was feeling rather

sorry for herself and had been for the past two days.
She had arrived at the apartment set on the hill above
Paleokastritsa with her friends Joan and Anne a week
ago, determined to have a month of rest and relaxation.
Only it hadn't quite worked out like that.

It was very true—two was company and three a crowd,
she thought ruefully. Joan and Anne had met a couple
of young German tourists and decided to go with the
young men on their very organised three-week walking
and camping holiday around the whole island. Jacy
couldn't help thinking that it was a very Teutonic trait
to divide a beautiful island like Corfu into squares on a
map and decide to camp in every one. It certainly wasn't
Jacy's idea of a holiday; but then neither was being left
on her own in a three-bedroom-apartment for the rest
of the month.

She stretched out her long legs and dabbled her feet
in the water, putting her hands behind her on the ground
to support her lounging position. She was completely
unaware of how stunning she looked. Her youthful face
glowed with health and vitality, her long golden hair
trailed over her shoulders in a mass of glittering curls,
and the brief sea-green bikini she wore revealed every
line of her curvaceous figure.

Paleokastritsa was perhaps the most beautiful place
on Corfu, but today Jacy had walked from the tourist
beach across the promontory to a small harbour, with
the ferry-boats docked along one side and the glass-
bottom boats that ran excursions from the harbour. A
few fishing-boats also lay idly at anchor. Jacy had chosen
the spot simply because the café only a few yards behind
her was much less expensive than the ones around the
main beach. She had just finished her lunch, a pizza and
a glass of wine, and was wondering how she was going
to spend the rest of the day when she'd spotted the
lobster prison.

'With your colouring, you should be careful, lady—unless you want to end up looking like my lobsters.' A slightly accented voice broke into Jacy's reverie, and, straightening up, she turned her head to look at the man who had spoken.

She was struck dumb. She'd heard of Greek gods and seen pictures of the same, but the man standing to the left and slightly behind her was over six feet tall and breathtaking. Her eyes lifted up over a pair of long, muscular bronzed legs, parted as he straddled the sharp rocks at his feet. Skimpy denim cut-offs barely covered his essential maleness, and a line of black hair arrowed from beneath the denim over a hard flat belly to branch out over a broad chest in curling splendour. Wide shoulders supported a strong neck and proud head. Thick black curly hair tumbled over a wide brow and beautifully arched black eyebrows framed the deepest brown sparkling eyes Jacy had ever seen. A straight classic nose topped a generously curved mouth that widened in a brilliant smile.

'Your lobsters,' she murmured, and blushed scarlet at the sensual appreciation in his dark eyes. Thank God she hadn't set them free, she thought! He was obviously the fisherman, and she instantly hated the idea of upsetting the gorgeous man in any way.

'Yes, and perhaps I can persuade you to share one with me tonight.' He lowered his large frame down on to the ground beside her, seemingly impervious to the rocky terrain. 'That is if you don't already have a date?' he queried, his handsome face now much closer to her own.

'No—no, I don't,' she hastened to tell him, and found herself explaining her friends' desertion, unconsciously revealing the loneliness she had been feeling for the past two days.

'Friends like that you could do without,' he said shortly.

'Oh, I'm not blaming them,' she said hastily. She didn't want this lovely man to think she was a whingeing kind of girl. 'They...' She had been going to say 'fell in love', but somehow it seemed rather infantile, and not strictly true. She had slowly realised over the past few weeks that Joan and Anne were far more sophisticated and experienced than she herself was. They had dated quite a few men on their travels, sometimes staying away all night, and Jacy had begun to feel like a naïve child in comparison.

'They will have my undying gratitude, little girl, if you will just tell me your name and allow me to entertain you for the rest of your holiday.'

Jacy lifted her head and looked at the man now sitting beside her. 'It's Jacy,' she said shyly.

'Jacy—a lovely name for a lovely girl.' And, placing his large tanned hand over hers on the earth, he added, 'I am Leo.' He lifted her hand and without the support she fell sideways against him as he solemnly shook her hand.

The brush of her bare arm against his chest sent quivers tingling down her spine. She blushed hotly at the unfamiliar feeling that his touch aroused but, remembering her manners, with a shy smile she murmured, 'How do you do?'

'So formal. I like that.' His brown eyes twinkled with laughter as he studied her flushed face. His gaze dropped to the gentle curves of her breasts exposed by the tiny green bikini top, then back to her scarlet face. 'And you blush so becomingly,' he teased, then jumping to his feet he dragged her up to stand beside him. 'I'm delighted to make your acquaintance, Jacy, and if you will permit I will show you my beautiful island. I will be your own personal tour guide, hmm?'

'Yes please,' she said breathlessly, completely be-
witched by the glint in his dark eyes and the warm smile
lighting his handsome face. 'But what about your work?'
she asked, glancing down at the lobster cage.

'What do you know about my work?' he demanded.

Jacy looked up into his now unsmiling face, surprised
at the sudden harshness in his tone. It hit her forcibly;
the laughing young man suddenly looked older, more
mature, and she wondered just how old he was.
'Well...noth...nothing,' she stammered. Perhaps he
felt she was belittling his job as a simple fisherman?
Hastily she reassured him, 'I think being a fisherman
must be very hard work—I only meant, can you take
time off whenever you like?' She watched as his harsh
face relaxed once more into a friendly smile.

'Let *me* worry about that, Jacy.' And, once more
catching her hand in his, he led her along the shore to
the pier. 'Come and I'll show you my boat, and if you're
very good I'll teach you how to fish...'

For Jacy, the next two weeks turned into a dream.
Leo's boat was her first surprise: a very modern motor-
boat fitted out with a galley and large comfortable cabin
and shower-room; and on deck all the fittings for big-
game fishing. Leo briefly explained that he sometimes
took people out shark-fishing. She automatically thought
he meant tourists; it was only much later that she realised
her mistake.

Their first dinner-date was spent on board the boat,
sitting on the deck sharing succulently cooked lobster
with a simple salad and a bottle of wine. The night sky
was a mass of glittering stars and the moon on the dark
water a perfect back-drop for the romantic meal. When
after midnight he drove her back to her apartment in a
rather beaten-up jeep, he kissed her lightly on the lips
and murmured a husky goodnight, promising to call for
her early the next morning. In bed she had gone over

every minute of the evening in her mind. She'd learned
that he was twenty-nine, and had been born in Corfu.
Later when she looked back she realised how clever he
had been. That was about all she had ever found out
about him.

They spent long hot days sailing, swimming, laughing
and joking, sharing almost every meal; it was paradise
to Jacy, and day by day her fascination with Leo grew
until she finally admitted to herself that she was for the
first time in her young life in love.

The sight of Leo standing on the bow of the boat
dressed in brief black Spandex trunks ready to dive into
the deep blue of the Ionian Sea was enough to stop the
breath in her throat. He was so male, a glorious golden-
brown god, and she couldn't believe her luck that he had
chosen her from all the lovely girls staying around
Paleokastritsa.

'Come on, lazybones, join me!' Leo shouted from the
water.

Jacy needed no further urging and, running to the side
of the boat, she dived into the welcoming depths. 'Race
you to the shore,' she shouted, and set off at a fast crawl
for the small beach some two hundred yards away. They
had dropped anchor at a small cove that Leo assured
her was inaccessible from the land and completely
private.

Suddenly something hard fastened around her slender
ankle and she felt herself pulled beneath the surface of
the water. Two strong arms wrapped around her bikini-
clad body and a firm mouth closed over hers. She clung
to his broad shoulders, the water around them doing
nothing to cool the searing heat inside her as the kiss
went on and on. She wrapped her long legs around his
and their limbs became entwined. Finally, they floated
to the surface and, breaking the kiss, both gasped lung-
fulls of fresh air.

Still clinging to her, Leo looked into her dazed golden eyes. 'God, but I want you, Jacy!' His feet found the sea-bed, but Jacy was still out of her depth—in more ways than one.

'And I want you,' she sighed, her small hands curving around his neck and ruffling the long dark curls plastered to his proud head by the warm water. He was everything she had ever wanted, she realised; nothing else in the world mattered to her as much as this man. For a second her golden eyes shadowed. Was it wise to be so obsessed with one person? But then Leo's lips once more found hers and all her doubts vanished.

'Open your mouth for me,' he husked against her lips, and willingly she complied. His tongue explored the moist dark cavern and she reciprocated in kind. Her heart pounded in her chest as Leo slipped one hand around her neck and removed the halter-top of her bikini before sliding to cup one perfectly formed breast in the palm of his hand. His thumb stroked lightly over the rosy nipple, and she gasped into his mouth as her breast hardened with his touch. Her head fell back as he trailed a row of soft kisses down her throat to the now pouting peak of her breast, then his mouth closed over the rigid tip and a small cry escaped her parted lips. Her slender legs gripped his muscular thighs even tighter and she heard him groan low in his throat as he reluctantly lifted his head from her breast.

She felt the heated pulse of his arousal hard against the most sensitive part of her; only two tiny fragments of cloth separated them from the completion they both ached for. The gentle lapping of the water around them did nothing to assuage the burning desire reflected in the black eyes that met her dazed golden ones.

'I don't think I can stand much more, Jacy,' Leo rasped, and began walking to the beach. He stopped a few feet from the shore and slid his hands down over

her waist to her thighs, and gently eased her on to her
own two feet before curving his large hands around her
buttocks and pulling her firmly against his bulging
thighs. 'If you want me to stop, it will have to be now,
Jacy. Feel what you do to me,' he demanded harshly.
'No woman has ever affected me the way you do.'

'It's the same for me,' Jacy whispered; and it was true.
She was standing in two feet of water, naked except for
tiny briefs, but she felt no shame, no embarrassment:
everything that had happened over the last few days,
every touch, kiss and caress had led her to this moment.
Her eyes, wide and worshipping, wandered in awe over
his magnificent torso, the sun beating down on his golden
skin, the black curling hair on his chest tipped with glittering pearls of water. She watched the heavy rise and
fall of his broad chest, his rapid breathing, and knew
hers was the same. She shivered as he lifted his hands
and cupped her full breasts, his brown eyes glittering
almost black as he feasted on her near naked form, and
then she was swept up in his arms and carried the last
few feet to the water-line.

Leo laid her down on the hard wet sand and she
stretched out her arms to him in the age-old symbol of
surrender. 'God, but you're beautiful,' he rasped as he
lowered himself down beside her. In one deft movement
he removed her bikini briefs so that she was lying naked
before him.

The bright sun burning down from a clear blue sky
dazzled her eyes for a second, then she gasped as Leo
rolled on top of her, his arms supporting him either side
of her shoulders. With one leg he nudged her thighs apart
so he was cradled in the well of her hips. She gave a
startled gasp as she realised he was also naked, but then
his dark head swooped down, his mouth finding her
willingly parted lips.

With hands, tongue and teeth he caressed and stroked every naked inch of her until she was a molten, quivering mass of need. She clutched his broad shoulders and her mouth found the strong column of his throat and bit lightly as her nails raked down his broad back. His long fingers stroked between her parted thighs, finding the soft damp curls and parting the tender flesh beneath. Her back arched in sudden convulsion as his seeking fingers found the most sensitive feminine heart of her, and she groaned aloud at the exquisite tension, the new fluttering sensations in her womb, the almost painful anticipation of something miraculous. Then Leo's mouth closed over the turgid peak of one breast and drew on the sensitive tip in rhythm with his wickedly stroking fingers. She writhed beneath him, crying, 'Please . . . please.'

'I can't wait,' Leo moaned against her swollen breast. 'Are you protected?'

'No, but . . .' She didn't care: she loved him . . .

A string of what could only have been curses erupted from his mouth in a furious tirade, and with appalling abruptness he leaped to his feet and dived back into the sea.

Jacy was too stunned to move; she lay on the beach where he had left her, a shivering mass of frustration. Slowly she became aware of her surroundings—the glaring sun, her completely naked state, the water lapping at her feet. Broad daylight! No man had ever touched her before and yet with Leo she had lost all modesty, all her inhibitions vanishing at his slightest touch.

She sat up. Leo was almost back at the boat, his strong arms scything through the water as though all the hounds of hell were after him. She groaned out loud. What a fool she was! Of course Leo would expect her to be protected. He was a sensitive, caring man and he would never take the chance of making a girl pregnant. She should be grateful for his restraint, but somehow all she felt was a burning frustration, and deep down a secret wish that he had been as carried away as herself. She would quite like to have Leo's child; in fact, she would love to. A little brown-eyed, black-haired boy. She smiled to herself—maybe some day. Getting to her feet, she picked up her bikini bottom and slipped it on before setting off at a steady crawl for the boat.

'Sorry, Jacy.' Leo's rather stern countenance stared down at her as she reached the small ladder at the stern. 'I had to leave, or else...'. He held out a hand to her and she took it and scrambled back on board.

'Or else what...?' she said breathlessly. Still topless, she had no notion of how seductive she looked. Her high breasts, the nipples hard, stood out pertly; whether it was because of the water or lingering traces of arousal— it didn't make much difference to the man beside her.

'Not what, where,' Leo growled, and, swinging her into his arms once more, he strode across the deck and down into the cabin, dropping Jacy on to the bunk from quite a height.

Laughing up at him, she met his eyes with hers and the laughter died in her throat. His handsome face was stern, almost angry. He had wrapped a towel around his waist, but that was all he wore. 'What's the matter?' she asked uncertainly; she had never seen him look so serious.

'Nothing's the matter now!' he said oddly. 'Hell, even swimming two hundred yards can't cure it,' he muttered, almost to himself, before joining her on the bunk.

'Do you think this is wise?' she managed to ask before once again his lips met hers in a long drugging kiss. Within seconds the passion that had flared on the beach was once more ignited and Jacy cried out as with lips and hands he once more aroused her to fever pitch: but this time there was no stopping.

Leo lifted his head from teasing her swollen breasts, and holding out a small foil package he murmured, 'Put it on for me, Jacy.'

For a second she didn't know what he was asking, and when she did she still trembled. Her hot, curious gaze slid down between their two bodies, the evidence of his manhood intimidating. 'I . . .' She tentatively stroked her slender hand over his hard flat stomach. How could she tell him that she'd never seen a naked man before? Never made love? Explain her virginal fear? How could she explain all this when her body reacted with wanton delight to his every touch?

'You're shy,' he groaned, 'and I can't hold out.'

Then once more their lips met and Leo slid his hands beneath her buttocks and lifted her up to him. Jacy tensed for a split-second, felt one last lingering flash of fear at what was about to happen, and then he was inside her. She flinched at the swift stab of pain, and Leo stilled.

'Jacy, why didn't you say?' he rasped, his dark eyes black with passion burning down into hers.

'Please don't stop,' she pleaded, all her love and longing there for him to see in her huge eyes, and with a muffled groan he buried his head in her throat and began to move slowly and firmly.

'I love you, I love you, Leo,' she heard herself scream as her slender body convulsed in a mind-bending explosion of rapture; and she only vaguely heard Leo's equally exultant cry as with one last thrust his great body shuddered out of his control before he collapsed on top of her.

For a long lingering moment the only sound was of their heavy breathing mingled with the gentle lapping of the water against the hull of the boat. Jacy had never felt so happy, so contented, so sated in her whole life. Leo's sweat-slicked body covered hers like a great loving security-blanket. He was hers for all time, she thought delightedly.

'My first virgin,' he breathed raggedly against her throat, and as he lifted his head his dark eyes, still dilated with passion, studied her softly flushed face. 'But you should have told me, Jacy. I would have been more gentle. Are you all right?'

'All right? No,' she murmured, and thrilled at the quick flash of concern in his eyes. 'I'm ecstatic, in heaven, in love. I never knew anything could be so wonderful,' she freely confessed, before asking, 'Is it always like this?'

'Between you and me, I have a suspicion it will always be perfect.'

'Just a suspicion?' she teased, confident in her new-found love.

Leo's head lowered and he breathed against her lips. 'God help me, it's a certainty.'

CHAPTER THREE

JACY SANG as she rushed around the small apartment
making sure everything was perfect for the intimate
dinner for two she had planned. A quick look in the
oven . . . yes, the fillet of lamb was almost cooked to perfection. Straightening, she glanced out of the window;
it was already dark but even at night the view was spectacular. The apartment was one of a block of four
perched halfway up the hill-side above the bay of
Paleokastritsa, and the twinkling lights below, the moon
on the water, all added to her sense of wonder at the
paradise she had found herself in—and the man who
had made it all perfect . . .

Leo would be arriving any minute, she thought happily
as she walked back into the living-room. It was a simple
room: white-washed walls and one or two pictures of
the island added for a bit of colour. A large, comfortable
sofa-bed, a couple of chairs and a coffee-table—the
minimum of furniture needed to equip an apartment to
be rented to tourists, but still she loved it.

The past three days had been magical; from the
afternoon on Leo's boat when he had made her his, she
had been living in a rosy glow of love. A soft, reminiscent smile curved her full lips. It had been night by
the time they'd finally upped anchor and made for the
harbour, after spending hours making love. Leo was
everything she had ever dreamed of. A tender, sensitive
lover and an expert teacher.

By the time they had finally reached the harbour, Jacy,
confident in his love, had jumped from the boat and

following his instructions had helped him tie it up. Unthinkingly she remarked, 'I think I will make a great fisherman's wife,' and his laughing reply, 'I'm sure you will, Jacy,' had only confirmed her happiness.

Jacy frowned slightly; the only cloud on her horizon was her mother. She had rung England earlier today and spoken to her. There were only four days of her holiday left, and it had seemed only fair to tell her mother that the chances were she would not be returning home, or going to university in September—because of Leo. Unfortunately, her mother's reaction had not been enthusiastic. She had responded by telling Jacy that her father was at present in England, and she'd better get home and discuss the future with both of them before doing anything rash. Jacy hadn't quite had the nerve to confess that she was already committed body and soul to her Greek fisherman.

The banging of a car door wiped the frown from her forehead, and with a leap of her pulse she dashed to open the door. 'Leo.' She said his name, her eyes drinking in the sight of his tall, hard body that was dressed casually in cream pleated trousers and a cream polo-shirt. He lounged elegantly against the door-frame, and in one hand he carried a bottle of champagne, in the other a bunch of gorgeous yellow roses.

'Golden flowers for a golden girl.' Leo smiled down at her, then, bending his head, he brushed his lips lightly across hers.

Her breath caught in her throat. He was so handsome and somehow different from the laughing fisherman she had fallen in love with: more mature, sophisticated. If she hadn't known better she could have quite easily mistaken him for a debonair man-about-town. She shook her head, her long golden hair shimmering in the half-light. She was being fanciful; it *was* her Leo, and tonight she was sure would be a milestone in their relationship.

Her feminine intuition was working overtime: surely tonight he would formally propose? She took the flowers he offered and, suddenly inexplicably shy, buried her face in the sweet-scented blooms.

'Thank you, they're beautiful,' she murmured huskily.

Putting his arm around her shoulders, Leo chuckled. 'Be careful, sweetheart. Don't forget the thorns. I would hate to see your lovely face spoilt.'

Lifting her head, she beamed up at him. 'So you only love me for my looks?' she teased. In the security of his embrace, she felt the most treasured, the most loved girl alive.

'Well, maybe not just your looks—your body has an awful lot to do with it,' he drawled with a lascivious grin.

Their joined laughter set the tone for the evening. They ate in the kitchen, by candlelight; two lovers in a world of their own, joking and laughing in between eating the typically English meal that she'd prepared: roast lamb, mint-sauce, and roast potatoes with Yorkshire pudding plus a selection of vegetables.

'What are you trying to do to me?' Leo groaned, a lazy smile twitching the corners of his sensuous mouth as he laid down his spoon, having finished the final scrap of cold summer-pudding. 'Get at my heart through my stomach?'

She grinned back. 'Would you mind?'

'No.' He looked surprised. 'No, I don't think I would.' He was silent for a moment, his dark eyes narrowed assessingly on her young face before, with an impatient gesture, he pushed back his chair and jumped up. 'Come on, let's finish this bottle in the living-room.'

Jacy had an uneasy feeling that something had upset him, so she meekly picked up the two glasses and followed him through into the other room. But she quickly dismissed her fears as Leo, reclining on the sofa with his long legs stretched out in front of him, beckoned her into his waiting arms. She placed the glasses on the coffee-table and curled up beside him, welcoming the warmth of his arm around her naked shoulders. Tonight she had worn the only dress that she had with her: a slim blue fine jersey sheath that tied with a draw-string between her breasts—more a beach dress than anything else, but when one's only luggage was a haversack there was no room for fancy clothes.

'You're quiet, sweetheart—something wrong?' Leo murmured, nuzzling her ear.

'No,' she sighed. 'I was just wishing I had a wardrobe of beautiful clothes to beguile you with.' She chuckled, lazily running her small hand over his broad chest. 'All you've seen me in so far is a bikini, or shorts and trousers, and...'

'My darling girl——' his mouth slid down over the soft curve of her neck, and lower '—I don't care *what* you wear—in fact I prefer you naked any time.' His teeth pulled at the draw-string bow between the soft curves of her breasts.

Jacy looked down at his dark head resting on her breast and, lifting her hand, stroked her fingers through the thick black curling hair of his head, delighting in the silky feel, the subtle scent of him, all male... and all hers. 'Time is another problem,' she murmured faintly.

Leo raised his head. 'A problem?'

'Yes.' And, taking her courage in both hands, she told him, 'The girls will be back any day now, and my ticket back to England is for Friday, in three days' time.' The thought of leaving Corfu and Leo terrified her. 'I don't want to leave you,' she blurted. With one slender finger she traced the outline of his eyebrow, the strong line of his nose, and around the generous curve of his mouth that could delight her in ways she had never thought possible. She loved him with all her heart, mind and body, and, leaning forward, she pressed her mouth to his, her tongue darting between his strong teeth. She wanted him; God, how she wanted him...

Leo allowed her to take the initiative for a moment before folding her tight in his arms, his tongue meeting and moving with hers as the kiss deepened into a flaring of passion so intense that liquid heat flooded Jacy's body and she burned with need. Her hands curved around his neck, her fingers tangling in the night-black hair of his head while Leo lifted her legs across his lap and laid her back against the sofa.

'Don't go, then,' he muttered thickly as he broke the kiss, his strong hand stroking down over her breast, taking the bodice of her dress with it. 'Stay here with me.' His fingers found her tender nipple and rolled it between thumb and forefinger. His brown eyes, gleaming with growing desire, captured hers. 'You want to. You want me,' he said hardly. 'You know you do.'

His hand at her breast, the darkening glitter in his eyes, and the heat of his hard body against her promised everything. It was what she had been longing to hear. He wanted to marry her.

'Oh, yes, Leo. Yes. I want to spend my life with you.' She felt the tremor through his huge body at her words; his hand fell from her breast and, as if in slow motion, he leant back to stare down at her flushed, beautiful face.

'You're very young, Jacy—your whole life is a long time,' he said, with an odd inflection in his throaty voice.

Guilelessly she traced her small hands up over his hard biceps to his shoulders. 'Not long enough for the way I feel about you, Leo.' At last, after two weeks of waiting, they were finally making a commitment, she thought ecstatically. Leo loved her, he wanted her to stay; her dream had come true. She slid her hands from his shoulders to cup his beloved face in her small palms. 'Kiss me,' she demanded, wanting to seal their future. But before his lips met hers a loud knock on the door interrupted their idyll.

'Are you expecting someone?' Leo demanded, drawing away from her.

Hastily she scrambled off his lap and adjusted her dress. 'No, no one—unless the girls have come back early.' The banging on the door continued. So much for her romantic evening, she thought sadly and with some frustration.

'You'd better answer it,' Leo commanded, leaning forward to pick up his glass of wine from the table. 'And get rid of them, if you can.' He glanced up at her flushed, woeful expression and grinned. 'If you can't, we could go night-fishing!'

Relieved that their evening wasn't to end so precipitately, she grinned back before heading for the door and opening it.

'What took you so long?' a hard male voice demanded.

'Daddy! What are you doing here?' she got out, before being swept off her feet in a bear-hug and carried back into the living-room.

'I came to see you, Ja . . .' She was dropped to her feet so abruptly that she nearly fell as her father caught sight of Leo. 'My God! Kozakis!' he exclaimed, completely ignoring his daughter.

Jacy stirred restlessly in the bed. Ten years on and the memory was still painful. She could see the whole scene in her mind's eye as if it were yesterday, the players moving seemingly in slow motion.

The small room, and her father, a tall slim man with fair hair, about the same height as Leo but a good deal older. He stood motionless, a questioning light in his pale eyes.

But Leo jumped to his feet, overturning in the process the small occasional-table that held the wine and glasses.

'What the hell are you doing here, Carter? Hoping to get a follow-up for your filthy rag?' he snarled, and in two short strides he was standing within inches of the other man and grasping him by the throat. 'Get out before I break your damn neck.'

'No, no!' Jacy didn't know what was happening, but there was no mistaking the burning hatred in Leo's eyes. 'Please, Leo, this is my father,' she cried.

Leo's hands fell to his sides and he turned slowly to face Jacy. For a moment he watched her in a bitter, hostile silence. 'This man is your *father*? You *knew*. You knew all the time who I was.'

She flinched at the icy contempt in his tone, and couldn't speak: fear had closed her throat. The dark man towering over her, who only minutes earlier had been making love to her, had vanished, and in his place stood a stranger. A steely-eyed, furious stranger.

'I suppose you're following in your father's footsteps as a budding reporter?' he queried with deadly softness.

'I thought about it,' she responded meekly, hoping to defuse the violent tension in the room. But...

'I should have guessed all that dewy-eyed innocence was too good to be true. What was it to be? A scoop to launch your career? How Kozakis seduced an innocent girl?' His lips curled in sneering contempt, his dark eyes narrowed to mere slits. 'Just you try it, Jacy—you *or* your father—and I will make you out to be the biggest slut in Christendom.'

Jacy, her legs trembling and her eyes filling with moisture, fought back her tears. She didn't know what had gone wrong. She could not understand what was happening—why Leo, her lover, was behaving this way. And she was too terrified to ask.

'Or perhaps you were going for the biggy, a wedding-ring, then the fat settlement and an exposé. My God! I nearly fell for it.'

She heard Leo's ranting, and her rosy dream of love and marriage to her fisherman disintegrated before her eyes. Her glance swung to her father, and she was hurt anew by the look of stunned disbelief on her father's face.

'Now, wait a damn minute, Kozakis. You can't speak to my daughter like that.' Her father finally found his voice; but as Jacy watched Leo pushed past the older man and strode towards the door. With his hand on the door-handle, he turned and spoke.

'Carter, I always knew you were a slimy rat.' His dark, furious gaze slanted between father and daughter. 'And the old adage is certainly true: like father, like daughter.' His black eyes caught and held Jacy's. 'At least a whore has the basic honesty to state a price, but women like you turn my stomach. Your type bleed a man dry before the poor sod even knows he's paying for it.' And with one disgusted shake of his dark head he stormed out of the apartment, slamming the door after him.

Jacy gave one despairing little cry. 'Leo...' But in her heart she knew it was too late. She staggered to the sofa and collapsed on to it in a heap. Burying her head in her hands, she cried and cried as her heart splintered into a million pieces. She was barely aware of the comforting arm of her father around her shaking shoulders. She didn't fully understand what had happened, but Leo's parting words had cut into her very soul. The icy contempt in his dark eyes was indelibly burnt into her brain.

'Hush, Jacy, please. The man's not worth it.' Her father's quietly voiced words finally penetrated the black depths of her sorrow.

'But I love him,' she rasped, her throat dry with crying. 'I don't understand...' she wailed and, lifting her head, with her eyes swollen and red with weeping, she beseeched her father, 'What happened? We love each other,' she ended on a sob.

'I don't know what has been going on here, Jacy; your mother gave me some garbled story about your wanting to marry a fisherman.'

'Yes, Daddy—Leo. But...'

'Sorry, my pet.' He held her close, an arm around her shoulder. 'But Leo Kozakis is no fisherman. He's a very wealthy businessman, with offices in all the major capitals of the world. Whatever he told you was a lie: his family home is a luxurious villa not far from here, and it's guarded like Fort Knox.'

As her father spoke Jacy felt the full weight of Leo's betrayal sink deeper and deeper into every fibre of her being. She felt sick and, worse, utterly humiliated and ashamed. She had given her most precious gift to a liar and a cheat. 'Are you sure he's the same man?' She made one last appeal, hoping there might be some mistake.

'Jacy, I'm sure,' he confirmed soberly. 'But if he's hurt you in any way, I'll make him pay—even if I have to follow him for the rest of my days.'

She looked into her father's familiar face and was shocked by the grim determination in his usually easygoing features. His pale eyes gleamed as cold as the Arctic Ocean. 'If that man has seduced you, my baby...'

'No, Daddy.' She stopped him. 'It didn't go that far,' she lied. Even in her distress she recognised that there was no way a man like her father would ever win a fight against Leo.

Suddenly, all the little things that she'd puzzled over in the past few weeks made complete sense. The luxurious boat—of course he didn't take out tourists; he probably enjoyed game fishing... The lobsters she'd seen on the very first day they'd met—obviously he had *bought* the catch. The amount of free time Leo had spent with her; no fisherman could afford that kind of leisure.

She groaned inwardly at her own naïve folly. The *look* of the man alone should have told her. Tonight, when he'd arrived at her door elegantly dressed, she had wondered for a moment how a Greek fisherman could afford that kind of attire. But perhaps most telling of all was his complete grasp of the English language, with hardly a trace of accent. She had once queried it, and Leo had laughingly said he'd picked it up from English friends.

'You're sure, Jacy? I know the man's reputation.'

'Positive,' she declared, and was amazed to hear how emphatic she sounded when it was taking every ounce of control she possessed to stop herself from screaming hysterically at the fate that had dealt her such a devastating blow. But somewhere in her subconscious she recognised the ruthless power of a man like Leo, and instinctively she knew that he was the type to crush her father without a second thought, if it suited him.

Exactly *how* she knew, she could not analyse. Her chaotic emotions weren't conducive to clear thinking. All she *did* recognise as she stood curved in her father's arm, was that the man she loved did not exist, and all she had left to cling to was her father. Later she would question every word, every gesture in bitter self-recrimination; but at the moment she just wanted some explanation, some excuse for the pain she was feeling. She recalled her father's face as he'd walked in the door and spotted Leo.

'But how do *you* know Leo, Daddy?' she asked, unconscious of the pained puzzlement in her delicately expressive features.

'Oh, baby, it's a long story, and not very pleasant.'

'Please, Daddy, I need to know, to understand.'

'I guess I owe you that much, Jacy.' A deep frown marked his even features, the lines around his pale eyes exaggerated as he stared down into the trusting, up-turned face of his daughter. 'It's not a pleasant story, child.' Taking a deep breath, he continued speaking in an even tone, showing little emotion. 'You know the paper I edit in Los Angeles? Well, a few months back Leo Kozakis was the headline story for quite some time. The lady he'd lived with for three years in San Francisco was suing him for palimony.'

Jacy's face went even paler, if that was possible, at the mention of another woman. 'Palimony?' She had never heard the word.

'Yes, Jacy; in California, a man doesn't have to be married to a woman to be sued for alimony—it's enough if they've lived together for a few years as man and wife. In Leo Kozakis' case, the woman claimed that she'd lived with him for three years in his penthouse apartment, and then he'd thrown her out. She applied to the court for palimony, and Kozakis fought the case. His ar-gument was that the lady was his mistress, nothing more, and that she'd clearly understood the situation before she moved into the apartment.'

'That's disgusting,' Jacy murmured.

'Yes, well, Kozakis reckoned that it was a common arrangement in Europe. He gave the lady presents when he saw her, and when she declared that she was homeless he allowed her to use the company apartment. But at no time had he made any commitment to her. It was a very nasty fight.'

Jacy could not bear to believe it. It was something so outside of her teenage idea of love and life. To fight in a Court of law, not even over a marriage but simply over one's *love-life*, was too horrible to contemplate. 'What happened?' she whispered.

'Kozakis won, of course. Unfortunately for you, my
pet. It was my paper, my decision to break the story to
the public, and we tended towards the lady's side of the
problem. Kozakis knows that, and he's never forgiven
me. Obviously when I walked in here tonight, and you
told him that I was your father, he must have thought
it was a set-up—you and I working together on another
exposé of his lifestyle.'

'Oh God! So *that's* why he asked if I was going to be
a reporter!' Jacy spoke her thoughts out loud. The worst
thing was that she'd confirmed Leo's suspicions by
agreeing that she *had* considered a career in journalism.
He'd cut her off before she could add that she wasn't
going to.

'I'm sorry, truly sorry, if I've ruined your budding
romance, but as your father I've got to tell you that the
man would never have married you. His type never do:
he just enjoys beautiful women.'

Each word her father spoke was like a knife in Jacy's
heart, but she didn't doubt for a moment that he was
telling her the truth.

'He's known to have girlfriends dotted all over the
world, wherever the firm of Kozakis does business. I
had heard that his father is ill, which is probably why
Leo is here at the family home in Corfu. I hate to see
you disillusioned, child——' his hand gently stroked over
her golden hair in a consoling gesture '—but I imagine
that he found a young girl like you nothing more than
a novel diversion while he has to stay here in Corfu.'

A blessed numbness had enveloped Jacy as she listened
to the horrible truth, and she knew that her father was
right. Almost dispassionately she recalled the first time
Leo had made love to her, and a bitter, ironic smile
twisted her full lips. He had almost taken her on the
beach, but he'd been nowhere near as out of control as
she herself had been. She understood clearly now why,

when she'd admitted to being unprotected, he had quite cold-bloodedly left her and swum back to the boat. Later, when he was adequately protected, only then had he made love to her. While she'd been dreaming of wedding-bells and little brown-eyed babies, he'd been making quite sure that he wouldn't be compromised into a hasty marriage.

'You've had a lucky escape, Jacy. At least the man had the decency not to seduce you completely. You're young, and it's your first crush on an older man. I know it hurts, but believe me, child, you'll soon get over it. Once you get home and go to university, all this will seem like a brief holiday romance that didn't come to anything.'

Jacy turned over on her stomach and buried her head in the pillow. Her father had been right, in a way. They had left Corfu together the next day, and she'd gone on to university; but she had never been the same carefree young girl again. That summer in Corfu she had grown up... Then in the autumn, her parents had told her that they were getting a divorce—apparently they'd only stayed together until she left home.

It had been another blow to her, and she had seen little of her father over the next few years. Then when her mother was so tragically killed he had returned to London and bought this house, and Jacy had shared it with him until his death.

With hindsight, she could see why her faith in men and marriage was non-existent, but for a long time she'd been terribly hurt by what she saw as betrayal by the only men she had ever known. Her student years were spent studying hard and taking little part in the social side of college—and avoiding men like the plague. She obtained a First in Economics, and joined Mutual as an

executive; and until tonight she'd been completely happy
with her career and lifestyle.

Yawning widely, she snuggled down into the depths
of her single bed. So Leo Kozakis had reappeared in her
life! She would not allow him to ruin her happiness
again. She was a mature, successful woman, not the silly
girl he had known. She could handle him, she told herself
as her eyelids drooped. In fact, it would be a pleasure
to teach the arrogant devil that he couldn't have every
woman he desired. She had read articles about him over
the years, and it appeared to her that he'd never changed
at all: he was still the womanising rake he'd always been,
whereas Jacy considered that *she* had grown into a
strong, capable woman—a match for any male chauvinist
pig of the Kozakis type. And on that thought she finally
drifted into sleep.

Jacy was naked on a beach. The sea, a raging grey
torrent, lashed the shore-line, barely missing her feet as
she ran along the hard sand as though her heart would
burst. A terrified glance over her shoulder showed her
that he was still in pursuit—a large, dark, faceless man.
Her lungs expanded in raw agony with every step she
took. He was gaining on her. She felt hot breath and
the hairs on the back of her neck stood upright in terror;
harsh breathing mingled with her own rasping breath,
and then in the distance a bell rang, getting louder by
the second. She gasped and struggled violently.

Opening her eyes, Jacy groaned out loud. She was
lying upside-down in the bed, the sheet twisted like a
strait-jacket around her and her slender body damp with
perspiration. Battling her way out of the tangled mess
of covers, she swung her long legs over the side of the
bed and, brushing the long mane of her hair from her
face, she reached for the jangling phone on the bedside-
table. God! That was some nightmare, she thought with
a shiver as she lifted the receiver to her ear.

'Hello, Jacy here.' It was Liz's cheerful voice at the other end. 'What time of the morning do you call this?' Jacy demanded, casting a glance at the clock beside the telephone.

'Seven—but I wanted to catch you before you left for work. How did it go last night with Leo? Did he make a pass at you?'

'Please, Liz, one question at a time,' she groaned, rubbing the sleep from her eyes with one hand. 'It went fine. He brought me home and said goodnight at the door and, no, he didn't kiss me.' Thank God Liz couldn't see her fingers crossed behind her back.

'Well, that's something, I suppose. Listen, Jacy, I don't think it's a good idea for you to date Kozakis. We'll just forget about the bet, hmm?'

Jacy straightened, suddenly aware of the unease in her friend's voice. 'And what's brought about this change of heart? Frightened you might lose the *netsuke*? As I remember, last night you were doing your damnedest to fix me up with Mr Kozakis,' she drawled mockingly. Liz was up to something...

'Yes, I know, but I only have your best interests at heart. I'd only met Leo once before, and I found him charming. Well, let's face it—the man *is* charming! But I had a talk to Tom last night, and he told me that Kozakis is a brilliant businessman, but where women are concerned, he's strictly the love 'em and leave 'em type. You're much too naïve to get mixed up with a man like that.'

'Naïve?' Jacy snorted. 'Hardly, Liz.'

'You know what I mean. You might be good in business, but your relationships with men are virtually non-existent. I don't know how you knew Leo Kozakis before, or what happened—you can tell me some time—but I don't think he's the right sort of man for you.'

'Is there something you're not telling me?' Jacy
queried. Liz's mission in life for years had been to fix
her up with a man, and now, in a complete turnabout,
she was trying to do the opposite.

'All right, I'll come clean. Leo Kozakis returned to
the party last night. Now, I know he's supposed to be
taking you out to dinner on Saturday, and yet quite
brazenly in front of me he offered to take Thelma home.
The cheek of the man!' Her indignation echoed down
the telephone.

Jacy burst out laughing, but there was very little
humour in it. Thelma was the tall blonde she had seen
Leo dancing with earlier last night. The man was certainly running true to form. 'Oh, Liz, I would love to
have seen your face.'

'It wasn't funny. Thelma might be a great interior designer, but her reputation for trying out all the beds she
instals is well-known. That isn't the sort of date I had
in mind when I made the bet with you.'

'Sorry, Liz, the bet still stands,' Jacy heard herself
saying firmly. 'Look at it from my point of view. I get
wined and dined for free, and win the *netsuke*, while the
great man gets nothing from me in return except my
company. His baser instincts he can indulge with the
lovely Thelma.'

'That's a dangerous game to play—Kozakis is a devious man. I wasn't going to say anything, but Tom admitted last night that he'd known all about the party for
a week—the boys had told him. He said nothing so as
not to upset me, but, apparently, when he mentioned it
to Kozakis the man insisted on coming back with him
last night for some papers that weren't all that important, after enquiring if you would be attending. He'd
seen a snapshot of you at our place in Surrey last week.
Tom thinks the man is hunting you down,' Liz warned.

'But I suppose you know what you're doing. At least, I hope you do...'

Jacy sat for some minutes after replacing the telephone, going over the conversation in her head. So Leo had known she was going to be there last night. But why bother after all this time? She frowned... But of course, the explanation was simple and so true to form... Leo was in London for the first time in ages—how much quicker it was to take up with an old flame, a meal and then straight to bed, than to have to find a new woman and waste time building a relationship.

She smiled. It was a good feeling to know that Liz cared about her well-being. But the information about Leo and his involvement with Thelma was the one thing designed to strengthen her determination. Leo Kozakis would get a taste of his own medicine for a change, she vowed.

Later that morning, when she walked into the foyer of the Mutual Save and Trust Company and saw Barbara at the reception desk, the young girl's face puffy and her eyes red-rimmed from crying, all her previous anger resurrected. Jacy had suffered like that herself at Leo Kozakis' hands. She'd never considered herself to be a vengeful person, but a burning desire to get even with Leo for herself and all her sisters who'd suffered at the hands of such men consumed her usually logical mind. Confidently, she told herself that this time she would turn the tables on the conceited swine. She was looking forward to Saturday night...

CHAPTER FOUR

JACY wasn't a conceited girl, but the reflection that stared back at her from the mirrored-door of her wardrobe brought a self-satisfied smile to her wide mouth. She had swept her long blonde hair into an intricate twist on top of her head and fastened it with a black and gold antique clip. She had taken time with her make-up, using slightly more than usual, and the taupe eyeshadow skilfully blended with a touch of dark gold emphasised the strange yellow glint of her wide eyes. A brown mascara elongated her already long lashes, the whole outlined with the faintest touch of brown kohl. The addition of blusher to her foundation highlighted her classic cheekbones, and the subtle plum-coloured lipstick outlined her full mouth in a sensuous curve.

She turned sideways and back, the better to admire her ensemble. The extravagantly rainbow-coloured, beaded swing-jacket moved subtly as she turned, and the matching black bustier, with identical colourful beading tracing the curve of her full breasts, fitted to perfection. It was a Diane Freis design, purchased that very afternoon from the designer room on the first floor at Harrods, and, yes—it had been a good buy. She'd teamed the jacket and bustier with her favourite black silk, short evening skirt that clung lovingly to her slim hips and ended just above her knee. Her stockings were a muted barely black, and her shoes were soft black leather mules with a bobbin-shaped inch-and-a-half heel. The overall effect was stunning.

After spending all morning going through her
wardrobe, she had finally decided to treat herself to
something new. She didn't question the reason behind
it, telling herself that it was a justifiable purchase. Yet
she had a very good wardrobe. A selection of classic
suits for work, plus a good range of casual gear. Calvin
Klein figured largely in her wardrobe: she loved the
American designer's easy, elegant style. She also adored
his perfume, Obsession, and, picking up a bottle from
the dresser, she liberally sprayed the long curve of her
neck. Finally she fitted a pair of black and glass beaded
cascade earrings to her ears, and she was ready. The
epitome of sophisticated womanhood, she told herself
with a grin.

She was lucky in one respect, she supposed. As a single
girl living in London she didn't have the expense of
buying or renting an apartment, having inherited her
father's mews cottage and also a fairly decent amount
of insurance money on his death. She wasn't wealthy,
she would always have to work, but she did have a very
nice nest-egg that allowed her to indulge herself
occasionally.

A knock followed by the ringing of the doorbell made
her stiffen imperceptibly; but with a last look around
the bedroom she picked up a small clutch handbag and
hastily made her way downstairs to the front door.
Taking a deep breath, she opened it.

All the mature confidence in the world couldn't
prevent her mouth falling open in stunned shock at the
sight that met her eyes. Leo stood negligently against the
door-frame, immaculately dressed in a formal evening
suit, a pristine white dress-shirt with an elegantly tied
bow-tie in deepest navy settled at his strong throat.
Across his broad shoulders was casually draped a long,
navy cashmere overcoat; but it was his face and hands
that caused her stunned immobility. His dark eyes

gleamed with a secret knowledge and his sensuous lips
were parted in a wide smile as his large hands held out
towards her a bunch of yellow roses and a bottle of
champagne...

'Golden flowers for a golden girl.' He pressed the roses
into her cold hand.

Mechanically she took them, muttering, 'Thank you.
I'll just put them in water.' And turning she fled through
the living-room and into the kitchen. How dared he
remind her of their last date all those years ago? she
fumed. Either he was the most insensitive clod on God's
earth or he had done it deliberately to discover her reaction; and she had a sinking feeling that the second
premise was correct.

Standing in the kitchen, she took a few deep breaths
before opening a wall cupboard and removing a large
pottery vase, the first one she touched. Filling it with
water, she stuffed the offending roses in the container.

'That's no way to treat such delicate flowers.' Leo's
breath moved the short hairs on the back of her neck.
He had followed her into the kitchen.

Jacy spun around. He was much too close, his tall
presence was overpowering in the small room. 'Yes,
well—I can arrange them later. I thought we were going
out to dinner. I'm starving.' She was babbling, she knew,
but suddenly it hit her. Her crazy idea to teach this man
a lesson was just that: crazy.

'Oh, I think we have time for a drink, Jacy. A glass
of champagne, a toast to old friends, hmm?'

'A little less of the old,' she drawled mockingly. 'And
I never drink on an empty stomach.' Bravely facing him,
while trying desperately to regain her shattered nerves,
she added, 'Shall we go?' She just wanted to get the
evening over with as quickly as possible, and then she
would never see Leo Kozakis again. His deeply tanned
face and the overt sexual gleam in his seductive brown

eyes threatened her in ways she had thought long
forgotten.

An unfathomable expression flitted across his
handsome features, and she wondered for a second if he
would be quite so easy to get rid of. She should never
have agreed to see him, she realised, when to her astonishment she found herself crushed against his hard body.

Her head fell back against his arm, and her lips parted
to object when his mouth swooped down on hers, taking
full advantage of her half-open mouth. Her bag fell to
the floor as she clutched at his upper arms in an effort
to restrain him, but his tongue darted provocatively into
her mouth in an achingly familiar kiss. She tried to
remain frozen in his hold, but as his shockingly sensual
mouth ravaged hers she could feel the fierce curl of
longing knot in her stomach.

She was going mad. She hated the man, but then as
his hands moved lower and slid beneath her jacket,
hauling her slender body tightly against his hard frame
and flattening her breasts against his broad muscular
chest, she trembled. But Leo wasn't immune either; she
felt the shudder that ran through him and the sudden
hardening of his thighs before, with a rasping groan, he
pushed her slightly away from him, breaking the kiss.
She was mortified at the ease with which he had evoked
her response and a red tide of colour suffused her throat
and face.

'How dare you?' she blurted like some Regency virgin.

'I always think it is best to get the first kiss out of the
way early, otherwise it can quite spoil one's dinner wondering if the chemistry is there,' he opined mockingly
and then, retrieving her bag from the floor, he held it
out to her.

She took it without a word, too furious to speak. But
Leo had no such problem.

'You're looking beautiful, Jacy, and I could happily stay here all night.' He ran a comprehensive eye over her, then smiled suggestively. 'But you were right, I find I am rather hungry myself. The champagne can keep until we return.'

To Jacy's stupefaction, acting as though he owned the place, he opened the refrigerator door and placed the bottle inside before turning to catch hold of her elbow and lead her out of her own house. She was seated in the front seat of his car, her seat-belt fastened securely over her body by an attentive Leo, before she could regain some control over her wildly fluctuating emotions. She wanted to scream at him for his high-handed treatment of her, but common sense prevailed and, with a degree of civility, she managed to ask conversationally, 'Where are you taking me to dine?' She cast a sidelong glance at her companion.

His handsome profile looked carved out of granite, and as she watched the firmly chiselled mouth tightened imperceptibly, almost as if he were reluctant to answer her simple question. Finally he turned slightly towards her, taking his eyes from the road for an instant. 'I hope you don't mind, but I have to attend a private dinner-dance at the Ritz; a cousin's twenty-first.'

'A private party?' she repeated. That wasn't what she had expected. A quiet dinner for two in some fashionable restaurant was Leo Kozakis' style, but certainly not an introduction to the Kozakis clan. 'But...'

'I know it is not what you expected——' Leo cut off her objection before she could voice it, his attention once more on the road ahead '—but we needn't stay long, and later I will take you somewhere more intimate, if you like,' he drawled provocatively.

Jacy said nothing, ignoring the challenge in his statement. But she couldn't help but recognise the irony of the situation. Years ago she would have been delighted to meet Leo's family; now, the idea horrified her.

Jacy entered the glittering room on Leo's arm, and hesitated slightly at the sight before her. At the end of the room, on a raised dais, was a typical Greek quartet, playing ethnic music with great verve. A quick glance around the rest of the room showed her that every woman present was dressed to impress. Designer gowns everywhere.

She breathed deeply. She had been right to splash out on her Diane Freis, and she gave thanks for the fact that in her job she'd become adept at mixing with the super-wealthy—for quite a few of her cases had been the theft or loss of jewellery collections insured by Mutual, and in one or two instances the owners themselves had been responsible.

A waiter appeared in front of them, and spoke to Leo. Tilting her head a notch, Jacy walked confidently at Leo's side, smiling politely as he addressed a variety of friends with a Greek greeting, while the waiter preceded them to a table for eight at the far side of the room.

'Leo, so glad you could make it.' A short, heavy-set man arose from his seat at the table that was already occupied by five other people—three women and two more men. 'And who is your charming companion?' The small dark man turned sparkling black eyes towards Jacy.

Leo, with a brilliant smile, urged her forward. 'My Uncle Nick, and this is Jacy, a very special friend of mine.'

She held out her hand and it was engulfed in a broad fist. The next few moments were taken up in a flurry of introductions. She accepted a seat next to Nick, with Leo at her other side. She quickly logged in her mind the various names. Apparently the pretty dark girl opposite was Nina, Nick's daughter, whose birthday it was. Beside her was a handsome young man, her fiancé,

whose name Jacy missed. Then Nick's wife, Anna, a
rather heavy lady. But it was the last couple that was the
real shock to Jacy: Leo's father and mother. His father
was a carbon copy of his uncle Nick—short and dark,
with a keen intelligence in his black eyes. But Mrs
Kozakis was a tall, angular woman, impeccably gowned
in black with a fantastic diamond necklace around her
throat that must have cost a fortune. One look at the
older woman's face and it was obvious whom Leo
favoured. The features that were ruggedly attractive on
a man somehow made the woman austere and vaguely
forbidding in appearance.

'All right, Jacy?' Leo's breath feathered against her
ear as he bent his dark head towards her. 'Don't be intimidated, they won't eat you.'

'I'm not,' she snapped back.

'Drink your wine and watch your temper,' he
prompted, his hard thigh pressing against hers under the
table as if in warning.

The contact was like an electric shock down the length
of her leg; she could feel the colour rising in her face as
she swiftly moved her leg, at the same time lifting the
crystal glass in front of her and taking a long swallow
of the wine. Luckily, no one seemed to notice her mo-
mentary distress—except Leo. With a sardonic glance at
her flushed face he murmured so that only she could
hear, 'Don't overdo the shy act, Jacy; we both know
what we want.'

She almost choked on the wine, and then had to grit
her teeth to prevent herself swearing at the conceited
swine. By the time she had regained control of her
temper, the conversation was flowing around her in
quick-fire Greek.

The meal that followed was typical Greek fare, and
to Jacy's surprise she actually enjoyed it. As course followed course and the wine flowed freely she found herself

quite readily accepted by Leo's family. In fact, if she hadn't known what an immoral animal Leo was she could quite easily have been fooled into believing that he genuinely cared for her.

Replacing her wine glass on the table, having drained it, she frowned slightly. It might be a happy family party but she must never forget she wasn't part of it. Leo had asked her out for a *good time*, a brief fling while he was in London. He had been bluntly honest about it at Liz's party. Her *own* reason for going out with Leo was no more laudable than his: a bet! And she couldn't help thinking that revenge would be sweet... Engrossed in her thoughts, she was unaware that Leo's father had spoken to her.

'Jacy. I asked if you would care to dance?'

At the sound of her name, she lifted her head and with an apologetic smile she answered the older man. 'Yes, please.'

'Tell me, Jacy,' Leo's father asked quietly as he propelled her in a perfect turn to an old fashioned waltz, 'how long have you known my son?'

'Years,' she replied lightly.

'Ah, that would explain why he brought you here tonight. Obviously you are different—a lady friend of long-standing, no?'

Jacy was beginning to feel uncomfortable under the direct gaze of the older man. 'Sort of,' she responded non-committally.

'Do you intend to marry my son?'

The directness of the question staggered her. Her golden eyes widened in shocked surprise, and then twinkled with a touch of humour. 'Good God, no,' she laughed. 'Whatever gave you that idea?'

'We will see,' he replied enigmatically, and as the music ended led her back to the table.

'What has my father been saying to you?' Leo demanded as soon as she sat down. 'You were laughing.'

But before she could reply to his question a laughing
Nick was grabbing his arm and something was said in
a flurry of Greek. As Jacy looked on in surprise Leo
and his father, Uncle Nick and the good looking young
man all shed their jackets and ties and, in a group, walked
on to the dance-floor.

The next ten minutes were a revelation to Jacy. The
band started playing a slow Greek tune. The four men,
arms linked at shoulder height, began moving with slow
deliberation to the firm beat of the music. Jacy's eyes
were drawn to Leo and she couldn't look away.

His brown eyes flashed wickedly and a broad grin
curved his handsome face. His chest heaved, the muscles
rippling beneath the fine silk of his shirt as the music
gradually speeded up. The rest of the party began to
clap in time to the music, all eyes fixed on the four men,
dancing in a wild, weaving snake across the smooth floor
in perfect time to the music.

Jacy couldn't contain a gasp of pure feminine appreciation at the picture the men presented. It should
have been effeminate, but the opposite was true. Her
golden eyes traced down the length of Leo; his dark
trousers were snug on his suggestively swaying hips, the
muscles of his thighs bulging beneath the soft fabric.
She could feel the heat rise in her face and her eyes were
glued to the stunning masculine vibrancy of Leo's tall
form. A hot flush of feminine arousal flashed through
her body, and she gasped as a plate flew through the air
to break at his feet.

He was laughing out loud while never missing a step
of the now frenzied pace of the music. Plates were thrown
from all sides at the energetic dancers, smashing into
smithereens on the hard floor.

Jacy swallowed hard; there was something so primitive, so basically pagan but undeniably sexual about the dance. She sighed, a long, low expulsion of air as the music finally stopped. She hadn't even been aware that she'd been holding her breath. Leo strode towards her, the sweat glistening on his brow, his short dark hair curling damply on his forehead. Rivulets of perspiration ran down his strong throat to mingle in the matt of black hair on his chest. In the exertion of the dance his shirt had come unbuttoned almost to his waist.

The crowd were shouting what she supposed were congratulations in Greek, but her eyes never left the approaching man. She was transported back in time to Corfu and her fisherman lover. Leo looked years younger and just as she remembered him from the first time they'd met.

His glittering, triumphant gaze caught and held hers, and with a panther-like speed he was at her side. His dark head swooped down and, with one hand at the back of her head, he kissed her firmly on her softly parted lips. For a second she made no demur, lost in a sensual haze of years ago. But suddenly the noise around her, and the sound of Leo's name being shouted, made her stiffen in instant rejection. It was too late, though, as Leo, chucking her under the chin with one finger, said, 'Nice, but I need privacy for what I have in mind. Shall we go?'

Blushing furiously, her lips still tingling from his openly possessive kiss, she glanced wildly around the room. Leo's family—aunts, uncles, cousins, the whole lot—seemed to be grinning at her. Leo urged her to her feet and before she knew it they had said their goodbyes and were walking out into the night air. She took a few deep breaths as they waited for the valet to bring the car. She was much too susceptible to Leo's powerful masculinity, and the clasp of his hand around her wrist was checking her pulse-rate, she was sure. She glanced sideways and caught the look of glittering anticipation in his eyes, and her heart shuddered.

In the car, she rested her cheek against the cold glass of the side-window. She didn't understand herself at all. For years she'd been all but immune to members of the opposite sex. She had dated, true, but she had always been in control. Tonight, in a few short minutes, watching Leo dance had aroused all her latent sensual emotions with a ferocity that had left her shocked and trembling.

'To a night club?' Leo asked shortly. 'Or home?'

'Home, please,' Jacy replied as the powerful car sped quickly through the darkened streets. She was tired, emotionally distraught, though she hated to admit as much. Leo was having just as powerful an effect on her senses tonight as he'd had years ago, and she would have to be the biggest idiot alive to think for even one second that she could possibly get the better of such a man. Did she even want to? she asked herself wryly. And the answer was no. Whatever had been between them in the past was long since dead. There was certainly no future for them. Leo wanted a roll in the hay, to put it crudely— and she should have had more sense than to encourage him. The problem was, her body had a completely different idea; she seemed to be plunging like a heat-seeking missile to its target—and the target was Leo.

'Overall I think it was a very good evening.' His deep voice broke into her troubled thoughts. 'My family liked you, and you appeared to get along with them very well.'

Jacy swung around in her seat to look at him, and in that instant she recognised her surroundings. The car had stopped at her own front door. 'You're lucky. You have a lovely family,' she said huskily, and, finding the passenger door-handle, she opened it and stepped out, then started walking towards her front door.

Leo appeared at her side just as she was fitting the key into the lock.

'Such haste; I'm flattered.' Taking the key from her shaking fingers, he opened the door.

'Thank you for a lovely evening, and goodnight,' she shot hurriedly, and made to dash into the house.

'Not so fast, Jacy.' His hand caught her elbow, and before she could protest they were both in the hall and Leo was closing the door behind them. 'Dancing is hot work; I'm looking forward to our chilled champagne,' he drawled silkily, urging her forward.

She stood still, and he paused to look down at her, his height dark and intimidating in the dimly lit hall. 'I would rather you left; I'm very tired.'

'In a few minutes. You wouldn't deprive a thirsty man of refreshment, would you?' he enquired mockingly.

She gave him a grudging, 'OK,' and preceded him through the living-room to the kitchen. The light of challenge in his dark eyes was enough to warn her that the simplest course of action was to give him the drink and then get rid of him. That way he would have no excuse to return for his damned champagne! she thought, finally practising some caution. She reached for the handle of the refrigerator, and was stopped by a large, tanned hand catching hers.

'Go and sit down, Jacy. I'll bring it through.'

'You don't know where the glasses are kept,' she argued, reluctant to have him take charge.

'I'll find them. Do as you're told,' he commanded, lifting his other hand to the nape of her neck and urging her around.

Meekly she walked back into the living-room and sat down on the sofa, rubbing the back of her neck with her hand. She was tired, she told herself, and the tension down her spine had absolutely nothing to do with the lingering effect of Leo's touch . . .

She watched him warily as, within seconds, he appeared with two glasses in one hand and the champagne bottle in the other. With a minimum of fuss the glasses were placed on the low table in front of her, and the champagne expertly opened with a satisfying pop and then poured into the waiting glasses.

'You should have been a waiter,' Jacy remarked as she took the glass Leo offered her, while carefully avoiding touching his fingers.

His dark gaze flashed from her face to her hand and back to her face, as good as telling her that he had noticed her not so subtle avoidance of his touch; but he said nothing. Instead he smiled broadly, picked up his own brimming glass, and sat down beside her.

'I was a waiter for quite some time, and a very good one.'

'A waiter? I don't believe you!' she exclaimed.

'It's perfectly true,' he confirmed, and, casually leaning back, stretching his long legs out in front of him, he raised his glass to his mouth and drank the sparkling wine.

She watched the muscles in his throat move beneath the bronzed skin as he swallowed, and had to swallow herself. He was a dangerously attractive man, and he was much too close for comfort. Hastily Jacy drained her own glass as Leo continued conversationally, 'My father is a firm believer in starting at the bottom and working one's way up. When I was young, our business was not so diversified as it is now. We owned a few hotels and a shipping line. So as a boy of fifteen I was put to work in one of our hotels—then every summer after that until I was twenty-one and had finished university.

'That accounts for your expertise with the bottle,' Jacy said, for the moment forgetting her dislike of the man. Fascinated by this insight into his youth, she unconsciously began to relax in his presence.

'Yes, but I was not always so efficient. I can re-member one summer, my first time serving in the dining-room, and I asked a lady if she wanted more hol-landaise sauce. The lady was wearing a very low-cut summer dress, and I was momentarily distracted and in-advertently poured the sauce down her shoulder.'

'Oh, no,' Jacy chuckled.

Leo flashed her a quick grin. 'It wasn't funny, I can tell you. It turned out that the scrap of a dress had a designer label, and my father made me pay for it. I worked the whole of the summer for that damn dress.'

Jacy burst out laughing. 'I wish I could have seen you,' she declared, all her antagonism vanishing under the warm smile in Leo's dark eyes.

'I was a skinny teenager, you wouldn't have liked me. But the episode did teach me a valuable lesson.'

'What was that?' she asked, still smiling.

Leaning forward, Leo placed his glass on the table and slid his arm around her shoulders. His dark eyes held hers, his gleaming with devilment. 'I never ogled the female guests ever again. But, I have to say, if ever a garment was made for ogling it's a bustier. I am having the greatest difficulty keeping my eyes off it, and no luck at all with my hand.' As he spoke his free hand lifted, his long fingers tracing along the soft swell of her breast above the beaded cups of her bustier.

Jacy, from being relaxed, was instantly tense. The touch of his fingers on her soft flesh was like a ribbon of fire and she jerked upright, instantly on the de-fensive; pushing his marauding hand away, she jumped to her feet. 'Obviously you never learned the lesson well enough,' she said drily. 'And I think it's time you left.'

'But we haven't finished the bottle.' His dark eyes gleamed wickedly up at her as he lounged back against the soft cushions of the sofa. 'I can remember the last

time we shared a bottle of champagne, and we finished
it off with you curled on my lap.'

'Did we? I don't remember.' She *did* remember, all
too well, and she also remembered how that night had
ended with Leo storming out. This time it was her turn
to call a halt. 'You're driving, you can't have any more.'

'Come and sit down and share the champagne. If I'm
over the limit for driving I'm sure that, as a gracious
hostess, you will give me a bed for the night.'

'No way,' she shot back, hovering over him, willing
him to get up and go. The thought of Leo anywhere near
her bedroom was enough to send warning signals to every
nerve in her body.

'Frightened, Jacy?' Reaching up, he grabbed her wrist
and with one swift tug she found herself back on the
sofa, and curved into Leo's side.

'Let go...'

'Don't worry, Jacy. I don't go in for rape: subtle persuasion is more my style.'

'And you're always successful, if the Press is to be
believed,' she flung back tautly, and saw his eyes narrow
fractionally in a brief flash of anger.

'I was with you!' he shot back mockingly, and, capturing her chin in one of his hands, he turned her face
towards his. For a long moment his intent gaze lingered
over her beautiful features.

Jacy stiffened with tension and, paradoxically, something more—a heady anticipation of the kiss she was
sure was to follow. But she was wrong.

Leo, holding her eyes with his, declared arrogantly,
'And I will be again, and we both know it.' One long
finger mockingly tapped her full lips as he added, 'But
I'm not so crass that I can't appreciate a little conversation over a fine bottle of champagne first... To old
friends, together...' He raised his glass and drank. 'Join
me, hmm?'

It was the *together* that bothered her. With his muscular thigh pressed against hers and the warmth of his hand cupping her chin, it was oh, so easy to forget how he had hurt her and to relax into his masculine warmth. But his conceited conviction that she would fall into his arms like a ripe plum stiffened her resolve to teach him a lesson. 'I seem to remember your saying the other night that you had a month in town and fancied a good time.' She drawled the last two words deliberately. 'Old friends we are not . . . Or is this another ploy in your subtle persuasion technique?'

'What do you think?' he asked sardonically, his hand falling from her face. He reached out and picked up the wine bottle, and topped up both their glasses. 'And while you're considering, how about a different toast?' Offering her a glass, he raised his own. 'To old lovers and new friends,' he drawled mockingly.

'*Possible* friends,' she amended lightly, and sipped the wine.

'Possibly a friend, but certainly a lover . . . Yes, I'll drink to that.' Leo drained his glass and replaced it on the table, and, turning sideways on the sofa, his fingers brushed hers as he took the empty glass from her hand and put it down with the other.

Fury or fervour flooded her face at the picture his words evoked. She closed her eyes briefly, fighting for control of her wayward emotions. She wanted to slap his mocking features and yet he only had to touch her to set every cell in her body alight.

'Blushing, Jacy? You're an odd girl—beautiful, intelligent, and yet at times tonight, and now this minute, you look like the shy young teenager I once knew.' His brown eyes smouldered with a deepening gleam as they held hers captive. 'Odd, I know. You are an intrepid investigator for your firm and have travelled world-wide

for them. India, wasn't it, last month? And you uncovered some chemical-factory arson?'

Jacy's eyes widened in amazement. 'How did you
know that?' she blurted unthinkingly.

'I had you investigated. A man in my position can't
be too careful,' he said with dry cynicism. 'You may not
have followed your father into journalism, but you have
obviously inherited his investigative instincts. One would
hope with more honesty...'

She was on her feet in a flash, fury winning. 'How
dare you have me investigated? Of all the bloody nerve!
Do you do that with all your dates? My God, it must
be an expensive exercise.' She couldn't believe the audacity of the man, or his snide remark about her father.

'Calm down, Jacy.' Rising to his feet, he grasped her
upper arm. 'It was nothing personal.'

'Nothing personal?' she parrotted. 'Delving into my
private life!'

A cynical grin spread over his handsome face. 'Actually, I didn't have much luck there. You appear to be
very discreet with your lovers—a good thing. But I am
curious as to how a young woman can afford a house
to herself in central London. You must have had some
wealthy bed-fellows.'

'Get out, just get out,' she cried, her temper ex-
ploding. He still thought of her as little better than a
whore and yet he was quite happy to make love to her
as a brief diversion while he was in London. If she had
needed further proof of what an immoral swine he was,
he had just supplied it. She swung her free arm up to
swipe his grinning face, but he caught her wrist in mid-
air, his long fingers digging into her flesh.

'Such passion should be reserved for the bedroom,
Jacy.' And he actually had the gall to laugh. 'Come on...
You're a woman of the world, and we both know the

score. I don't mind a little feminine reluctance for modesty's sake, but violence——' his grip relaxed slightly on her arm '—isn't my scene, so quit pretending. And don't worry, sweetheart, you won't find me ungenerous...'

His black head descended while she was speechless with rage at his assumption and conceit. But it didn't stop her heart-beat accelerating until it shot out of control as his mouth took hers in a deep, hard kiss. She closed her eyes helplessly, and subtly the kiss changed as he felt her surrender to a long and languorous seduction of her senses, filling her with a warmth that made her mind spin. She only regained her senses as he drew back, and she felt herself swept off her feet.

'Put me down.' She began to struggle so he complied, dropping her on to the sofa and following her down. She lay winded for a second—and Leo wasn't even breathing heavily, she noted bitterly. But then he was a superbly fit male, it was evident in every move he made. He sat on the edge of the sofa, one arm along the back and the other placed firmly on her breast-bone, pinning her down.

'I find your behaviour intriguing,' he pondered, and the very softness of his tone sounded like a threat to Jacy's overstretched nerves. His dark head bent lower and the musky male scent of him teased her nostrils as his mouth covered hers yet again. She was helpless to resist the potent intimacy of his kiss, and slowly all the anger drained out of her, to be replaced with a burning frustration. She wanted to reach up to him, stroke the close-cropped hair, bury her head in the warmth of his neck. But with a terrific effort of will she kept her hands at her sides, her fingers curling into fists.

He raised his head, his brown eyes speculative on her flushed face and desire-hazed eyes. 'I could make love to you now; I could have you begging in minutes.' He traced the soft curve of her breast and watched her

tremble helplessly. 'But tell me, I'm curious. Why did
you accept my invitation? I made it obvious I wanted
you. We are two consenting adults, and yet you're trying
your utmost to pretend indifference...' He glanced at
her clenched fists. 'Why?' he demanded hardly.

She made no response. She couldn't, she was fighting
to control the heavy thumping of her heart.

'It's been apparent all evening that you can barely hide
your resentment,' he tagged on musingly.

She lowered her lashes over her golden eyes to mask
her expression from the far too astute Leo. Fool, she
thought hollowly. Revenge was a stupid idea, and she
was far too aware of the man for her little plot ever to
have worked. Forcing herself to think sensibly for the
first time in half an hour, she hit on the solution for her
erratic behaviour and a way to get rid of Leo all in one
go. Raising her eyes, she looked up into his dark, knowl-
edgeable face.

'I'm sorry, Leo. I should have cancelled our date.' She
hesitated. 'A touch of PMT the past couple of days, and
now...' She let her voice trail off...

'You poor darling, you should have told me.' And she
was instantly enfolded in his strong arms, her head
pressed against his broad chest in a comforting hug. Then
he eased her back on the soft cushions, and his brown
eyes gleamed down on her small face.

She had to suppress the hysterical laughter that
bubbled in her throat at the look of tenderness tinged
with pure masculine relief in his expression. 'Stay where
you are and I'll make you a hot drink... Then I'll call
a cab. All right?'

She smiled her thanks. His easy acceptance of her
excuse was comical. But so like Leo—his ego couldn't
stand the thought of any woman refusing him; it was
much simpler for him to accept that it was the wrong
time of the month for her. God, but the man's ego was

monumental, Jacy thought wryly, sinking gratefully into the sofa. It might even be interesting to see how he would avoid making a date with her for the next week. He was a man of carnal appetites, and as she was out of commission he would have to find his relief somewhere else . . .

CHAPTER FIVE

BUT her supposition was wrong. Ten days later Jacy stood before the mirror in the bathroom of Leo's opulent London apartment in Eton Square, and surveyed her reflection. Tonight she had opted for the casual look—a plaid skirt in autumn shades, topped with a tangerine silk shirt. It should have clashed with her hair, which was brushed loose around her shoulders in soft curls, but somehow it worked. Huge eyes, wide and luminous, reflective, stared back at her and she barely recognised herself. She had excused herself to go to the bathroom in a last-ditch attempt to regain control of the fluttering nervous anticipation that was tying her stomach in knots, and it was all Leo's fault. At this very minute he was sprawled on the sofa in the lounge, waiting for her to join him, having just dismissed for the night the couple who'd served the intimate dinner they had shared. For the life of her she couldn't understand how she had got herself in this position with a man she had despised for the past ten years.

She reviewed the past week in her mind and to her surprise she was forced to admit that Leo Kozakis had been the most attentive and charming companion. On the Sunday after the party at the Ritz, he had called around to collect his car, and insisted on Jacy joining him for lunch. Monday evening he had escorted her to the latest musical in the West End; Wednesday it was the opening of a new art gallery—one that Leo had an interest in, she had discovered on talking to the young man whose paintings were on exhibition in the place.

Saturday night it had been an intimate dinner at the re-
nowned celebrity restaurant, the San Lorenzo in
Knightsbridge.

A worried frown marred her smooth brow. It was
Sunday evening and he'd suggested a relaxed, lazy night
at his apartment. The trouble was, she thought uncomfortably, although Leo had behaved impeccably, her own
behaviour she had difficulty coming to terms with. She
kept telling herself that it was the bet, and a desire for
revenge, that had made her accept his invitations; but
her own innate honesty forced her to admit that neither
reason was the total truth. The bottom line was—she
enjoyed Leo's company. At eighteen she hadn't really
known the man on an intellectual level, but this past
week she had delighted in his conversation, his sharp
intellect, and surprisingly she'd discovered that they had
a lot of common interests, from painting to music and
a love of 'whodunnit' books...

She tried reminding herself that he was a womaniser,
but it didn't stop her heart beating faster when she met
him, or defuse the sexual tension that constantly simmered just beneath the surface when they were together.
His dark eyes lingered on her shapely body, the brief
kisses they shared on parting, were subtle reminders to
Jacy that Leo was a virile, intensely physical male—and
that he wanted her. The lie she had told over a week ago
had protected her so far, but she had an uneasy feeling
tonight that Leo intended a lot more than a goodnight
kiss.

Straightening her shoulders, she took a deep breath
and exhaled slowly, and, fixing a polite smile on her face,
she opened the door of the luxurious bathroom and
walked straight into the hard wall of a very masculine
chest. A pair of strong arms wrapped around her, holding
her steady.

'I was beginning to think you'd got lost.' Leo murmured the words against the top of her head.

Jacy eased back. He was dressed casually in
comfortable hip-hugging designer jeans and a soft, baggy
blue chambray shirt, open at the neck to reveal an enticing glimpse of crisp, curling body hair. She swallowed
hard and, tilting her head, looked up into his ruggedly
attractive face.

'Are you all right now?' he demanded huskily, not
trying to hide the avid hunger in his gaze. His brown
eyes, dilated to almost black, captured hers and she had
the sinking feeling that he was not asking her solely about
the shock of bumping into him.

Jacy could feel the heavy beat of his heart beneath
the small hand she had defensively splayed across his
chest. She felt the heat building in her lower stomach,
the warmth of his muscular thighs hard against the soft
wool of her skirt, and she chewed her lip nervously,
unable to answer him. The problem was that her own
feelings were no longer so clear-cut. Her *head* said she
should despise him, but she was beginning to realise that
it would be a very simple step to being completely enthralled by him all over again, and the thought terrified
her.

'Yes, I'm fine,' she managed to respond in what she
hoped was a cool tone, but the huskiness of her voice
betrayed her conflicting emotions.

'In that case, my bedroom's next door,' Leo said
thickly, his eyes grazing over her upturned face and lower
to the enticing cleavage revealed by the V-neck of her
silk shirt, then lower still to her narrow waist, the soft
feminine curves of her hips, and her flat stomach. His
fascinated gaze fed on every inch of her before slowly
drifting up to her mouth and finally to her wide, honey-
gold eyes.

She swallowed hard. An image of her younger self and Leo, naked limbs entwined, flashed into her mind, and she felt light-headed at the thought of once more experiencing the potent force of Leo's lovemaking. But that way lay madness, she reminded herself, all her defensive instincts coming to the fore. He wanted her, but wanting wasn't enough for the mature Jacy. Or was it, when every nerve-end in her body cried out for fulfilment?

'Still the same egocentric Leo,' she said tightly, trying to defuse the atmosphere of electric tension surrounding them. Pushing against his chest, she made to slip past him.

His expression snapped from hungry need to puzzled bewilderment. 'What are you playing at?' he countered hardly, one hand sliding down from her shoulder to slip loose a button of her shirt, his thumb brushing the swell of her breasts.

She gasped and inhaled sharply at the contact, her hand reaching to cover his. 'Don't!'

'Why not? We have spent the last week together and I've made it perfectly clear that I want you, and you know you want me; the chemistry between us is as powerful as ever.' Deliberately his fingers played with the fastening of her shirt, teasingly brushing her breasts. 'You're no shy young virgin, and I should know,' he drawled mockingly, his glance dipping to where her hand ineffectively rested on his and then back to her face, fully aware of her obvious response to his caress.

Jacy quivered. He was right, damn him! But she had no intention of admitting as much, certainly not after his last crack. 'I don't go in for one-night stands,' she protested, fighting down the incredible urge to lean into his hard, hot body.

'It could never be a one-night stand for us, Jacy,' he declared throatily. And, as if losing all patience, his

fingers tightened around hers at her breast and he hauled
her against him, trapping their joined hands between
them while his other arm encircled her waist, his hand
stroking suggestively up her spinal cord. 'We've been
lovers before and we will be again. I've tried to be
reasonable,' he mouthed against the top of her head.
'How I've stopped myself from touching you these past
few days is a miracle of self-control. I'm not trying to
rush you, Jacy——' his grip tightened around her slender
waist '—but celibacy doesn't suit me.' And with his other
hand he raised hers to his shoulder and placed it there
before dropping his hand back to the opening of her
shirt and burrowing beneath one soft, silk-cupped, lacy-
clad breast. 'Or you either, by the look of things.' His
dark eyes were fixed on her hardening breast, his voice
thick. 'Don't try to deny it. You want me.'

'No,' Jacy murmured, but with little conviction,
unable to resist his intimate touch as heat-waves of desire
coursed down her spine. He moved his thighs restlessly
against her, the hard heat of his masculine arousal
pulsing against her abdomen. The fact that she could so
easily arouse him fuelled her own growing excitement.
Her body, with a will of its own, arched into his, but as
his head bent to find her mouth a last thread of self-
preservation had her turning away to avoid his kiss. Was
she such a fool as to fall again for the same suggestive
talk and hard body?

'Don't play games with me, Jacy,' he said thickly, a
sharp edge of angry frustration in his voice. 'I'm too
old and too experienced for teasing females.'

'I'm not playing games,' she got out shakily.

'No? Then come to bed,' he demanded arrogantly.
'You know you want to.'

It was his supreme arrogance that finally gave her the
strength to pull out of his arms and dash into the lounge.

Leo followed, grabbing her wrist before she could reach the entrance-hall and escape.

'What the hell is the matter with you?' he asked furiously. 'Do you make a habit of leading men on? Is that something you've learnt in the past ten years?' His eyes darkened as he looked down at her. 'I'm nobody's fool, and I don't take kindly to frustration...'

'My God, you've some nerve,' Jacy flung back at him, her mature sophistication flying out of the window as her barely controlled emotions were overtaken by a rush of anger. 'You think a few dinners and a show entitle you to a woman's body... well, let me tell you, buster— not *this* woman's. The last ten years have taught me to be a lot more discerning than the young girl you seduced. When and if I have a lover I will want a hell of a lot more than a couple of dates and into bed.'

'My apologies,' Leo said in a menacing voice. 'I forgot for a moment that all women have a price. What's yours—a diamond bracelet? Or perhaps you'd prefer a necklace? No wonder you own a house in London; you've used your body well. But if it's marriage you're holding out for, don't hold your breath.'

He had regained his cool control with an insulting ease that infuriated her and underscored how little he actually thought of her. She swung her arm in a smooth arc, her hand connecting resoundingly with his tanned cheek. 'And to think I thought I'd misjudged you, that perhaps you weren't the lecherous liar I had you pegged for,' she spat disgustedly. 'My father was right about you.' She stopped suddenly, afraid of what she might reveal in her angry panic, and appalled at how quickly the anger had flared between them.

The silence that followed her outburst lengthened until the tension was almost tangible. Jacy raised her eyes to Leo's darkly flushed face, noting the imprint of her hand on his tanned skin, and then her eyes met his and she

flinched beneath the indomitable anger in their black
depths.

'I won't retaliate in kind, not this time.' He hauled
her hard against him, his arm around her waist, and
with his other hand forced her chin up so she had to
face him. 'Because I think that, at last, we are getting
to the truth,' he said softly but with a deadly intent.
'You're a sophisticated lady, a delightful companion, and
yet all week I have sensed a certain antagonism just below
the surface of your so charming exterior.'

Unfortunately for Jacy, she couldn't stop the guilty
colour flooding her face; he was much closer to the truth
than he realised. 'I don't know what you mean.' She
tried to shrug but his arm tightened around her, his hand
at her chin sliding to circle her neck, his thumb resting
on the pulse that beat erratically in her throat.

'Oh, I think you do. You're twenty-eight, not eighteen
any more.' His smile was chilling. 'There have been other
men in your life, other lovers over the years, so why this
pretence of outraged virtue? It doesn't become you, Jacy.
You might try to fool yourself but you can't fool me. I
can recognise a sexually aroused woman and I know
you're burning with the same sexual frustration I feel.'

If only he knew, she thought helplessly, frightened of
the way her body reacted to him. Her knees felt weak
and her heart thudded. She lowered her lashes to block
out the intense speculation in his dark gaze. He had
spoiled her for any other man. Only Leo brought forth
this aching response in her traitorous body.

'You mentioned your father,' he said so slowly that
she could almost hear the cogs in his brilliant mind
ticking over. 'And my womanising ways.'

Jacy flicked a glance up at him and was suddenly wary
of the speculative gleam in his eyes.

He laughed softly, his fingers relaxing on her throat
and stroking gently. 'Now I get it,' he drawled huskily,

obviously having reached a satisfactory assessment of the situation in his own mind. 'You think I'm still carrying a grudge against your father. Is that it, sweetheart?' he asked encouragingly, his eyes defying her to look away from him. 'Well, forget it—I don't give a damn about the past and, anyway, the man is dead.' He bent his head and pressed his lips to the pulse beating madly at the base of her throat. 'Come on, Jacy, you know you want to. Take a gamble on me and I'll bet you will enjoy it.' His teeth bit lightly, teasingly on her neck. 'I won't hurt you. At least, not intentionally,' he added, his voice rich with sensual meaning.

Jacy was stunned into immobility. That he could come up with such a suggestion just about took the biscuit, and his mention of gambling rang oddly sinister in her ears. Leo couldn't possibly know about her bet, could he? She flushed furiously and jerked her head back, fighting down the fierce tide of pleasure that surged through her veins at his caress.

'*You* carrying a grudge against *me*?' she said scathingly. 'You've got to be joking. Shouldn't that be the other way around?' She was positively sizzling with anger and resentment. 'As I recall, you walked out on me after feeding me a pack of lies about being a poor fisherman. You—the high and mighty Kozakis—filling in a few weeks with a naïve teenager while your lawyers were blackening some poor innocent ex-girlfriend's name back in America.'

It would have been funny if it weren't so tragic, Jacy thought as Leo stepped back, his arms falling by his sides and an expression of shocked amazement on his face. It had obviously never occurred to him that she might consider he was at fault. She was free, but she was also furious.

'Really, Leo, you have a hell of a selective memory. You called me worse than a whore, and you actually

expect me to forgive and forget——' flinging out her arm,
she snapped her fingers in his face '—just like that?'

Leo swung on his heel and crossed the room to stand
in front of the elegant Georgian window, his back to
Jacy. He savagely pulled a cord and the heavy cream
velvet drapes slid back to reveal the flickering glow of
the street lights of London.

Jacy saw his dark head shake slightly. His broad
shoulders looked oddly taut. She knew that now was her
chance to leave, walk out and never see Leo again; but
for some reason her feet were reluctant to move. Her
gaze wandered around the room, lingering on the huge,
over-stuffed, soft cream hide sofa and its smaller
matching counterpart, then moved on to the ornate
marble fireplace, the functional antique walnut desk and
occasional table, where coffee-cups and the glasses and
bottle of wine that they'd shared half an hour earlier
still stood, looking somehow intimate.

A crack jerked her attention back to the man who
stood by the window. Leo, one hand balled into a fist,
slapped the palm of his other hand. 'My God, I never
realised...' He stopped, but Jacy knew that he hadn't
been speaking to her. Suddenly he swung back around,
his dark eyes clashing with hers.

For a second Jacy could have sworn she saw pain
etched into his handsome features, but it vanished as his
dark brows drew together in an angry scowl as he
searched her pale face with unwavering scrutiny. Nervously she ran her damp palms down over her slender
hips and, unable to hold his gaze, dropped her eyes to
stare at the floor.

'Now I understand, Jacy. This past week has been your
way of seeking revenge for what you obviously saw as
my scornful treatment of you in the past,' he said icily.

'No, of course not,' she denied, but her denial didn't
carry much conviction.

'How long did you think you could string me along with the promise of your body?' he asked silkily. 'A month?'

Her head shot up; why had he picked a month? 'No, I never thought ... I ...' She stopped, eyeing him warily as he walked towards her.

He placed his large hands on her shoulders. 'You never thought ... Yes, I can believe that. In my experience, women rarely do.' She almost sighed with relief, but then was stunned as he continued, 'I never realised until tonight how I might have hurt you by my furious outburst years ago.' Like a sheep she allowed him to lead her to the sofa and pull her down beside him. One strong arm rested on her slender shoulders. She stiffened at the enforced intimacy, then relaxed as he said, 'We need to talk ... You were very young, and perhaps I *was* a little hard on you. Maybe I treated you shabbily. But it was a difficult time for me.'

Maybe! There was no maybe about it ... And *he* had been having a difficult time? What about her? Jacy wanted to ask. She couldn't see Leo ever finding life difficult: he strode through it with money and power and a blatant masculine chauvinism that prevented anything or anyone ever hurting him ... She glanced sideways at him. '*You*, in difficulties—I don't believe it's possible,' she said drily.

'I know. I didn't think it was possible either, but I can assure you it did happen.'

Her lips quirked in a grin at the arrogance of his statement. She might have guessed that Leo wasn't the sort to admit to a weakness like lesser mortals. At least not for long.

'I never explain my actions to anyone, but in your case I am willing to make an exception, and then hopefully we can get back to what we really want— each other.'

'Big of you,' she snorted inelegantly.

'Yes, it is rather,' Leo drawled mockingly, and Jacy felt like hitting him. But, guessing her intention, he settled his arm firmly around her shoulder while his free hand caught her hand in his. 'Listen...' he said, and she did.

'I don't know how much you know about the trial I was involved in. But, for a start, the lady concerned was no innocent young girl.' His mouth twisted with cynical humour. 'I, on the other hand, was twenty-four, and in America for the first time—sent by my father to head up our business interests there. I met Lily in a nightclub; she was a singer and a good ten years older than me. We were lovers. But I only saw her on my infrequent trips to California, a month or two at most in any one year. Anyway, I had known her for almost two years when she told me she had been thrown out of her apartment, the building having been taken over by a development company, and I, feeling sorry for her, told her that she could stay in the Kozakis company apartment until she found something that suited her. My one mistake.' He shrugged his shoulders. 'I thought it would cost me nothing; in fact, it was a hell of a lot less expensive than the jewellery I used to give her. I wasn't quite as wealthy then. My father was still in charge,' he said with blunt practicality.

Jacy, watching his face, was struck by the hard cynicism in his dark eyes. But she couldn't deny the ring of truth to his words.

'Barely a year later I found out from the security guard at the apartment block, on one of my very rare visits, that not only was Lily entertaining a variety of men, she had also been caught with drugs in her possession. The papers were right, I did throw her out—but I also gave her enough money to lease another apartment. Lily, however, was a greedy lady, and with the compliance of a less than honest lawyer thought she would try to hit me for more money. Hence the palimony case. The one time I acted the gentleman and it cost me dearly—not in money, that didn't matter, but in aggravation. Your father's paper ran the story, and for a few months my life was disrupted...'

Disrupted. Jacy couldn't help smiling. Anyone else would have been traumatised, but not Leo...

'But happily the Court found in my favour and awarded the lady one dollar...'

'One dollar!' Jacy exclaimed. She had never read the newspaper reports; in fact, except for that one night in Corfu, she and her father had never mentioned the subject again: it had been too painful for the younger Jacy to even contemplate. But now she instinctively believed Leo.

'Yes. But the damage to me was much greater. My reputation was worse than mud, and it hurt my family. I don't allow *anyone* to harm my family.' His mouth tightened into a hard line, and he looked somewhere over her head, a remote expression in his dark eyes. Jacy shivered. No one would ever cross this man and live to tell the tale, she knew, and she had been a fool to try...

Leo dropped his gaze to Jacy and regarded her silently for several seconds, then his lips twisted into the beginnings of a smile. 'Then one summer day in Corfu I met you on the beach. A lovely innocent young girl. I didn't lie to you, Jacy. I never actually said I was a fisherman, but it was so refreshing to meet a girl who didn't know who I was or the sordid details of my immediate past. You were a welcome balm to my dented ego.'

Jacy's heart sank. So *that* was what she had meant to him. A young girl to ease his battered ego, nothing more. While she had imagined they were in love...

'The night your father arrived I saw red. He was the editor of the paper that had first run the story, and you were his daughter and a budding reporter. I was so furious, I stormed off.'

'I remember,' she murmured, a lingering sadness tingeing her tone. 'I never had any firm intention of being a reporter, and after your denouncement of the whole breed ... well ...'

'Jacy, I couldn't care less about your work. When I met you again at Liz's party, I saw a beautiful woman and asked you out simply because I want you. It was only tonight when you lashed out at me that I realised how it was possible I might inadvertently have hurt you in the past. So, now that I have put the past in perspective, can we finally get on with the present—and hopefully to bed?'

Leo had been brutally honest with her, and she could understand why he'd behaved the way he had. It must have been very difficult for a man with Leo's supreme confidence to accept the fact that he'd been made a fool of. She could even understand why he'd lashed out at her all those years ago. But what she found harder to accept was his casual assumption that, having explained himself, probably as near an apology as Leo was capable of making, they could swan off to bed!

She pulled herself upright and, perched on the edge of the sofa, she turned her body slightly to look at him. He was lounging back against the sofa, his long legs stretched out in front of him in negligent ease, his hands resting lightly on his thighs, his dark face expressionless. Only a nerve beating beneath the bronzed skin of his cheek told her that he wasn't as relaxed as he was trying to appear.

'So, what's it to be, Jacy? It's up to you,' he prompted tautly.

Her golden eyes searched his dark features. He was a proud man and he had made a great concession in even explaining about his past. He wanted her, and in all honesty Jacy knew she ached for him. But could she be as mature as Leo and forget all her old resentment and bitterness? Take what was on offer—a few weeks of sexual satisfaction—and play the game by his rules? She looked into his eyes and was fascinated by the tinge of uncertainty that even the masculine need blazing fiercely in their depths could not quite disguise.

She could say no! She knew that Leo would accept it—he'd told her last week that violence wasn't his style, but subtle persuasion...

She should say no! Then his thumb traced the vein in her wrist. She saw the black flare of passion in his eyes, and she knew the same emotion was reflected in hers. The decision was made for her; the trembling inside her gave her the answer.

'I believe you're not quite the rat I thought you were,' she murmured teasingly, holding out her other hand, her body swaying towards him as she added, 'And who am I kidding? I'd rather have a tycoon than a fisherman any day.' She knew that it probably only confirmed his less than flattering view of her, but it was better than admitting that she'd loved him years ago, and could quite easily again. He was offering nothing but a brief affair; at the very most she might possibly win her bet, she thought with bitter irony.

Leo caught both her hands and cradled them in his own. Then, in a potently erotic gesture, he kissed the centre of each palm. 'I knew you were a sensible female.' His dark voice was a whisper of rough velvet against her skin as his mouth trailed kisses over her wrist while he gently urged her towards him. 'You won't regret it.'

Sensible was the last thing she was, Jacy admitted, but she could deny the urging of her body no longer. Her gaze fastened on his sensuous mouth and her tongue flicked out unconsciously over her suddenly dry lips.

Dropping her hands, Leo grasped a handful of her hair, his long fingers tangling in the silken gold locks. He urged her face to his. 'Jacy, what are you doing to me?' he groaned, before covering her mouth with his own.

She made a tiny moue of protest before sweetly opening her lips. Leo was inside at once, his tongue tasting, searching, provoking, until she was responding with the intense excitement only Leo could arouse. Jacy raised her arms, her hands sinking into the gleaming thickness of his hair, trailing to curve the nape of his strong neck as the kiss went on and on. She felt the sofa at her back and the pressure of Leo's hard body forcing her down, but she didn't care.

Then Leo raised his head and his dark eyes blazed with masculine triumph as he demanded, 'No turning back this time, Jacy.'

With a soft, throaty groan she linked her hands around his neck and pulled his head back down to hers, her lips giving him the answer he wanted.

The soft silk of her shirt was pushed aside, her front-fastening bra quickly unclasped and her firm, full breasts were freed to his searching hands. When his palm grazed lightly over one nipple, teasing it into a hard peak, Jacy moaned. Leo swallowed her small sound of passion and slid his hand to the other pouting breast. By the time his subtly teasing fingers were finished, Jacy's breasts were achingly sensitive.

Deftly Leo removed the blouse from her shoulders and swung her long legs from the floor across his lap, his hand lingering on the back of her knee. Slowly he stroked up to her thigh and she gasped as his fingers found the naked flesh where her stockings ended. His fingers closed over the tiny lace strap of her garter-belt, and snapped the elastic.

'A welcome addition since last time,' he drawled, but not quite steadily. Straightening, he quickly divested himself of his shirt. His dark head thrown back, he stared down at her. 'Garter-belts turn me on something wicked.' He smiled wolfishly as he studied her naked thighs; her skirt was rucked up around her hips. 'But everything about you turns me on.' His dark eyes deepened to black as he greedily scanned her naked breasts, the hard tips pleading for his caress.

Jacy was enthralled by the sight of his bare torso, the matt of black hair, the glistening bronzed skin. She reached out for him with impatient hands. Her fingers traced through the hair on his chest, over small, flat male nipples until Leo, with a throaty growl, slipped his hand to her waist and eased down the zip of her skirt, his hand slipping downwards over her stomach.

'Leo.' She said his name softly, breathlessly, then his dark head bent and his mouth closed over the turgid point of her breast, licking and nibbling, his teeth lightly grazing first one and then the other. Her arms went around his broad back, her fingers digging into the hard muscle as his other hand found the edge of her panties, his long fingers sliding inside to stroke her hot moist centre...

Jacy clung tightly to the strong, massive bulk of his shoulders as she felt the delicious tremors flood her body. Dear heaven! How had she done without this man, this feeling, for so long? She turned her head into his shoulder and bit into his sleek satin skin with a cat-like savagery.

Leo trailed kisses from her breast to her throat while with a firm hand he urged her thighs apart. 'You're ready for me, Jacy; hot, wet and wanting.' He growled the words, lifting his darkly flushed face to stare down at her softly parted lips. 'And God knows I've been waiting for you long enough,' he rasped, before once more covering her mouth with his own, his fingers still working their indescribable magic.

Jacy whimpered her need as the tension spiralled in her body. She stroked her small hand down over his chest, wanting to give him the same pleasure, and slid her hand down his taut thigh, tracing his hard manhood through the fabric of his trousers. She heard his muffled groan of pleasure while drowning in the musky masculine smell of him, her slender body vibrating with pleasure.

'Jacy, Jacy. . .' Leo growled, his hand covering hers at his thigh. Then she felt his hand at the snap of his jeans and tried to help him, her fingers grazing his flat belly.

A string of throaty Greek words encouraged her endeavours, as soft moans and sighs interspersed with the long, drugging kisses that he showered on her swollen mouth. She was lost in the molten passion of his desire; she could hear bells ringing in her head and it seemed as if Leo would steal the very breath from her body.

'No, no, no,' Leo grated, his hard thighs grinding her into the sofa. 'I don't believe it.'

Reluctantly he lifted his dark head and rolled off her, sitting on the side of the sofa. His broad shoulders shook as he took great gulping breaths, and only then did Jacy realise that the ringing wasn't in her head but was in fact the strident bell of a telephone, echoing in the heavy, passion-laden atmosphere. 'Ignore it,' she whispered breathily.

Leo turned to stare down at her, at her golden eyes beckoning him back, and he gave a mighty sigh. His sensual mouth twisted in a wry smile of self-mockery. 'I can't—it's the company apartment so it must be business.' He bent and lightly brushed her lips before striding across the room to pick up the offending instrument.

Jacy watched him, mesmerised. His broad back was all rippling muscle and sinew, and his dark hair was mussed in appealing disarray. He was gorgeous ... and hers. She tensed and shivered slightly at her thoughts. No. He was not hers. It was lust, pure and simple ...

He slammed the phone down and turned back to her. 'I have to go, Jacy. You'd better dress.'

'Yes,' she quietly agreed.

With a ragged sigh Leo ran a hand through his short hair. 'God! I'm sorry, I think I will very probably die of frustration, but unfortunately that was from the shipping office in Athens. One of our cruise-liners is in trouble in mid-Pacific. I'm flying to America immediately; I've got to find out what has gone wrong. The company jet is standing by at Heathrow.'

'Oh, Leo, I'm sorry,' she murmured. But was she? she wondered, carefully pulling on her clothes and smoothing her skirt back down over her hips. Perhaps she needed more time to accept the kind of adult relationship that Leo was offering, and the telephone call was in a way a reprieve. But the screaming frustration of her body didn't appear to agree with her, she thought wryly.

'Not half as sorry as I am,' Leo declared bluntly and, crossing to where she stood, he lifted her chin with one finger and drawled throatily, 'Promise me we can carry on where we left off when I return.'

'Yes, all right,' she said, kissing him teasingly on the nose. This is the best way, she told herself. Keep it light.

His arms closed tightly around her. 'And a word of warning: I insist on an exclusive relationship with my woman—so no other men.'

'There has never been any other man.' The words popped out unconsciously and she felt the tell-tale colour rising in her cheeks.

Leo arched one dark eyebrow sardonically. 'You don't have to go that far, Jacy; just behave yourself from now on.'

She didn't know whether to be glad or sorry that he hadn't believed her, but she had no opportunity to think about it as Leo called her a taxi and saw her into it, his parting words, 'I'll call you tomorrow night.'

CHAPTER SIX

JACY snuggled down under the rose-covered duvet, determined to put Leo out of her head and sleep. But his cool explanation of their past relationship still lingered in her mind. It shouldn't, but it still hurt to have it confirmed that ten years ago he had never loved her. That was obvious from his revelations tonight. She had been a balm to his bruised ego, and that was all... She sighed, and turned restlessly.

Haughty, handsome Leo... He thought he had some God-given right to ride roughshod over lesser mortals, using them when it suited him and discarding them without a second thought. Unfortunately, knowing the ruthless power of the man didn't stop her whole body flushing with heat as she thought of the liberties she had allowed him earlier that evening. Where had her ice-maiden act gone? No man had got to first-base with her in years, but Leo, in one week, had reduced her to a mindless wanton. If the telephone hadn't rung, they would have been lovers—again...

She lifted a finger to her swollen lips, the memory of his kisses still fresh in her mind... Perhaps the maturity of her working life was finally spilling over into her private life, because she knew that she wanted Leo and she was going to wait for him. And was it so wrong? She was a bit old to be hankering after the hearts and flowers, and wedding-bells. It was time she was more realistic, she told herself, and she crushed the tiny voice of conscience reminding her that she wasn't the kind of girl to settle for anything less. With a bit of luck she

might even win the bet! With that thought, she fell into
a deep, dreamless sleep.

'You're looking remarkably pleased with yourself this
morning, Ms Carter. Can I guess why?' Mike, the office
junior, stood in front of her desk, a cheeky grin on his
freckled face.

'Thank you, Mike. And what are you after?' Jacy responded, looking up from the pile of papers in front of
her with a smile. Mike was a dear but he was also always
on the dodge; for him to pass a compliment meant that
he was after something.

'Nothing, nothing at all. Only I thought you might
like to see my newspaper.'

'That rag.' She knew from experience that young Mike
had a great interest in the seedier tabloids, which, considering he was a university graduate and supposed to
be training as a financial consultant, seemed somewhat
out of character. 'You've got to be joking.'

'Oh, I don't know, there's a good photograph of you
in it. You can look real sexy when you let your hair
down.' He leered suggestively.

Jacy was out of her chair and reaching over the desk
to snatch the paper out of his hand in a flash. 'Me ...
where?' she exclaimed in horror.

Mike laughed out loud. 'Got you that time. Try page
five.'

Rapidly she flicked through the pages, and stopped.
With a low groan she collapsed back into her chair and
spread the offending page on the desk in front of her.
There, in glorious Technicolor, was a picture of herself
and Leo leaving the restaurant on Saturday night. But
it was the caption that brought the colour to her face.
'Leo Kozakis, once noted for always having a glamorous
blonde on his arm, but over the past few years becoming
adept at avoiding the Press, has returned to the London

scene in style. Miss Jacy Carter, who shared an intimate dinner with the fabulously wealthy Greek, is not only beautiful but—my sources in the City tell me—she is known as a high-flyer in the prestigious firm, the Mutual Save and Trust company—a directorship is not out of the question. Quite a change from Kozakis' usual bimbos. Well done, Leo!'

Of all the patronising, chauvinistic pigs. Jacy swore at the author under her breath. 'Thank you, Mike,' she snapped. Rolling the paper up and throwing it at him, she added, 'Take your rubbish and go.' She was furious and long after Mike had left her office, closing the door quietly behind him, she was still burning with resentment. Congratulating Leo! Because she had brains! What a nerve!

Work—that was what she needed; and, deliberately returning her attention to the papers in front of her, she began to read. It was an interesting case. Over the last six months, five hair-care clinics dotted around the country had mysteriously caught fire, all owned by the same firm. The insurance liability was Mutual's but they were very reluctant to pay, and Jacy could see why. The thing smelt to high heaven. Half an hour later she had cooled down enough to call her secretary on the intercom and ask apologetically, 'If you see Mike, Mary, tell him I'm sorry for yelling, and if it's not too much trouble can I have a coffee?'

She had over-reacted about the article, she knew. If she was going to continue seeing Leo she would have to get used to this kind of scurrilous Press-reporting; but she couldn't help thinking it was distasteful. Probably it had been an unfortunate choice of restaurant on Saturday. It was noted as a favourite of the Royals—not that there had been any there on Saturday. No doubt some member of the paparazzi, bored after a fruitless vigil outside the restaurant, had snapped Leo and Jacy as better than nothing...

Jacy looked up as her office door opened and Mary, her secretary, entered with a coffee-cup in her hand and a broad grin on her plump, friendly face. 'So, tell all, do. Is Kozakis as good as they say?'

'Not you too, Mary, please.' Taking the cup, Jacy swallowed thirstily before replacing it on the saucer and looking up into the laughing blue eyes of her secretary. 'All right, Mary. For the office grape-vine, and to avoid any exaggeration, yes, I do know Leo Kozakis. I've known him since I was a teenager and we're just good friends. Got that?'

'Yes, ma'am! Whatever you say!' She saluted cheekily and added, 'By the way, Liz rang and said would you call her back after one?'

Jacy worked through her lunch-hour, only grabbing a couple of sandwiches from the staff canteen, and, having eaten them, she reluctantly called Liz. No doubt her friend had seen the same paper, and wanted a blow by blow account. But in that she was wrong.

'Hi! Jacy, listen, I can't stop now, I have to dash— it's my afternoon helping out at the day-nursery. But I'm coming up to London on Wednesday. Can we meet for lunch?'

Jacy happily agreed, and arranged the time and place then spent the rest of the afternoon studying the case before her. At four a surprising development had her re-planning her week. A call from the head-office in Manchester of the hair-care clinic revealed that on the Sunday night a bottling-plant they owned had been burned down.

Drastic action was called for, Jacy decided, and after meeting with her immediate superior, Mr Brown, it was agreed that she should travel to the north-west at the earliest opportunity. As she left the office that night Mr

Brown's instructions echoed in her head. 'And don't come back until you've solved it, Jacy.'

A rueful grimace curved her full lips as she drove home. After consulting her desk diary, she realised that the earliest she could get away was Thursday. And where did that leave her relationship with Leo? He would probably be back in London and she would be stuck up in Manchester.

By eleven o'clock that night, Jacy's cautious optimism of the previous evening—that perhaps this time she could handle an adult relationship with Leo Kozakis—had dwindled to nothing. She had hovered over the telephone all night until finally, at midnight, she'd climbed into her lonely bed, calling herself fifty kinds of fool. She had exposed herself to the gutter Press, risked her business reputation, and almost allowed Leo to make love to her again. And all for nothing. She obviously meant no more to him than any other woman he had dated. His promise to call her was just so much guff.

She burrowed down under the duvet and curled up in a little ball, squeezing her eyes shut against the tears that threatened to fall. She had vowed ten years ago not to shed another tear over Leo, and she had held true to that vow until now. She was damned if she was going to weep over the man again, she told herself, but that didn't stop a single drop of moisture easing between her long lashes. With a hard hand she brushed her cheek. Stupid, stupid, stupid, she castigated herself.

Then the telephone rang. In her haste to answer it, her travelling-clock was knocked off the bedside table, but she barely noticed as breathlessly she said, 'Hello...'

'Jacy. Leo here.' His rich, dark voice echoed down the telephone-wire as clear as if he were in the room with her.

Jacy's heart skipped a beat and then raced like crazy.

'Jacy, are you there?' Leo demanded urgently.

'Do you know what time it is?' she blurted, finally managing to speak. 'Almost one in the morning, and I was in the papers today—you as well.' She was babbling but she could not seem to stop. 'I don't...'

'Jacy, calm down and forget about the papers. It means nothing.' Leo cut in hardly and then, in a much softer tone, apologised. 'I'm sorry—I forgot about the time-zone. It's a lovely sunny afternoon in California.'

'It's a miserable wet night here, and I'm in bed.'

'I hope you're alone, and missing me,' Leo drawled softly.

'I'm certainly alone, and as for missing you...' she almost said yes but substituted '...maybe.'

'I suppose I can be content with alone, and maybe,' he responded roughly, satisfaction evident in his tone. 'But the frustration is killing me after last night and what nearly happened. A few more minutes and you would have been mine again. God! I wish I was there with you now.'

'It would be a tight squeeze,' she teased, thinking— keep it light, sophisticated. 'I'm in bed and it's only a single.'

'Oh, I'm sure if I tucked you underneath me we could manage,' he drawled sexily.

Her stomach clenched with an ache of longing so fierce that she groaned out loud, and Leo recognised the sound.

'Don't *do* that, Jacy. Not when I am half a world away and unable to cover your sensuous mouth with mine and swallow those aroused, erotic little noises you make that turn me inside out.'

'Leo, please.'

'Oh, I *will* please you, and that's a promise,' he vowed throatily, and continued to tell her in graphic detail exactly how...

Her breasts hardened in taut arousal, the duvet suddenly too hot to bear against her aching flesh. She flung the cover back and it was all she could do to say softly, 'I don't think you're allowed to say things like that on the telephone.'

A throaty chuckle greeted her comment. 'Playing Miss Prim, Jacy? And yet in my imagination I have a vivid image of you splayed naked on a bed, your golden hair tumbling down over your superb breasts.'

'Leo, enough.' His name came out as a groan; his words turned her on even when he was thousands of miles away.

Triumphant masculine laughter greeted her comment. 'Perhaps you're right. I'm using a public phone in a restaurant. As it is I will have great difficulty walking out of here for the next half-hour.'

She chuckled. 'Serves you right for talking dirty.'

'Talking is about all we can do for the next few days, and you would not want to deprive a man of a vicarious thrill, would you?' he declared with wry mockery.

Some imp of mischief made her reply in a low throaty drawl, 'I wouldn't like to see you deprived of anything.' She dragged out the last word.

'Oh, Jacy, what are you trying to do to me? Let's get down to business quickly, or I shall have to spend the rest of the day in this place.'

Laughing, Jacy sank back down on to the pillow, holding the telephone to her ear and listening intently as Leo described what had happened.

Apparently the cruise-liner wasn't too badly damaged and was limping towards the nearest port, a small island in the Pacific. Leo still had a few loose ends to attend to, but he hoped to be back by Friday.

'But I have to go to Manchester on Thursday, and I don't know how long for,' she told him regretfully, and briefly outlined the case she was working on.

'Not to worry, we'll work something out and I'll call you Wednesday night,' he promised.

By the time they finally broke the connection, Jacy was floating on cloud nine. But half an hour later, lying restlessly in her bed, she was scolding herself for being such a fool. Leo wanted to bed her, nothing more—and she'd better remember that if she wanted to avoid being hurt. Sex was the name of the game, she told herself; and they didn't come any sexier than Leo...

Jacy was still trying to remind herself to keep her feet on the ground, and that it was an adult affair when she strode into the restaurant in Harrods on Wednesday to meet Liz.

'Should I curtsy—given your celebrity status?' A grinning Liz stood up as Jacy approached the table.

'Fool,' she said with a grin and, pulling out a chair, sat down. Liz looked lovely as usual in a winter wool suit in bright red, reminding Jacy of 'Little Red Riding Hood'.

'As long as you're not being a fool as well,' Liz responded quietly, her blue eyes fixing her with steely intent. 'I know I said you should get a man, but Leo Kozakis! Tom showed me the paper with your picture splashed across the gossip column. I didn't expect you to dive in at the deep end—are you sure you can handle it, Jacy? I know you knew him before, and obviously it didn't work out, so...'

Jacy didn't respond immediately, instead she gave her order to the hovering waitress. A smoked salmon salad. 'Have you ordered, Liz?'

'No. Make mine the same—and don't change the subject.'

Jacy sat back in her chair, resigned to revealing at least some of the truth to her friend. 'OK, I met Leo on holiday in Corfu over ten years ago. We had a holiday romance, nothing more. It fizzled out and I returned home, went to university and never saw him again until your party. Since then I've dated him a few times, and that's it.'

'I see,' Liz said slowly. 'That explains a lot. So are you still seeing him? After all, it's two weeks today since you met—a record for you, Jacy.' Her friend smiled, and at that moment the food arrived.

'He had to go to California—a bit of an emergency— but, yes, I am still in touch.' Jacy's face lit up with a wide grin, her golden eyes sparkling. She couldn't resist teasing her friend, 'The *netsuke* is as good as mine, Liz.' Not that she would take it, even if she *did* win; but she saw no harm in letting Liz sweat a little. 'As for Leo, he called on Monday and he's calling again tonight. And, yes, he will be back soon. Satisfied? Now can we eat!'

'You lucky dog,' was Liz's only comment, and for the rest of the meal they indulged in the usual women's talk.

On leaving the store, Liz reminded Jacy not to forget the races at Cheltenham a week tomorrow.

'What are you trying to do? Turn me into a hardened gambler? First the bet on the *netsuke*, and now a day at the races.' Liz had explained over lunch how Tom's bank had rented a private box at the Cheltenham Gold Cup meeting, corporate-entertainment stuff, and Liz had persuaded Jacy to go as the party was sadly lacking in females.

Liz laughed. 'Take a day off, it's good for you, and if you stick with Leo another two weeks the prize is yours.'

'Oh, I don't know if I could stand the man that long.' Then she spoiled it by giggling. Jacy was still grinning when she returned to the office.

Her humour deserted her when Leo called that night. 'I'm sorry, Jacy, but I won't get back for at least another week.'

'But I thought you said the ship was due to dock tomorrow? Surely after that there's nothing to worry about?' She admired him for taking care of what was just one small part of his vast business empire, but she ached for him to be back. She saw his face in her mind's eye a hundred times a day. His tall, virile body haunted her dreams, and if her voice sounded sulky she couldn't help it.

'Yes, I know, but I hadn't realised that a cousin of my mother's is a passenger on the boat—an elderly lady not in good health, and I've promised my father I will fly out to the island and personally escort the old dear back to Greece. I have to. She is family.'

'You must have a huge family,' Jacy mused, 'if that party at the Ritz was anything to go by.'

'Yes——' his deep voice sank to a throaty drawl '—and over the past week or two I find I keep having this inexplicable urge to add to it.'

Jacy's breath stopped in her throat. Was he saying what she thought he was saying? She didn't dare believe it, but she couldn't stop the hope that blossomed in her heart. She didn't know how to respond and her hand gripped the receiver, her knuckles white with the strain. Was he suggesting a commitment? Then he burst her bubble by adding, 'But I'm fighting it. I picture Tom's twin boys, have a stiff drink, and it's gone. Enough about me. When can I call you again?'

She gave him the address of the hotel she would be staying at in Manchester, and long after she had put the phone down she was still mulling over Leo's surprising admission, and his equally quick retraction. She would be a fool to read more into his words than he meant. He didn't even *like* her, she reminded herself. He actually thought her home was financed by past lovers. It was sex, a chemical attraction, nothing more; and as long as she went into the relationship with her eyes wide open Leo couldn't hurt her.

The next eight days seemed to Jacy to be the longest of her life. Her trip to Manchester was successful. After spending four days going through records and interviews, she had her culprit, and a good laugh... When Leo called her on the Tuesday she finished the case she could not wait to tell him.

'You sound happy without me,' Leo remarked curtly. 'I hope you're behaving yourself.'

'I am.' She couldn't hold back her chuckle. 'You know the case I was working on with the string of hair-care clinics and then the bottling plant? Well, you'll never guess who was setting all the fires.'

'I have no doubt that, with your inherited talent for unearthing the dirt, you will tell me. But isn't the owner the usual culprit?'

'Not in this case. It was a handsome young man who had unfortunately gone prematurely bald. He'd been a customer for three years. It turned out he was so furious that none of the treatments or the hair restorer had worked after he'd spent thousands trying them that he systematically set out to destroy the whole company by burning the clinics down.'

Deep laughter greeted her revelation. 'Ah, Jacy, you're so good for me; I can always depend on you to lift my spirits. Look after yourself. I'll see you at seven on Saturday, if not sooner.'

Unfortunately Jacy could not depend on Leo to lift her spirits, she thought sadly as she replaced the receiver. His derisory crack about her talent for 'unearthing the dirt' left her in no doubt. Leo might be temporarily eager for her body, but his opinion of her as a person was negligible. He was a sophisticated, expert lover, and she wanted him; lying in bed at night, she

couldn't sleep for the physical ache of frustration that
gnawed at her body. But in her heart of hearts she knew
such a hedonistic arrangement as Leo had in mind would
not suit her.

'Come on, Fredsaid. Come on . . .' Jacy screamed at the
top of her voice. The chestnut with the white blaze, the
jockey wearing the pink and blue colours of an Arab
sheikh, shot past the winning post half a length in front
of its nearest rival. 'I've won, I've won!' Jacy cried in
delight and, turning around from her vantage-point of
the box window, she pushed her way through the crush
of people to where Liz was standing at the sumptuous
buffet. 'Guess what?' She tapped her on the shoulder.
'Guess what?'

'You've won again.' Liz groaned in mock-horror, and
popped a cracker covered in caviar into her mouth.

'By my calculation, a fiver at ten to one means fifty
pounds and my stake back.' Jacy had no idea how
stunning she looked, her beautiful face alight with joy,
her smart cream and black dog-tooth jacket hung open
to reveal a clinging cream silk blouse tied in a cravat
around her neck, not unlike a jockey's tie; but there all
resemblance to the male ended. A wide black leather
belt emphasised her tiny waist and the matching checked
skirt fitted snugly over her hips to end an inch above
her knee. Plain black high-heeled shoes accentuated her
long legs.

'You'll have to tell me your secret, Jacy. That's the
fourth time you've won today, and muggins here has yet
to back a winner.'

Jacy, her golden hair swept back from her face to fall
in a tumbling mass of curls down her back, laughed out
loud at Liz's woebegone expression. 'Just lucky.'

'You know what they say: lucky with money, unlucky
in love,' a deep, dark voice drawled mockingly behind

her head, and Jacy's heart somersaulted in her chest. Liz melted tactfully into the background. Jacy spun round and saw the distinguished figure of Leo standing about a foot away from her. He looked magnificent in a pale grey business suit, and pristine white silk shirt. His glittering dark eyes swept her from head to toe and then he added, 'But if you play your cards right you could get both.'

'What? How did you...? Why?' The shock of seeing Leo so unexpectedly made her intelligence desert her. His hands were warm and strong as they curved around her upper arms, drawing her closer. She gazed up at him, speechless, and saw what was in his eyes: he was going to kiss her. They were in a room full of people. 'Not here,' she warned.

'You would be insulted if I didn't,' Leo mocked and his dark head descended, his mouth covering hers.

Her heart pounded against her ribcage. He was right, damn him! she thought wryly as her body swayed boneless in his hold. Her skin felt hot; she felt her nipples tighten, pressed hard against the firm wall of his muscular chest. His tongue invaded her mouth, and she stopped thinking altogether...

Leo recovered his composure first, and with a self-satisfied smile, his dark eyes intent on her flushed face, he said softly, 'You still want me, Jacy, but patience. I need to see the last race and then I will take you home.'

She should have objected to his arrogant assumption that she was his for the taking, but her body had already betrayed her. Fighting to regain her self-control, she stepped back. 'You never said why you're here,' she queried. Had he returned to England earlier than expected and checked with her office and followed her? she imagined happily, very flattered.

'Tom invited me, but I didn't expect to be back in time. But I got in a couple of hours ago, and as I have a horse running in the last race I thought I might as well drive down and pick up the trophy personally,' Leo explained with casual arrogance as he turned and took a glass of champagne from a passing waiter.

So much for her over-active imagination, Jacy thought drily, and was glad Leo had not seen the flash of disappointment in her face as he turned back to her, taking a sip from the crystal glass.

'I didn't know you kept racehorses,' she said coolly. 'And aren't you being just a little premature?' One finely arched brow rose mockingly. 'There are seven other horses in the race, Leo.' She was proud of her sophisticated response. Even though her insides were churning with sexual excitement...

'Not at all, Jacy, sweetheart. Haven't you realised yet? I always win.' His dark eyes held hers and she had the oddest feeling there was a warning in his statement, but as he continued talking she dismissed the disturbing thought from her mind, seduced by the deep, rich tone of his voice. 'I had Greek Legend sent over from my racing stables in France specifically for this race. It is one of the best of my string, so take my advice and have a flutter on it.'

She glanced down at the race card in her hand, and sure enough number three, Greek Legend, with the owner's name Kozakis next to it, was there. Some perverse sense of independence made her say, 'I don't know, Leo, I rather fancy Royal Speedmaster.'

'You're joking; what on earth for? It's only won once in two years.'

'Well, this meeting is patronised by the Queen Mother,' she said defensively.

'And that's your reason for picking it?' He threw back his dark head and burst out laughing. 'Jacy, you will never make a gambler. If I were you I would keep your investigative instincts for your career. They won't help you on the race track, but I can if you do as I say.'

'For your information,' she grinned, poking him playfully in the chest, 'I have won a considerable amount of money today.'

Leo put his glass down on the table and took her hand in his. 'OK, please yourself; far be it from me to come between a woman and her intuition,' he drawled cynically, his dark eyes grazing over her smiling face. 'But be warned...' He drew her forward, taking her hand behind her back to hold her hard against his tall frame. 'You won't win.'

His nearness was like a potent force enveloping her. She felt the leashed power in his body; she had never known a man who could affect her as physically as Leo did. The smile left her lips and she stared up into his glittering dark eyes, and inexplicably a shiver of fear slithered down her spine. 'How can you be so sure?' she asked softly, and she saw something dark and dangerous flash in his eyes.

'Because I always do, Jacy...'

CHAPTER SEVEN

JACY, held captive in his hold, her golden eyes trapped by the desire she recognised in Leo's, felt the shiver turn into a tingling sensation down the length of her spine. He was a hard man, all steel, the toughest man she had ever met or was ever likely to. Yet she knew with a deep feminine instinct that Leo was as aware of her as she was of him. The words he spoke were probably true. But they were secondary to the invisible tension that enveloped them.

'And also because I'm a genius,' he opined, his voice harsher, and, as though he resented the tension between them, he released his hold on her.

'And modest with it,' she murmured sarcastically.

'Of course.' The corner of his mouth quirked in the beginnings of a grin and with a slow, salacious study of her feminine curves, neatly displayed by the high-necked blouse and hip-hugging skirt, he added, 'And you are immodest enough for both of us in that outfit.' His arm curved around her waist under her jacket. 'The tie at your throat is begging to be unknotted. How anything so masculine in design can appear so feminine is one of the mysteries of life.'

'Well, we women need some secrets,' she responded with a mock-flirtatious flutter of her long eyelashes, playing his sophisticated game.

'And you, I think, have more than most. Gambling appears to be another one of your vices,' he said hardly.

'Another one? I wasn't aware I had any vices.' Until I met you, she wanted to add. Her lust for Leo was her one great weak spot, and inside she died a little. Leo desired her, but it was becoming more and more obvious that his opinion of her as a person had not changed at all.

'If you say so, my sweet. I won't argue; your character or lack of it isn't what I am interested in.' His dark head bent and he pressed a swift, hard kiss on her full lips, and before she could take him up on his comment an announcement over the public address system announced that the horses were going down for the last race.

Suddenly they were besieged by the rest of the party—businessmen demanding from Leo if his horse stood a chance, a rush to place bets, and a hasty scramble for the best view of the track by some, while others were content to watch the race on the television screen provided in the private box. Throughout it all Leo kept Jacy pinned to his side, making it very obvious she was his woman.

For the next half-hour she lived in a mad whirl of excitement. She deliberately squashed any lingering doubts about the wisdom of taking up with Leo again. She only had to look at him to recall the hard potency of his superb male form, and feel the heat curl in her belly. She smiled and laughed, entering wholeheartedly into the various discussions with the ease that long years of working in a high-powered job and travelling extensively to interview and investigate businessmen from the bankrupt to the multi-millionaire had given her.

On a purely practical level, she acknowledged, at eighteen she had been no match for Leo, but now she could confidently move in his sophisticated world with comparative ease, and the thought was oddly comforting, in that they had something in common other than sex. Still, it did not stop her eyes from lingering on

his impressive features or her pulse from racing like a
gauche teenager's every time he smiled down at her.

Finally the race was off, and she watched along with
everyone else as the horses chased around the two-mile
four-furlong course. She couldn't repress a groan as hers
fell at the fourth jump, but by the final straight she was
cheering Greek Legend along with everyone else. Her
own stubborn pride had made her stick to her choice,
and when Leo's was first past the post she was picked
up in his arms and swung around while Leo grinned like
an overgrown schoolboy on his first date. When he
finally set her back on her feet and she recovered her
breath she managed to say, 'Congratulations. But don't
say it...'

'I told you so...? As if I would be so cruel...' He
laughed, and insisted she join him at the presentation
of the trophy in the winners' enclosure.

Leading in the winning horse, standing in the ring with
Leo as he accepted the trophy and fat cheque, cameras
whirling, and then joining him for a cheerful walk back
up to the box for a celebratory toast, Jacy was beguiled
into believing he cared.

Liz caught her arm as Leo was accepting the congratulations of Tom and his boss. 'Leo taking you back
to London, is he?'

'I——'

'Of course I am, Liz,' Leo cut in briefly before turning
back to Tom. 'Thank you, Tom, I'll be in touch.'

'It's customary to ask first,' Jacy muttered, not realising she had spoken out loud.

'Oh-oh, I smell a fight,' Liz quipped. 'Good luck,
Leo.' And she was swallowed up by the crowd.

'Why? Are you going to refuse?' Leo queried silkily.
'I was under the impression you had missed me the past
couple of weeks, but perhaps I was misled.' His arm
tightened around her waist.

'No,' she admitted. Her golden gaze rested helplessly on his bronzed face. What was the point in denying herself or Leo? 'And I did miss you,' she answered honestly.

'I find that hard to believe. You're a very beautiful, very sexy woman. Didn't you feel just a little deprived, waiting for me?' he queried with a cynical smile that did not quite reach the deep brown eyes lingering watchfully on her glowing face.

But Jacy didn't notice his cynicism, or the lack of humour in his smile. She was too hypnotised by the overpowering masculine aura of the man, and with unconscious feline grace she curved her body more snugly into his.

'Well, Jacy?' he demanded. 'No reply, or frightened you might incriminate yourself?'

'Deprived of you,' she drawled languidly. 'But the wait was worth it,' she whispered and felt the rising pressure of his masculine arousal as his hand slid lower to her buttocks and turned her hard against him. She sucked in her breath as fire coursed through her veins. It was as though the rest of the room, the people, had disappeared, and there was only Leo. He filled her mind and her senses to the exclusion of all else.

'Let's get out of here. I can't wait any longer,' Leo growled impatiently, holding her for a long moment, still and rigid against him, as the sexual tension shimmered in the air around them, heavy with need and unspoken desire.

She was unaware of the knowing looks, and the surprised glances, as minutes later Leo, with admirable restraint, made their polite goodbyes and ushered her downstairs and out into the pale evening light. Meekly she followed him across the grass to the car park.

'Get in the car,' he said curtly, opening the door to a long black Jaguar, and then swinging into the driving seat.

The fresh air finally broke through the sensual haze Jacy had been living in for the past few minutes, and rather nervously she pulled the hem of her skirt down to her knees as she sank into the soft leather upholstery of the passenger seat. Was she ready for this? she asked herself.

With a squeal of burning rubber the car shot forward down the entrance drive to the racecourse and out on to the open road towards London. 'It's about two hours' drive to the city; would you like to stop somewhere *en route* for dinner?'

'Not really, I've been munching on caviar, chicken and just about anything else you can name all afternoon. Tom's bank certainly knows how to entertain,' she said conversationally, hoping to defuse the air of electric tension filling the car.

'In that case we'll go to your place; it's slightly nearer,' Leo opined bluntly, casting her a brief sidelong glance, and, as if sensing her growing awareness of their abrupt departure, he dropped one hand from the wheel and gently stroked her thigh through the soft wool of her skirt. 'Your trouble is, you think too much, Jacy. Relax and enjoy; we've waited a long time to be alone together.' His dark voice deepened perceptibly.

She looked across at his starkly etched profile. She could not see the expression in his eyes, but as his long fingers teased towards her inner thigh she swallowed hard, the sexual tension back in full force. Jacy covered his hand with her own. 'My place is fine,' she managed to say. 'But I would like us to get there in one piece, so both hands on the wheel, please.' She tried to lighten the atmosphere, but in the close confines of the car his nearness seemed to affect her breathing and heighten her awareness of him.

'I'll please you; don't doubt it, sweetheart,' he murmured, and squeezed her slender hand for an instant before returning his own to the wheel.

She breathed out shakily. What was she afraid of? Hadn't she decided it was time she grew up? Leo wanted her and, dear heaven, she wanted him. They were friends now. Of a sort, a little voice taunted, and soon to be lovers. She sat up straight in the seat, and with a terrific effort of will managed to ask almost levelly, 'Did you see your aunt safely home all right?'

'Yes.'

'Was it a good trip?' she blundered on, trying to ignore the play of muscles in his thigh as his foot worked the pedals. She raised her eyes to his hands on the wheel— such strong, tanned hands, and she could almost feel them on her naked flesh.

'Yes.' Another blunt reply.

'You're not very talkative,' she prompted huskily.

'We've talked enough over the past few days. What I have in mind now is something else again,' he drawled huskily. 'At the moment my priority is reaching your damn house.' He shot her a quick dark glance, and returned his attention to the road.

Jacy's lips curved in a secret feminine smile. Leo was suffering from the same frustration she was feeling, and the discovery wasn't at all displeasing. She laid her head back against the seat, and, whether it was the champagne or simply the smooth motion of the car, in minutes she was asleep.

'We've arrived, sleepyhead.'

She opened her eyes and for an instant did not know where she was. Leo was leaning over her, his handsome face only inches from her own, and she smiled softly.

Lifting her hand, she stroked his cheek. 'Leo,' she murmured, and his lips covered hers in a deep, drugging kiss.

Minutes later she was standing on the doorstep of her home, and with shaking fingers trying to find the doorkey in the bottom of her bag. Leo wasn't helping as, with one arm around her waist, his dark head bent and his firm lips nuzzled provocatively on her neck. She found the key, but had great difficulty trying to put it in the lock, her hand was trembling so much.

'For God's sake, Jacy, give it to me.' And, taking the key from her, he opened the door and propelled her inside.

Automatically she switched on the hall light, and turned back to glance at Leo. Suddenly nervous, all her self-protective instincts coming to the fore, she was about to mouth the obvious cliché, Would you like a coffee? But when her golden eyes met his, for a second she was struck dumb by the flash of barely controlled violence in the depths of his dark eyes.

Dynamic and all male, he projected a raw virility that was almost frightening in its intensity. An involuntary shiver snaked down her spine. Tall and dark, he towered over her; she could sense the unbridled masculine aggression in his still form. 'Leo...' His name a question on her lips, she stepped back.

'No, Jacy,' he gritted. 'Not this time.'

Jacy made a feeble effort to restrain him as he pulled her to him, but they both knew it was only a token gesture. His mouth found hers and in moments all her last-minute doubts had vanished.

She should have been horrified by the savagery of his kiss, but instead her mouth opened and she welcomed the fierce sexual demand apparent in the hard force of his mouth and tongue. His teeth pulled on her lower lip and she swallowed his hot breath with her own. His strong hands stroked up her back and down to her buttocks, hauling her into the hard masculine heat of his taut thighs. Her feet left the floor as he lifted her, better to fit the muscled contours of his superb physique, and then somehow he was carrying her up the narrow stairs, his mouth grazing her cheeks, her throat, urgent and enticing.

Her slender arms wrapped around his broad shoulders. She exulted in his passion and returned it whole-heartedly. This is what the last few weeks had been leading up to; what she had been aching for for the last few hours, and even if she had wanted to she could not have stopped Leo. Her mind might query the wisdom of her response, but her physical being was incapable of denying him anything.

She wasn't aware when or how they reached her bedroom. He lowered her slowly down the long length of him, making her achingly aware of every muscle and sinew in his tall frame, then deliberately stepped back, setting her free. Dazedly she recognised by the landing light slanting through the door her familiar room and narrow bed. Her eyes sought his in the semi-darkness, and she was captivated by the glittering intensity in his black gaze. She lowered her eyes against the fire in his, and watched as he slipped off his jacket and, flinging it and his tie to the floor, unfastened his shirt and dropped it to join the rest on the floor.

'What are you waiting for, Jacy?' he demanded harshly, his voice throbbing with some emotion. 'Or do you want me to do the honours?'

Her heart was pounding like a sledge-hammer, her palms damp, her whole body flushed with heat. She could not tear her eyes away from the thick mat of black hair across his broad chest. Surely he had not looked so good years ago? His presence now surpassed any memory she had ever had of him. She shrugged off her jacket and skirt and then stopped, suddenly shy. Nothing that had happened before could compare with the sheer intensity of her want, her desire for him. She swallowed convulsively, her eyes flicking to his finely chiselled mouth, and then she was in his arms again.

Her lips parted willingly at the intimate insistence of his tongue, and she gave herself up to the incredible sensation his kiss aroused. She never noticed as he pulled the tie at her throat and her blouse fell to the floor; she was lost in examining with tactile delight the breadth and strength of Leo's torso. Then Leo's dark head lowered, trailing down her throat until his mouth covered one aching nipple through the soft silk of her last garment, a brief white silk teddy.

A low groan escaped her; her head fell back over his arm as her body arched wantonly, offering him her breasts. The teddy fell away and she was naked, but she felt no shame. Her small hands slid and clung to his shoulders, then with a will of their own stroked down to claw at the fastening of his trousers.

Leo moaned deep in his throat as her fingers inadvertently scraped over his hard muscled belly. In seconds he was naked and with strong arms he gripped her upper arms, holding her away from him. 'First I want to look at you,' he growled, his dark eyes narrowed to mere slits in the hard contours of his handsome face as he studied her: the high, full breasts, the deep rose nipples, swollen and taut, her narrow waist and the soft feminine flare of her hips. His eyes lingered on the golden crown of curls at the apex of her thighs; his throat worked jerkily. 'God, but you're even more exquisite than I remembered. How the hell do you do it? So innocent on the outside and so...'

Leo stopped on a rasping groan, as Jacy, no longer in control of her own desire, reached out as if in a dream and wound a short, silky chest curl around her index finger and tugged gently.

For Jacy the room turned and she was on the bed, Leo's hard body pinning her to the mattress. Naked, flesh against flesh, she whimpered little erotic sounds of want and almost pain, as Leo, in a frenzy of tumultuous action, fed on her lips, her throat, the curve of her breast. His mouth suckled feverishly on her nipples, first one and then the other, as his strong hands traced the outline of her slender body, his fingers stroking, nipping, teasing, searching out every pulse and pleasure point, and finally, splaying her legs apart, he sank his hard weight between her thighs, his hands biting into her buttocks, lifting her off the bed, as in one savage, demonic thrust he joined his body with hers.

Jacy gasped aloud at the raw, driving urgency of their coupling, and felt a second's pain, a tightness that made her cry out again. Leo, conscious of her action, stopped, and held her for a moment suspended in time, allowing her body to adjust to accept his vital, utterly male possession. Her arms wrapped round his broad back; her fingernails raked down the satin flesh, drawing blood as his mouth covered hers and the fire of his passion seared her innermost being. Her long legs wrapped tightly around his waist and it was the final action that shattered Leo's rigid self-control, as with a tormented cry he tore his mouth from hers, and, burying his head in her throat, he thrust hard and fast, building to a shattering crescendo he was incapable of controlling.

For Jacy the world spun away, her body one pulsating mass of indescribable ecstasy. She heard Leo's hoarse, triumphant cry as his life force exploded into her in a shuddering convulsion that went on and on in a tidal wave of pleasure.

How long they lay locked together, the aftermath of their tempestuous coupling still sending rippling shockwaves through their sweat-slicked bodies, Jacy had no idea. Slowly the real world began to infringe on her

consciousness, and the dawning realisation that there was
no going back from here. She was once again in Leo's
arms, his lover...

This time would be different, she told herself with a
soft sigh of satisfaction, and, glorying in his weight above
her, she tenderly pressed her open palms to his pounding
chest, thrilled at the chaotic beating of his powerful
heart. Proof, if proof were needed, that he was as shaken
as she by the white heat of their passion.

Leo reared up and looked down at her hot, flushed
face. He lifted a hand and stroked the tumbled mass of
her hair from her brow. 'I'm sorry if I hurt you, but it's
been a long time.'

'For me too,' Jacy admitted, while ruefully recognising that it had probably been a heck of a lot longer
for her than Leo, but she was not about to tell him that
and upset their new-found relationship. 'And you didn't
hurt me,' she added breathlessly, raising a finger to lightly
tap his nose. 'But you did get a bit carried away.' She
grinned. 'I seem to remember you used to be a very gentle
lover.' And he had been. But she realised tonight it had
been the fierce, unbridled passion of two equally frus-
trated adults.

'Gentle? I lost that long ago,' he said cynically, but
in an oddly possessive gesture he swept her hair to one
side and across the pillow. 'I used to dream of your
golden hair splayed across my pillow,' he mused, almost
as though he was talking to himself. 'How many blondes?
How many nights? The face became...' He stopped abruptly, and in a flurry of Greek he swung off the bed
and to his feet.

Jacy stretched languorously on the bed, and rolled over
on her side to watch him make for the bathroom, she
presumed, but she was wrong. 'What are you doing?'
she asked, sitting up on the bed and pulling the cover
up over her breasts. It was a stupid question, she knew.

Leo had quickly found his clothes and was pulling them on. 'Leo.' He turned to look at her and a shiver of fear had her clutching the cover between her breasts with both hands.

Wearing only his pants and standing in the middle of the room, he looked every inch the powerful, magnetic tycoon, no trace of his previous lack of control, or any trace of emotion in his hard gaze. A sardonic glint of amusement lit his dark eyes as he answered, 'I'm dressing, Jacy, darling. Surely you've seen a man dress before now.'

'Yes... No...' she stuttered, his endearment grating oddly on a raw nerve. She suddenly realised she had no idea of how to act in the aftermath of their lovemaking. What had she expected? That he would hold her in his arms and declare his eternal love? Well, maybe not that, but at least she had thought he would show he cared. But this stony-faced man standing in her bedroom bore no relationship to the man she had only minutes earlier shared her bed and body with.

'What's wrong, Leo?' she asked quite steadily, fighting back her uncertainty.

'Nothing's wrong, Jacy; if anything you are even better than I remembered,' he drawled silkily, fastening his shirt.

His words should have reassured her; instead they sounded suspiciously like an insult. She eyed him warily, her gaze puzzled and slightly fearful. 'Thank you, I think,' she murmured.

'The pleasure was all mine, Jacy. But you were right about the bed—it is too small. Before you entertain any other man I suggest you invest in a bigger one,' he derided mockingly, and slipped on his jacket.

Before she entertained... She could not believe her ears, and with a sinking heart she studied his shuttered face. 'I never bring men home.'

'In that case I am suitably grateful.'

Jacy recognised the sarcasm, but could find no reason for it. 'Grateful?' she parrotted.

'Yes.' And, slipping his hand in the inside pocket of his jacket, he withdrew a long jeweller's box. 'I did intend to give you this earlier, but in the heat of the moment I forgot.' Walking towards her, he dropped the box in front of her on the bed.

There was something dreadfully wrong; every nerve in her body screamed the warning, but she could not bring herself to believe it. She picked up the box, and glanced questioningly up at Leo, unaware of the pleading light in her golden eyes.

'Here, allow me.' Sitting down, he took the box, snapped it open, and before her startled gaze withdrew an exquisite pearl and diamond pendant in the shape of a heart on a heavy gold chain. Lifting the heavy fall of her hair from her shoulders, he placed it around her neck, and with a quick adjustment settled the jewel between the soft curve of her breasts.

The touch of his fingers against her flesh, the warmth of his breath against her cheek, and she could feel the stirring of renewed arousal. 'It's beautiful, Leo, but you shouldn't have bought me anything.' Maybe she was im- agining his coolness, and everything was all right, she told herself, and she stretched out her hand to him, but with an abrupt movement he shrugged her away and once more stood up.

'Rubbish, you deserve it, darling, and I can only apologise for not managing to obtain an antique *netsuke*; I know that is what you prefer.' He walked across the room and stopped with his hand on the door-handle, the light from the open door illuminating his harsh features. 'But you understand pressure of business; I had no time to go hunting in antique shops. My visit to London was only for a month and then, of course, there was my unforeseen trip to America. You know how it is; you're in a high-powered business yourself.'

'How did you know I collect *netsuke*?' she asked, but she was horribly afraid she already knew the answer. Wrapping the cover firmly around her naked body, she slid off the bed and walked towards him, her eyes searching his hard, handsome face. 'I don't remember telling you.'

'You didn't; I overheard you at Liz's party. The picture you drew was very erotic; what was it you said? ''Mr Kozakis will not ask me out, even if I were to strip naked in front of him.'' Wrong, Jacy.' He shook his dark head; a slow, sensuous smile curved his hard mouth. 'You grossly underestimate yourself, my dear. I determined to have you the minute I set eyes on you again. As for your bet with Liz, I'm afraid you're going to be disappointed. I'm leaving London tomorrow, and I don't know when I will be back.'

Jacy realised in stricken apprehension that Leo had known about the bet all along. Surely he couldn't believe that was the reason she'd gone out with him? She lifted her free hand and placed it on his shirt front. 'You've got it all wrong, Leo.' If she explained...

With a dismissive gesture he flicked her hand from his shirt front. 'No, I was right about you the first time.' He slashed her a scornful glance, his mouth compressed in a tight line. 'Then it was to help your career, and now for an ornament.'

She could not speak; her tongue was glued to the dry roof of her mouth as she stared at him in shocked horror. Leo really thought so badly of her...

'A word of advice, Jacy...' And with one hand he reached out and tore the cover from her fingers so she was left standing naked before him. His dark eyes roamed over her in blatant cynical appraisal. 'You're a beautiful woman, but certainly no saleswoman. You sell yourself far too cheap, and, as for gambling, let this be a lesson to you—forget it. Your face is far too expressive; you will never make a poker player,' he derided mockingly.

Jacy was incapable of movement, stunned by his cutting words and the dawning realisation that their lovemaking had meant less than nothing to him.

Tanned fingers closed around her wrist. He jerked her up against his hard body. 'Mute, always the silent act when you're found out. But God! I still fancy you.' Her golden eyes widened fearfully as Leo's fingers pushed up her chin, devilish amusement burning in his gaze. 'Don't worry, not again tonight; I haven't time.'

The stark assurance in his deep-timbred drawl held her mesmerised, but as the full import of his words sunk in she shivered, suddenly aware of her nakedness and the ice creeping through her veins.

'I'll give you a call the next time I'm in London.' With an icy smile his fingers fell from her chin and his hand left her wrist. 'Get back to bed; you'll catch cold.' And, picking the cover from the floor in an oddly gentle gesture, he wrapped it around her shoulders. 'I'll let myself out.'

He left her standing there. How long Jacy stood looking vacantly at the open bedroom door she had no idea; she was listening intently to the loud hammering of her heart. Why hadn't it stopped? A broken heart should stop, she thought fuzzily, and then like an old woman she staggered over to the bed and lay down on it, pulling the cover firmly around her like a shroud. She curled up in a little ball and willed the pain to go away as tears fell unchecked from her pain-hazed eyes.

Jacy awoke slowly, a niggling warning teasing her consciousness. She struggled up into a sitting position and rubbed the sleep from her eyes with her soft hands, and then it hit her...

She doubled over in pain, her stomach somersaulting, nausea clawing at her throat. She dragged herself to the bathroom and was physically sick. She lifted her head and, grasping the wash-basin, ran the cold water tap, splashing her face over and over again. Finally she straightened and stared at her reflection in the mirror over the wash-basin. The laughing, glowing woman of yesterday had vanished and in her place stood a poor replica. Her eyes were red, and her colour ashen. Between her full breasts lay the pearl and diamond heart. With slow deliberation she loosened the clasp and held it in the palm of her hand. Her payment for sex. She let it drop through her shaking fingers to the floor.

Leo Kozakis, her nemesis. Was she never going to learn? she asked herself bitterly. He had made love to her and walked out to teach her a lesson! It would be laughable if it didn't hurt so much, but she had only herself to blame. How simply she had fallen into his arms, just as she had ten years ago. Only this time it was a hundred times worse. At least at eighteen she had been in love with him and had believed Leo loved her. Last night she had been under no such illusion. She had been perfectly well aware of Leo's reputation, but had justified her own surrender on the strength of a few conversations with the man and a foolishly held belief that, with age and maturity, this time with Leo would be different. She groaned out loud; she had reduced her expectations of love and marriage in favour of a more realistic adult relationship, only to find herself used once more.

Well, that was it! Never again, she vowed, and walked back into her bedroom and forced herself to follow her usual morning ritual. Dressing in a pair of old, well washed jeans and a soft blue cashmere sweater, she applied a minimum of make-up to her pale face, but could do nothing to disguise the dark circles under her eyes, or the haunted look she was unable to hide. Thank God she had taken the Thursday and Friday off work in lieu of working last weekend. There was no way she could have gone to the office today.

She glanced at the rumpled bed; a brief image of herself and Leo, naked, entwined in the throes of passion, flashed vividly through her mind. Clenching her teeth, she marched out of the room. Passing the door to the main bedroom, she hesitated and, pushing it open, walked in. No memories of Leo here, only of her father.

A deep sigh escaped her. Her father, bless him, had returned to England as the editor of a serious British newspaper after the death of her mother, and bought the house, quite happily making a home for Jacy as well. She crossed to the wide bed and sat down. It was a pleasant room, decorated in shades of beige and brown, and very reminiscent of her father. Unbidden, she recalled her father's words when she had once asked him if he was going to marry again. At the time he had been going out with a very attractive lady reporter, and Jacy had had visions of having to move out to make room for his new wife.

'Jacy, my pet, whatever advice your mother gave you about sex, the only thing you need to remember is an old Scottish saying, "A man will never buy the bottle if he can drink of the whisky free".' And then he'd laughed.

She should have remembered his advice, she thought, rising to her feet and walking slowly to the door. All men were basically the same. Leo, even her own father... She had loved him dearly and after he'd died she had never bothered changing her bedroom for his much larger one. Perhaps now it was time she did. She knew in her heart she would never again sleep happily in the bed she had shared with Leo. In a flurry of activity—anything to stop herself thinking—she transferred all her belongings to the master bedroom.

Finally by mid-afternoon she collapsed on the sofa in her living-room, a cup of coffee and a plate of sandwiches which she had no desire to eat on the table in front of her. She drank the coffee and laid her head back against the soft cushions. It was no good; she could not hold back the memories of yesterday any longer, however hard she tried.

The events of the evening ran through her head like a recurring nightmare. Leo had known about the bet all along, from the very night she had made it with Liz, and yet the devious swine had never mentioned it. Not until last night after he had finally got her into bed. Then he had cold-bloodedly thrown it in her face, and added a chilling denouncement of her character. To top it all he had then had the audacity, after once again just about calling her a whore, to turn around and say he'd call . . .

With hindsight she could see there had been plenty of clues. More than once she had wondered if he knew about the bet, but after he'd gone to America, and their long conversations, she had put it out of her mind. But Leo quite obviously hadn't. He had delighted in throwing it in her face.

She cringed with shame as she recalled the frenzied lovemaking. He had wanted her; that was some consolation, she tried to tell herself, but it was poor comfort when she considered how the evening had ended. He had used her and she had let him. She was an astute businesswoman, but she might as well admit that in the male-female relationship stakes she was a non-starter and resign herself to the fact. Her body ached for the satisfaction only Leo could provide, but with a steely determination she resolved to put him out of her mind for good. She had done it once and she could do it again, she vowed silently.

The phone rang and she reluctantly answered it.

'Hi, Jacy, are you alone?' Liz's happy voice queried.

'Yes,' Jacy said flatly.

'Do I discern a lovers' tiff so soon?'

'No lover and no tiff.'

'Don't tell me you've blown it, Jacy. You only had to keep in with Leo until next Tuesday and the *netsuke* was yours.'

'As I have no intention of ever seeing Leo Kozakis again, tell me when you want me to baby-sit.' And for the first time in her long friendship with Liz she lied. 'Sorry, Liz, someone at the door, I must go. Bye.'

CHAPTER EIGHT

JACY had only delayed the inevitable as at four in the afternoon a knock on the door heralded the arrival of Liz.

'You sounded funny earlier and I was coming up to town to meet Tom, so I've told him to pick me up here. I thought I'd call and see how you are. The speed Leo carried you off yesterday was unbelievable. He was eating you with his eyes. So come on, what went wrong?'

'Nothing. We returned here. Leo had coffee. We talked and he left.' Jacy did not tell lies easily, but even for Liz, her best friend, she could not bare her soul. It still hurt too much...

'Washed-out complexion, red-rimmed eyes, and you're not going to tell me, hmm?' Liz queried, sitting down in the wing-backed chair, her pixie face full of compassion. 'It might help to talk, and I'm a great listener.'

A wry smile brightened Jacy's face for a second. 'You never give up, Liz, but this time I'm afraid you'll have to. Suffice it to say you were perfectly correct when you warned me about Leo after Tom's birthday party. He is too much the cynical sophisticate for me. So now can we change the subject? Please...'

Liz regarded her candidly. 'Are you going to be OK?' she queried. 'Or shall I get Tom to punch Leo out for you...? No, perhaps that's not such a good idea. Tom is hoping to clinch Leo's considerable business for the bank and end up chairman. Breaking the bloke's nose might not enhance his prospects.'

Jacy laughed at that, and until Tom arrived the conversation carefully avoided any mention of Leo.

It was only after they had left and the silence of her home began to press in on her that Jacy realised sadly just how much subconsciously she had been hoping this time with Leo would be different. The house had never seemed so empty before, and she had never felt so alone. Much to her own self-disgust she found herself praying for the telephone to ring.

Rubbish, pull yourself together, girl! There was life after Leo before, and there would be again, she told herself firmly, and of course this time she didn't love Leo! That had ended years ago. She could not deny the physical attraction between them. Last night it had reached breaking-point. A temporary madness, she assured herself, but as she ascended the stairs to her changed bedroom she could not help recalling how only a few hours ago she had been carried tenderly up the same stairs in the arms of her lover.

She shuddered, her blood turning to iced water in her veins. It had been hard enough admitting her mistake the first time, but at least she had the excuse of extreme youth and naïveté. This time it was a much greater humiliation. She was a mature woman and the blow to her own self-respect, self-image, doubly hard to endure.

Almost three weeks later Jacy sat curled up on the sofa in her 'Save the Whale' night-shirt, a plate of raw mushrooms and a huge strawberry cream cake on the table in front of her, with a pot of tea, and the daily paper open at 'What's on TV'.

Yes, she congratulated herself quietly, the hurt was easing. Leo hadn't called, but then she hadn't expected him to. He hadn't lied to her; he had suggested a brief affair, and that was all it had been. She couldn't really blame Leo. Anger at Barbara's treatment had encouraged

her to make the stupid bet. How could she expect a proud
man like Leo Kozakis to react when he found out other
than to take delight in turning the tables on her? He had
told her himself he always won. Now she knew it was
true... Leo had shown himself in his true light. His relationships with women were, and always would be,
shallow. He had made love to Jacy because he wanted
to teach her a lesson, while she had secretly nursed the
hope that their relationship might develop into something more. In her business life she was a tough go-getter,
but she could never handle the kind of meaningless,
sophisticated relationships Leo Kozakis indulged in. How
she had fooled herself otherwise on the strength of a few
telephone calls she couldn't bear to contemplate.

Instead she had immersed herself in her work, and she
was not without friends. Next weekend was Easter and
she was spending it looking after the twins, while Liz
and Tom went to Paris. More immediate, she loved
opera, and tomorrow, Friday, Simon was taking her to
Covent Garden to hear Placido Domingo in *Tosca*.

She picked up a mushroom and popped it into her
mouth before turning her attention to the paper. She
was trying to decide between *Roseanne* and the ten
o'clock news when the telephone rang. Damn! Who
could it be at this time of night? she wondered and,
strolling into the hall, unsuspecting, picked up the
receiver.

The breath wooshed out of her body in one long gasp
of amazement. Leo...

'I'm back in London for a while; I saw Tom yesterday
and he tells me you're still free. Sorry I couldn't get in
touch sooner. I don't usually kiss and run, but business...
You know how it is.'

The cool cheek of the man took her breath away. But
with remarkable self-control she managed to respond
with biting sarcasm, 'Think nothing of it. I haven't...'

And read what you like into that, she muttered under her breath.

'Good, I knew you would understand. So how about coming to Covent Garden tomorrow evening, the opera, with——?'

Jacy cut in, 'Placido Domingo. I know, I have a ticket; I'm going with Simon.' Nothing in her life had ever given her so much satisfaction, she thought elatedly, delighted at the coincidence that had enabled her to turn Leo down flat.

'The red-headed guy at the party.' The dark voice cracked like broken glass.

'Yes. But thank you for thinking of me.' In a voice sickly sweet, leaving him in no doubt that she was sure the opposite was true, she added, 'I hope you enjoy it; I'm sure I shall.'

'No doubt I will; he's a marvellous singer,' Leo responded smoothly, sounding not in the least put out by her refusal. But the deep, rich sound of his voice reawakened all the hurt and longing Jacy had been so desperately trying to suppress, and when he ended with, 'Goodbye, I'll see you around,' she had to bite her tongue to stop herself asking when.

She ate the plate of mushrooms and the cake, washing it down with cold tea. She had saved her pride by turning him down, but a tiny devil whispered in her head that Leo hadn't been very insistent. He could have asked her out another night... Why did he have to ring now? Damn him! Just when she had begun to get her life back on an even keel. Because he was a sadist; he got his kicks out of stringing women along. The answer was obvious, she thought morosely.

Sitting in the front stalls with Simon beside her the next night, even the enormous talent of Placido Domingo could not shake off her dread of bumping into Leo.

It happened in the interval. Simon had managed to secure them two glasses of wine, and after a sip or two she was finally beginning to relax. Simon lounged tall and elegant against the wall and Jacy stood in front of him. Teasingly she said, 'What a waste to womankind, Simon; you really do look incredibly attractive.' And he did, along the lines of a male model, impeccably dressed in a fashionable dinner suit.

'I know, darling, but right now I have a more pressing problem than my sexual predilections. A certain dark Greek is standing across the room and if looks could kill I'd be dead.'

Jacy's hand trembled, spilling a little of the wine. She breathed in deeply and, resisting the urge to turn around, she held her head high, her eyes going to the mirror on the wall beside Simon, reflecting the room behind her. Leo, clad in a perfectly fitting conventional black dinner suit, the plain white silk evening shirt in stark contrast to his swarthy complexion, looked absolutely devastating. He was standing with his arm around Thelma, but his glittering dark eyes were fixed firmly on Jacy. Her stomach felt as though it were on a roller-coaster ride, while her heart pounded against her ribcage until she was sure everyone must hear it. Her throat went dry and she could not tear her eyes away from Leo.

His firm mouth twisted in a polite social smile as he mockingly saluted her with the glass in his free hand.

She couldn't pretend she had not seen him, and stiffly she raised her own glass in greeting, then was struck with a wave of jealousy so intense that she clenched the stem of her wine glass till her knuckles turned white with the strain, as Leo lowered his dark head to his companion and whatever he said had the other woman smiling up at him in adoration.

Jacy wanted to scream bitchily, 'You weren't his first choice,' and a treacherous feeling of regret flooded her mind. It could so easily have been her with Leo tonight, if her stupid pride had not got in the way. Taking a hasty swallow of her drink, she looked away. She knew she wasn't being fair to Thelma. The woman was really quite pleasant, a very attractive blonde and an excellent interior designer. But Jacy had no doubt that the designs the other woman had on Leo had nothing to do with furniture. Telling herself not to be so stupid, she breathed a sigh of relief as the bell rang for the next act.

Once more in the auditorium, she was determined to enjoy the second half of the performance. But it was not that easy. A thousand unanswered questions swirled around her troubled mind. Had she been too precipitate in refusing Leo's invitation? Who was she kidding? She meant nothing to the man. Surely seeing him with Thelma at his side had taught her that much. A blonde— any blonde—would do for Leo. Jacy had too much pride, too much self-respect, to be any man's plaything.

'Aunty Jacy, Aunty Jacy,' two young voices chorused in unison. 'It's morning...'

Opening one eye, Jacy glared at the bedside clock. Six a.m. She groaned and turned over just as the terrible twins arrived with a thump on top of the bed. The reverberations ricocheted through her body, and stopped in her stomach.

'Yes, OK.' She hauled herself up to a sitting position and eyed the two pyjama-clad little bodies balefully, before gingerly swinging her long legs over the side of the bed. Then it happened: nausea rose up in an overwhelming surge; she could taste the bile in her throat as she made a headlong dash for the bathroom.

Five minutes later, wearily lifting her head from the toilet bowl, she swivelled around and sat on the tiled floor, her face on a level with two angelic-looking blond-haired angels, only the angels sported identical worried frowns.

'Are you sick every day, Aunty Jacy?' Tomas, the older by one minute, asked seriously.

'Apparently,' she murmured, getting to her feet. 'But it's nothing to worry about,' she reassured them, and wished she could reassure herself so easily. The past few days had been hell. She adored Tomas and Jethro, and when she had arrived on Thursday to take care of them for the weekend she had firmly waved Liz and Tom off, prepared to spend a pleasant Easter weekend in the comfort of their luxurious house. But it hadn't turned out like that. Friday morning had seen her waking up sick for the fourth day running, and she knew she could no longer pretend it was something she had eaten. The same thing had happened on Saturday, and now this morning. She could fool herself no longer. A brief calculation in her head confirmed her suspicion. She was two weeks overdue. She couldn't believe her own stupidity...

Luckily, with the twins to look after, she did not have time to brood over her problem, as they occupied every minute of the day. Speedily she washed and dressed, then performed the same service for the boys, amid much giggling and horseplay. Half an hour later, with breakfast prepared, she sat down with her first cup of tea of the day, and a slice of dry toast. She could not face coffee— hadn't been able to for the past week... A warning she had chosen to ignore...

'Don't put your toasted soldiers in your ears, Tomas; they are meant to dip in your egg,' she said bluntly.

'I'm Dr Spock.'

'Dr Spock had pointy ears, not toast sticking out of them,' she said matter-of-factly, adding, 'Now what are we going to do today?'

'Sunday school this morning, Sunday school this morning,' both boys started to chant.

Jacy breathed an inward sigh of relief. She could drive them to the village church for ten o'clock and have a couple of hours to herself before she had to pick them up again at twelve.

It had not been a very productive break, she thought with wry self-mockery as once more she let herself out of the Tudor house and locked the oak door behind her. She had spent most of it chewing her thumbnail and cursing Leo Kozakis. Still, she might be wrong, she told herself, pulling the soft blue cashmere sweater rather self-consciously down over her jeans-clad behind. Was she already subconsciously trying to hide an imaginary bump? Striding across to her car, she inserted the key in the lock, and then hesitated. Lifting her head, she looked down the drive to see another car speeding up. Who could it be? Tom and Liz weren't due back until tomorrow. She waited and as it drew closer, her golden eyes widened to their fullest extent in shocked horror.

The car stopped two feet from her own, and with a rising sense of helplessness she watched as the driver's door opened and out stepped Leo.

'What the hell are you doing here?' she demanded peremptorily, more in self-defence than any real anger. She was too fragile this morning to deal with Leo Kozakis.

One dark eyebrow arched in silent query. 'Is it any business of yours?'

'I'm in charge,' she said sullenly. He was too arrogant, too thoroughly male, she thought with an overwhelming sense of inadequacy. Her pulse was racing and she could do nothing about the nervous fluttering in her stomach.

Leo, casually dressed in a thick cream Aran-styled sweater teamed with designer jeans, the lighter patches sexily outlining the points of tension in the denim, covered the distance between them in a few lithe strides.

'What of?' He glanced derisively around the obviously empty garden, then back to Jacy. 'You sound like a two-bit general who's lost his troops,' he drawled with mocking amusement as he stopped a hand's breadth away.

'I am not interested in your opinion, and if you're looking for Tom and Liz they're away. I'm taking care of the twins.'

'And who is taking care of you?' Leo demanded cynically. 'The red-headed pretty boy?'

'Certainly not,' she snapped, instantly on the defensive. He was too near; the spicy scent of his cologne mingled with the fresh spring air was having a disastrous effect on her breathing. Then to her astonishment Leo suddenly smiled, a breathtaking, face-splitting grin that deepened the slight laughter lines around his sparkling brown eyes and took years off his age.

'I'm glad to hear it, Jacy.' And for a ridiculous moment she thought she saw a flicker of relief in his expression and wondered if he had been jealous of her friendship with Simon, but quickly dismissed the thought as he continued smoothly, 'I know Tom and Liz are away for the weekend, but I promised the boys I would bring them an Easter egg each. So where are they?'

She wanted to ignore him, leap in her car and drive off. He was much too dangerous to her emotional well-being. But he made the request sound so natural that she had no choice but to tell him. 'I'm just going to collect them from Sunday school.'

'Great, we'll take my car; there's more room.' And before she could object Jacy found herself in the front seat of the gleaming Jaguar, as near to the door as she could get, and reluctantly giving Leo directions to the village church.

For a while the only sound was the swish of tyres on tarmac. Jacy determinedly looked out of the side window, keeping her face averted from Leo, but she was achingly aware of every move he made.

'So how are you managing as a surrogate mother?' His deep voice drawled seductively along her overstrung nerves, and the word 'mother' gave her a sinking feeling in her already upset stomach. She said nothing.

'Are the twins running you ragged? You look a bit washed out.'

'I'm fine,' she snapped. So what if he did think she looked a mess? It didn't matter to her. But if he ever found out what was the matter with her, her life would not be her own, she recognised instinctively. Then, frightened she had been too emphatic, she tagged on, 'I love the boys, I can manage perfectly.'

'I wasn't suggesting you couldn't, Jacy,' he said, quietly stopping the car at the entrance to the church. Turning sideways, he studied her huddled form in the corner of the seat. He stretched out a hand and flipped the end of her long blonde hair over her shoulder.

She knew it looked a mess, but this morning she had scraped it back in a ponytail with an elastic band simply for ease. The touch of his hand made the hairs on the back of her neck prickle in alarm, and her hand grasped the door-handle, ready to bolt...

'Still the mute defence, hmm?' he prompted, his hand curved around her shoulder, preventing her exit, quite deliberately allowing the tension to build until finally Jacy could stand no more; she had to look at him.

His dark eyes, strangely intense, held hers and for a long moment something inexplicable passed between them, an emotion so strong that Jacy shivered in fear. Her eyes fell to his mouth; the firm, sensual lips were parted slightly, and she knew if he made a move to kiss her she would not be able to resist. She had refused to go out with him, but only over the telephone, and soberly she realised face to face she had no defence against him. But his next words broke the tenuous thread that held them together.

'Would it be so hard for you to behave as a normal human being for the next couple of hours?' he demanded bitingly, his dark eyes never leaving her pale face. 'I have no desire to upset the children, but if you insist on trying to ignore me or keep a foot of space between us the boys are bound to notice.'

He wasn't interested in her. When was she going to get it in her thick head...? It was the boys he was worried about, and he was right, she knew. He was here to see the twins, and at that moment two voices could be heard screaming in delight at the sight of the long black car.

Opening the door, Leo prompted, 'Well, Jacy—friends?'

'Yes, all right.' She slid out of the passenger seat and greeted the twins.

For the next few hours Jacy was treated to a totally different Leo Kozakis. The ruthless businessman was replaced by a laughing friend who thought nothing of driving to the outskirts of London to lunch in the nearest hamburger restaurant. They returned home to a frantic football game on the front lawn, with a wild disregard for Liz's recently planted flowerbeds, and by six in the evening two bathed, shiny-faced boys lay comfortably on the floor in the elegant drawing-room, a tousled Leo sprawled out beside them while they attempted to build a castle with Lego.

Jacy, stretched out on the sofa, was pretending to read the Sunday paper, but her gaze kept straying to the three on the floor, or more particularly to the man, and remembering the last time she had seen him lying down; then he had been naked and in her bed, his handsome face taut with passion...

'What's wrong? Have I a smut on my nose or something?'

With a guilty start the paper fell from her hands as Leo caught her staring at him. How could she tell him what she had been thinking? 'No, no, nothing like that,' she blurted. 'I was just thinking how good you are with children.'

With the speed and grace of some sleek jungle cat he rose to his feet and came towards her.

'I like kids, and I'm very good with my nephew and nieces, I'll have you know,' he offered, grinning smugly.

'You just don't like how you have to get them?' she said, thinking of his aversion to marriage and his host of casual relationships.

A roar of laughter greeted her comment. 'You couldn't be more wrong, sweetheart.' Collapsing on the sofa beside her, he flung his arm around her shoulder, and, his breath like a summer breeze against the soft curve of her cheek, whispered huskily, 'I love how one has to get children; I couldn't do without it. Shall I show you later?' Then he leant back, still chuckling.

Jacy turned a fiery red with embarrassment. 'I didn't mean that... I meant getting married,' she corrected him furiously.

'True, I have always avoided that particular trap, but——' Whatever Leo might have added was forestalled by the boys.

'Can we have some more of our chocolate egg?' Jethro asked, pulling on Jacy's arm, while his twin was pulling on Leo's arm, demanding another game.

Relieved at the distraction, Jacy eyed her two little charges' flushed faces and tired eyes. 'You have both had enough for one day.' They had been delighted with the huge chocolate eggs Leo had presented them with and had eaten almost half already. 'And Leo has to go now, so how about we see him off, and then bed and a story, hmm?'

'But I want Leo to stay, and I want some more chocolate,' Jethro demanded fractiously.

'Sorry, darling, but it will make you sick; you'll be ill and you wouldn't like that.' She tried to placate the little boy.

'I don't mind,' he said staunchly. 'You're sick every day, Aunty Jacy, and you're all right.'

The blood drained from her face, and for a moment she was speechless. She didn't dare look at Leo; instead, finding her voice, she said, 'Yes, OK, you can have some chocolate, and then bed.' She half stood up, but a large hand around her wrist forced her back down on the sofa. She shot a furious glance at Leo, but his attention was fixed on Jethro and Tomas.

'Has your aunty Jacy been making herself sick with chocolate?' he asked the twins with a grin.

Jacy burnt with humiliation as the boys delighted in giving Leo graphic details of her morning stints with her head in the toilet bowl, ending with the information that after her tea and toast she was fine.

His dark eyes narrowed to slits in the harsh contours of his handsome face as he flashed her a look of such glittering hatred that she flinched as though he had struck her; his fingers dug into the flesh of her shoulder through her sweater. Then abruptly he set her free, as though just to touch her was a contamination.

How she got through the next hour she didn't know. One look at Leo's hard face and she knew her hints that he should leave were pointless. He had guessed she was pregnant . . . and was furiously angry, though he hid it well with the cheerful face he showed the children.

Finally she could delay the confrontation no longer. The boys were in bed and asleep, and with Leo at her

back, following her out of the room, she walked down
the stairs to the drawing-room.

'I need a drink.' Leo crossed to the drinks trolley and
poured himself a large Scotch. 'I won't offer you one.
In your condition I believe it is unwise.' His hard mouth
twisted in a mockery of a smile.

'I have no idea what you're talking about. I'm perfectly all right, and I think it's time you left.' Her legs
were trembling and it took all her will-power to stand
in front of him and try to bluff it out in a last desperate
attempt to deny the inevitable, but it was no good. Leo
slammed his glass down on the trolley and, reaching out,
grabbed her wrist.

'Don't lie to me, Jacy. You're pregnant, aren't you?'

'What the hell has it got to do with you?' She knew
as soon as the words left her mouth that she had made
a mistake. Leo went white about the mouth, his features
settling into a hard, impenetrable mask that filled her
with fear.

'Everything, if it is mine,' he announced in a icy, impersonal tone. 'And don't try to fool me, Jacy. I will
insist on tests to make sure. You're not sticking me with
that red-headed wimp's offspring.'

She couldn't help it; she started to laugh. It was ironic.
She had been terrified he would find out, and he was
equally terrified in case it was his child. He had said he
didn't want to be trapped, and now, with his insistence
on tests, he would trap himself. It would be hilarious if
it weren't so sad.

'Stop it, Jacy.' His curt command, the pressure of his
fingers on her arm, silenced her laughter.

She sobered instantly. 'It's all right, Leo. I haven't
been to a doctor. It's not certain I'm pregnant; you have
nothing to fear. Even if I am there will be no tests,' she
declared scornfully. He had shown his true colours; he
was a bastard, but then she had always known that, she

thought with rising fury. She didn't notice the flash of enlightenment in his dark eyes, or the fact she had given herself away by her declaration; she was too enraged. Ten years ago she would have been incapable of standing up to Leo, but not any more.

'I am perfectly capable of taking care of everything myself. I may not be wealthy according to the law of the great Leo Kozakis, but I'm not a pauper. I have my own house.'

'And we both know how you got it; you're hardly likely to be able to continue with that particular moonshine activity.'

His sneering condemnation served to fuel her anger. 'That crude assumption was about what I would expect from a rat like you. But you're wrong: my father left me the house.' She was too furious to notice the quick flash of shocked relief in his expression. 'I won't be pregnant forever; I have a good career. I don't need a man, and certainly not you.' Lunging back, she was free and, swinging on her heel, she would have stormed out. She couldn't bear to look at him . . .

A strong hand spun her back around, his fingers biting into her narrow shoulderblade. Dark eyes glittered down at her in barely controlled fury. 'You bitch. It is mine and you had no intention of telling me.'

'Get your hands off me,' she ordered, her anger wavering as she collided for a brief moment with his hard body. She jerked back as though hit by lightning, an odd breathlessness making her breasts heave. His arm snaked around her waist; deliberately ignoring her command, he increased his hold on her. 'Leo, let go of me.' But a constriction in her throat made the sentence sound like a husky plea, instead of the adamant demand she had intended.

Dark colour swept up over his high cheekbones, and a flash of demonic rage lit his glittering gaze. 'You would abort my child, and return to your career without a qualm.'

Her eyes widened to their fullest extent as she stared at him in horror. That was not what she had meant. How could he so misjudge her? He really did not know her at all if he could imagine for a second that she would abort her unborn child. Her mouth worked, but no words came out...

'No denial, Jacy!'

His eyes hardened until they resembled polished jet, then he drew her even closer until her breasts pressed against his broad chest. Slowly his hand at her shoulder slid to hold the nape of her neck, while his other hand moved down the base of her spine, moulding her so close that the pressure of his powerful thighs was almost a pain.

'You don't need a man, do you?' The query was silky-soft, but she sensed his rage was held by the slenderest of threads. 'Liar.' And with a deadly intent he lowered his head and took her mouth in a savage, bitter kiss that, although she recognised it was an insult, slowly drained all the resistance from her body.

His mouth gentled on hers, and her arms slid around his broad shoulders; her fingers dug into the soft wool of his sweater, while her lips parted helplessly beneath his. She melted into the hard heat of his long body, the blood flowing through her veins, the heavy thudding of her heart deafening her to everything but the exquisite taste and touch of Leo.

Suddenly, with an angry oath, he flung her from him, she almost fell; only Leo's quick reaction saved her, as he once more caught her arm. She was completely disorientated, still under the spell of his embrace, until her eyes focused on his face, and she felt as though someone had thrown a bucket of iced water over her.

His lips twisted in a hard, contemptuous smile. 'You want me; you can't help yourself.' And with that knowledge he appeared to have regained control of his temper. Leading her to the sofa, he pushed her trembling body down. 'Sit down before you fall down, and from now on you are going to do as I tell you...understand?'

He towered over her, tall and indomitable. 'I'm not...' she gasped.

'You and I are going to be married as soon as possible.'

A brittle laugh escaped her. 'You're mad. I'm not marrying you. You said yourself marriage is a trap, and you are not the only one who has no desire to fall into it.'

A dark brow lifted sardonically. 'Oh, I think you will.' Coming down beside her, he gathered her into his arms.

'Sex is no solution,' she managed to get out before his lips closed over hers once more.

Her head fell back against the cushions and her mouth opened instinctively for his. His fingers pulled the band from her hair and wound into the tangled curls. His other hand edged beneath her wool sweater, easing it up, her lacy bra along with it, until his hand was cupping her breast, his long fingers stroking her rosy nipple into instant arousal, while his tongue searched the dark, moist hollow of her mouth to devastating effect. She tried to tell herself he was deliberately seducing her, but his onslaught was too practised, too intense. Before she knew it she was lying full-length on the sofa, her sweater pushed up under her armpits, his hard body over her, as his hands continued their tormenting, wandering over her breasts, the firm swell of her hips, and down her long legs, encased in clinging denim, in confident knowledge of her helpless arousal.

He seduced her utterly. It had been too many weeks since she had felt his touch, and her body writhed against him in aching need.

Abruptly he released her love-swollen lips and lifted his dark head. 'You want me; you can't deny it. I could take you now.' His fingers trailed teasingly over her turgid breasts. 'You will marry me next weekend. Our child will have two parents, and we ... we will have this,' he growled, his head once more lowering, but this time to nip teasingly at her breast.

Jacy could barely breathe, her nipples tight, engorged with her surging blood. An ache was arrowing from where Leo's hand covered her groin through every nerve and sinew in her body.

'Say yes ...' His mouth whispered the words against her throat. 'You know you want to.' And, raising his head, his derisory gaze lingered on her swollen, pouting lips.

That was the terrible part, she thought in self-hatred. Leo was right, and he knew it. He drove her crazy—he always had and probably always would—but that was no basis for a marriage. 'Anyway, I may not even be pregnant,' she stalled.

'How late are you?'

'Two weeks,' she mumbled, and, glancing warily up at him, she noted the dull flush of passion along his cheekbones. It was a two-way street, she realised, this explosion of the senses whenever they touched.

'Well, then, I'll make arrangements for you to see the doctor on Tuesday and we will be married next Saturday.' His fingers trailed seductively over the soft, creamy mound of her breast, and she couldn't think straight.

'But we don't love each other,' she objected.

'Love is a vastly overrated emotion. What we have is much better.' His fingers plucked at her breast and he chuckled as her body instinctively arched beneath him. 'You're the most responsive woman I have ever bedded, the chemistry is perfect between us, you're pregnant with my child ... Many a marriage started with less.'

'No, I won't.' She tried to push him away, the thought of all his other women cooling her over-heated emotions immediately. 'There are other solutions.' He could have visiting rights or something, she thought feebly. She just wasn't cut out for his kind of open-ended commitment, and sadly she recognised it.

'Well, you're not aborting my child.' He swore furiously and hauled her upright and in a deft movement had her sweater back down where it belonged. 'You haven't got a choice.' His jawline hardened. 'Liz and Tom are your friends. He has a glittering career before him, possibly chairman of the bank, but only with my contract under his belt. Do I make myself clear?'

'You ruthless bastard,' she swore unsteadily.

'Maybe.' His hard, dark eyes held hers with cruel mockery. 'But I'll make damn sure my child is not . . .'

CHAPTER NINE

LEO and Jacy were flying direct to Corfu; Leo's parents had insisted on it. His father, unable to fly because of recent heart surgery, had not been able to attend the simple civil marriage ceremony that morning in London. Instead, Leo had informed Jacy that a large family party had been planned for the evening at the Kozakis villa.

'They know the circumstances of our marriage and it will be easier for you to meet them all at once and get all the ribald comments over with immediately,' he vouched with wry amusement.

Jacy saw nothing amusing in the situation at all; her full lips tightened in a grim line. The past week had been sheer hell. On Tuesday Leo had dragged her to a Harley Street doctor, and her pregnancy was confirmed the same day. After that Leo had overridden her every objection like a steamroller flattening everything in its path. How he had convinced Liz and Tom of their hasty desire to marry she had no idea. But they had quite happily stood as witnesses at the ceremony. Leo—damn him!—had done his work well, she acknowledged. Even Liz, her best friend, had been totally convinced it was the love match of the decade.

The two girls had spent last night together and Jacy could have told Liz the true state of affairs, but her conscience wouldn't let her. She would not destroy Tom's career and she had no doubt that Leo would carry out his threat without a second thought. Suddenly it struck her as rather odd! Liz had made it easy for her. She had not been her usual inquisitive self at all last night, or this morning when the limousine had called at the house to collect them for the nine o'clock service. Liz had hurried her along with a few platitudes. Jacy had pinned a smile on her face and played her part to perfection. The wedding breakfast had been just that, except in the glamorous surroundings of the Dorchester Hotel.

A shaky sigh escaped her; now she was strapped into an aircraft seat next to Leo in the rear of an elegant lounge of a private jet, flying into a totally alien lifestyle with a man she despised. But did she? Deep in the secret corners of her mind a tiny voice reminded her that once her only wish in life had been to marry Leo.

'Are you worried at meeting my family again?' Leo reached for her hand, and she shrugged him off.

'Not in the least.'

'Then why the long sigh?'

'It's not every day one gets forced into marriage,' she said curtly.

'Keep your voice down.' She had not seen the cabin steward approaching. 'The world does not need to know of your childish grumbles.' Leo surveyed her with angry dark eyes. 'I don't find marriage any more agreeable than you do, but it is a necessity. Remember that...' The hard implacability of his tone brooked no argument, and she made none.

Leo ordered a whisky from the steward, adding, 'No alcohol for my wife. A cup of tea, perhaps?' He cast a sidelong, enquiring glance at Jacy.

'Nothing,' she snapped and, avoiding his eyes, she picked a magazine from the table in front of her and was soon deeply engrossed in an article on the European Community and the likelihood of the ECU eventually becoming the sole European currency. When she had finished she looked up and found Leo watching her, a strange expression in his eyes.

'You loved your work, didn't you?'

'I still do,' Jacy said bitterly, recalling the way he had calmly walked into her managing director's office last Wednesday afternoon and informed her boss she was leaving immediately.

They had argued all the way back to her mews cottage until finally Leo had snarled, 'You are carrying my child, albeit reluctantly. There is no way I am letting you out of my sight until the birth. I don't trust you.'

Knowing he actually believed she would try to get rid of the baby at the first available opportunity hurt her more than she was prepared to admit, and his closing comment, 'Think of Tom,' shut her up completely.

Dismissing her troubled memories, she glanced briefly at Leo and caught a glimpse of something oddly like compassion in his brown eyes, but it was angry resentment that made her answer his question spitefully. 'Hopefully in twelve months' time I will return to it, if not before.'

Long fingers caught her chin. 'Dismiss that idea from your mind; as my wife, you will stay by my side.' And she sensed it wasn't his side he had in mind. His face was much too close to her own, and with only a few inches between them she was vitally aware of his raw masculine appeal...

'Chauvinist,' she flung bitterly.

'I'm Greek; where my wife and child are concerned I freely admit to being chauvinistic. But you will not find me totally unreasonable. Mine is a large company; if at some later date you wish to work I will find something for you. Failing that, your boss has assured me he will quite happily give you some consultancy work, when you are able to do it.'

She was surprised and oddly flattered that Leo had actually discussed her resuming work with her boss, but she had no intention of telling him so.

'Am I supposed to thank you?' she gibed, her eyes icy-cold. 'Well, I'm not that generous. You've got a wife and hopefully in a few months a child. But that is all you're getting from me.'

'What are you trying to do, Jacy?' he raked in an undertone, his dark eyes narrowed angrily on her pale face. 'Turn our marriage into a war of the sexes before it has even had a chance? Well, it won't work.' And with the hand at her chin forcing her head back against the seat he leaned across her, and pressed his mouth to hers; his teeth bit down on her bottom lip and her mouth opened to give him entry.

She didn't want to respond; she caught her breath, trying to fight back the flood of feeling that threatened to engulf her, but Leo, with a throaty chuckle, merely increased the pressure, while his other hand slipped the jacket of her classic cream Calvin Klein suit open to caress her breast through the fine silk of the pale peach camisole.

'Stop it,' she whispered breathlessly.

Leo released her and leant back in his own seat. 'You're right,' he agreed with a triumphant smile. 'I can wait until tonight.' And, lowering his gaze to her breasts, the nipples outlined in stark relief against the fine fabric of her blouse, he added, 'But I'm not sure you can.'

Her face flamed and, dropping her head, she quickly fastened her jacket, then turned to look sightlessly out of the cabin window.

The Kozakis villa was enormous, set within what seemed to be miles of white walls. The limousine that had collected them from Corfu airport whisked them between massive wrought-iron gates, and up a long drive to the magnificent entrance portico. Dozens of cars were parked all along the drive. It looked as if half the island had turned out for the party.

'You look a little flustered. Don't worry; it will be fine,' Leo said softly, helping her out of the car. 'Trust me.'

'It's only the heat,' she defended swiftly, trying to disguise the mounting tension she felt. On the drive from the airport she had been vividly reminded of her first visit to Corfu. She had forgotten how beautiful the place was, the rocky hillsides covered with olive trees, and, to her surprise, the ground covered in a million different colourful spring flowers. Then there were the quaint villages, perched in the most unlikely places, and overall a hot, sweet fragrance peculiar to the island. She had not realised April would be so hot, and the light wool suit that had been perfectly acceptable for London was sticking to her back with perspiration.

Meekly allowing Leo to lead her up the large white steps to the front door, she ruefully acknowledged that sitting for the best part of an hour in the back seat of the car with Leo hadn't helped. She was disturbingly aware of his every move as, with complete disregard for her presence, he had busied himself on the journey with a pile of papers from his briefcase. Now, with his hand firmly curving her elbow, he ushered her inside.

The next few hours were sheer hell. The diamond-studded gold band Leo had placed on her finger earlier was marvelled over by what seemed to Jacy to be a thousand people. She gave up trying to remember the names after the first fifty or so. She had shed her jacket, but even the brief camisole with the shoe-string straps was beginning to cling to her.

Leo's father asked her to dance and teased her unmercifully. 'I knew you would marry my son. It was in your eyes the last time we danced, but you denied it.' And, patting her stomach, he laughed uproariously. 'But my Leo, he is all man; he always gets what he wants.'

'What was my father saying to you, Jacy?' Leo came up behind her and, placing his arms around her waist, he turned her around to face him.

She explained indignantly, and Leo laughed with the same masculine triumph as his father.

'It's not funny,' she fumed, the heat, the music and the crowd of laughing people making her head whirl.

'Poor Jacy, you look as bewildered as the first time I met you on the beach a couple of miles from here.' And she felt it, she realised solemnly. 'You have nothing to worry about; my family adore you.'

'I am surprised,' she drawled, nerves making her strike out at him sarcastically. 'I thought you Greeks only married virgins; I hardly fill the bill.'

His proud profile tautened. 'My father knows you were pure when we met. That is enough for him.'

'And does he know what you called me and how you dropped me like a ton of bricks?' she queried bitterly. Ten years ago this would have been the happiest day of her life. Now it was too late...

'I didn't deliberately set out to hurt you then. It was an unfortunate set of circumstances—a mistake, if you will. But now I have corrected the wrong I did you; what more could you want?'

The saddest part of all, Jacy realised, was that Leo was actually arrogant enough to believe what he said. 'Nothing, nothing at all,' she murmured, and he swept her into his arms and began to move to the haunting strains of the Greek love-song the band were playing.

With her slender hand held in his, the diamond band, its many facets sparkling brilliantly, caught her attention. To her surprise Leo had insisted on wearing a ring as well, a broad gold band. He moved her closer in his arms and she deliberately turned her head away, allowing her gaze to roam around the crowded room. Huge chandeliers hung from a high, ornately carved roof.

There were long, elegant windows from ceiling to floor, the cerise silken drapes blowing in the breeze. The people were all Greek, but not the stereotyped black-garbed women of the travel brochure. This was a different world, one of great wealth and designer dresses. The jewels of the women alone were worth a king's ransom.

'You're slipping away from me, Jacy. I don't like it.' Lost in her own thoughts, and oddly safe wrapped in Leo's arms, she had let her mind wander, but, coming back to the present with a shock, she was instantly aware of the tension in his magnificent body. 'It is time we left,' he said softly.

A great roar went up as Leo swept her up high in his arms and, with an ease belying his huge frame, lightly ran up a huge circular marble staircase. Jacy, her slender arms wrapped around his neck, in self-preservation, cried, 'What's going on?' All the guests were chasing them.

Then they were inside a huge bedroom. Leo had dropped her to her feet and speedily locked the door behind him just as what sounded like a hundred fists hammered on the door.

Catching her breath, she looked around in awe. In the centre of the room was a huge carved and canopied bed, a four-poster draped in pure white silk trimmed with gold in the classic Greek design. The white walls were hung with exquisite embroidered tapestries. The dressing-table and wardrobes were of the finest yew, and obviously antique. Intricate marquetry was inlaid on the finely polished surfaces. The floor was an impressive marble mosaic in blue and white, with huge rugs interrupting the design around the bed. She caught sight of herself in a long-mirrored door, and saw a stranger. Her golden hair was brushed free and tumbling around her shoulders in a mass of curls; the strap of her camisole was hanging off one shoulder. She looked a mess, she thought numbly, and she felt as nervous as any young virgin. How had it all happened? Where was her sophisticated, competent self?

'At last.' Two strong hands settled proprietorially on her slender shoulders, and spun her around.

She jumped and said the first thing that came into her head. 'Why the noise?' she asked breathlessly, and lifted her eyes to meet his. Her chest constricted in shock. He had stripped to a pair of black silk boxer shorts while she had been dumbly admiring the room, she realised, horrified... Instinctively she put up her hands to ward him off, but when her palms met the crisp hairs of his chest her fingers, with a will of their own, splayed with tactile delight in the seductive curls, the heat of his skin burning her fingertips.

'A tradition carried over from primitive days. Everyone at a wedding celebrates the moment of consummation. In ancient times they circled the bed.' His eyes gleamed with devilish humour. 'Now, thank God, voyeurism is out, and they stop at the door.'

She gasped, her eyes wide with horror at the picture his words portrayed. Then her gaze fastened on Leo, tall and bronzed, his muscular near-naked frame gleaming in the half-light, his head thrown back as he laughed out loud at her shocked expression. In that moment she fancied he looked like the devil himself, the white wings of hair at the side of his dark head resembling two horns. His eyes, black as jet, held hers with almost hypnotic fascination. His hands lifted to frame her face, raising it slightly, and she closed her eyes against the unmistakable passion burning in his.

'Open your eyes, Jacy,' he drawled throatily. 'There is nothing to be afraid of.'

'I'm tired.' And it was true, she realised, her long lashes fluttering briefly. She had been living on her nerves, in a state of permanent tension all day. No, not

just all day, but all week, and now she felt the last remnants of her strength slipping away.

'I know, Jacy.' His voice softened huskily. 'I'll put
you to bed.'

Her eyes flickered open. What exactly did he mean?

Gently he reached for the straps of her top and slid
them off her arms; next he unclasped her bra, and then
his fingers unzipped her skirt and let it fall to the floor
before edging beneath the fine lace panties.

'Don't. I can't. No.'

'You would say no on our wedding night? Shame on
you, Jacy,' he mocked arrogantly, totally ignoring her
plea, his fingers easing her panties down over her thighs.

She knew exactly what he meant; he would put her to
bed all right, but with him. It was there in the dull flush
on his high cheekbones, the sensuous curving of his
mouth, and from somewhere she gathered her defeated
spirit, pushed hard against his chest, and stepped back.

'No, I said,' she cried. She would not let the arrogant
devil walk over her again! She would not give in to her
baser instincts, although her heartbeat raced and his
blatant masculine virility tempted her to do just that.
'I'm pregnant already; what the hell more do you want?'
She almost laughed at the expression of dumb
amazement that flashed across his handsome face, before
his eyes filled with icy anger.

'I want my wife in my bed, and using our child as an
excuse will not work. I know you...' And with ridiculous ease he caught her by the shoulders and inexorably drew her towards him. His raking, sexual,
explicit gaze appraised her near-naked form and left her
in no doubt of his intentions.

She began to struggle, but her bare breasts came in
contact with his broad chest, and his dark head descended to fasten with unerring accuracy over hers. She
opened her mouth to say no, but the denial died on her

lips as he began a ravaging exploration of her mouth
that went on and on, until she felt the taste of her own
blood on her tongue.

Then mercifully the kiss ended and she took great
gulping gasps of air, but Leo, nowhere near as breathless
as she was, swung her in his arms and deposited her on
the bed. Quickly following her down, his splendidly
muscled frame trapped her beneath him.

The dim glow of the bedside light outlined his harsh
features. She gazed mutinously up at him, her golden
eyes spitting fire.

'Why fight it, Jacy?' His heavy weight anchored her
to the bed, and with one hand he caught her wrists and
placed them above her head. His black eyes burned
pitilessly down into hers. 'You want me, and I intend to
show you just how much.' His head bent, but he did not
kiss her, instead his lips touched her defiantly jutting
chin and trailed down her throat to settle for a moment
over the hollow that housed her madly beating pulse,
then slipped lower to the softness of her breast.

His free hand skimmed down to cup the soft mound
of her breast, rolling the tight nipple between finger and
thumb at the same instant as his mouth covered its
partner.

A spasm of agonising want shot through her trembling body; her back arched, offering her breasts to him,
begging for his seductive caresses. Her golden eyes glazed
and she gasped out loud, all thought of denial vanishing
as his hand slid lower over her still flat stomach to the
tangle of golden curls at her groin. One heavy muscled
leg nudged between hers, spreading her thighs, as his
fingers delved into the damp warmth of her female core.

He raised his head. 'You're my wife, and tonight we
consummate our union,' he stated in a husky growl; his
black eyes, simmering with heat, burnt into hers. 'In
fact you will beg me to.'

Jacy wanted to refuse him. With her arms pinned above her head, his long length half over her, she felt like some primitive sacrifice from a classic Greek legend. Except that the hard, pulsating force of his own arousal pressed rigidly against her hip told her Leo was as helplessly trapped, as much a slave to his passion as she was, and she was filled with a wild feminine satisfaction. Then his long fingers found the nub of her sexuality, and when he bent lower over her her lips parted provocatively. 'Make me,' she teased with an adult sensuality that she had never realised she possessed.

He reared up over her, setting her hands free to roam over the hard wall of his chest and lower to his narrow waist and the flat muscled stomach. He dragged her hands away and threw off his shorts. 'I never refuse a challenge,' he rasped, his hard-boned face taut with savage desire.

With one hand he spread her golden hair out over the white satin pillow. 'When I saw you at that party, I knew, I knew you would be mine again,' he groaned as his mouth covered hers in a long, drugging, passionate kiss, while all the time his other hand worked an erotic, sensuous magic on her tender flesh.

The blood raced through her veins like quicksilver, her breath strangled gasps between a moan or a whimper of ecstasy. The musky male scent of him filled her nostrils. She wanted him! Her small hand stroked down his stomach to his belly, desperate to touch him, but he caught her hand in his and placed it at her side.

'Not yet, Jacy! Tell me what you want.' His teeth bit on her tight, aching nipple, first one and then the other, and then in a soothing gesture he repeated the action with his tongue. 'What do you like?' he grated. 'Is it this?' And his mouth suckled her breast. 'Or perhaps this?' His fingers teased the hot, fluid centre of her.

Jacy cried out her need, her hand clawing around his waist and lower over his firm buttocks, urging him towards the ultimate act of possession. 'Yes, yes, please...' she begged, her body arched like a bow string, and with a muffled roar of masculine triumph Leo reared up and, sweeping her legs wide, lifted her up from the bed to accept his awesome male power. His mouth met hers in a frenzied all-consuming kiss as their two bodies locked into a rhythm uniquely their own.

Jacy woke up completely disorientated; her head felt fuzzy, and a great weight seemed to have settled over her waist. Her stomach churned and she wriggled, her bottom coming into contact with hard naked flesh. She heard a grunt and the events of last night came flooding back in sharp etched detail.

She stifled her own moan, not wanting to wake the sleeping Leo, and carefully moved towards the edge of the bed. Last night had been an education in the pleasures of the flesh; she would never forget it as long as she lived. How had she ever fooled herself into believing she could resist Leo? The question tormented her. He had taught her in the long hours of the night more about her own sexuality, her own wanton desires, until she had burnt in the fiery furnace of her own voracious appetite, avidly taking all he had to give and then greedily reciprocating in kind, until finally she had fallen asleep in his arms, satiated to the point of exhaustion.

She turned her head to look at him. His eyes were closed in sleep, his long, dark lashes curled over his hard cheekbones, his hair short, damp, ruffled curls on his broad brow. He looked younger and somehow defenceless. It was odd: they had been lovers years ago and again weeks ago, she was carrying his child, and yet this was the first time she had ever actually slept the night with him.

Her heart squeezed in her breast. 'My husband...' It was the first time she had said the word, and she lifted her hand to touch his face tenderly, then dropped it again. She swallowed hard as she thought about all the other women he must have spent the night with over the years. Simply because he had married her, it didn't make their relationship any different. A deep sadness welled up inside her, and with it the recognition she had tried to deny for years. She loved this man...always had...and probably always would... Fool that she was...

Her stomach churned, reminding her of her other foolishness, and, scrambling off the edge of the bed, she prepared to dash to the bathroom, but a large hand caught her wrist and forcefully dragged her back.

'No. Let go...' she cried, as she fell backwards on to the bed.

'No way. No woman cuts and runs on me,' Leo grunted angrily. 'Certainly not my wife.'

'You don't understand,' she tried to explain, her feet searching for and finding the floor, and with an almighty tug she was free and running for the bathroom, a hand over her mouth.

'Oh, God forgive me!' Leo leapt stark naked out of bed and caught her as she shot into the bathroom. With a strong arm protectively around her shoulder, his other around her stomach, he carefully held her while she was violently sick in the toilet bowl.

Jacy was utterly mortified, but too weak to object, as an oddly gentle Leo wrapped a large white fluffy towel around her naked body like a cocoon and sat her down on the bathroom stool. She watched fascinated as, totally unconscious of his own magnificent nudity, he put the plug in the large circular bath and turned on the taps. Then, rinsing a face cloth at the vanity basin, he came over and knelt in front of her. Taking her chin in his hand, he tenderly bathed her ashen face, talking all the time.

'I'm sorry, Jacy, truly I am. I forgot the baby; I never realised. I thought you were running... Hell, I don't know what I thought. I was just being my usual arrogant self and determined to keep you in my bed, until I said different.'

'It's all right,' she murmured, finally lifting her eyes to his face, and she was stunned to see the deep remorse in his dark brown eyes.

'Is it always like this?'

'Most mornings.'

'And I did this to you. You must hate me.' Straightening to his full height, he ran a tired hand through his rumpled hair. 'At this minute I don't much like myself,' he muttered.

For the next half-hour Jacy was treated to so much tender, loving care that she could hardly believe it. Leo insisted on helping her into the bath; he washed her hair with as much care as a mother would give a baby. He left her for a few minutes and she heard him giving staccato orders on the telephone. Then he was back and lifting her from the bath and, carefully wrapping her in another huge bath towel, he gently patted her dry, before carrying her back into the bedroom and tucking her tenderly back into the bed.

'Stay there and don't move.' He straightened, an impatient grimace twisting his hard mouth. 'Where the hell is the maid? I've already ordered the...tea and dry toast, isn't it...? I seem to remember the twins telling me.' He walked towards the door. 'I thought they exaggerated your sickness; now I know different. I'll see what the delay is.'

'Leo...' She said his name huskily.

'Yes?' He hesitated, a hand on the door.

Jacy started to smile, her honey-coloured eyes tracing over his magnificent body. 'Haven't you forgotten something?'

'What? Tell me.' His brown eyes, worried and flustered, searched her lovely face. 'Anything you want you can have.'

'Well, far be it from me to give you orders, Leo, but I think as your wife I would prefer you not to walk out of the door stark naked. I wouldn't want you frightening the staff.' And she burst out laughing as probably for the first time in his life the great Leo Kozakis blushed scarlet. Her laughter turned to a roar as she realised the blush wasn't confined to his face but suffused his whole body.

'Oh, hell.' He dashed across the room and into the bathroom, to reappear a second later in a short navy towelling robe. 'You could have mentioned it sooner, Jacy,' he opined, crossing to the bedside.

'What, and deprive myself of a sight for sore eyes? No way.' She chuckled and Leo's masculine laughter rang out to mingle with hers.

He reached over the bed, and pressed a light kiss to her forehead, still grinning. 'Now who's the voyeur? Behave yourself, woman, I'll be back.' And he sauntered out of the room.

Resting her head back against the pillow, Jacy felt better than she had in weeks. She loved Leo and she had finally admitted it to herself, but the question was what was she going to do about it? Using her analytical skills, she tackled the problem as she would a case.

On the positive side she listed: A, she was married to the man. B, he was a magnificent lover. C, he had shown her a tender, caring side to his nature. D, she knew he liked children—she had seen him with the twins—and so would love his own.

On the negative side: A, he did not love her. B, he was a womaniser and C, not above using blackmail to get his own way.

She sighed; the positive outweighed the negative, but only just. Jacy thought of Liz and Tom, and the surprise party. It was unbelievable that what had started as a stupid bet could make such a change in her life. She had gone out with Leo for a bet, and ended up married to him, which if she was honest was what she had probably subconsciously always wanted. So why not take another chance and continue her gamble? she asked herself. Leo might not love her, but he wanted her and she certainly wanted him. Time and propinquity, plus a child, and who knew? The solution was simple. This time she would gamble on passion and pray that she won Leo's love...

CHAPTER TEN

LEO returned almost immediately carrying a loaded tray bearing a china teapot, a delicate matching cup and saucer and plate, a full toast-rack and a variety of small pots of jam. Pride of place in the centre was a silver bud vase with one exquisite golden rose in it. She glanced up and caught the glint of humour in his dark eyes as he placed it carefully in front of her.

'Thank you.' She smiled, touched by his gesture, then cheekily added, 'If you used to serve the guests in the hotel wearing only a robe I bet all the women ordered breakfast in bed.'

Leo laughed. 'No, you lose the bet again. I reserve this service strictly for my wife.' Bending over her, he kissed the tip of her nose. 'But thank you for the compliment. I think it's the first nice thing you've said to me in weeks.'

He was right. 'I'll have to practise, then,' she murmured, her eyes lingering on his face, the dark early morning stubble giving him a piratical air.

'You don't need to practise, Jacy, you're perfect just as you are,' he responded throatily. 'Well, apart from your penchant for gambling,' he mocked, adding, 'Now eat your breakfast while I take a shower; you're much too tempting, and you've been sick.' Jacy chuckled when she heard him mutter worriedly under his breath, 'I must practise self-control,' as he headed for the bathroom.

It had been a marvellous honeymoon, Jacy thought tiredly as she stepped into the Jaguar at London airport.

They had stayed at Leo's uncle Nick's private island near Crete, where they had lived for one day at a time, swimming, laughing and making love.

She glanced lovingly at Leo sitting next to her, then yawned widely and closed her eyes. She had no idea how beautiful she looked. The sun had streaked her hair almost white in places, her creamy skin had developed a soft golden tan, and the man beside her glanced with unrestrained adoration at her sleeping form.

'Wake up, sleepyhead.'

She opened her eyes and stretched. They were parked outside the company apartment in Eaton Square. 'Back to the grind.' She smiled at Leo.

'Unfortunately that is true. I do have a lot of work to catch up on, and your monthly medical check is due.'

She had deliberately put it out of her mind in the euphoria of the past few weeks. Leo's reminder of the real reason for their marriage damped her spirit somewhat. But, walking into the apartment with Leo's hand curved around her elbow, and accepting the effusive congratulations of Mr and Mrs Belt, who looked after the place, before they left for the night, Jacy couldn't resist smugly congratulating herself. Her gamble appeared to be working. A more attentive husband didn't exist, she was sure, and, as for their sex life, it was just about perfect, day or night. She would feel Leo's eyes on her in a certain way and within minutes they were making love.

The only restraint she put on herself was that of silence; in the throes of passion sometimes she had to bite her tongue to prevent herself crying out her love. Leo, on the other hand, was a very verbal lover, but as he spoke in Greek she had no idea what he said. Once she had asked him to translate. He had joked, saying, 'You once told me not to speak dirty; you don't want to know.'

'Would you like a warm drink before we go to bed?' asked Leo now, his eyes narrowing faintly as they took in her sleepy features.

They had been watching the news on the television, and Jacy had found herself nodding off once or twice, lulled by the large beautifully cooked meal she had eaten courtesy of the Belts.

She lifted lazy eyes. 'No, I'm all right,' she refused, watching him, with feminine appreciation, walk to the drinks cabinet and pour himself a small whisky. He was lithe and compellingly masculine in dark trousers and a fine-knit shirt; suddenly she couldn't get to bed fast enough...

'You're sure?' He turned back to her, glass in hand, concern showing clearly in his dark, probing scrutiny. 'It's been a long day for you.'

His attentiveness warmed her heart, and various other places of her anatomy, she thought sexily. 'Yes,' she insisted huskily. 'I think I'll get an early night. I want to go home tomorrow. I forgot to ask my neighbour to water my plants. They're probably all dead by now.' She grimaced and, standing up, she threaded her hand through the wild tumble of her hair in an unconsciously provocative gesture.

'This is your home.' Leo slammed the glass he was holding down on the table, his dark eyes raking over her in glittering fury, his illusion of concern abruptly cast aside. 'And don't you forget it,' he commanded crushingly.

Suddenly the ease of the past three weeks vanished, and tension sizzled in the air.

Shock kept her immobile, that and a growing feeling of reciprocal anger at his high-handedness. She might be gambling on winning his love, but did that mean she had to turn herself into a doormat for the man? No way, she thought mutinously, and responded in kind. 'You don't give me orders!' She had not meant to shout, but she found some satisfaction in seeing the surprise in his autocratic features. 'And as for this being a home——' she waved a disparaging hand around the immaculate room '—it is a company apartment you admit yourself you rarely use. It makes much more sense to live in my house.' She hadn't actually thought about it until now, but suddenly the spirit that had made her a success in business had reasserted itself, the sensual daze she had been in for weeks was beginning to clear.

'This is where we will stay until I decide otherwise,' he declared icily, and stalked towards the door.

'But why? I have a perfectly good house, and you will be away a lot. I have neighbours...' She trailed off, shaken by the cool detachment in his dark gaze as he turned, his hand on the door, and watched her stumble through her reasoning.

'You are my wife; you will do as I say,' he continued ruthlessly. 'Now I suggest you go to bed; you look tired. As for your house, I will make arrangements tomorrow for the sale of the property.'

Jacy bit her lip, anger giving way to hurt at his dismissive tone. Had the past few weeks meant nothing to him? She had fondly imagined they were growing closer, but now she was no longer so sure. 'That is unnecessary, Leo.' Crossing to him, she laid her hand on his arm. 'Surely you can see the sense of my proposal? It will be much better for me and my child,' she pressed.

'*Our* child. And I decide what is necessary. I don't wish to hear any more about it.' The dark-lashed black eyes clashed with hers, and his hand covered hers on his arm. 'Go to bed; I have work to do in the study. I will join you later.'

She said nothing. She was infuriated by his arrogant assumption that she would do exactly as he said, and afraid as the warmth of his hand on hers sent the all too familiar shivers of pleasure down her spine.

He carelessly brushed his other hand through her long hair, adding, 'I won't be long,' and her brief defiance vanished as her pulse raced hectically, anticipation curling in her stomach. He only had to touch her and she melted.

'Leo, about the house——' she began, lifting her free hand and running her fingers teasingly down his throat to his chest.

'Enough, woman.' His icy control broke, and he kissed her with hard hunger before thrusting her away. 'Don't try it,' he snarled.

'Try what?' she muttered shakily, still reeling from the unexpected force of his kiss.

'I will not be manipulated by sex, not even by you.' Swinging on his heel, he left, the door rocking on its hinges behind him.

Later, lying in the unfamiliar bed in a room decorated efficiently in shades of brown and blue, waiting for Leo to join her, Jacy silently seethed. She loved him, and yet he dared to accuse her of using sex to manipulate him. If anything, the reverse was true. It was Leo who managed to get his own way every time simply because she could not say no to him.

How long she could continue with the gamble that her love would be returned she did not know, but she had a sinking feeling that this was one bet she was not going to win. She knew herself well enough to realise she was not cut out to play the little *hausfrau*. Eventually Leo, with his abrupt mood swings, and his arrogant assumption that she would obey his every whim, would try her temper too far.

A humourless smile curved her lips. She had always known Leo was ruthless, but because of her love for him and their unborn child she bit her tongue and held her

temper. But her patience wasn't finite—anything but . . .
Eventually she fell into an uneasy sleep alone. But in
the morning she awoke to find Leo standing by the side
of the bed, staring down at her, a cup of tea in his hand.

He was wearing an immaculate charcoal-grey business
suit. His handsome face, tanned even deeper by their
holiday in the sun, was somehow remote. But to Jacy
he looked every inch the perfect male animal, and her
heart expanded with love. Still drowsy, she reached a
hand out sleepily. 'Come to bed.'

'Sorry—work.' Lowering his dark head, he kissed her
lightly on the cheek, adding perfectly calmly, as though
he were addressing a board meeting, 'Don't go out
without telling me where you're going. Here is my
number. Ring if you want anything.' And, pressing a
piece of paper in her hand, he left.

It was all very well for Leo; he had his work to keep
him occupied, Jacy thought a few days later, but for her
it was a vast adjustment from being a busy career girl
to lying around in an apartment all day. Leo had taken
her out twice, once to the doctor for her medical check,
and once on a very expensive shopping spree in
Kensington, culminating in lunch in a small Italian bistro
next to the Kozakis office block. He had bundled her
into a taxi and sent her home, but he rarely managed to
get home himself before eight, and the apartment was
beginning to feel like a prison.

On impulse she rang Liz and after an exchange of
greetings she made a date to meet her the same day for
afternoon tea at Harrods. Feeling much better, she
bathed, washed her hair, and really went to town on her
make-up. Even so, she was ready before noon.

She wandered around the empty apartment and,
catching sight of herself in the large mirror in the hall,
thought, Not bad, Jacy! Her skin was still tanned a nice
golden brown from her honeymoon and her sun-streaked

hair was brushed back from her face and tied with a silk scarf to fall in a curling ponytail down her back. She was wearing one of the new outfits Leo had chosen and paid for, a pale blue and yellow patterned silk blouson jacket with a plain blue sleeveless scooped-neck blouse and matching patterned culottes. It was a lovely summer May day and she wore no stockings, just low-heeled strappy blue sandals. Her only jewellery was the pendant Leo had given her; she had retrieved it from the bathroom floor weeks ago and remembering the angry scene that had followed at the time, she had an urge to see Leo. Her insecurities were showing, she knew, but what the hell! He was her husband. She knew where his office was. Why not?

The decision made, she walked jauntily out of the apartment, and hailed a cab. She would surprise him; they could eat at the little bistro again and then she would go on and meet Liz for tea. After all, she was feeding two; she could afford to make a pig of herself for once.

An hour later, as she turned the key in the lock of her own house, food was the furthest thing from her mind. Pale and shaking, she staggered to the bedroom and fell down on the bed, the tears rolling helplessly down her cheeks.

She cried and cried, great racking sobs that shook her whole body. She bent her knees up to her chest and wrapped her arms around them. Curved into a near foetal position, she wept until there were no more tears. Her throat dry and parched, her head aching, she finally turned over on to her back and lay staring sightlessly at the ceiling.

Jacy couldn't believe the pain; it seared her flesh like a million lash strokes. In her mind's eye she saw once again the entrance to Kozakis House, the impressive office block in the centre of the city. The glass doors parted automatically and out on to the pavement stepped a couple. The man, tall and dark, his handsome face wreathed in smiles, turned his head to the blonde woman, and, curving an arm around her shoulders, kissed her cheek. Leo and Thelma...

Like a spectre at a feast Jacy saw herself fall back against the wall of the building and watch them stroll along the street and turn into the entrance of a familiar restaurant.

Betrayal... Deception... Emotive words, but who was at fault? she asked herself brutally. Her husband of a few weeks had betrayed her with another woman, but she could not accuse him of deception. He had made no promise to love her. He had married her for the child she was carrying. He had quite openly blackmailed her into the marriage; he had not tried to deceive her with soft words or avowals of undying love.

No, she had done that herself. Deliberately she had deceived herself, by imagining that their marriage was anything other than a convenient deal between two people responsible for a child. She had betrayed herself, the strong, mature Jacy with a clear knowledge of her own self-worth, which she had deliberately suppressed in a futile gamble to win the love of a man who wasn't worthy of her love.

Sitting up, she swung her feet to the floor and, sweeping her tangled mass of hair from her face, she cupped her head in her hands. How could she have been such a complete and utter idiot? Leo was a highly sexed virile man. Last night he had not touched her, now she knew why: he had a date for today... He could afford to go without for a few hours. It was that basic, that simple...

Getting to her feet, she looked around the familiar room. A photograph of her father in a brass frame had pride of place on the bedside table. She stared at it for a moment, remembering the first time Leo had betrayed

her, and how she had found comfort and strength from
her father. He might have been wrong about the
palimony case, but he had been right in his reading of
Leo's character; of that she had no doubt. When she
was eighteen he had warned her. God! The cry was from
her very soul; how she wished she had heeded the
warning.

But it wasn't too late, she vowed silently. Her parents
had brought her up to be strong and independent. Was
she going to disgrace their memory by wallowing in despair and self-pity? No way! She ran a hand over the
soft swell of her stomach; this was her baby, their grand-
child. For the baby's sake she would survive the heart-
break, and the first thing she needed to do was eat. The
empty feeling in her stomach was not just despair but a
genuine need for sustenance.

She made her way downstairs and stopped in her
living-room, and looked with dismay at the row of large
packing-cases stacked against one wall. Another sign of
her spineless behaviour where Leo was concerned. Rather
than argue with him again, she had meekly handed him
a key for the house and allowed him to arrange the sale.

With his usual ruthless efficiency he had obviously
already contacted the removal firm to have her personal
things packed. A slow-burning anger built up inside her
and erupted in fury.

'The bastard. The low-down, arrogant, over-sexed
bastard,' she swore out loud. 'Well, this time the swine
is not going to have his way.'

Her violent outburst acted like a catharsis. She could
see things clearly at last. She had come to her senses just
in time. She still had her home, and here she was staying.
Even if she had to fight Leo Kozakis in every court
in the land, she would keep her child and
her independence ...

The decision made, she took a few deep, calming breaths, and an icy calm pervaded her being. Blank-faced, she crossed to the mantelpiece and picked up one of a group of tiny little figures, a dragon's head, the first *netsuke* she had acquired, as a present from her father. She turned the smooth ivory figure over in the palm of her hand. Who would believe the desire for such a tiny object could bring so much pain? Perhaps it was fitting, she thought with irony, replacing the dragon on the mantel. The ivory trade was a disgusting business; maybe it was only right the recipients of the dirty business should feel some pain. And she knew in that moment that she would never buy another *netsuke* ...

The sound of fists thundering on her front door stilled her hand for a second before she continued methodically raising the fork to her mouth and eating the dish of baked beans set in front of her on the kitchen table. It was all she had been able to find in the near-empty cupboards. But the sound of Leo's angry voice shouting to her to open the door did get through to her.

'Jacy, are you there? Are you all right?'

She stopped and replaced the fork in the dish, her hand shaking. He actually sounded as if he cared. What a liar! 'Get lost,' she screamed back, not actually expecting him to hear her, but it made her feel better ...

The pounding on the door intensified. 'Open this door, Jacy. What the hell are you playing at? Liz was worried sick when you didn't turn up.'

Tea! She'd forgotten all about it. She might have guessed Liz would call Leo, and of course he had to play the caring husband and come looking for her. What a joke! She stood up and, rinsing her plate under the tap in the sink, walked slowly through to the hall. She was going to bed, and he could hammer till doomsday for all she cared.

'Jacy, if you don't open this door I will break it down.'

Jacy hesitated, her foot on the first stair, and thought about it for a second. He would do it, she didn't doubt. Turning around, she straightened her shoulders, and, head high, she marched to the door. If it was a confrontation Leo wanted, that was what he would get. Hadn't she spent the last hour convincing herself she was worth more than what Leo was offering, and determining to do something about it? Well, now was the time to start. No longer was she a slave to his sexual expertise; she could learn to live without him, and the sooner she began, the better.

She flung open the door and Leo was captured with a fist up above his head. 'Lost your key, Leo?' She had given him it only yesterday. 'But then I shouldn't be surprised; after all, you must have an awful lot to juggle with,' she opined with thinly veiled contempt. He must have the keys to more women's apartments than a locksmith!

'What the hell are you talking about?' he said in a hard voice, lowering his hand to his side. 'And why did you stand Liz up? She waited two hours for you. She was worried about you and called me.'

She stared at him. He had changed from the suit he had left the apartment in that morning into a soft denim shirt and jeans. For a second she wondered if it had been for Thelma's benefit, and frowned, before responding. 'Sorry you've been troubled, but, as you can see, I am perfectly OK.' The words were clipped and she had to stifle the desire, even now when he had hurt her beyond belief, to reach out and touch him. The first three buttons of his shirt were open, his hair was rumpled, and he needed a shave, but even so he exuded a raw animal magnetism that it took all her strength to ignore.

His rapier-like glance raked her from head to toe as though he had never seen her before. 'And of course it

never once occurred to you to inform me where you were
going,' he drawled derisively.

'No, why should I? You're not my keeper.' With a
defiant toss of her head she turned on her heel, and
would have slammed the door in his face, but she was
too slow...

Leo grabbed her around the waist, swung her high in
the air, and carried her across the hall and into the living-
room. She struggled furiously, her arms flailing wildly,
but with her back to his chest she had nothing to strike
out at. He spun her around to face him, and for an instant desire flared between them, but brutally she crushed
it.

'Let me go,' she said curtly.

Leo's mouth curled. 'Over my dead body.' His grip
tightened on her upper arms, his dark eyes narrowed
assessingly on her pale face. 'Now what happened? You
are not OK. You've been crying; your eyes are red. What
the hell are you playing at, Jacy? I demand an
explanation.'

He demanded! And of course what the great Leo
Kozakis wanted he got, she thought bitterly. Well, not
this time. And, schooling her features into what she
hoped was cool disdain, she responded by acting for all
she was worth.

'It is quite simple, Leo. I have decided to live here in
my own house. I'm sorry I forgot about Liz, but I will
call her and apologise. As for the red-rimmed eyes, I
was looking at a photograph of my father; it's the anni-
versary of his death this week,' she improvised quickly.
His touch was getting to her again, and, clenching her
hands at her sides, she evaded his eyes as she continued,
'Maudlin, I know, but...' She tried to shrug, and
swallowed hard. The silence seemed to stretch intermi-
nably between them.

Finally Jacy had to look up at him, and choked back a gasp at the expression on his hard face. She had expected him to lose his temper, rant and rave. Instead his dark brown eyes were curiously empty, but in the emptiness she glimpsed an edge of...was it torment?

He was staring at her and when he finally broke the tense silence even his voice sounded different, defeated. 'All right, Jacy, we will live here for now.' Letting go of her arms, he turned and lowered his long frame on to the sofa.

Her mouth fell open in shock. She shook her head to try and clear it, her long hair flying around her face. What did he mean, *we* will live here?

'Do you think I could have a coffee? I left the apartment in rather a hurry.' He shot her a wry glance. 'Obviously I need not have worried about you; you appear to have everything under control.'

Jacy took a step forward to stand in front of him. 'No. No...' she repeated desperately. This wasn't supposed to happen. Leo had to go.

'No coffee.' One black brow arched sardonically. 'And I have to give up a luxury apartment for this? Tut tut.' He shook his head mockingly, and Jacy saw red.

He wasn't defeated. He wasn't tormented. He was his usual bloody-minded arrogant self, and laughing at her to boot. In a split second something seemed to snap in Jacy. Tears of rage half blinded her, and she jumped on him like a wildcat. Her hands curled into fists, she hit out at his cold face. She was bitterly angry, thwarted by his bland acceptance of her story, and filled with burning jealousy and resentment.

Leo's hands gripped her wrists, and with insulting ease he swung her on to the sofa and pinned her beneath him.

'Get off me,' she screamed. 'You bastard.' She bucked wildly beneath him. 'You lecherous old goat, pig...' She screamed at him every vile name she could think of and then some, before he bent his black head and shut her mouth with his. His mouth burnt hers, his hard body pressing her into the sofa as the kiss grew deeper, more urgent, until with a despairing moan she felt herself succumb, liquid fire flowing through her veins with an urgency that was terrifying. Her head spun and she reached up to him, her hands sliding around his neck.

Leo ended the kiss, lifting his head. His gaze burnt on her swollen mouth for a second, then he slowly raised his black eyes to hers. 'Name-calling won't help you,' he said thickly, an edge of steel in his tone. 'I want the truth. You were running, and I want to know why.'

He wanted the truth, the one thing she could not give him; she had too much pride. She could not speak.

Leo moved to one side, his big body urging hers against the back of the sofa. He flung a heavy thigh over her slender legs, keeping her prisoner, but relieving her of his weight. 'Not the mute treatment again, Jacy; it won't work. I know I'm no expert with women—you only have to look at my track record to realise that—but——'

'You're joking, of course,' she prompted snidely, but Leo did not take her up on her sarcasm.

'No. But I honestly thought since you and I married I had finally got it right. You accepted me as your husband although I know I was less than honourable in blackmailing you into marriage. I thought we were making a go of it. But tonight when I returned to the apartment and discovered you'd gone I couldn't believe it. I almost went crazy when Liz rang. I have just spent the worst few hours of my life, imagining you hurt or worse. I rang all the hospitals before I thought of here.'

She wanted to believe his concern was genuine, but she didn't dare. She stared at him in silence, and felt the rapid beat of her heart quicken. Leo slid his hand to her neck, and he watched her intently as he felt the tell-tale beat of her pulse in her throat.

'You want me.' His thigh moved restlessly over her long legs, his arm around the end of the sofa slipped beneath her head, and he urged her face up to his. His lips brushed hers. 'Sex has never been a problem with us, so tell me what's wrong, Jacy.' For an agonising moment she was tempted to pour her heart out, but fear of further humiliation stopped her.

'Haven't you realised yet? I would do anything in the world for you,' he murmured against her lips. 'But I need to know what you want, what you need.' And all the time his hand strayed lower to stroke lightly over her breast.

His hands, his voice, the pressure of his hard body were all seducing her. She tilted her head back and her eyes met his, and she was mesmerised by what she saw there. His ruggedly attractive face was taut with some unbearable pain and his black eyes glittered as if with fever.

'I love you, Jacy,' he said in a raw voice. 'You're the best thing that's ever happened to me, and I don't want to lose you.'

Jacy was too choked to speak. She began to tremble violently, and his arm tightened about her, drawing her more firmly against his muscular body.

'For God's sake, Jacy, say something. I'm baring my soul here, and you——'

'Is it true?' she said shakily. 'You love me?'

Leo stared at her fixedly, his body rigid. 'God, you know I do. I've told you a hundred times every time we've made love. I married you. How can you doubt it?'

She wanted to believe him, more than life, but... 'I thought it was only because of the baby.'

He stared at her for a moment in shocked disbelief, and then he laughed, a harsh, mocking sound devoid of all amusement. 'Your opinion of me is so low, you might as well know it all. I got you pregnant deliberately; at least I hoped I had.'

'What?' She gasped. Though, thinking back, it was strange that Leo, who had made such a point of being protected the first time they had ever loved, should ignore the same precautions when they were both much older and wiser... 'You did it deliberately?' The enormity of his admission stunned her.

'Yes. I know—despicable of me. But from the first time I saw you again at Liz's I determined to have you for myself. I thought I had succeeded that night in my apartment when we cleared up the mistakes about the past and would have made love but for the telephone call. When I was in America I lived every day for the sound of your voice, and when I returned to London I couldn't wait to see you, and I thought you felt the same.'

'I did,' she said without thinking.

'But you went out with me for a bet,' Leo reminded her, drawing away to look intently down at her. 'I knew all along, but it didn't stop me wanting you. When I made love to you that night it was stupid male ego that made me throw the knowledge of the bet in your face. I knew I had to return to Corfu and I thought it would do you no harm to lose the bet, and I'd be back in a week and we'd take up where we left off. Unfortunately I got held up in Corfu. But I can't regret that night; because of it you married me.'

'And a little blackmail,' Jacy teased. Suddenly her heart felt lighter and she snuggled into his hard warmth. She felt his lips against her hair, and then they dropped lower to brush against her ear, and a shiver of pleasure raced down her spine.

'Blackmail aside——' he tilted her chin with one finger
and gave her a crooked smile '—I thought I had won.
In and out of bed, you're everything and more than I
ever dreamed of.' His dark eyes, the pupils dilating to
almost black, seared hers as he reached up and ran his
fingers through the silken mass of her hair, sweeping it
back from her brow. 'I'm not asking for your love,
Jacy—I know I don't deserve it—but I want you to stay
with me.' He crushed her against him and groaned into
her fragrant hair. 'I went through the torment of the
damned tonight when you disappeared and I don't think
I could stand it a second time.'

Jacy tried to speak, but couldn't for the emotion that
blocked her throat. She swallowed hard, and Leo eased
her back against the cushion. She searched his face for
the truth. The rigidity of his features was betrayed by a
muscle jerking wildly under the dark skin. Her golden
eyes clashed with his and for a second she saw his heart
in his eyes, the mask of cool arrogance stripped away
to reveal the vulnerable man beneath.

She believed him. 'Leo...' she breathed, but he did
not seem to hear, too intent on his confession.

'So if living here means so much to you, we will.
Because there is no way on God's earth I will let you
go.' His dark head lowered, his hand once more dipping
to cup her breast. She felt the curling of desire and closed
her eyes, lifting eager lips to his. He loved her. He would
never let her go. They would live here... Then the reason
she was here in the first place hit her, and with an
almighty shove she dislodged him from the sofa.

'My God,' she exclaimed, her voice cracking with fury,
unconcerned that Leo was lying flat on his back on the
floor. 'I almost fell for it... And to think you accused
me of sexual manipulation. Love? You don't know the
meaning of the word. I saw you today with your girl-
friend Thelma. What do you take me for—a complete

idiot?' She was shouting, but didn't care. She never saw
the look of incredulity on Leo's face as she swung her
feet to the floor and sat up.

'Thelma? That's what this is all about.' And, tossing
his head back, he roared with laughter.

Flushed, dishevelled and furious, Jacy jumped to her
feet. His laughter was the last straw, and she aimed a
hefty kick at his most vulnerable part, but before she
could connect Leo had caught her ankle and brought
her tumbling down on top of him. His arms closed
around her in a vice-like grip and her face was buried
on his chest. The curling body hair through the open
neck of his shirt tickled her nose and she tried to raise
her head. She got one arm free and planted it on his
shoulder to push herself up, but his long legs twined with
hers and she was caught between his thighs.

'You fight dirty, Jacy.' His triumphant smile beamed
up at her. 'We are a lot alike, you and I.' And, tangling
his hand in her long hair, he forced her head down to
meet his mouth.

Jacy tried to fight it, but it was no use. Sprawled on
top of him, their bodies provocatively entwined, she felt
her last shred of anger vanish in the wonder of his kiss...

'You were jealous, you little she-cat,' he murmured
against her lips. 'You've no idea how great that makes
me feel.' He pulled her head back and his darkening eyes
searched her flushed face. Recognising her uncertainty,
he continued, 'You had no need, my love. I don't know
what you saw.'

'You and Thelma walking out of the office; you kissed
her.' She wanted there to be an explanation, but she had
been hurt too much by this man already.

'Jacy, I have never, ever even thought of being un-
faithful to you, not from the first moment I saw you
again at Liz's.'

'But I saw you...' It was a cry from the heart.

'You saw me with an arm around the shoulder of a woman who I had just congratulated on doing some excellent work for me, hence the kiss on the cheek—and that was all it was.'

'What work?' she asked suspiciously.

Leo chuckled, his dark eyes lit with laughter. 'I suppose I will have to tell you, but it blows my surprise. You know when we collected the boys from Sunday school that day... well, did you notice the old vicarage with the scaffolding around it?' he asked, but, without waiting for her reply, continued, 'Anyway, it's a large stone-built house set in a small wood a hundred yards down the road.'

'Yes, but what's——?'

'Shut up and listen.' But the quirk of his lips belied his serious tone. 'When I was in America I arranged with Tom to buy the vicarage, and Tom put me in touch with a local builder and hired Thelma, as the best interior designer, to get a woman's opinion on what you would like.'

She stared at Leo dumbly, unable to speak. His brown eyes watched her with a compelling intensity, as if willing her to believe him. 'You bought a house for us, near Tom and Liz? When you were in America, before you even knew...' She spoke her thoughts out loud. 'You were that sure...'

'I've always known from the day I met an eighteen-year-old on the beach at Paleokastritsa, only it has taken me until just recently to finally admit it. I thought you knew how I felt on our first date, when I introduced you to my family.'

'Your father asked me if I was going to marry you...' she remembered.

'I know; I had already told him of my intentions. I had lost you once and I swore I would not let you slip through my fingers again. I tried to tell you how I felt when I called you from America. I hinted I wanted a family.' His strong fingers picked up the pendant that hung at her neck. 'I bought you this as a symbol. You had my heart. But I am ashamed to say I still did not quite trust you; this house, the bet, rankled with me. I have never been so relieved as when you told me your father left you the house, but the damage between us was already done when you let slip that piece of information,' he chided gently, and she had the grace to blush.

'I should have put you right straight away, but you were so contemptuous that I got angry...'

'Anyway, when we made love here in this house I still hadn't the courage to openly declare my love; instead I hid my feelings behind taunting you with the bet and sarcastic comments about your lifestyle, but I seem to recall I let slip that, with every woman I'd tried to bed in the last ten years, the face on the pillow had always been yours. Why did you think I always dated blondes? Before I met you my preference was for brunettes.'

'Really? I'm flattered, I think...'

His dark eyes fused with hers. 'If I had thought for one second I would be away from you another three weeks I would never have behaved with such conceited arrogance. Please, Jacy, say you forgive me.'

'There is nothing to forgive.' She sighed and licked the skin showing through the open neck of his shirt.

'You're very generous,' he rasped huskily, his arms tightening around her. He buried his head in her sweet-smelling hair.

Jacy realised she believed him, and, if he was telling the truth about loving her, then surely it followed that he was also telling the truth about Thelma. Suddenly her heart felt lighter. Her golden eyes shone with love as she lifted her head and smiled down at him. 'You bought a house for us.' Only one thing bothered her. 'Then why

were you so adamant we had to stay in the apartment?
If we are going to have a home in the country, surely
we could just as easily have stayed here?'

Leo sighed and stroked his hands tenderly up her back,
but his brown eyes avoided her questing gaze, fixing on
some point on the ceiling, almost as if he was afraid to
look at her. 'Jealousy. You've lived here alone a long
time, and the thought of sharing the same bed you've
shared with other men...'

Jacy began to chuckle. Her head fell down on his chest
and she curved her slender arms around him, hugging
him to her. 'You fool,' she admonished, a wide grin en-
hancing her beautiful face. 'I told you once—no man
has ever slept in my bed but you.'

'You called me a chauvinist and I am. I know it's old-
fashioned... What did you say...?' Suddenly her words
had registered and in a second he had rolled her over on
to her back, his large body poised darkly above her, but
the glitter in his deep brown eyes was not in the least
threatening. 'You never...'

'No, never! I loved you at eighteen and I never
stopped.' The look of wonder and love on his bronzed
face made her heart sing, and she knew he deserved it
all. 'I didn't go out with you just for the bet; in fact
when I saw you were the first man in the room I told
Liz the bet was off. But you got under my skin with your
arrogant assumption that because I was no longer supposedly a reporter I was all right to date.'

'Was I that bad?'

'Yes, but I knew when you went to America I wanted
you back. I tried to tell myself it wasn't love, simply that
I had spent too long celibate, and it was time I joined
the adult world and plunged into a relationship. Only it
didn't work. After the night we made love I was furious
and felt used and vowed to forget about you all
over again.'

'I know; I could have killed you when you turned down my date for the opera and turned up with that red-haired Adonis. Thank God I found out about him before I destroyed him.'

Jacy's eyes widened in surprise. The arrogant Leo was back with a vengeance. 'Destroyed him?'

'I thought about it until the investigator told me he was a homosexual, so I let it go.'

'You are ruthless, Leo,' she said uncertainly. She didn't like the idea that he had investigated Simon, but somehow it did not surprise her.

'Only to protect the people I love, Jacy.' And, swooping down, he pressed a soft kiss to her parted lips.

For a long time the only sound in the darkening room was that of clothes being hastily discarded, and then Leo's deep, melodious voice, sounding like the rustle of satin sheets, huskily declaring all the erotic delights in store, and to Jacy the floor became the most luxurious bed as she gave herself up to her husband's loving...

Later, lying enfolded in his arms, she smiled mischievously up at him. 'Well, you weren't a bad bet after all, Leo. But tell me, what would you have done if I wasn't pregnant, and didn't have to marry you?'

He didn't return her smile; instead he sat up and turned his body to stare down at where she lay naked on the carpet, a flash of anguish in his deep brown eyes. 'Does it bother you that I forced you into this marriage and the baby?'

'No, oh, no. And you were wrong, you know, Leo; I never even considered getting rid of the baby.'

'I think I always knew that, but it was another way to keep you at my side.'

Jacy knelt up beside him and wrapped her slender arms around his strong neck, pressing tiny kisses to his cheek, and chin, anywhere she could reach. 'I love you, and I finally admitted it to myself on our wedding night. In fact I made another bet.'

'You what?' His roar shook the house. 'Who with this time? Not Liz, because I confessed everything to her days before our wedding.'

So that was why Liz was so reticent the night before the marriage, Jacy realised, but all such thoughts were knocked of her head by Leo hauling her to her feet.

He clasped her hands to his naked chest. 'Gambling is a mug's game, Jacy,' he said urgently. 'What was it this time?' he demanded, and she could feel the heavy thud of his heart beneath her clasped hands. 'I'll find out and cancel it; your betting has caused us both enough heartache already.'

She looked up at him with a secret smile playing around her full lips, and sighed dramatically. 'Cancel it, you say... Well, if you insist.'

'I'm your husband; I do insist.'

'It seems a shame,' she murmured, her eyes lingering over his naked body in deliberate sensual invitation. She freed her hand and stroked down his chest and lower to his flat muscled stomach. She heard his stifled moan of pleasure, and her cheeks dimpled in a wicked smile at the sight of his obvious masculine response. 'I do enjoy gambling.' She tapped him lightly and stepped back.

'Jacy...' He gasped and reached for her.

She lifted molten golden eyes to his, and murmured, 'On the first day of our marriage I gambled on passion making our marriage work, but as an obedient wife I bow to your superior judgement,' and burst out laughing.

'You witch.' Leo laughed, shaking his head in disbelief, and, grabbing her around the waist, he kissed her until she clung to him. Then he lifted his dark head, gently brushed back a lock of unruly hair from her brow, and stared at her, his black eyes leaping with devilment and banked-down desire.

'Well, I am an extremely wealthy man, Jacy, darling,' he drawled throatily as his hand slid to her hips and pulled her in tight against his thighs. 'Perhaps I was a bit hasty. You can gamble every day of your life, as long as it's only with me.'

Sara Craven was born in South Devon, and grew up surrounded by books, in a house by the sea. After leaving grammar school she worked as a local journalist, covering everything from flower shows to murders.

Sara started writing for Mills & Boon® in 1975. Since then she has written more than 50 novels and has had them translated into more than 15 languages. Apart from writing, her passions include films, music, cooking and eating in good restaurants. She now lives in Somerset.

Sara has also appeared as a contestant on the Channel Four game show Fifteen To One and last year became the last ever winner of the *Mastermind of Great Britain* championship.

FLAWLESS
by
SARA CRAVEN

CHAPTER ONE

'BUT you hate this kind of occasion,' said Clive. 'You always have. You call them "meat auctions" and "slave markets". You know you do.'

Carly, seated at her dressing-table, applying blusher with a practised hand, gave his irate reflection the smile the camera loved. 'That's quite right.'

'Then why in hell are we all going to the Flawless reception?'

'I changed my mind.'

'Now, that I don't believe.' Clive turned on his wife who was lounging on Carly's bed, leafing through a copy of *Harpers Bazaar*. 'Speak to her, Marge.'

'Waste of breath,' said Marge serenely. She eyed wistfully a photograph of a reed-slender black cocktail dress. 'Oh, why haven't I got thirty-four-inch hips?'

'Because you have three children,' said Clive, and brightened. 'Now there's a thought,' he said beguilingly. 'Why don't we scrap the Flawless do, go back to the house, and challenge the monsters to a team game of Trivial Pursuit?'

'No,' Marge and Carly said in unison, and he glared at them.

'Why not?'

'Because they always beat us,' said his wife.

'And because we're going to the Flawless party.'
Carly reached for a mascara wand, and began to
pay minute attention to her eyelashes. 'It's important to me, Clive.'

'Oh, for heaven's sake.' The end of Clive's tether
seemed to be fast approaching. 'They want a pretty
girl to launch a new range of cosmetics, that's all.
Just because they've hyped it into the search for
the new Scarlett O'Hara, it still doesn't make it any
big deal.'

Carly sighed. 'Clive, you're my agent. Don't you
want me to get work?'

'You do get work. I get you work. I have things
in the pipeline now that will make the Flawless deal
look like yesterday's news.' He dragged a chair
forward and sat down. 'Sweetie, you're at a crucial
point in your career. I don't think the Flawless job
would be a particularly good move for you.'

'Is that what you've told all your clients?'

'Of course not,' he said. 'It will be a fabulous
chance—for somebody.'

'Then why not me?'

'Because it would place you under an exclusive
contract to them for a year and probably far longer.
You wouldn't be able to take other assignments,
and you'd be typed as the Flawless Girl for ever
after.'

'I'm ready to risk that.'

'But why?' howled Clive. 'You've trusted my
judgement in the past. Why are you doing this to
me—to yourself?'

Carly replaced the mascara in her make-up kit.
'I have an instinct about it. Besides,' she paused,

'it's an ambition of mine to be photographed by Saul Kingsland.'

Marge looked up. 'Now you're talking,' she said. 'I hear he's an absolute dish. Good-looking and sexy as hell.'

'Oh, do you?' snorted Clive. 'Well, I hear he's a complete bastard. His models end up in tears, and his assistants have nervous breakdowns.'

Carly's brows rose. 'But he's a genius with a camera. And I suppose genius has to be allowed a certain amount of—artistic temperament.'

'That's not all Flawless are allowing him,' Clive said sourly. 'He also gets a free hand to pick The Girl.' He exhaled, frowning. 'Carly, every hopeful in modelling will be there tonight, parading themselves in front of him, and a few that should have given up hope by now,' he added grimly. 'You don't need to do this. If you're really so set on the damned job, I'll get on to Septimus Creed. His agency's handling the campaign, after all, so he should be able to pull some strings with Kingsland—and he owes me a favour...'

'No!' Carly banged her fist on the dressing-table, making the jars and bottles jump. Clive and Marge jumped too, and stared at her.

She bit her lip. 'I—I'm sorry. But I don't want any string-pulling. I want to go to the reception, and be chosen on my own merits.'

'And if you're not? It could be a pretty public rejection, sweetie. Everyone there will know you tried for it and failed.' Clive's face was sober.

'O, ye of little faith,' she said lightly.

'I'm serious. Supposing Saul Kingsland's idea of flawless is a five-foot blonde with baby-blue eyes, and a peaches-and-cream complexion?'

'That's your fantasy woman, darling, not Mr Kingsland's,' his wife said, getting to her feet. 'You've badgered Carly long enough. Now let's leave her to finish dressing in peace.' At the door, she paused. 'Have you ever actually met Saul Kingsland before, Carly?' she asked casually.

'Of course she hasn't met him,' Clive cut in impatiently. 'How could she have? She'd have still been a kid at school when he took off for America four years ago. And he hasn't been back since. I never thought he would come back.'

Marge shrugged. 'I only wondered,' she returned mildly, leading her still fuming husband into the sitting-room, and closing the door behind them.

Carly released a long, deep breath, letting sudden tension flow out of her.

'Take it easy,' she whispered to her mirrored image. 'You have a long night ahead of you.'

She eyed herself with a kind of clinical detachment, trying to see herself as Saul Kingsland would later that evening.

Her hair cascaded to her shoulders in wave after wave of burnished mahogany. Her eyes under the long sweep of mascaraed lashes were as cool and tranquil as aquamarines. She had a pale skin, a small, straight nose, a chin that was determined without being obtrusive, and a well-shaped mouth, the top lip clearly defined, the lower one curving in discreetly sensual promise.

'Flawless,' she said aloud, and with irony.

Her dress was aquamarine too, a simple, supple shape that left one shoulder bare, and she wore no jewellery, not even a watch.

I don't want to know when it's midnight. I might turn back into a pumpkin, she thought, and for a moment her hands clenched into fists at her sides.

But it couldn't happen. Here she was, after all, Carly North. One of modelling's newest and most successful faces. An up and coming name. Someone to be reckoned with in the cut-throat world of promoting beauty and fashion.

Just for a second, she wondered what the assignments were that Clive had been lining up for her, and allowed herself a brief pang of regret. Quite apart from the fact that he and Marge had become almost her second family, she had nothing but praise for the way he'd handled her career so far.

But she couldn't have second thoughts now. She'd waited too long for this chance. Her decision was made, and there was no going back.

She was going to be the Flawless Girl. She had to be.

She picked up her flask of First by Van Cleef and Arpels, and drew the glass stopper delicately over her pulse points. By the time she got to the reception, the fragrance would be blooming and alive on her skin.

Then she smiled at herself. It wasn't a smile that Marge, Clive, or the children would have recognised, or, indeed, any of the photographers she'd worked with in the past, who spoke of her warm vitality.

It was a harsh, almost feral twist of the lips.

'Saul Kingsland.' She said his name aloud like
an incantation. 'You won't choose anyone else. You
won't see anyone else.'

She picked up her wrap and went to join the
others.

It was a warm night, and the long french windows
of the hotel's banqueting suite had been thrown
open. The balcony outside overlooked the hotel's
sunken garden, a square of paved walks inter-
leaving beds of crowding shrubs and roses.

Carly stood beside one of the open windows, and
drew a deep, grateful breath. Clive had been so right
about her loathing of this kind of party, she
thought, grimacing inwardly. The clash of most of
the popular scents on over-heated bodies vied for
supremacy with the smell of alcohol, and the all-
pervasive reek of tobacco smoke.

The champagne had been flowing freely all
evening. Carly's own glass was almost untouched,
but other people hadn't been so abstemious.
Around her, voices were being raised, and laughter
was a little too strident. Some of the other girls
were looking flushed, too, and their immaculate
grooming was becoming frayed round the edges.

If he keeps us all waiting much longer, people
will start passing out, Carly told herself. But
perhaps that's how he's going to make his choice—
the only girl still vertical at the end of the evening.

Her mouth curled in distaste at the thought. In
fact, Saul Kingsland's delayed appearance at the
reception spoke of arrogance of the worst kind. But
maybe the man who was being spoken of, since his
recent return from the States, as the natural suc-

cessor to David Bailey and Patrick Lichfield, felt himself above the consideration of other people's feelings or convenience. If so, he would undoubtedly be a swine to work with.

Good, Carly thought, lifting her hair away from the nape of her neck for a moment so that the faint breeze could caress her skin. That suits me just fine.

'Carly, I thought it was you.' Gina Lesley, with whom she'd worked on a bathing-suit feature in the Bahamas, appeared from nowhere. 'Isn't this whole thing unbelievable? It's like being in some harem, and waiting for the Sultan to appear and pick one of us for the night.'

'They say it's exactly like that,' an elfin-faced girl, her red hair exotically tipped with gold, broke in eagerly. 'Lauren reckons that Saul Kingsland sleeps with all his models. Do you suppose it's true?'

Gina gave Carly a speaking look. 'I shouldn't think so for a moment,' she returned crushingly. 'If he went in for that kind of bedroom athletics he wouldn't be able to focus his eyes, let alone a camera.'

The other girl pouted and walked off.

'Incredible,' Gina muttered. 'In fact, the latest whisper from the powder-room says that we're all wasting our time because the great man has no intention of showing here tonight.'

Carly was very still. 'I hope that isn't true,' she said sharply.

'So do I, darling. And to add to my depression, one of the hacks from the Creed agency is spreading the word that Saul Kingsland is going for a total

unknown—someone he'll see in the street, or
serving in a shop, maybe.'

'I don't believe it,' Carly said. 'They wouldn't
be throwing away their money on a bash like this
if that was the case.'

Gina grinned at her. 'Positive thinking,' she said.
'That's what I like to hear.' She paused. 'Oddly
enough, you were the last person I expected to see
here tonight.'

Carly shrugged. 'I have to eat, too,' she returned. 'I just wish it was all over, and we could
go home.'

'Well, something seems to be happening at last.'
Gina craned her neck. 'Some of the Flawless
bigwigs are milling about, and Septimus Creed is
doing his marshalling act. I think someone's going
to make a speech.'

The chairman of the company producing the new
cosmetic range mounted the flower-decked dais at
the end of the room, and tested the microphone a
shade uncertainly. After the usual words of
welcome, he launched into an enthusiastic de-
scription of the new range.

'Flawless,' he told them, 'is not just another
brand of make-up. We regard it as a total look—
part of today's woman's complete way of life—
hypo-allergenic, yet highly fashion-conscious at the
same time. And we pride ourselves on the fact that
we are leading the way in banning animal testing
from our laboratories.'

Carly joined in the dutiful ripple of applause,
and took a sideways step towards the open window
to gulp another breath of fresh air. And in that
moment she saw him.

He was standing at the head of the short flight
of stairs which led down into the banqueting suite
from its main entrance, his eyes restlessly scanning
the crowded room.

He was tall, she thought, her gaze devouring him.
Broad-shouldered and lean-hipped. He was by no
means conventionally handsome. His features were
too strong—too assertive with those heavy-lidded
grey eyes, jutting chin, and a nose that was almost
a beak. He shouldn't even have been attractive,
Carly told herself. His face was too thin, and the
lines round his face and mouth altogether too
cynical. His hair was too long, and the formality
of his dinner-jacket sat uneasily on him, Carly told
herself critically. His tie was slightly crooked, as if
he'd wrenched at its constriction with an impatient
hand.

Yet in spite of this—because of this?—he was
attractive. Devastatingly, heart-stoppingly, un-
equivocally attractive. All man, someone had called
him once, and it was true. A man who spent his
life among beautiful women, and enjoyed that life
to the full.

But no one else had noticed his arrival, Carly
realised as she stared across at him. They were all
facing the dais, listening to the chairman's
peroration.

With total deliberation and concentration, she
focused all her attention on him, willing him to turn
his head, and see her.

Look at me, she commanded silently. Look at
me now.

Slowly, as if she was operating some invisible magnet, Saul Kingsland's head turned, and across the room their eyes met.

For a long moment Carly held his gaze, then she deliberately snapped the thread, turning to watch Septimus Creed who'd followed the chairman on to the dais and was outlining the thinking behind the plans for the campaign.

'The Flawless concept is one of total freshness—naturalness—even purity,' he was saying. 'And this is what we want our Flawless Girl to represent.'

'Well, that cuts me out,' Gina whispered with a humorous grimace.

Carly forced a smile in return, but said nothing. Her mind was working feverishly. She'd made him notice her, but was it—would it be enough?

It means so much, she thought. It has to be enough. Has to.

'My goodness!' Gina's eyes were widening. 'Do you see who's here—who's actually arrived? How long do you think he's been standing there?' She took a breath. 'I'm going over to say hello. Introduce myself. Coming with me?'

Carly shook her head. 'I'll catch up with you later, Gina. I—I need some air.'

It wasn't an excuse. The force of her emotions was making her feel dizzy. She slipped out on to the balcony, and stood leaning on the stone balustrade looking down into the garden. Lamps had been lit now among the tall shrubs, and the scent of the roses was warm and strong in the evening air. Above the bulk of the hotel building, a crescent moon hung like a slash of gold in the sapphire sky.

Carly looked up at the moon, and inclined her head to it, as the old superstition dictated.

'Oh, moon,' she whispered silently. 'I wish—oh, how I wish...'

'Good evening.' The sound of his voice from the doorway behind her made Carly start violently. She spun to face him, the fragile wine-glass falling from her hand to shatter on the tiles at her feet.

'Are you all right?' Two long strides brought him to her side. 'You haven't cut yourself?'

'No,' she forced from her taut throat. 'I—it's just some champagne on my dress.'

'Damnation.' He produced an immaculate handkerchief. 'Let me see...'

She took a step backwards. 'I can manage—really.'

He'd followed her, and that was incredible. But it was also too soon. He'd caught her off guard. She wasn't ready for this confrontation—and she certainly wasn't ready to be touched by him.

'Just as you wish.' He sounded faintly surprised, but he passed her the handkerchief, and she dabbed at her dress, her hands shaking, sharply aware that he was watching her.

He said abruptly, 'You're very nervous.'

'What do you expect? You—startled me.'

'I shouldn't have sneaked up on you like that.' Saul Kingsland's smile contained both repentance and charm. He paused. 'But then, you knew I'd follow you—didn't you? Isn't that exactly what you intended?'

He certainly believed in the direct approach, Carly thought, rallying her defences.

'You're a free agent, Mr Kingsland.'

He shook his head. 'Not tonight. I'm here to do a job—fulfil an obligation. I have to find a face—a body around which an entire advertising campaign can pivot. Frankly, I thought it was impossible—a gimmick foisted on me by Septimus Creed. How could I choose anyone when I didn't know what I was looking for—what special qualities I needed?' He broke off, the cool eyes skimming over her, missing nothing.

Carly found the intensity of his scrutiny and the continuing silence unnerving. She broke it deliberately, moving backwards, resting an elbow on the balustrade. 'And do you know now?'

He said slowly, 'Yes, I think I do. It's totally incredible.'

His gaze went down the curve of her body as she lounged against the stonework, lingering on breast and thigh. It was as if he'd put out a hand and touched her intimately, and she was hard put to it not to flinch.

She thought, I don't know if I can go through with this. But I must . . .

She laughed. 'Is this your usual line, Mr Kingsland? "Put yourself in my hands, little girl, and I'll make you famous"?' She pulled a face. 'A little tacky, don't you think?'

'Yes—if it were true.' He sounded impatient. 'But I assure you I'm not just shooting a line. I should know your name. Why don't I? Who's your agent?'

'My name is Carly North,' she said. 'My agent is Clive Monroe, and if you're not careful, I shall begin to think you mean this.'

'Believe it,' he said shortly. His brows drew together in a frown. 'Or is there some problem?'

She shrugged. 'Perhaps I'm not sure I want to be the Flawless Girl.'

'Then what are you doing here?'

'Natural curiosity. Normally I avoid this kind of situation like the plague.'

'Then we have something in common at least.' He gave her a long, speculative look. 'So, I have to persuade you, do I?'

'Not easy,' she said, lightly. 'I have a mind of my own, and my career is going well. Ask Clive.'

'I intend to. But that doesn't let you off the hook.' He paused. 'I have to stay at this thing for a while, but will you have dinner with me when it's over?'

'With my agent?'

'If necessary.'

'He's a family man. He might not be able to make it.'

'All the better.'

'You don't waste any time.'

'Why should I? The deadlines have been drawn— quite apart from any personal considerations.'

Carly's brows lifted. 'You seem to be living up to your reputation.'

'I don't have a reputation,' he said. 'These days, I'm a stranger in town.'

'Hardly,' she said. 'There can't be a person in the country who hasn't heard of you.'

'Professionally, maybe. On other levels, they know nothing, and nor do you. So, ignore rumour and hearsay. Use your own instincts—your own judgement about me, Carly North.'

'Perhaps my instincts are warning me to run.'

'Then they're playing you false,' he said slowly. 'Besides, if that were true, why did you want me to notice you so badly just now?'

'Is that what I did?' Alarm tingled on her skin.

'You know it is. And if it wasn't for strictly professional reasons, then it must have had a personal basis.'

She said coolly, 'That's a rather arrogant assumption.'

Saul Kingsland shrugged. 'Then that could be something else we have in common.'

'What do you mean?'

'Isn't it a form of arrogance to come here tonight, looking as you do, when you don't really want the Flawless job?'

'I didn't say that,' she said quickly. 'I said I wasn't sure.'

'So, I'm asking again, will you have dinner with me later, and let me convince you?'

She felt as if she was being swept along, caught in a current she couldn't control. A voice in her head was screaming at her to refuse, warning her frantically that this was all too much, too soon.

She said, 'Very well.' She shot him a veiled look. 'But I'm promising nothing.'

'Professionally?' Saul Kingsland asked silkily. 'Or personally?'

'Both.'

'Fine,' he said equably. 'Then we know where we stand.' He smiled at her. 'And now I'd better justify my presence here—mix a little—talk to some people.' He paused. 'Don't run away.'

'I gave that up,' she said, 'a long time ago.'

She watched him walk away, back into the lighted room. Leaving her alone.

Relief flooded through her, making her feel almost light-headed. She sagged against the balustrade, her legs trembling, staring sightlessly in front of her as her mind revolved over and over again everything that had happened, everything that had been said between them.

In the end, it had been easy. Too easy, perhaps. Certainly not what she'd expected.

What have I done? she thought, a pang of unease shivering through her. What have I started? I've got a tiger by the tail, and I can't—I dare not let go.

There was no turning back, not now. And perhaps there never was.

Squaring her shoulders, she went to find Clive.

CHAPTER TWO

SAUL KINGSLAND'S car was long, sleek and powerful. Of course, Carly thought, her lip curling as she settled herself into the passenger seat.

Their departure from the reception together had caused something of a sensation. The atmosphere of disappointment and frustration among the other girls had been almost tangible.

'I just hope you know what you're doing, that's all,' had been Clive's valediction.

And Marge had said softly, 'Oh, I'm sure she does.'

I shall have to be careful with Marge, Carly thought, as Saul eased the car into the traffic. She's altogether too shrewd.

'Do you like Italian food?' Saul asked. 'Or are you on some kind of permanent diet?'

'Good lord, no.' She gave a slight shrug. 'I suppose I'm lucky. I seem to burn up a lot of calories.'

'Yes, I can believe that. You're very cool on the surface, but underneath I suspect there's a mass of tension.'

She bit her lip. 'Not that I'm aware of.' She gave him a small cool smile. 'I'm a very uncomplicated person, actually.'

'I'll let you know about that,' he said, 'when we're better acquainted.'

20

'Comments like that make me nervous,' she replied. 'I like my privacy.'

'But if we're going to work together—achieve some kind of rapport, we can't remain strangers.'

'You think it's all decided, don't you? All sewn up.' There was an edge to her voice.

'I'm taking nothing for granted where you're concerned, lady. That's why we're having this meal together—to see if we can establish some kind of basis to proceed from.'

'And if we can't?'

It was Saul's turn to shrug. 'Then I find another Flawless Girl from somewhere. No one's irreplaceable, after all.'

'Is that Public Warning Number One?'

'You're in the business,' he said. 'You know the score as well as I do.' There was a brief silence, then, 'Your agent really doesn't want you to do this, does he?'

'Clive has—reservations.'

'But he said it was your decision.' He sent her a sideways glance. 'He made me wonder if you were just playing games with me—playing hard to get.'

'Of course not. Why on earth should I?' Her mouth was dry suddenly.

'You tell me,' he said laconically.

Carly was quiet for a moment. Then she said, 'Perhaps I should put my cards on the table. I was in two minds about the Flawless assignment when I went to the reception tonight. I—I still am, come to that.' She ran the tip of her tongue along her lower lip. 'But you were right about one thing—I did want you to notice me, and that was even before I realised who you were.'

'I'm flattered.'

'And I'm ashamed,' she returned. 'I shocked myself this evening. I don't usually—come on so strong.' She forced a little laugh. 'There—confession over.'

'You won't be made to do penance,' he said. 'I'm glad to know the attraction was mutual. Now, all we have to do is relax and enjoy the rest of the evening.'

He found a parking space, and they walked the remaining hundred yards to the restaurant's entrance. Carly had half expected Saul to put his hand under her arm, or clasp her fingers with his as they walked along, but he made no attempt to touch her even in a casual way. In view of her recent admission, she found this restraint intriguing, but she was relieved by it too.

It wasn't a large restaurant, and it relied heavily on the intimacy of its atmosphere. The lights were low, the tables screened from each other by trellis-work covered in climbing plants, and in one corner a lone guitarist played music which was pleasant without being obtrusive.

'The food here used to be wonderful,' Saul remarked, handing her a menu.

It still was. They ate stuffed courgette flowers, and scallops grilled in their shells, followed by *osso buco* and roast quails with *polenta*. To finish the meal Carly had a frothy chocolate concoction, rich with cream and liqueur, and Saul asked for cheese. The coffee was strong, black and aromatic, and served with Strega.

While they ate, the conversation had been general. Carly had encouraged Saul to talk about his life in America, and the glossy magazine scene in New York. He also told her about a book he had coming out.

'I did a hell of a lot of travelling while I was over there,' he said. 'So, it's a kind of odyssey in pictures. My tribute to everything I liked best about life Stateside. Places and people that I loved.'

His tone gave nothing away, but Carly found herself wondering how many of those people had been women.

'It sounds—illuminating,' she said. 'Do you intend to go back to America?'

Saul signalled for more coffee. 'At the moment, I'm not sure,' he said. 'My plans are—fluid. I need to see how things work out for me here, once the Flawless assignment is finished.' He paused. 'And, while we're on the subject, have you come to any decision yet?'

Carly gasped. 'I've hardly had time to think,' she began.

'Really?' He gave her a straight look. 'I had the impression several times tonight that you were so deep in thought you were a million miles away.'

She flushed a little. 'I'm sorry if I've been poor company...'

'I didn't say that.' He leaned forward. 'If you're still not sure, spend the day with me tomorrow, and I'll take some pictures of you—convince you that way.'

Carly shook her head. 'I can't tomorrow. I'm going home to visit.'

'Where is home?'

'In the country. Very quiet and dull.'

'With you there?' He slanted a smile at her. 'Impossible. Tell you what, why don't I come with you? I was going to walk you along the Embankment and through the parks, but a rural background would be even better.'

'I'm sorry, but it's out of the question.' Her flush deepened. 'It's going to be rather hectic—a houseful of people. My sister's getting engaged.'

'Not so quiet and dull, after all,' he said.

'It usually is. My family is—very conventional. I don't think they altogether approve of my life in London.'

'And what heinous sins do they think you commit? Perhaps I could reassure them.'

'But you don't know me,' she said. 'You don't know what I'm capable of.'

'Not at this moment,' he said. 'But I intend to know you, Carly North, in every way there is.'

He was smiling, but as the grey eyes met hers Carly was conscious of a curious intentness in their depths. She felt vulnerable suddenly, and afraid, as if Saul's gaze was probing too deeply, staring straight into her mind, laying bare all her innermost secrets.

Her heart missed a beat, and her throat felt tight. She said huskily, 'I find remarks like that—distasteful.'

'Then I apologise.' He didn't sound sorry at all. 'I'll begin our acquaintance solely through the lens of a camera, and in no other way, I swear.' He stretched out a hand to her across the table, and reluctantly she allowed his fingers to close round hers. 'Will you work with me, Carly North? Will you be my Flawless Girl?'

'I can't tell you now. I have to think about it.'
She withdrew her hand from his grasp. 'May I have
the weekend?'

'I won't argue with that.' He took a diary out of
an inside pocket of his dinner-jacket, tore out a page
and scribbled down a telephone number. 'Call me
on this when you've decided.' He paused. 'You say
that your sister's getting engaged. What about you,
Carly? You're not wearing any rings, but that
doesn't mean a whole lot in these liberated days.
Are you attached? Are there any lovers or husbands lurking in your vicinity?'

'There's nobody.'

'You astound me.'

'It's through my own choice.' She despised the
defensiveness in her own voice.

'I'm sure it is.'

'Am I allowed to ask you the same question?
How many ex-wives have you left sighing over you?'

'None at all—and no present Mrs Kingsland
either.' He was laughing openly. 'I am entirely
without encumbrances.'

Of course he was, she thought. Saul Kingsland
was a rolling stone, a man who would never settle
or opt for an ordered existence. He would walk into
a woman's life, take what he wanted, and walk on
without a backward look. A wreaker of havoc,
unknowing and uncaring. And you didn't even have
to be a woman to suffer at his hands.

Abruptly, Carly pushed back her chair. 'I really
should be going.'

'Already? It's still relatively early.'

'I have to leave first thing in the morning. My
mother will be needing help with the arrangements.'

'Ah, yes,' he said softly. 'The devoted daughter
rushing back to the bosom of the family. Oddly
enough, that's not the impression I had of you.
When I saw you standing in the moonlight, I
thought I'd never seen anyone look so solitary—so
used to being alone. It just shows how wrong one
can be.'

'First impressions are often misleading.' She
made her voice deliberately dismissive. 'Would you
ask someone to find me a cab, please?'

Saul looked at her in surprise. 'There's no need
for that. I'll drive you home.'

'I—I don't want to take you out of your way.'

'That's very thoughtful of you.' His smile was
sardonic. 'How do you know that you will be?'

'I—don't, actually.'

'Then there's no more to be said,' he told her,
indicating to the head waiter that he required the
bill.

Carly bit her lip, trying to hide her annoyance.

'Do you never take "no" for an answer?' she
enquired acidly, when they were in the car, and he
was following her reluctantly given instructions.

'It depends on how positive the "no" is,' he said.
'In your case it was just a ploy to prevent me
knowing where you lived for some reason, and a
useless ploy at that.'

'Why do you say that?'

'Because there are plenty of ways of finding your
address if I were sufficiently desperate,' he said.
'There's the phone book, for starters.' He slanted
a frowning look at her. 'So, for goodness' sake calm
down, and stop being so damned uptight,' he went
on. 'There's nothing to be scared of. You have my

word on that. I'm not going to pressure you, or make a nuisance of myself by camping on your doorstep. Perhaps events have moved rather too fast tonight, but from now on we'll take things just as easily as you wish.'

'Thank you.' Her hands gripped tautly together in her lap.

'I learned some relaxation techniques in the States.' He didn't miss a thing. He added, with a smile in his voice, 'If you asked me nicely, I might be prepared to teach them to you.'

'I'll bear it in mind.' She made herself speak lightly. She'd let him think she'd been instantly attracted to him, for heaven's sake. Now she was treating him as if he was some plague carrier. 'Actually, you're quite right. This evening has been—totally outside my experience. I'm in a state of complete confusion.'

'I'm still in shock myself,' Saul said drily. 'Perhaps the weekend will help us get our heads together.'

The remainder of the journey was completed in silence, to Carly's relief.

Saul stopped the car, and glanced up at the block of flats. 'Very nice,' he commented. 'Your career really is doing well.' He paused. 'Do you live by yourself?'

She shook her head. 'I share with another girl. She works for a television company.'

'Is she there at the moment?'

'No,' Carly said, before she could stop herself. 'She's abroad with a film crew.'

'Then I'll go up with you,' he said.

She looked at him in total dismay, and his mouth tightened.

'And not for the reasons you seem to think,' he added bitingly. 'My motives are actually quite chivalrous. I want to make sure you get home safely.'

'Don't you feel you're being rather over-protective?'

'No, I don't. I took a girl home from a party in New York over a year ago. She was independent, too, and insisted on saying goodnight on the pavement. When she got up to her apartment, someone had broken in, and she was attacked and badly injured. If I'd insisted on escorting her to the door, it might not have happened. I'm not taking the risk again.'

'In case you hadn't noticed, this is London, not New York.'

'Just a different part of the jungle, lady.' He walked up the steps beside her, and opened the swing doors.

She stood beside him in the lift in resentful silence. Walked along the passage to the door, still without speaking.

''May I have your key?' Saul held out his hand.

'Oh, this is silly,' Carly burst out in exasperation as she gave it to him. 'Just how many times do you think I've come back here alone at night? Lucy's away a lot.'

'That was in the bad old days.' He unlocked the door, and pushed it open. 'Now you don't have to be alone any more, unless you want to be.'

Carly lifted her chin. 'Is that a hint that you want to stay for more coffee—or a nightcap—or whatever the current euphemism is? How very obvious.'

'No,' he said calmly. 'It's more a declaration of intent.'

He was standing very close to her. She could actually feel the warmth of his body. Suddenly Carly found it difficult to breathe. Any moment now, she thought wildly, and he would reach out for her, take her in his arms, and she was terrified. She felt as if she was balanced on a knife-edge, every nerve-ending tingling in alarm and anticipation.

Kiss me, she thought, her heart beating violently against her ribcage. Kiss me and get it over with.

As he moved, her eyelids fluttered down, and her lips parted in a little unconscious sigh. Her whole body tensed, waiting to feel his hands on her, his mouth against hers.

He said quietly, 'Goodnight, Flawless Girl. Call me after the weekend, and let me know what you've decided.'

The door closed softly, and he was gone.

Carly's eyes flew open, and she stood rigid for a long moment, staring at the enigmatic wooden panels; then, with a small sob, she hurled herself forward, putting up the chain and securing the interior bolt with hands that shook.

She'd been so sure that, in spite of her protestations, he would offer at least a token pass. Now, paradoxically, she felt that he'd made a fool of her.

And that's ridiculous, she thought. Because Saul Kingsland is the one who's been fooled. I've done it. I've succeeded. I've won.

She laughed out loud, and the sound echoed eerily in the quiet flat.

She walked into her bedroom, shedding her few clothes as she went, and straight into the bathroom

which separated her room from Lucy's, stepping
into the shower, and turning the warm spray full
on. She stood motionless, letting the water pour
over her, soaking her hair, and running in rivulets
down her skin.

Washing Saul Kingsland away.

But only for the time being, she reminded herself
with a sharp stab of excitement as she reluctantly
turned off the water, and stepped back on to the
thick mat, reaching for a towel.

On Monday, she would make that call, and after
that—she drew a breath. After that, whatever would
be, would be.

As she turned, she caught a glimpse of herself in
the mirror, and almost recoiled. It was like seeing
a stranger, or her own bad angel, eyes glittering
with malevolence, bright, febrile colour along her
cheekbones, the soft mouth starkly compressed.

Revenge might be sweet, but, dear heaven, what
would it cost her in human terms?

The image in the mirror blurred suddenly and,
bending her head, Carly began to weep—for the
girl she'd been, and for the woman she'd become.

The sun was pouring into the bedroom the next
morning, as she packed a weekend bag with her
usual economy. The dress she had bought specially
to wear for the party was already waiting in its protective cover, and she grimaced slightly as she lifted
it down and carried it out to her car.

A greater contrast to the dress she'd worn the
previous night could not be imagined, she thought
wryly. But then, she hardly looked the same girl at
all. She was simply and casually dressed in tailored

cream linen trousers with a matching jacket over a
short-sleeved khaki T-shirt. Her hair was gathered
into a single plait, and allowed to hang over one
shoulder, and her face was innocent of all cosmetics but a touch of moisturiser.

As she loaded the car, she couldn't resist a furtive
look round. In spite of his assurances, Saul
Kingsland might be there watching her, perhaps
from one of the row of parked cars across the street.

Oh, stop it, she adjured herself impatiently.
That's the way to paranoia.

Traffic was heavy, and getting out of London required all her concentration. She couldn't relax until
trees and fields began to replace suburban sprawl.
She lowered the window a little, to enjoy the sunlit
breeze, and put a cassette of Vivaldi's *Four Seasons*
into the tape machine, then sat back to savour the
remainder of her journey.

An hour later, she turned the car into the grav-
elled sweep of the drive and saw the familiar red-
brick Georgian bulk of the house awaiting her. She
drove round to the rear, and parked in the former
stables, slotting her Polo in between her father's
Bentley and the sedate estate car her mother
preferred.

She sat for a moment, staring in front of her,
then, with a smothered sigh, collected her things,
and walked down the covered way to the side
entrance.

There was a lot of activity already, she saw. A
large marquee had been erected on the lawn, and
folding tables and chairs were being carried into it.
As she watched, a florist's van drew up in front of
the house, and two women dressed in pink overalls

got out. Presently, no doubt, the caterers' vehicles would also be arriving.

Mother will be in her element, Carly thought, her mouth twisting. She'll be able to use it as a trial run for Susan's actual wedding. And I'm about as necessary in all this as an extra thumb.

She caught a movement in the large conservatory which flanked the lawn and, smiling a little, trod quietly across the gravel and stood in the doorway watching the tall, grey-haired man who was deftly repotting some plants.

'Hello, Father.'

He turned with an obvious start, and peered at her. 'Why, Caroline,' he said, 'so you've come. Your mother wasn't sure... Well, this is splendid—splendid.' He paused, then added another vague, 'Splendid.'

Carly bit her lip. 'I did say I was coming,' she said, quietly. 'If I'm not expected—if my room's being used, I can always try the pub.'

'Certainly not. I'm sure your room's ready and waiting for you, my dear, although, of course, your mother always handles those arrangements. She's in the drawing-room, having coffee with your Aunt Grace. I said I'd join them once I'd finished this and washed my hands, but now...' His voice tailed off expectantly.

'But now that I've arrived, it will let you off the hook,' Carly supplied drily.

'Well, all this talk about engagements and weddings,' he said. 'Not my sort of thing at all, you know. They'll start on christenings next, I dare say,' he added with disfavour.

'I can imagine.' Carly slanted a smile at him. 'Stay with your beloved plants, Dad. I'll try and ensure you're not missed.'

As she entered the hall, she could hear Aunt Grace's authoritative tones issuing from the drawing-room. She pulled a small face. Her mother's older sister held strong views on everything, from the government in power down to the deplorable attitude of today's shop assistants. Since her only daughter's marriage and departure for New Zealand a few years previously, she had lived in Bournemouth, which she rarely left. Carly couldn't help wishing that she had not decided to make an exception to this excellent rule for Susan's engagement party.

She resolutely pinned on a smile as she went into the drawing-room. 'Hello, Mummy, Aunt Grace. How are you both?'

There was an immediate surprised silence. Carly was aware of both pairs of eyes riveted on her, taking in every detail of her appearance. She put down her case, and draped her dress-carrier over the back of a chair.

'Is that coffee? I'd love some.'

'Of course, dear.' Mrs Foxcroft filled the third cup waiting on the tray and proffered it to her younger daughter. 'Did you have a good drive down?'

'Marvellous, thank you.' Carly bent and kissed her mother's cheek, and, more fleetingly, her aunt's. 'You're both looking very well.'

Her mother smiled awkwardly. 'And so are you, darling. Positively—radiant. Isn't she, Grace?'

'Hm,' said Mrs Brotherton. 'Try as I may, Veronica, I still cannot accustom myself... However,' she turned to Carly, 'I saw a photograph of you in a magazine at my hairdressers' last month, Caroline. You were wearing an extraordinary garment in white taffeta, and seemed to be standing in an area of slum clearance.'

'Oh, the Fabioni. I remember it well.' Carly laughed. 'It was incredibly cold that day—the middle of winter, in fact—and we were down by the river. Did you manage to count my goose-pimples?'

'I find it very odd,' said Aunt Grace majestically, 'that a reputable journal should find it necessary to photograph an evening dress outdoors in broad daylight, and inclement weather.'

'It's because of publishing schedules,' Carly told her. 'Fur coats in August, and bikinis in December. The bane of a model's life.' She looked at her mother. 'Where's Susan? Resting for the big occasion?'

'She's gone with Anthony to look at the house his father is giving them as a wedding present. Apparently it needs a great deal doing to it, and work will have to start almost at once if it's to be ready for them to move into after the wedding.'

'Have they set a date yet?' Carly asked casually. 'I'll need to know fairly well in advance.'

'I believe they're thinking of October,' her mother returned. 'I know Susan wants to talk to you about it,' she added, after a pause.

'Oh, good.' Carly drank some of her coffee, feeling another silence about to press down on them all. She decided to prevent it. 'How are James and Louise?' she asked her aunt.

'They seem happily settled. The farm is not too isolated, fortunately, so Louise can get into the nearby town for shopping, and other essentials. She is expecting another baby in July.'

'So soon?' That made three in just over five years, Carly thought, blinking. 'Maybe Louise should consider spending even more time in town,' she joked feebly.

'Caroline, dear,' her mother said repressively, while Aunt Grace looked more forbidding than ever.

'I'm sorry.' Carly drained her cup, and rose to her feet. 'I'll go and unpack. Am I in my old room?'

'Well, actually, dear, I was wondering if you'd mind using the nursery—just this once, of course. Jean and Arthur Lewis found they could come, after all, and as it's such a long way for them to travel I did offer...'

'...my room to them.' Carly completed the hesitant sentence. 'Of course they must have it. They're such old friends, after all. I quite understand. Well—I'll see you both later.' She paused at the door. 'If there's anything I can do to help, you only have to ask.'

'That's very sweet of you, dear, but everything's under control.'

'Yes,' Carly said gently, 'I'm sure it is.'

Susan's engagement to Anthony Farrar, the son of a local landowner, had been hoped for and planned for over a very long period, she thought with irony as she climbed the broad sweep of stairs. Susan had first met Anthony at a hunt ball when

she was eighteen, and had made up her mind there
and then to marry him. Everything that had happened since had been like a long and fraught
military campaign, with triumphs and reverses in
almost equal proportions.

Carly herself had wondered more than once if
Anthony was worth all this agonising over. He was
attractive enough in a fair-haired, typically English
way—certainly better-looking than either of his
sisters, she allowed judiciously—but she'd always
found him humourless, and suspected as well that
he might share his father's notoriously roving eye.

But Susan clearly regarded her engagement as a
major victory, Carly thought wryly, as she went up
the second flight of stairs to the old nursery
quarters. So, heaven forbid that she should be a
dissenting voice amid the jubilation.

Not that Sue would listen if I was, she thought
with a sigh, as she opened the nursery door.

It was hardly recognisable as the room she and
her sister had once shared. All the old furniture
had gone, and so had the toys—the doll's house,
the rocking-horse, and the farmyard animals. It was
now, very obviously, a very spare bedroom, she
thought, dumping her case down on the narrow
single bed, furnished with unwanted odds and ends
from the rest of the house. Only the white-painted
bars across the windows revealed its original
purpose.

She opened her case and put the few items it contained into the chest of drawers.

The photograph, as always, was at the bottom
of the case. She extracted it, and placed it carefully
on the dressing-chest next to the mirror.

She stood for a long moment, staring at it. The child's face looked back at her, its eager brightness diminished by the heavy glasses, and the protruding front teeth that the shy smile revealed.

Slowly, her hands curled into taut fists at her sides, and as gradually relaxed again.

An object lesson in how not to look.

And one, she thought, that she would never forget.

CHAPTER THREE

CARLY adjusted the neckline of her dress, and gave it a long, disparaging look. As a garment, she supposed it was adequate. The material was good—a fine, silky crêpe—and it had been competently put together. But the Puritan grey did nothing for her, and with her hair twisted up into a smooth topknot she looked bland and unobtrusive, like a Victorian governess.

But that, of course, was precisely her intention.

It had been a long afternoon. She'd made another diffident offer of help downstairs which had been kindly but firmly refused. Instead she'd found herself being subjected to an exhaustive commentary on the problems of sheep farming in New Zealand by Aunt Grace.

In the end she'd taken refuge in a sunny corner of the garden, so far untouched by the demands of the party, with an armful of books from her childhood which she'd rescued from the attic. It had been wonderful to discover that *The House at Pooh Corner* had lost none of its old magic and step once more into *Tom's Midnight Garden*. She found a new serenity burgeoning within her as she relaxed with them.

Over tea in the drawing-room she'd looked at the multitude of snapshots Aunt Grace had triumphantly produced of James, Louise and the children, and said all the right things. Or she hoped she had.

James looked flourishing, tanned and handsome. The kind of man who'd be an achiever whatever he set his hand to. But Louise, she thought privately, looked weary, her radiant blonde prettiness muted somehow, as if the everyday demands of babies and farming were becoming too much for her.

But then Louise had always enjoyed the urban life—London with its buzz, its theatres and parties. For her, the country had been somewhere to spend the occasional weekend. Strange then that she should have married James, and accepted the radical change of life-style he was offering, rather than one of his wealthy and sophisticated friends.

Of course, Louise might consider that the world she was used to was well lost for love, but Carly didn't think so. Not on the evidence of these photographs, anyway.

As soon as she could, she escaped upstairs again, and had a lingering, scented bath, mindful of her mother's adjuration to vacate the bathroom in good time, ready for Susan's use.

'It is her night, after all, dear.'

Carly felt that the reminder was unnecessary. She was conscious too of a nagging disappointment that Susan's house-viewing trip was taking so long. It had been ages since she'd seen her sister—talked to her. In fact, it was Christmas, she realised. Each time she'd been home briefly since, Susan had been preoccupied with Anthony.

She took one last look at herself, and turned away from the mirror, glancing at her watch. Well, Sue

was bound to have returned by now. She could go
down to her room and chat to her while she got
ready, as they'd done when they were younger.

She went down the short flight of stairs, and
walked along the passage. As she lifted a hand to
tap at the door, it occurred to her that once she
would simply have barged cheerfully in.

'Come in,' Sue called, and Carly turned the
handle and walked into the room.

Sue swung round on her dressing-stool. 'Oh, it's
you.' Her smile was perfunctory. 'How are you,
Caro?'

'I'm fine.' Carly deposited herself on the bed.
'You don't mind if I stay—talk to you while you
dress?'

Sue shrugged. 'If you want. But I don't have a
lot of time to spare. I stayed longer than I should
have done with Anthony's mother, talking about
the wedding.'

'Oh.' Carly hesitated for a moment. 'Would you
like me to do your make-up for you?'

'No, thank you.' Sue's voice had an edge to it.
'I may not have the professional touch, but I've
managed adequately up to now. Besides, Anthony
prefers me to look natural.'

Carly felt herself flush. 'I—wasn't criticising. I
thought it might relax you.'

'I'm perfectly relaxed,' Sue said shortly, reaching
for the moisturiser.

Carly bit her lip. 'I can always go away, if you
prefer.'

'No, you may as well stay. I've been wanting to
talk to you anyway about arrangements for the
wedding.' She fidgeted for a moment with the lid

of the jar, then burst out, 'Caro, would you mind awfully if you weren't a bridesmaid?'

Carly stared at her, feeling as if she'd been pole-axed. She said slowly, 'Not a bridesmaid? But Sue, we promised each other ever since we were little . . . Of course I'd mind.'

'Yes, I know that.' Sue's tone was impatient, dismissive. 'But things change—circumstances alter. And I've decided to have just Anthony's sisters instead. They're both shorter than you, and blonde. It would be practically impossible to find a colour you all could wear, and next to them you'd look like a giraffe anyway.'

'I—see.' Hurt and disappointment were warring inside Carly with a growing anger. 'It didn't occur to you to have me alone?'

'No, it didn't, frankly.'

'Even though I'm your only sister?'

Bright spots of colour burned in Sue's cheeks. 'Listen,' she said, 'whether you like it or not, I only intend to get married once, and it's going to be my big day, from beginning to end. I'm not prepared to be—outshone by anyone. I want them all to be looking at me as I walk up the aisle, not at whoever's following me.'

'You think I wouldn't take a back seat—that I'd push for attention?' Carly spread her hands. 'Sue, I wouldn't—I swear it.'

'You couldn't help it. If you walked around with a bag over your head, people would still look at you. It's the way you hold yourself—the way you move—everything.' Sue slammed down the jar. 'Anyway, there's no use in arguing about it. My mind's made up. I've already spoken to Tess and

Sarah.' She paused. 'And Lady Farrar's delighted,' she added deliberately.

'Oh, I understand,' Carly said stormily. 'This is all to do with last New Year's Eve, and the fact that your future father-in-law can't keep his hands to himself. I suspected I hadn't heard the last of that, even though it wasn't my fault, and you know it.'

Sue shrugged again. 'Nevertheless,' she retorted, 'you can hardly expect to be her favourite person.'

'You're quite sure you even want to invite me to the wedding?'

Sue's hesitation was just a fraction too long. 'Don't be silly.'

'I'm not.' Carly rose. 'I think I'm just beginning to see sense.' She gave Sue a long, level look. 'I'm really not wanted here, am I? I'm aware of it more and more each time I come home—that I'm an outsider.'

'Not an outsider,' Sue said angrily. 'A complete stranger—in every way. What do you think it's been like for Mother and Father—for me, listening to people talking about you—about the change in you? Seeing your picture in magazines—on television—all over the place? You know how they've always hated any kind of gossip or notoriety. How they've valued their privacy—their quiet family life. Well, you've ruined that. You've become spectacular, Caro, a media person. But you're not going to spoil my wedding. I want it to be a dignified occasion, not a field-day for a lot of camera-happy idiots.'

'Don't worry about that,' Carly said with supreme bitterness. 'I promise to be somewhere on the other side of the world when that happy dawn breaks. Just let me know what you want as a present, apart from my absence, that is.'

It took all the control she was capable of not to slam the door as she left. She was trembling violently as she walked back to the nursery. She lifted her hands, and began to unfasten her hair, shaking it free on her shoulders in a scented mahogany cloud, scattering the pins piecemeal on the carpet uncaringly.

She knew all about her parents' shock and resentment over her choice of career, and the means she'd chosen to achieve it. That was why she'd tried so hard, each time she returned home, to revert to being plain Caroline Foxcroft in the subordinate role of younger daughter. She thought she'd succeeded on the whole. But clearly she'd made a terrible mistake.

The incident at the New Year party when Sir Giles Farrar, flushed with whisky, had cornered her in the hall, thinking he was unobserved, had been embarrassing, but basically trivial. A more tolerant woman than Lady Farrar would have laughed it off.

Sue would make her the perfect daughter-in-law, she thought, anger stirring within her.

She collected her things, ramming them into her bag with swift, jerky movements. She kept on the grey dress. She could change when she got back to the flat. She didn't want to remain here a minute longer than necessary.

As she carried the case downstairs to the hall, her mother appeared in the drawing-room doorway, Aunt Grace inevitably behind her.

'Caroline?' She stared at the case, raising her brows. 'What are you doing?'

'Leaving,' Carly said briefly. 'Isn't that what everyone wants?'

'Of course not.'

'Well, it's certainly what Susan would prefer.'

'But you can't go,' her mother almost wailed. 'The first guests will be arriving soon. Everyone will think it's so odd.'

Carly shrugged. 'They may also find it relatively eccentric that my own sister doesn't want me as her bridesmaid,' she retorted, her voice brittle.

Mrs Foxcroft sighed. 'So Susan told you. Oh, dear, I rather hoped she'd wait. I knew you'd be upset.'

'That,' Carly said, 'is putting it mildly. Mother, I can't stay for the party, as if nothing had happened. You must see that.'

'Your mother sees nothing of the kind,' said Aunt Grace. 'You're spoiled, Caroline. Spoiled, and selfish. You can hardly wonder that Susan doesn't want you as an attendant. No one's forgotten your behaviour at Louise's wedding.' She snorted. 'Claiming you had a virus only hours before the ceremony—insisting on being taken home, without a thought for anyone but yourself. The balance of the bridal procession was completely destroyed, and it was all your fault. You should have taken an aspirin, and played your part.'

Carly threw back her head. 'Don't tell me I was missed,' she said. 'Louise only asked me because she felt obliged to. It must have been a relief to her not to have me trailing behind her, the ugly duckling among the swans.'

'You were certainly not a prepossessing child,' Aunt Grace said. 'But you've definitely taken drastic steps to remedy the situation since then,' she added disapprovingly. 'I, of course, have never agreed with tampering with nature. And poor Susan must feel it badly, having always been the pretty one.'

'All the more reason for me to go back to London.'

'But everyone will be expecting to see you.' Mrs Foxcroft sounded distracted. 'They'll be asking where you are.'

Carly turned towards the front door. 'Tell them I have another virus,' she flung over her shoulder. 'Or, better still, make it an infectious disease.'

She was still shaking as she drove back along the lanes towards the main road. A tractor pulled out of a gateway ahead of her, and she had to brake sharply to avoid it. She pulled the car over on to the verge, and sat for a few minutes, her arms folded across the steering wheel, and her forehead resting on them, waiting for her heartbeat to steady, trying to regain her equilibrium.

It was stupid to drive when she was so upset, so on edge. She couldn't risk an accident now. It would ruin everything. She had to keep her hard-won beauty intact—flawless.

For Saul Kingsland.

At the thought of him, her whole body tensed uncontrollably.

During those innocent sunlit hours in the garden, prompted by the nostalgic memories of the child she'd been, she'd almost begun to have second thoughts about taking the Flawless assignment. But

the confrontation with Susan had hardened her resolve to granite. She still could hardly believe that
it had happened, that the girl with whom she'd
grown up could resent her so deeply. When they'd
been children, they'd been so close, the four-year
difference in their ages seeming immaterial.

Sue let me tag around after her everywhere, Carly
thought. And I was so proud that she was my big
sister. I never minded when people said how lovely
she was. I never cared about the comparisons they
drew when they looked at us, side by side.

Her throat constricted painfully. But perhaps
Susan had enjoyed the contrast, she thought.
Even—needed it, to reassure herself about her own
looks and popularity. *Mirror, mirror on the wall*...
In those days, there'd never been any doubt as to
what the mirror would answer.

But then had come Louise's wedding—shattering her—turning everything upside-down. And
in its aftermath her whole life had changed—
totally and irrevocably.

And with that change had come first bewilderment, then awkwardness and withdrawal, and
now, finally, estrangement from her family.

Saul Kingsland, she thought. Saul Kingsland, you
have so much to pay for. And I'm going to extract
every last penny. Starting now.

The flat seemed emptier than usual as she let herself
in. She tossed the case into her room, and went
straight to the kitchen. The fridge-freezer held a
selection of packet meals which could be micro-
waved. She chose the first that came to hand, and
slid it into the oven.

She filled the coffee percolator, and switched it on. Assembled crockery and cutlery.

Then she went to the telephone. She didn't have to look up the number. She already knew it by heart. She dialled, and waited.

'This is Saul Kingsland.' He sounded, disturbingly, as if he was there in the room with her. 'I'm sorry I can't talk to you in person right now, but if you'd like to leave a message after the tone, I'll get back to you as soon as possible.'

'It's Carly North. If you still want to take some pictures of me, I'm free tomorrow.' She put down the receiver.

That's that, she thought, and went back to the microwave and her instant meal. By the time she'd eaten it, the small kitchen was filled with the aroma of coffee. She poured herself a cup and took it through to the bedroom.

She peeled off the grey dress, and let it fall to the floor. On Monday, she decided, she would take it to a nearly-new shop. Certainly, she never wanted to see it again. She dropped bra, briefs, tights and slip into a linen basket and put on her dressing-gown. Its almost tailored style, with padded shoulders and deep revers, slashed to reveal the cleft between her small, high breasts, was in stark contrast to the sinuous peach satin it was made from. It was the most expensive robe she'd ever bought, but the colour warmed her skin, and acted as a magnificent foil to the tumble of her hair.

Barefoot, she wandered back into the sitting-room and switched on the television set. I don't want anything significant, she told it silently. I just want some mindless entertainment—to prevent me

from thinking. Because if I start rehashing everything that's happened I shall cry, and I don't want
to give way to that kind of weakness.

A film was beginning—a classic thriller which
she'd seen many times before—and she subsided
into it gratefully, sitting curled up on the sofa, her
hands clasped round the warmth of her cup.

It was ridiculous, because it was a beautiful night
in early summer, but she still felt chilled to the bone.
Perhaps in a minute she would switch on the electric
fire.

The sound of the front door buzzer brought her
head round sharply. All her circle of friends thought
she was at home, enjoying herself at Susan's party.

She got up and trod over to the intercom. 'Yes?'
Her voice was not encouraging.

'It's Saul. Open up.'

She had the door half-open before it occurred to
her that she had no reason in the world to obey his
authoritarian command. But by then it was too late.
He was already in the room.

'Isn't it rather late for social calls?' she asked
coolly.

'I was intrigued by your message,' he said. 'Also
by the fact there were no party sounds in the background. You rang off before I could cut in and talk
to you, so I decided to take a chance and come
round.' He gave her a narrow-eyed stare. 'What are
you doing back so soon from the family reunion?'

Carly shrugged. 'I found I wasn't in a party
mood, after all.' She paused. 'If we're going to work
together, I hope I'm not going to have to explain
every facet of my behaviour.'

'Only if it directly impinges on our relationship.' He was still watching her. 'You look tense.'

'I had a near miss on the drive back,' she said shortly. 'It shook me, rather.' She gave him an edged look. 'Is that sufficient explanation?'

'It will do for now.' He walked forward, dropping the denim jacket he'd been carrying, slung over his shoulder, on to a chair. 'That coffee smells good.'

His jeans were denim too, clinging closely to his lean hips, and long legs, and he wore a plain white shirt, open at the neck, and with the cuffs rolled back to reveal muscular forearms.

'I'm not really in the mood for company.' She stayed by the door, holding it open.

'Then I'll have to change your mood,' he said pleasantly. 'Is the kitchen through there?'

Trembling with temper, she banged the door shut and followed him.

His sudden appearance had unnerved her. She wasn't ready for this kind of intrusion.

She said tautly, 'You really do take over, don't you?'

He poured the coffee into a beaker. 'Tell me what I want to hear, and I'll leave.'

'I—haven't made up my mind yet.'

'Liar,' he said. 'You wouldn't have called me if that were so.'

'I want to wait,' she said, 'until you've photographed me. After all, I might photograph like a dog, and you'd have to change your mind.'

'I've seen how you photograph. This morning I saw some of the work Lonnie Attwood did with you. Now I want you to see yourself through my eyes.'

She shrugged again. 'A rag, a bone and a hank of hair. What's new in that?'

'Some rag.' His eyes slid lazily over her, making her aware without equivocation that he knew she was naked under the robe. 'And some hank, too,' he went on, studying the gleaming waves spilling over her shoulders. 'Is that its natural colour?'

'Hardly.'

'What was it before?'

'Difficult to say. Maybe a sort of—fieldmouse brown.'

'Sounds cute.'

'Very boring, actually.'

He smiled and shook his head. 'Oh, no, lady. Nothing about you could ever be boring. But I approve of Hank Mark Two.'

'I'm sure you do.' Swift, overwhelming anger stung through the words, and he gave her a surprised look.

'Did I say something wrong?'

She wrenched herself back into control. 'Not really. I've had a fraught day, and you're catching the backlash, that's all. When I'm like this, I'm best left in peace.'

'That's one theory.'

'You have a better one?'

He leaned back against the sink unit, very much at ease. His eyes went over her again, slowly, definitively, lingering on the deep V formed by the lapels of her robe, and down to where the satin clung to the line of hip and thigh. She felt her body begin to burn under the long, sensual appraisal. Her breasts seemed swollen and oddly tender as they thrust against their thin covering, and her legs were suddenly like water. Standing there suffering the intimacy of his gaze was a major problem, she thought faintly, so how could she possibly contemplate any other kind of involvement with him, however inconclusive?

'Infinitely better,' he drawled, breaking the thrall of silence she was locked in. 'Making love is a fantastic way of releasing aggression and ironing out the kinks. Pure therapy.'

'Pure,' she said, 'is not the word I'd have chosen.' To her chagrin, her voice sounded very young, and rather breathless.

He grinned at her wickedly. The force of his charm—his attraction, when he chose to exert it, was like being caught in the glare of some arc light, she thought crossly.

'Do I take it you're rejecting my infallible remedy?'

'I'm afraid so.'

'Don't be afraid,' he said. 'That's something you need never be with me. In bed, or out of it.'

'Please don't talk like that.' She felt colour wash into her face.

'Like what?'

'As if it was all a *fait accompli*,' she said wildly. 'As if you were taking over my life.'

'I'll take it by degrees,' he said. 'Starting with your working life. You'll find it completely painless.' He paused. 'I take it your passport's in order?'

'Of course. Why?'

'Because we may be going abroad fairly soon for location work. The Flawless UK chairman, Athol Clement, has suggested that we use his private villa on Thyrsos as a base both for the television commercials and the still shots.'

Her eyes widened. 'Is he serious?'

'Apparently so. He says it's the perfect Greek island—fantastic light, tiny deserted beaches, even a ruined temple. And we'd have the run of it for the duration.' He gave her a meditative look. 'Tempted?'

'It sounds—ideal.'

'Septimus Creed thinks so, too. He wants to get this project off the ground as quickly as possible.'

'You—you said you wouldn't pressure me any more,' she said quickly. 'I'll give you my answer tomorrow. I promise I will.'

'Only now you'd like me to go.'

She nodded mutely.

'Then I suppose I must,' he said ruefully. 'But I'd much rather stay—begin exploring with you exactly what happened between us last night.'

'Nothing happened.' The protest sounded weak.

'Not physically, perhaps. Largely because I didn't trust myself to touch you. But then you already know that, don't you, Carly North?'

She looked down at the floor. 'Yes.'

'A touch of honesty at last,' he said mockingly.

'I'm not usually so evasive.' She tried to smile. 'I think I must still be in shock.' She gave a little helpless shake of the head. 'You see, I'm just not used...' Her voice tailed away.

'That makes two of us.' His expression gentled.

She'd struck the right note, she thought. That hint at her emotional confusion had appealed straight to his masculine ego.

Saul drained the remainder of his coffee, and rinsed the beaker under the tap.

He said abruptly, 'I wish you trusted me.'

'You want so much.'

'In actual fact, I want very little. But I would dearly like to know exactly what went wrong at your country retreat.'

'Oh, that's easily told. A little female squabble over my sister's choice of bridesmaids.'

His brows lifted. 'In other words, you're not one of them.'

'Quite right,' she said with forced lightness. 'I think it must be fate.' She paused, aware that her heart was hammering. 'The last time I was supposed to follow a bride up the aisle,' she went on, keeping her voice casual, 'I was taken ill, hours before the ceremony, and had to drop out. I'd hoped for better luck this time.'

'Only she can't stand the competition,' Saul said, and smiled at her stifled gasp of surprise. 'Well, it's her loss. But it still doesn't explain to my satisfaction the sadness in your eyes.'

'I think you're imagining things,' Carly said defensively. 'I'm tired, that's all.'

He grimaced. 'I suspect that's another hint for me to leave.' He walked across to her, and put a hand under her chin, tilting her face up towards his. He said, 'Goodnight, my elusive beauty. I'll pick you up around ten tomorrow.'

He bent and brushed her mouth with his, swiftly and lightly.

'You see,' he told her softly. 'There's really nothing to fear.'

He went past her, out of the room, and seconds later she heard the front door close behind him.

She lifted a hand and touched her mouth with fingers that shook. Saul's kiss had been so fleeting that it had barely existed, yet she'd felt it in every fibre of her being. Her body was tingling still, and her lips, ridiculously, felt bruised.

Although he'd gone, she realised wonderingly, the room still seemed full of him, as if he'd somehow imprinted his personality on it, indelibly and for all eternity.

Each time I come in here, she thought wildly, I'll see him, lounging there, watching me, his eyes devouring me. When all this is over, I'll have to have the place exorcised—or move.

She walked over to the sink, and picked up the beaker he'd used, studying it curiously as if it was some kind of alien artefact. Delicately, hardly breathing, she ran her finger round the rim where his lips had touched.

Nothing to fear, she thought. Oh, lord, nothing to fear.

And with a little inarticulate cry, she whirled round and threw the beaker at the tiled wall, smashing it beyond repair into a hundred tiny fragments.

CHAPTER FOUR

CARLY was ready an hour before Saul was due to collect her the next morning.

Usually when Lucy was there, Sunday was a lazy day for them both. They got up late, and spent some time lounging with the papers before preparing brunch. But this time she'd been up, it seemed, almost since dawn. She'd tried on half a dozen different outfits, experimented with make-up and her hair, and she still wasn't satisfied.

In the end, she put on a simple white cotton dress, sleeveless, and flaring gently from a deep yoke, and tied her hair back with a matching ribbon. She used eye-shadow and blusher with discretion, accentuating eyes and cheekbones with an artist's hand.

He'd seen her sophisticated, and next door to naked. Today it would be the virginal look, she thought detachedly, surveying her handiwork.

When she opened the door to him, his brows lifted slightly, but he made no comment.

'So, where are we going—Hyde Park?' she asked, as she sat beside him in the car, the sun pouring through the windows.

'A rather more peaceful environment than that.' He slanted her a swift smile. 'I hope you have no plans for the rest of the day.'

'Nothing definite.' She kept her tone neutral, in spite of an inner stab of alarm.

'Good,' Saul said laconically, and slid the car expertly through a gap in the traffic.

She was on tenterhooks to see the route he would take, but when she realised it was nowhere near the road she had followed yesterday she began imperceptibly to relax, although she still had no idea where they were going.

They didn't talk much, but Carly was aware of Saul's brief sidelong glance flicking towards her constantly as he drove.

And I should be watching him too, she thought. Persuading him with every half-smile, every flutter of my eyelashes, that my interest in him is real, and personal. Oh, I wish I was a better actress.

She was thankful when there was no city left, and she could concentrate with genuine interest on the scenery. She thought for a while that they were going to the coast, but Saul soon left the main road, and turned the car into a maze of lanes.

Drawing her deeper and deeper into some web of his own devising, she thought, but who was the one who would remain caught when it was all over?

She drew a deep breath, and felt him look at her again more sharply. To cover it, she said lightly, 'Will we ever find our way back?'

'Would it matter?'

She shrugged. 'I think we might be missed. Clive would be looking for his percentage.' She paused. 'And I'm sure someone, somewhere is keeping tabs on you.'

'A thankless task.' He was smiling.

'I'm sure it is.' She moved her shoulders, luxuriating in the sun's warmth. 'What a heavenly day.'

'And you're going to enjoy it in a tiny corner of Paradise.'

'No other clues?'

'I thought you'd like a touch of mystery.' The hedgerows they were driving between were bright with hawthorn. Carly could have extended a hand and picked some as they passed. 'After all,' he went on, 'you're something of an enigma yourself.'

Her heart missed a beat. 'Nonsense.' She extended slender bare arms. 'Nothing up my sleeves—look.'

'I'm looking all the time,' he said. 'I'm just not sure what I see.'

She forced a laugh. 'Well, they say the camera cannot lie.'

'It's not obliged to tell the whole truth, either.' His tone was wry. 'All in all, it promises to be an interesting day.' He paused. 'Are you hungry?'

'Yes, I am,' she admitted, slightly surprised. She'd made herself some toast back in that early daylight, but thrown most of it away.

'Then we'll eat.'

There was a signpost indicating a village half a mile ahead. It was a tiny place, just a few houses and a church clustering round the edge of a green, and the inevitable pub. There was already a handful of cars parked outside, and people were standing, or sitting in the sun, drinks in hand.

'It could be just bread and cheese,' Saul warned, as he swung himself out of the car.

'That would be wonderful,' she said. 'With a lager.'

She found the last vacant table, and sat down. He'd said, 'the rest of the day', she thought. What did that mean? How long did a day last, and what did he have planned for its ending? After all, they'd admitted a mutual attraction. She could hardly express outrage if he expected her to remain with him through the night.

She bit her lip. I'm going to have to be so careful, she thought.

'Still brooding over your family problems?' Saul put down the lagers, and sat beside her on the wooden bench, his thigh brushing hers.

'I'm sorry, does it show?' She resisted the impulse to edge away.

'I'm glad that it does. You don't need to hide things from me.' He was smiling as he said it, but Carly found her body tingling under the sudden intensity of his regard.

She ran her finger down the condensation on the outside of her glass. 'Am I allowed no secrets at all?'

Saul shook his head slowly. 'No,' he said quietly. 'I want to know everything.'

'That sounds—alarming.'

'It doesn't have to be instant knowledge. Learning should be a gradual and enjoyable process.' The caress in his voice was almost tangible, as if his hands had touched her intimately. 'I hope that you want to know about me, too. That I'm not just someone who can further your career.'

'No,' she said. 'No, I don't see you like that at all.'

'Good.' He took her free hand and carried it to his lips. 'Although I plan to make you the sensation of the year—of the decade.'

She pouted laughingly, covering up the swift, unwanted flare of sensation which the brush of his mouth across her skin had induced. 'Not the century?'

'That too,' he promised solemnly. 'Now, here comes our bread and cheese.'

It was more than that, of course. A waitress brought twin platters loaded with cheese, and slices of home-cured ham, flanked by chunks of french bread and a crisp salad, and accompanied by an assortment of chutneys and pickles. In spite of her inner turmoil, Carly found she was eating ravenously.

When they'd finished their meal, Saul walked her round the green to the church. There was an ancient lych gate, and beyond it in the churchyard a yew tree, its trunk thickened with the centuries, its boughs almost sweeping the ground.

Saul made her stand in front of it while he photographed her, a slim, pale shape against the tree's darkness, the faint breeze lifting her hair, and ruffling the white dress into a cloud.

He directed her sharply and succinctly, ordering every turn of her body, every motion of her head, making her kick off her sandals and stand barefoot and on tiptoe, as if about to take flight.

'Fantastic,' he said, finally, telling her to rest. 'Like Primavera—or Persephone escaping from the gates of Hell.'

'That was relatively painless,' she commented, slipping on her sandals again. 'I'd heard you were a terrible bully.'

'I can be,' he said. 'And the session's only just begun. We're off to a new location, that's all.'

His stride was long, and she had to trot to catch up with him. 'Are you leaving the car?'

'It's within walking distance.' He took her down a narrow lane, where the trees met overhead to form a sun-dappled canopy. The cottage was at the bottom of a short slope, set back from the road. It was an attractive building, whitewashed and half-timbered, with moss gathering on the roof tiles. Rambler roses and wistaria reached up to the first-floor windows in an ordered tangle.

'Like it?' Saul smiled at her bemused expression.

She drew a breath. 'It's fabulous. How did you know it was here?'

'I know the owner.' He pushed open the gate.

Carly hung back, giving him a suspicious look. 'Is it yours, by any chance?'

He laughed. 'No, I've never put down roots like this. But it's all right, she's away, and anyway, she wouldn't mind.'

Wouldn't she? Carly thought as she followed him round the side of the house, and through another wicket gate. Then she must be very tolerant. I wonder precisely who 'she' is?

Then, when she saw what was confronting her, she stopped wondering about anything, and just stood, filling her eyes with its beauty.

Beyond the confines of the cottage garden was the bank of a stream, and there someone had planted masses of azaleas, which were now blooming in full maturity, a carpet of vibrant scarlets, pinks and mauves all the way to the water's edge. The colours were almost a shock to the senses, she thought faintly.

'Stunned?' He came to stand beside her. 'I always am, too. I keep telling myself it can't possibly be as I remember, and yet it always is.' He put his arm round her, drawing her against him. 'As soon as I saw you, I wanted to put you in this setting.'

She gave a nervous laugh. 'It's too lovely. I don't deserve it.'

'You'll enhance it.' He turned her fully into his arms, looking down into her face. He gave a small, uneven laugh. 'Oh, Carly,' he said softly, 'I brought you here to work . . .'

He bent his head, and his mouth came down on hers. This time, his kiss was neither casual nor gentle. His lips were hungry, parting hers in an aching demand which would not be denied. His tongue invading her mouth, seeking her sweetness, was like silk—but silk that burned, she thought dazedly as the sunlight, the azaleas, the dazzle on the water and Saul's kiss became some sweet and fiery unity that threatened to consume her.

His hands stroked her back, tracing the supple length of her spine through the thin fabric of her dress, and her body arched towards his in startled and imploring delight.

He said huskily, 'Oh, my sweet,' and pulled her against him, moulding her body to his, making her aware that he was fiercely and heatedly aroused. At the same time, his hand sought the zip at the back of her dress.

The force of that realisation jerked her back to some semblance of reality. Her hands lifted in panic, pushing at his chest, thrusting him away from her.

'No,' she choked from her dry throat. 'Let go of me.'

He obeyed instantly. She took a step backwards, lips parting to drag air into her lungs, arms folding defensively across her body.

Faint colour burned along his cheekbones, and his mouth twisted as he noted the gesture. He said, 'Carly, you don't have to worry. In spite of appearances, I haven't brought you here to rape you.' He shrugged almost wryly. 'I hadn't planned on seduction either, but you were so—exquisitely responsive. I—lost my head for a moment.'

And she had lost hers too, she thought, in horrified disbelief. For a moment, she had forgotten everything, almost drowning in a pleasure that was totally new to her experience. Oh, how could it have happened—how could she have allowed it to happen—and with Saul Kingsland, of all the men on earth?

'I'm so ashamed.'

She didn't realise she'd spoken aloud until she saw his brows snap together.

'There's nothing to feel shame about. The point of no return was still a long way off. Surely you realise that.' He paused with a sharp intake of breath. 'Or don't you know? Is that what you're trying to tell me? That you haven't—that there's never . . . ?'

She lifted her chin. 'Is it so impossible to believe?'

'No,' he said quietly. 'Suddenly it's not impossible at all. In fact, it explains a great deal.' He threw back his head and looked at her, almost dispassionately. 'But what I can't figure,' he went on, 'is why? You're beautiful, and you certainly aren't frigid, so why hasn't there been someone for you?'

She turned away, looking across the rioting azaleas to the gleam of the water. 'There were always other priorities,' she said slowly. 'My career, for instance.'

And my revenge.

'But that isn't all.' His hands descended on her shoulders, holding her lightly and without threat. He said gently, 'I think at some time, Carly North, you've been hurt quite badly. I think it's made you wary—made you close in on yourself. Made you shut out other people. Well, I'm telling you that's all over now.'

'You're going to heal me?' Her face felt as if it had been turned to stone. She was glad that he was standing behind her, and couldn't see her expression.

'I'm going to try.' He paused. 'It would help if you could tell me a little about it . . .'

'Not now,' she said. 'But one day I'll tell you. I promise I will.'

'Then I'll be satisfied with that.' His lips touched her hair. 'So don't go tense on me again. From now on, we play this your way. I won't force the pace, or make any demands you're not ready for.'

'You're—very understanding, and very kind.'

'A misunderstood saint, in fact.' Amusement quivered in his voice. 'Don't be fooled, lady, I'm not that altruistic. I'm hoping that if I'm patient with you now, one of these days all that dammed-up passion is going to break through, and you're going to give yourself to me without holding back. In fact, I'm counting on it.' He turned her to face

him. 'And, as you don't yet want my body, I'm
going to make love to you with my camera instead.
Go and sit among the flowers.'

She obeyed, smiling, lifting her face to the sun.
Without knowing it, Saul had just delivered into
her hands the perfect weapon to use against him.

His patience, she thought, his self-control, tried
to the utmost limits. Oh, how she could make him
suffer.

And I will, she promised silently, picking a
handful of crimson blossoms and tossing them in
the air so that the petals drifted down over her face
and dress. I will.

He said, 'Tell me now, lady. Are you going to
take the assignment—become my Flawless Girl?'

She looked at him, her face wiped of all emotion
except that radiant professional smile. And said
once again, but aloud this time, 'I will.'

She sat beside him in the car, as they drove back
into London, feeling totally drained. It had been a
long, demanding session, and Saul had been un-
sparing with her, driving her relentlessly to give
more of herself than she had with any other
photographer.

When she'd tried to protest at one point, he'd
said shortly, 'I'm not interested in pretty masks,
darling. I want the woman beneath, or nothing at
all.'

But, exhausted as she was, she had to admit, reluctantly, that she had never felt more stimulated
or more alive during a session.

Working with Saul Kingsland could have been the experience of a lifetime, she thought, with a tinge of regret, instantly subdued.

He said, 'Will you have dinner with me tonight?'

'I—can't. I have a prior invitation—from Clive and Marge.'

It wasn't true, but Clive and Marge always kept open house on Sunday evenings, and people were welcome to drop in if they chose. There was nearly always a crowd, talking endlessly, playing music and silly card games, helping themselves from the huge pots of spaghetti and chili con carne in the kitchen.

Carly always enjoyed herself there, but tonight their home would be a refuge. Because she'd been shocked to realise how tempted she'd been to accept Saul's invitation, and let her day with him linger into evening, and beyond. The clean, warm taste of his mouth exploring hers, the stroke of his hands, the stark pressure of his lean body—all these returned to haunt her with total recall.

Because—just for a moment—she had been in genuine danger, much as she loathed to admit it, her untried flesh awakened and urgent.

And now she was tired, and therefore vulnerable. Apart from anything else, she'd allowed herself to enjoy their working rapport too much, she castigated herself. So it would be altogether unwise to risk spending any more time in his company.

He might be her enemy, but he was wickedly, frighteningly attractive, she thought broodingly, and she was going to need all her strength and all her wits about her to resist him physically and emotionally.

'Are you going to tell Clive your decision? Naturally Septimus Creed will contact him with the contract details.' Saul paused. 'You know the snags, I suppose. Exclusive rights to you. No pictures of you, other than as the Flawless Girl, to appear anywhere for the duration of the agreement.'

'Yes,' she said. 'I know.'

'I hope you do,' he said, a shade grimly. 'The company has invested a lot of money in pre-publicity—the search to find The Girl, and are spending even more on the campaign. If there was any kind of foul-up, they could get nasty.'

'Then I'll have to be ultra-careful.'

'We both will.' He drew up the car outside her block, and looked at her, reaching to draw his forefinger lightly round the curve of her lower lip. 'Sure I can't persuade you to change your mind, and stay with me this evening?' he asked quietly. 'It's dinner that's on offer. Nothing more.'

'I—know that, but it's still impossible.' She looked down at her hands, folded tightly in her lap. 'I'm sorry.'

'So am I.' His voice was rueful. 'But I can wait.'

When she got into the flat, her heart was hammering as if she'd taken part in some marathon, and she sagged weakly against the closed panels of the door, fighting to control her breathing.

Other men—men she'd liked—had kissed her, and she'd found it pleasant, without experiencing the kind of stir in her blood which would have tempted her to go beyond kissing.

So why must it be Saul Kingsland, whom she hated, who could make the lightest caress matter so terribly? It had taken all her will-power, she recognised, dry-mouthed, to walk away from him into the building.

Perhaps it was some kind of karma, she thought. A divine retribution being exacted in advance for what she was going to do to him.

She said aloud, 'Well, so be it.'

Marge said, 'You look different.'

Carly concentrated her attention on the bottle of wine she was opening. 'Different better, I hope.'

'I'm not sure.'

Carly sent her a glance of mock horror. 'Marge, darling, I'm going to be the Flawless Girl. Now is not the moment to tell me that my looks are going off.'

'I wasn't going to,' Marge said drily. 'You're as stunning as ever. All the single men here tonight are drooling with lust—and a few of the married ones too.' She paused. 'No, it's something in your eyes—a faraway look you get—as if you had some secret you were hugging to yourself.' She added deliberately, 'And I'd be much happier, Carly my sweet, if I thought it was a nice secret.'

Carly managed a careless laugh. 'You have a great imagination, Marge. No wonder you were such a whiz as a copywriter.'

'I wish it was just imagination,' Marge said with a measuring look. 'Are you planning to pour that wine, or just strangle the bottle with your bare hands?' She paused again. 'Did I see you chatting to Mark Clayfield earlier?'

'Do I hear your disapproval showing?'

'Yes, you do, actually.' Marge filled a bowl with crisps.

'Then why do you have him here, if he's *persona non grata*?'

Marge sighed. 'Because he and Clive were at university together, and he used to be a half-way decent journalist before he sold himself to that terrible Sunday rag. Now I feel I have to guard every word in front of him, in case they appear in the next edition as "bored housewife's kinky fantasies".'

'Well, I didn't say a word he could use against me,' Carly said. 'In fact, I found him quite pleasant.'

Marge snorted. 'No doubt he wants you to strip for that centrefold of his. Become one of his Sunday Sirens.'

Carly bent her head, letting her hair swing forward like a curtain. 'My goodness, can you imagine Clive's face?'

'Indeed I can, and not only his.' Marge tipped peanuts into a variety of small dishes, and put them on a tray. 'Following on from that, how did you enjoy dinner with Saul Kingsland?'

'It was fine.' Carly bit her lip. 'Do you think I should open another bottle of white wine?'

'On past experience, I'd open several. Is "fine" all you have to say on the subject?'

Carly shrugged neutrally. 'I've achieved my ambition,' she returned. 'He's taken my photograph. And he's going to take more.'

'Ah, yes,' said Marge. 'I suppose congratulations are in order. If the Flawless assignment is really what you want, of course.'

Carly opened her eyes wide. 'How could it not be? It's going to make me the most famous face in Europe.'

'For a little while, certainly,' Marge conceded ironically. 'What are you going to do as an encore?'

'I'll worry about that when the time comes.' Carly picked up the tray of glasses. 'I'd better take these round before they all go purple and their tongues start to swell.'

For goodness' sake, she thought, as she carried the tray into the big, comfortable cluttered drawing-room. It's as if she knows. But she can't. No one has the least inkling. She's just fishing.

But that was unfair. Marge had been a friend to her from those first, uncertain days when she'd tested whether her face was going to be her fortune or not. She'd been more of an older sister, more of a mother to Carly than the real incumbents of those positions. And her antennae were second to none. She knew there was something wrong—something off-key—and she was concerned.

And when it was over she would be devastated.

I wish I could tell her, Carly thought, as she laughed and chatted and passed round wine. I wish I could confide in her. But I daren't. Because she'd tell Clive, and that would be the end of it. And I've waited too long to allow that to happen.

In fact, it seems to have used up all my life—waiting for Saul to come back.

CHAPTER FIVE

As she was passing through the hall on her way back to the kitchen, Clive was coming down the stairs.

'I bear ill tidings,' he said. 'The Third Monster is asking for you. Claims the last time you were here, you promised to read her a story. Absolutely refuses to go to sleep without it.'

'Yes, I did,' Carly said remorsefully. 'I'll go right up.'

In the room at the far end of the landing, Laura was sitting up in bed, clutching a favourite teddy bear, her eyes turned expectantly towards the door.

'You've been such a long time,' she complained, lifting her face for Carly's kiss. 'Teddy's gone to sleep already.'

'Then I'll have to read specially quietly so as not to wake him.' Carly looked at the pile of books on the night table. 'What story is it to be?'

'*The Ugly Duckling,*' Laura said promptly. 'And will you act all the bits like you always do?'

'Yes,' Carly said gently. 'I'll act all the bits.'

The familiar tale of rejection and ultimate joy wound its familiar course, and Laura listened avidly, her eyelids drooping as Carly, her voice softening, reached the conclusion.

'I'm glad the other swans liked him,' she said sleepily, leaning her head against Carly's arm.

'What would he have done, poor thing, if they hadn't wanted him either?'

'I don't know sweetheart,' Carly said huskily. 'I really don't know.'

'Perhaps he'd have become something else instead,' Laura said. 'Something he didn't want to be . . .' Her voice trailed away, and her eyes closed.

Carly felt the sudden sting of tears against her own eyelids. Perhaps so, she thought. Perhaps so, indeed.

She knew from past experience that Laura, once asleep, would not stir, and there was nothing to prevent her from putting the little girl back on her pillows and rejoining the party downstairs.

Yet she felt in no hurry to do so. She stayed where she was, enjoying the peace in the room, the soft sounds of the child's breathing. Up to now, she'd seen and appreciated what Clive and Marge had in their marriage without envy. But, suddenly, she found herself wondering what it would be like to have a child of her own. To conceive it, protect it inside her body, and give it birth and love it.

She'd never even considered such an eventuality before, she thought wonderingly. She'd been too determined, too single-minded in her purpose to allow the possibility of a different kind of future for herself. So why was she thinking about it now, just when the victory she'd dreamed of was almost within her grasp? Surely she couldn't be weakening, now of all times?

She heard a small sound and, turning her head, saw Saul standing in the doorway staring at her. For a moment, she thought he was a figment of her imagination—a mirage created out of the mass of confused emotion within her, then he took a step forward into the room, and she knew he was only too real, and gasped, her hand flying to her throat.

Disturbed by the sudden movement, Laura muttered something, turning her head restlessly. Carly hesitated, then eased herself away from the child, lowering her on to the pillows and tucking the covers round her.

Saul was waiting for her on the landing. 'I seem to spend my life startling you,' he said wryly.

'What are you doing here?' She was angry, and more shaken by his sudden appearance than she wanted to be. 'How dare you do this? Are you following me—checking up on me for some reason?'

'Of course not, what do you take me for?' His brows drew together. 'Clive telephoned me to say you'd told him the news, and that although he still didn't approve he was putting some champagne on ice. He invited me over to share the celebration. Didn't he mention it?'

'No, he didn't.' Carly bit her lip hard.

'Then maybe he should have done,' Saul said coolly, 'as there's clearly some problem. But I can always leave, if that's what you'd prefer.'

He turned towards the stairs, and she flew after him. 'No—Saul, please.' She tugged at the sleeve of his jacket. 'I'm sorry I came on so strong, but I just wasn't expecting to see you there. Of course we must celebrate. It was a marvellous idea of Clive's.'

'Was it?' There was no softening in his dark face. 'I'll have to take your word for that, lady.'

She threw back her head. 'I've said I'm sorry. What do you want me to do—grovel?'

'No,' he said. 'Explain.' He shrugged. 'But I'm aware that's not possible, so we'll leave it there. Now I'll go down, drink Clive's champagne and go.'

She said in a low voice. 'That's—not what I want.'

Saul gave her a long look. When he spoke, his voice was slightly more gentle. 'Are you sure you really know?'

She nodded mutely. She couldn't let him walk away like this. Couldn't risk the possibility of a rift which might ruin everything. Not now.

For a moment he was still, then he shrugged again, and extended his hand. She put hers into it, and they walked downstairs together.

Clive's speech hailing Carly as the Flawless Girl was a masterpiece. The majority of his audience were left with the belief that it was all his own idea, and that it was due to his ceaseless efforts that she was fronting the campaign at all. Saul's gaze was ironic as it met hers.

They were, naturally, the centre of attention. But, as they laughed and talked, Carly was aware of a continuing reserve in Saul's manner towards her. She was conscious too of the buzz of excitement his arrival had created among the women present, and soon found, not altogether to her surprise, that he'd been cornered by one of Marge's actress neighbours. Mel Bolton was blonde, ambitious and predatory, and while her use of body language might not be subtle it was certainly effective, Carly thought grimly, observing from the corner of her eye how Mel's slender finger was playing idly with

the buttons on Saul's shirt, while she smiled beguilingly up at him.

Saul's response was rather more difficult to
fathom. Glass in hand, lounging back against the
wall, he looked relaxed, and faintly amused. But
Carly could swear there was growing appreciation
in his eyes as they studied the cling of Mel's seductive little black dress.

'At the moment, he's just flattered,' Marge said
in her ear. 'But I've seen Mel in action too often.
Give her another twenty minutes, and he'll be
leaving with her.'

Oh, no, he won't, Carly said silently, feeling her
nails curling like claws into the palms of her hands.

That was something she hadn't allowed for—the
intervention of another woman to muddy the waters
and provide another focus for Saul's attention. And
it was something she needed to deal with.

She walked over, and slid her hand through his
arm, giving Mel Bolton a swift smile.

'Saul, can I possibly drag you away? All that
fresh air this afternoon seems to have knocked me
out, and I'd like to go home now.'

Saul said equably, 'Very well,' but the quizzical
lift of his brows was a challenge.

As they crossed the room, he said softly, 'Leading
me out of temptation, darling? I wasn't aware you
required my services as an escort tonight.'

She flushed slightly. 'I—I need to talk to you.
To find out more about the assignment. This trip
to Thyrsos, for instance—is it definitely on?'

'A matter of supreme importance indeed,' he
commented sardonically. 'And the answer is, yes,

as far as I know. We'll probably get final confirmation in a day or two.'

As she sat beside him in the car, she said jerkily, 'You still haven't forgiven me, have you?'

'For what? For preventing my acceptance of the rather obvious invitation I was getting?' The glance he sent her was edged.

'Of course not,' she said too quickly. 'You're a free agent, after all. No, I meant for—sounding off at you as I did.'

'Well, let's leave it at that,' he said, after a pause. 'You're tired, and my sudden appearance was a shock to you. End of story.'

'I'm not usually this temperamental. Anyone will tell you that.'

'They have. You have a name for being totally professional and co-operative.'

He was still, she realised, keeping her at a distance. And that was bad news. She needed him involved—under any spell she cared to weave.

When they arrived outside the flat, she said, 'Would you like to come in for a drink—some coffee, perhaps?'

'I think I should let you get an early night instead.'

'It doesn't have to be—that immediate.'

He was silent for a moment, then he said, 'In that case, fine. I could use some coffee.'

This time, he stayed in the sitting-room while she made it and carried it through. She found him down on one knee, scrutinising her record collection.

'They say you can tell a person's character by studying the books they have on their shelves,' he said over his shoulder. 'I wonder if it's the same with music?'

'What does it tell you?' She sat down on the sofa.

'On the surface, fairly conventional.' He came to sit beside her. 'But underneath, a romantic streak which upbringing and conditioning hasn't been able to subdue, and a tendency to take risks. Hidden depths, and some surprising contradictions.' He paused. 'How am I doing, so far?'

She shrugged. 'You make me sound far more interesting than I really am.'

'Not just interesting,' he said. 'Fascinating.'

She poured the coffee and handed it to him.

'It's a very pleasant flat. How did you acquire it?' he asked.

'I was very fortunate. I had a wealthy god-mother. When she died, I found she'd left me quite a lot of money. I inherited it when I was eighteen.'

'And invested in this place?'

'Among other things.'

'A wise move. Property prices round here look set to go through the ceiling.'

'That doesn't really concern me. I'm not planning on selling.'

'So, what are your plans?'

She gave a slight shrug. 'I—seem to fall in with whatever life throws at me.'

'And right now, it's hurled the Flawless contract into your lap. Your face on hoardings, in magazine spreads and television commercials. Personal appearances at stores and beauty centres up and down the country, and across the Channel.'

'You make it sound—rather daunting.'

'But also extremely lucrative. Most of the models I've met are looking to the future, squirrelling away their earnings into some kind of business which will keep them when their faces are no longer their fortunes. Have you thought about that?'

No, she thought. Because everything I've done, every decision I've made, has had only one aim in mind—to bring you down—and I've never looked beyond that.

She shrugged again. 'Oh, I think I have a few good years left.'

'I'd say you had any number of spectacular years,' Saul said drily, putting down his empty cup. 'Thank you for the coffee. I shall now leave you in peace.'

She didn't look at him. Slowly she replaced her own cup on the table, beside his. 'Do you—really have to go so soon?'

She could sense the sudden tension in his lean body. 'No.'

She leaned back against the cushions. 'Well, then...'

As he bent towards her, she closed her eyes, sliding her arms up round his neck, drawing him down against her pliant body.

For a while, she remained passive while his mouth gently caressed hers, then, aware that he was about to lift his head, she delicately flicked her tongue along his lower lip.

Immediately Saul's arms tightened around her, and with a faint groan he deepened the kiss to passionate demand. She responded instantly, exploring his mouth with the same urgent intensity, stroking the hair at the nape of his neck with fingers that shook.

His weight was pressing her down into the softness of the sofa. Every bone, every muscle, every nerve-ending was aware of him. She felt the pulsing of his heart against her own.

His hand lifted, touched her breast through the jade and turquoise silk of her shirt. She felt her nipples peaking eagerly under the brush of his fingers and gasped.

Beware, a voice in her brain screamed at her. It's his self-control you're testing, not your own. This should stop here and now.

He lifted himself away and looked down at her, his eyes guarded, watchful, the lean body tense as whipcord. Her skin was tingling, greedy for his touch, as slowly—too slowly—Saul began to release the buttons on her shirt from their fastenings. His hands lingered on their task—even fumbled a little, as if he was uncertain or afraid.

She didn't want this gentle, almost tentative wooing, she thought dazedly. She wanted him excited, hungry for her, demanding—something she could turn against him into reproach when the time came to call a halt.

A heavy silence enfolded them. She could hear neither her own breathing nor his. Her consciousness, her entire being, seemed concentrated on the unhurried movement of his hands. The rustle of the silk sounded almost harsh in her ears as he pushed the shirt from her shoulders at last.

As his hands cupped her nakedness, her heated flesh seemed to surge beneath his fingers. Her whole body clenched suddenly in one agonising pulse of desire.

'Oh, Carly.' There was pain in his brief words, and yearning too, and when he kissed her again his mouth took hers with stark sensuality.

His hands stroked her breasts, fondling the rosy peaks lightly but sensuously, sending small ripples of a new and painful delight through her body. Making her achingly aware that Saul's caresses were engendering other desires, other needs, unfamiliar, but disturbingly potent.

She found herself wondering crazily what it would be like to have him touch her everywhere— to have his mouth and hands making a feast of her. The thought sent a shaft of longing piercing through her, so intense it made her moan out loud. Her arms locked fiercely round his neck, and her slender hips lifted, sharply, involuntarily to strain against his own.

'That's enough.' The words seemed to come from a million miles away, as if they'd been torn out of him.

Saul jackknifed away from her, flinging himself to the end of the sofa furthest from her. For a moment he sat motionless, eyes closed, trying to steady his breathing.

Then he said again, 'That's enough.'

'Why?' Carly hardly recognised her own voice. Could not believe she was asking the question.

'Because we either stop now, or we finish it in bed.' He saw her flinch from the sudden harshness in his voice, and added more gently, 'And I don't think you're ready for that. Not yet.' He paused. 'Are you?'

Slowly, mutely, she shook her head.

'That's what I thought.' He sounded resigned, almost grim, but he sent her the beginnings of a smile. 'For heaven's sake, lady, have you the slightest idea what you do to me?' He raked a hand through his hair, then leaned forward, pulling her shirt back into place, his mouth twisting ruefully as he tugged the edges across her bare breasts.

His hand touched her face, stroking the curve of her cheek. He said quietly, 'I can't kiss you again. I don't trust myself. So I'll just say goodnight and go.'

At the door, he turned and looked back at her. He spoke softly, a note in his voice of laughter and promise.

'A word of warning, my lovely one. When it finally happens, one or both of us may not survive.'

The door closed behind him, and she was alone.

For a while, she couldn't move, couldn't think, then slowly and stiffly she sat up, forcing the buttons of her shirt back into their holes with shaking fingers, trying to come to terms with the near-disaster which had befallen her.

For a brief while, in Saul's arms, she'd forgotten everything that had motivated her—driven her inexorably for the past five years. Put out of her mind the mental suffering he'd caused her, and the long months of physical pain which had resulted, which she'd deliberately invited.

He'd almost destroyed her. Now she intended to destroy him. It was that simple. So, how could she have allowed it to slip away from her consciousness even for a minute?

And all for a few moments of sexual pleasure—
the most transient experience known to the human
race, she thought in self-derision.

But what had she expected? When she set out to
play with fire, she could hardly complain when she
was the one who was scorched.

She'd thought that everything she'd once felt for
Saul was dead—eclipsed, stifled at birth by his un-
thinking cruelty. And that, at best, it had been a
naïve, adolescent stirring of emotion. Now, she realised, it was not so easily dismissed. When she'd
first met Saul Kingsland—first fallen so headily and
dizzily in love with him—she'd been a child on the
threshold of womanhood, with a woman's needs,
a woman's desires. And, while love had turned to
disillusion and hatred, she had to face the unwelcome fact that desire could continue and co-exist
along with that hatred.

A long shudder ran through her as she leaned
back against the cushions, wrapping her arms round
her body, feeling the sour ache of unsatisfied
arousal deep within her.

She needed to blot that out. Needed to block the
memory of Saul's hands and lips on her skin with
other more powerful remembrances.

I don't want to remember, she thought, wincing.
But I must.

She had to probe once more at those five-year-
old scars. Provide herself with a final, dark reminder of what she had become, and why.

Let her mind take her back, yet again, to the
tranquil summer day when it had all begun.

*   *   *

'Isn't it fantastic?' said Louise, her hair a golden aureole in the sun which poured through the window. 'Saul Kingsland, of all people, agreeing to photograph the wedding.' She gave a little laugh. 'When James told me, I could hardly believe it.'

Five of her bridesmaids, gathered in her bedroom for the final fitting of their dresses, looked and murmured their envy. Caroline, the sixth, and youngest, knowing that she was not required to give an opinion, stood patiently while Mrs Barlow and her assistant twitched irritably at the folds of fabric which enveloped her, and exchanged tight-lipped glances.

'How on earth did James get to know him?' Sue sprawled on the bed and helped herself from a box of chocolates. 'Saul must be years older than he is.'

'Only about five. They were at school together. Saul was James's head of house, and captain of the first eleven, and heaven knows what else. James absolutely hero-worshipped him when he was young. And then, when Alex was killed in that ambush in Northern Ireland, Saul was incredibly kind and supportive. Kept James from cracking up, and made him see that joining the army in his brother's place, and maybe getting himself killed in turn, was no answer.' She gave a slight, guilty giggle. 'For which he has my undying gratitude. And, of course, he and James have kept in touch since.'

'You are lucky, Louise,' Katie Arnold said with a sigh.

'Well, there are strings, of course. He doesn't want to take just the stock shots. He's thinking of bringing out a book—a complete record of a country wedding, warts and all.' Louise giggled again. 'Mummy wasn't awfully pleased when I told her he'd be arriving later today to snap her bawling out the caterers yet again over the phone.'

'Is he going to photograph us trying on our dresses?' Belinda Knox asked eagerly. 'I wish I'd worn my Janet Reger camiknickers.'

'You'll be lucky if any of you get to try your dresses with the time Caroline is taking,' Louise said with a shrug. 'What's the problem, Mrs Barlow?'

'It's the length, Miss Brotherton. We seem to have gained another inch and a half.'

'Caro's having one of her droopy days,' Sue said lightly. 'Do stand up straight, darling, and try and co-operate. You're keeping everyone waiting.'

Caroline sighed inwardly, and straightened herself, aware that a painful blush was spreading up from her toes.

It was all right for Sue. She and the others were the same relative height.

But I'm half a head taller, she thought forlornly. Everyone will notice when we all walk up the aisle. Her glasses were slipping, and she pushed them back up her nose with the little nervous gesture which had become a habit.

Mrs Barlow tutted. 'If you could manage to stand still, also, Miss Foxcroft.'

'Yes, for heavens's sake, Caro,' Louise said crossly, 'we do all have other things to do, you know. Mrs Barlow, I'm still not sure about the neck detail on my gown. It looked wonderful on the Princess of Wales, I agree, but . . .'

Mrs Barlow immediately sprang to the defence
of her design, and Caroline was thankful to have
attention diverted away from her own
shortcomings.

She'd been so excited when Louise had invited
her to be a bridesmaid, but it hadn't been a totally
happy experience so far. As the youngest, she felt
very much an outsider. Very much still the
schoolgirl, while her cousin, her sister and their
friends seemed like women of the world.

They even looked alike, she thought, as if they'd
been picked from a matching set. Whereas she . . .

She stole a sideways glance at herself in the long
mirror, and frowned. She didn't want to stand
straight. When she bent her head a little, she could
convince herself that her long nose was slightly less
obtrusive. And if she hunched her shoulders no one
could tell that her breasts hadn't really budded
under the draped mauve chiffon bodice, but had
to be helped with a padded bra. If only she could
put on some weight.

She stifled another sigh. 'Could I have a chocolate, Sue?'

'Certainly not. You know what sweets do to you.
The last thing you want is one of your horrible spots
in time for the ceremony. Do have a bit of sense.'

The tone of her sister's voice made Caroline realise it would be wiser to stand tall, allow Mrs
Barlow to make whatever adjustments were needed,
and then take herself off somewhere, out of everyone's way.

But it was a good half-hour later before she could
have her wish, and, dressed once more in the comfortable anonymity of jeans and T-shirt, run down-

stairs, and out into the sunlight. Reuben, Aunt
Grace's golden retriever, followed her. He seemed
to feel out of place in all the hectic preparations
too, she thought, stroking his head.

'Come on, old boy,' she whispered. 'We'll go for
a walk down by the river.'

It was a blissful time, that last golden hour of
her childhood, at the water's edge. She found a stick
and threw it for the dog, and let him bring it back
to her over and over again, until they were both
soaked and muddy.

Reuben had the stick in his jaws, and was half
crouching, growling in mock menace, his damp,
plumy tail waving in delight, while Caroline,
laughing, tried to wrest it from him, when she heard
a sound that was an intrusion, wholly unconnected
with their game, or the lapping of the water, and
the breeze in the trees. A buzz, followed by a click.

She looked round, and saw him, a young man,
a stranger, a few yards away, camera poised.

'Don't stop,' he ordered peremptorily. 'Pretend
I'm not here.'

She couldn't. She was frozen with embarrassment and, when she did move, it was to make
that swift, self-conscious adjustment to her glasses.

'Damnation,' he said ruefully, and put his camera
away. 'I hoped I'd manage a few more shots before
you saw me. You were having such a marvellous
time, and I've spoiled it.'

'It—doesn't matter.' She got quickly to her feet,
wiping her hands on her slender flanks. 'I ought to
be getting back, anyway. It's bound to be nearly
teatime, and Aunt Grace probably wants me for

something. There's so much to do—with the wedding.'

'So you are from the house. I wondered.' He gave her a meditative look. 'You're related to the Brothertons?'

'Yes, I'm Louise's cousin, Caroline Foxcroft. I'm going to be one of the bridesmaids. It's my very first time.'

There was an odd silence, then he said, 'Is it, indeed? Well, I'm Saul Kingsland, the honorary photographer.'

'Yes.' She flushed. 'I sort of guessed you were.' She paused. 'Won't they be wondering where you are?'

'I arrived a while ago, and got the introductions over. Then there seemed to be some problem with the florists, so I decided to be tactful, and take a look at the location.' Another brief silence. 'Did your cousin Louise tell you what I was planning?'

She nodded. 'A book—all about the wedding.' She smiled at him. 'We'll all be famous.'

He didn't return the smile. 'If it works. Maybe it isn't such a good idea, after all.'

'Oh, but you must do it. Louise—everyone—would be so disappointed if you didn't.'

'And that's all that matters, of course, at any wedding. Not to disappoint the bride.' His voice was dry. 'I'll have to try and remember that.' He paused. 'But I could always do a different kind of book. Children, maybe, with their pets, being happy as you were just now.'

'I'm not a child,' she said indignantly. 'I'm seventeen. I've got A-levels next year. And Reuben isn't mine. He belongs to Aunt Grace, really, only we both felt a bit in the way, so I brought him for a walk.'

'I'm sorry,' he said, but he looked more angry than regretful, she thought. 'But maybe it isn't such a bad thing to look younger than you are. When you're forty, you might be glad of it.' He glanced at his watch. 'Shall we still be in the way, do you think, or should we go back for tea now?'

'I expect so,' she said shyly. 'I'll have to take Reuben in the back way. Aunt Grace will be furious if I let him in the drawing-room in this state. I'll have to change, too,' she added, casting a stricken glance down at her bedraggled state.

'Well, don't take too long,' Saul Kingsland said. 'We outsiders have to stick together.' He held out his hand, and took her grubby fingers in his. 'Agreed?'

Words were suddenly impossible, so she nodded.

'Good. See you later, then.' At last he smiled at her, an easy, friendly grin which softened the rather saturnine lines of his face. Then, he turned and walked away along the bank.

Caroline took Reuben the other way, towards the gate which opened into the kitchen garden. She didn't hurry, and the dog frisked impatiently in front of her, running back constantly to see why she was taking so long.

Caroline was oblivious. Her mind was seething with a mass of confused impressions—half-remembered words and phrases. She thought of that final smile, and the clamour of her own heartbeat almost deafened her.

'Saul Kingsland,' she whispered. 'Saul Kingsland.'

And his name soared in her mind like some joyous, ecstatic song.

CHAPTER SIX

THE next time she saw him, at tea in the drawing-room, he was surrounded by other people, but he looked across at her, smiled and mouthed 'Hello', and Caroline felt a fresh burst of happiness explode inside her.

She was careful not to let it show. She melted into a corner of the window-seat, and took a cup of tea and a scone she did not want, for camouflage, and watched him from under her lashes, committing every feature, every gesture and turn of his head, every nuance in his voice to memory.

She was overwhelmed by what she felt for him, shaken by its swiftness and inevitability. Was this, she wondered helplessly, what people meant when they talked about love at first sight? And if so, why didn't they also mention how painful it could be when it was all on one side?

She watched Sue, Katie and the others moving round him, vying for his attention, and wished, for the first time in her life, that she could join in, that she had the confidence and experience to walk up to a man, and stake an unequivocal claim.

But, she hadn't, of course. And she wasn't so lost to all sense of reality as to dream he would welcome her advances. He was much older than she was, for one thing—at least twenty-eight, she thought. And he undoubtedly would have a girl-friend—no, a lover, she hastily amended, trying to be sophisticated about it, although her face warmed at the thought—even if she hadn't accompanied him to Elmsleigh.

Leaning back against the warm window-panes, Caroline gave herself up to a luxurious daydream where she found herself walking once again by the river with Saul. Felt his hand close round hers once more. Heard him whisper, 'I thought I knew about women, darling, but you're so young and sweet . . .'

'Caro, do pull yourself together, and help pass the sandwiches round.' Susan's irritable voice returned her to earth with a bump. 'Honestly, you look positively half-witted at times.'

And sometimes I feel it, Caroline thought, guiltily, as she got to her feet. Because hankering after Saul Kingsland has to be the stupidest thing I've ever done. But luckily it's my secret, and that's the way it's going to stay.

It wasn't a difficult resolve to maintain, as the countdown to the wedding began, because, she soon realised, he was totally absorbed in the job he'd come there to do. And even though he was surrounded by pretty girls, all sending out unmistakable signals that they'd be in the market for an enjoyable flirtation, or more, if he was willing, Saul seemed immune to their overtures. But then, in his profession, pretty girls were probably two a penny, Caroline realised ruefully.

Watching him in action with a camera was a revelation. He knew exactly what he wanted from them all, and he cajoled and commanded until he got it. Even Aunt Grace wasn't proof against his charm when he chose to exert it.

Caroline wondered what they would do when the book came out. Watching Saul as closely as she did, she knew that as well as the deliberately posed shots, designed to present the idyllic façade of an English country wedding, there were dozens, in addition, of a far more candid and unflattering nature. Alongside the pretty pictures of people smiling in their best clothes, there would be other, franker illustrations of the inevitable strains, tensions and sheer bad humour that were an inevitable part of such an occasion.

She tried to visualise Aunt Grace's reaction when eventually she saw herself, red-faced and bristling, browbeating the men who had come to erect the marquee. Asked herself if Katie and Meg had realised Saul had even been there as they bickered endlessly over how the bridesmaids' hair should be arranged for the great day. Wondered how Louise and James would feel about the shot of themselves glaring at each other with sudden active dislike.

Clearly none of them shared her own sharp awareness of his every movement, she thought wryly. She'd hoped that Saul hadn't noticed her either, but she was wrong, because on the third morning he said abruptly, 'If you're going to continue to shadow me, you may as well make yourself useful—help with my gear—hand me things.'

'Oh, all right.' She tried to sound offhand, but inwardly she was transformed with delight.

It was, she thought afterwards, the happiest morning she'd ever spent. Saul was a hard taskmaster, frankly dictatorial and even abrasive if she was slow or clumsy in carrying out his commands, but she didn't care. Being with him as he worked, being able to call herself, inwardly, his assistant was pure joy.

At lunchtime, he said, 'Come on, let's get out of this hothouse atmosphere for a while. Get Reuben, and we'll walk down to the village.'

In the doorway of the local pub, he looked at her with sudden compunction. 'Hell, you're not old enough to drink, are you?'

'I am nearly.'

'Well, nearly isn't quite,' he said grimly. 'It's lemonade for you, my child.'

As he gave the order, Caroline wished rebelliously that she'd been old enough to say, 'Thank you, I'll have a frozen daiquiri.'

She had no idea what they were like, but she loved the sound of them. Not that the Crown would be likely to provide such delights, anyway. Mrs Ransome, the landlady, went in more for real ale and traditional meals.

She got her lemonade, mixed with orange juice and ice, and tinglingly cool and refreshing, and a wedge of Mrs Ransome's homemade steak and kidney pie to go with it.

'What are we going to do this afternoon?' she asked, as she scooped up the last gravy-rich crumbs.

There was a pause, then he said, 'I'm going to do some individual shots of the bridesmaids. I thought I might use the rose arbour, for some extra romanticism.'

'It should be sweet peas, really. That's what we're all meant to look like—all misty pinks and blues.' She sighed. 'My dress is mauve, which is my least favourite colour.'

'Well, I doubt whether I'll get round to you today.' He smiled at her swiftly. 'You're far too useful in other ways.'

'Then I don't mind waiting.' She glowed, bending to fuss the recumbent Reuben to mask her embarrassed pleasure.

'Would you like some ice-cream?' Saul studied the menu. 'There doesn't seem to be a great deal else in the way of dessert.'

'I shouldn't really have it,' she sighed.

'You can't be watching your weight.' His brows rose.

'No, my wretched skin,' she admitted. 'If I break out in spots at this late stage, Louise will kill me.'

'Is that likely to happen?'

'Well, it could. I usually get spots if I'm overexcited about something, and being a bridesmaid is the most marvellous thing that's ever happened to me.'

'I see.' Saul drank some of his beer. 'And what future thrills await you, Caroline Foxcroft? What's going to happen once you've taken your A-levels? What do you plan for your life?'

'I don't really know. I'm quite good at English, so I suppose I could teach.'

'You don't sound wildly enthusiastic about it,' he said drily.

'It's a worthwhile career,' she said primly.

'Who are you quoting?' He sent her a sardonic look.

'My headmistress.'

Her heart was beating suddenly, wildly and painfully. If this was a fairy-tale, she thought, he'd say,

'Forget teaching. You're too valuable to lose. Come and work for me instead.' If this was a fairy-tale.

As it was, he glanced at his watch. 'We'd better get back. I told the girls to sort out their favourite casual gear as well, so I could do some contrast shots.'

'Oh.' She looked down at herself. 'Will I do like this?'

'I've already done yours,' he said. 'Down on the riverbank with the dog that first day. Don't you remember?'

'Well, yes.' She tried not to feel disappointed. That day, she hadn't even known he was there, she thought. But at least he would photograph her properly once, even if it was in the grotty mauve dress.

I'll still go and change when we get back, she decided, in case he changes his mind.

She had some new white trousers which made the most of her slim hips and long legs, and a pretty French shirt in turquoise which tied at the midriff. She put up a hand and touched her hair. And maybe she could find something more exciting to do with this than the short, straight bob which they encouraged at her school. Katie had some heated rollers which she might be prepared to lend, she thought doubtfully.

But, when she got back to the house, she never had a chance to ask. Upstairs was chaos, with all the others trying to get ready at once.

'Katie!' Meg's voice sounded shocked and envious at the same time. 'You're not going to wear that for the informal photograph.'

Katie airily waved the minute black bikini she had just unearthed from her case. 'Saul said to wear things we felt comfortable in.' She giggled. 'Well, I can feel incredibly relaxed in this.'

Meg was just about to say something else when she spotted Caroline hesitating in the doorway. 'So there you are,' she said sharply. 'Your aunt has been looking everywhere for you. Where on earth have you been?'

'I've been helping Saul.'

'Don't you mean following him round like a stray puppy?' Katie's face was unamused as she glanced over her shoulder at the younger girl. 'But I'm afraid he'll have to dispense with your services this afternoon. Mrs Brotherton has a list of errands for you as long as her arm, and rather you than me,' she added waspishly.

'Oh.' Caroline's spirits plummeted. 'Did—did she mean right this minute?'

'Actually, I think she meant half an hour ago,' Katie said absently, holding the bikini up against herself, and studying her reflection. Her full lips curved in a catlike smile. 'Yes,' she said, half to herself, 'I think this will do very well.'

'Caroline.' Aunt Grace's tones floated magisterially up from the floor blow. 'Where is that girl?'

'She's here, Mrs Brotherton,' Katie called back, sending Caroline a malicious grin. 'Off you go, ducky, like a good little girl,' she added in an undertone.

Perhaps Aunt Grace won't want me for long, Caroline thought without much hope, as she trailed back downstairs.

But her hopes were dashed instantly. Her first
task was to address a stack of envelopes enclosing
thank-you notes from the bride and groom to
people who had sent gifts. As James and Louise
were known to be going to live in New Zealand,
nearly everyone had sent money.

Caroline's hand was aching by the time she'd
finished the pile in front of her. She wished that
Aunt Grace wasn't such a stickler over personal
letters being handwritten in every respect. I could
have typed those envelopes in half the time, she
thought forlornly.

As she got up to make her escape, Aunt Grace
loomed again. 'Here are the stamps, Caroline.
When you've attached them, you can take these and
my other letters down to the post box in the village,
and then go on to Mrs Everett's house with this
note. She promised she would supply me with a list
of the music she proposed to play before the arrival
of the bride in church, but she hasn't done so.'

'Does it really matter?' Caroline's voice held a
hint of rebellion. 'It's only something for people
to listen to while they say rotten things about each
other's hats.'

'We are talking of a sacred occasion, Caroline,'
Aunt Grace said reprovingly. 'And Mrs Everett has
an unfortunate habit of including secular music,
even pop songs, I'm told, among her selections.'

'Heaven forbid,' Caroline muttered, *sotto voce*.

'So, you had better wait, and bring the list back
with you,' Aunt Grace decreed, and sailed off
again.

Caroline could have howled aloud. Her whole golden afternoon with Saul was slipping like sand through her fingers.

The sun was blazing down, and she felt hot, sticky and out of sorts by the time she reached Mrs Everett's. She found the parish organist on her dignity, and inclined to bridle when she heard Aunt Grace's request.

'Well, I remember Mrs Brotherton mentioning it, but I didn't really think she was serious. I've never had any complaints about my choice of music before, in all my years, and after all the fuss over the anthem I thought she might have been glad to leave it up to me.'

It took all Caroline's diplomacy to soothe her ruffled feathers and extract a grudging list from her.

'But I reserve the right to alter it,' was Mrs Everett's parting shot as Caroline began to trudge back to Elmsleigh.

Caroline stifled a groan. That was not the kind of message she wanted to pass on to her aunt in her present mood. But perhaps she could delay the evil hours, just for a while. After all, Aunt Grace wouldn't be expecting her back quite yet, she placated the unseen deity in charge of family obligations. So she could find Saul, apologise and explain, and hope against hope that he would still find something for her to do.

She chose the back way into the house yet again, and went round to the rose garden. The scent of the flowers hung heavy in the warm air, and bees drowsed among them. It was very quiet, and for a moment Caroline thought the photo session might be all over.

Then she heard Katie giggle, a small, soft sound
that seemed, oddly, to have little to do with genuine
amusement. There was something about it that
halted Caroline dead in her tracks.

For a moment, she stood very still, an inward
voice telling her it would be better—much better to
return to the house. But something impelled her
forward to the hedge of ancient shrub roses which
protected the arbour.

Within its shelter was an oasis of green lawn with
a moss-encrusted sundial as centrepiece. Katie was
kneeling near the sundial, her hands tangled in her
mane of blonde hair, lifting it away from her
shoulders. The pose was totally, consciously provocative, and so was her smile.

She looked stunning, Caroline thought numbly,
and incredibly sexy in that minimal black bikini.

'I feel like a Page Three girl,' Katie said, her voice
warm and throaty. 'Do you think I look like one,
Saul, darling?'

'You're rather overdressed.' Saul was putting
another roll of film in the camera.

'Well, that's easily remedied,' Katie said softly.
She put a hand behind her back to the clasp of her
bikini top, and let the tiny garment fall to the grass.
She arched her body slightly. 'How's that?'

'Spectacular.' There was amusement in his voice,
and a faint huskiness too. 'Hold that.'

She obeyed, pouting. 'Do you think I could
become a professional model?'

'It takes stamina. I'd stick to amateur status, if
I were you.'

'You really don't take me seriously, do you?'

'I certainly don't underestimate you,' Saul said, after a pause. 'Turn slightly. Look at me over your shoulder. That's good—that's fantastic.'

'Well, do you realise just how much manoeuvring it's taken to be alone with you like this?' Katie's voice was throaty and seductive.

'The manipulations haven't been totally one-sided.' Saul sounded faintly abstracted, but his words made Caroline's hands ball into taut, painful fists at her sides. 'I managed to deal with the others in record time, so that I could devote the rest of the afternoon to you.'

'I'm thankful to hear it,' Katie said, laughing. She paused. 'Of course, the hardest job has been getting rid of the faithful puppy constantly trailing behind you. Honestly, Saul, why do you encourage that grotesque-looking child to hang around you all the time?'

There was a silence. In spite of the heat, Caroline felt cold sweat breaking out on her forehead. Suddenly, she wanted to run, but her feet seemed rooted to the spot, holding her there captive and humiliated, waiting, without breathing, for his reply.

He said slowly, his words dropping like stones into Caroline's frantic silence. 'I suppose I'm sorry for her. For goodness' sake, she's practically an object lesson in how not to look!'

'Well, what do you think it's like for us, being saddled with her as the sixth bridesmaid?' Katie demanded pettishly. 'It's like taking part in some freak show.'

'As a matter of interest, exactly why was she chosen?'

Katie shrugged, her pert breasts bouncing. 'A case of needs must, apparently. Louise wanted Susan, but the family decreed that if she had the pretty cousin, she had to ask the ugly one too. We all prayed she'd refuse, but she didn't, of course, and James and Louise were absolutely furious. She's like a fish out of water, being so much younger. And I swear that nose of hers grows longer every day.'

'Well, she's given me one devil of a problem.' Saul's voice was angry. 'How the hell can I camouflage her—hide her away among the rest of you in the wedding groups tomorrow? Her height's against her, for one thing. She'll stick out like a sore thumb. I can leave her out of the book, except in the most marginal way perhaps, but I can't cut her out of the official photographs.'

Katie giggled. 'You're the professional, darling. Can't you arrange some convenient slip of the camera? I'm sure Louise would be eternally grateful, not to mention the rest of us.'

'Well, I'll have to do something.' Saul's tone was short. 'But she's my problem, not yours. Now, lean back on the grass. Draw up one leg slightly. That's good—that's amazing.'

'Is it enough?' Katie allowed one hand to toy almost idly with the strings which fastened her bikini briefs at the hip.

'That has to be your decision.' The amusement was back in his voice.

Katie pouted. 'You could—help me make up my mind.' She paused. 'These damned strings seem to have knotted.'

'How incredibly inconvenient of them.' Saul walked across the grass and dropped to one knee beside her. 'Let me see.' His hand moved, and the little black triangle of material joined its counterpart on the grass. 'There,' he said softly. 'It was really quite—simple, after all.'

Caroline heard Katie giggle again, and saw her arms go up to wind round Saul's neck and draw him down to her. The stark knowledge of what she was going to witness was enough, at least, to release her from the almost catatonic trance imprisoning her there.

She took a step backwards, slowly, quietly, terrified of revealing her presence. Then another. And another, placing each foot like an automaton. Backing away across the expanse of the garden with infinite, heart-rending care. Her hands were clenched into fists at her sides, her nails scoring the soft palms. She wanted to lift them, to cover her eyes, to block her ears, to press against her parted lips, and dam back the sounds of the pain which was beginning to tear her apart, and which she could not utter.

She shuddered, feeling the ground dip and lurch beneath her feet.

She thought—I'm going to faint. But I can't. Not here. Not now. I have to keep going. Have to.

She stood still for a moment, breathing deeply, forcing the swirling world to steady itself. Then, when at last she was sure she was at sufficient distance from the rose arbour for her retreat to be unseen and unheard by its occupants, she turned tail and ran like some small, frightened animal for the sanctuary of the house.

She just made it into the cloakroom leading off
the hall. She hung over the basin, retching mis-
erably, her whole being one silent moan of agony.

From some far distance, she heard approaching
feet.

'Caroline?' Aunt Grace's voice was shocked.
'Whatever is the matter with you? Your parents
have just arrived. I wanted you to show them to
their room.'

She tried to speak, to form coherent words, but
the world was spinning again crazily, out of control,
and she let herself slide down into the merciful, en-
compassing darkness.

Aunt Grace's anger when she learned that her
younger niece intended to return home, and take
no further part in the wedding, was formidable
indeed. At any other time, Caroline would have
been totally cowed by it.

But not then, or, in fact, ever again, Carly
thought, looking back over the years with a wry
smile.

On that nightmare afternoon there was no threat,
no browbeating or level of icy displeasure which
could make the slightest impression on her decision. For the first time in her life, she was
adamant, simply repeating over and over again that
she was ill—too sick to be a bridesmaid, and had
to go home at once. And eventually Aunt Grace
had, furiously, given way, at the same time making
it clear that this defection would not be forgiven
or forgotten in a hurry.

The journey home was a rapid one. She lay on
the back seat of the car, propped up with cushions,

pretending to be asleep while her parents conversed
in low, worried tones about her pallor.

The doctor, hastily summoned, and rushed off
his feet with cases of summer flu, gave her a cursory
examination, pronounced her another victim, and
left some antibiotics which Caroline flushed down
the toilet as soon as she was alone.

She had little difficulty in persuading her parents
that a couple of days in bed was all she needed,
and that they could return to Elmsleigh and enjoy
the rest of the wedding without her.

Once they'd departed, she locked her door
against the housekeeper's kindly concern and offers
of cool drinks and nourishing snacks and gave way
to the agony of misery inside her.

She wept until there were no more tears left, then
lay, harsh sobs still tearing at her chest, staring into
space.

She'd always known that Susan was the pretty
one, and she'd accepted this without resentment.
But that was before she had been taught in one
cruel, devastating lesson just how ugly, how un-
lovable she really was.

Saul's words jarred her mind, seemed to sear their
way into her wincing brain.

An object lesson in how not to look.

How could he? she moaned, grinding her
clenched fists against her teeth. Oh, how could he
be so unkind?

All those hours she'd spent with him, delighting
in his company. Eagerly treasuring every look, every
smile, her confidence in her burgeoning
womanhood blossoming every minute—each one
had been a lie, a total betrayal.

Because Saul Kingsland—her friend—her first love—didn't even like her. He pitied her, and that was bad enough. In fact, it was the worst thing that had ever happened to her. But he also found her an embarrassment, not just personally, but professionally, and that was even more terrible.

She was too plain—too gawky—too hideous to be photographed. She was a freak—a monster. That was what they all thought, talking and laughing about her behind her back.

In a way, it didn't matter what James and Louise thought. She supposed that she knew, subconsciously, why they'd asked her to be a bridesmaid. It didn't matter what any of them said about her—except Saul—only Saul.

Fresh pain lashed at her, and she moaned, wrapping her arms defensively round her body. She knew—she'd always known that eavesdroppers never heard any good about themselves, so why had she gone on standing there, listening, letting herself be wounded like that?

Because she'd been waiting—praying for Saul to defend her, she thought, wincing. She'd naïvely expected him to be angry at Katie's poisoned remarks—to contradict her—slap her down. But instead—instead...

She sank her teeth into her lower lip until she tasted blood. Every hope, every innocent fantasy had been shattered and there was nothing left. No dreams. Only the harsh reality of knowing herself unwanted, and a laughing-stock.

Only the memory of seeing Katie naked and willing in Saul's arms. And that was the greatest betrayal of all.

She kept her door locked and didn't emerge for over twenty-four hours. She didn't want to see anyone—face anyone, even her family when they got back from the wedding. The thought that perhaps their affection was a mask for secret pity was more than she could bear. Maybe even her closest friends at school felt sorry for her too, or perhaps she was the butt for their careless cruelty behind her back.

She shivered. It would be easy to stay shut up here. She could understand for the first time why people cut themselves off from the world—became reclusive. If it meant avoiding the kind of hurt she'd experienced, then it could almost be worth it, she realised with anguish.

I'll never be able to meet anyone again, she thought. Never be able to look them in the eye without wondering if they're laughing at me, saying things about me. I can't bear it—I can't . . .

She felt a scream rising inside her, and bit it back. She felt as if she was going mad. She wasn't even eighteen yet, and she was contemplating becoming some kind of hermit.

And Saul Kingsland had done this to her. She'd loved him. She'd trusted him and he'd destroyed her, she thought, and felt the misery inside her beginning to harden into anger and bitterness. Somehow she would make him pay for what he'd done. She would make him suffer as badly as she was hurting now.

She said aloud, 'I will destroy him,' and heard the words echo in the lonely silence.

All she had to do was find the way.

She spent a lot of her solitary vigil in front of her dressing-table mirror, examining herself minutely, carrying out the most complete and candid self-appraisal of her life.

By the time it was over, she knew what she was going to do.

'So there you are,' was Sue's greeting, when at last Caroline went downstairs. Her sister was reclining on the drawing-room sofa, flicking through a magazine. 'What a little idiot you are, letting everyone down like that.' She preened slightly. 'As it was, Louise asked me to be chief bridesmaid, and Megs and Katie weren't altogether pleased, I can tell you.' She giggled. 'In fact, it wasn't Katie's day at all. It seems Saul Kingsland cleared off back to London and didn't ask for her phone number. She was livid. But it serves her right. She was playing with fire, getting involved with him in the first place.' She paused. 'Are you all right, Caro? You've gone positively green.'

'I'm fine,' Caroline said quietly.

Sue yawned. 'Well, I'll take your word for it. You've got the most amazing shadows under your eyes,' she added critically. 'Are you sure you should be out of bed? You've got to be fit to go back to school.'

'I'm not going back.'

Sue gaped at her. 'What nonsense is this? Of course you are. You've got important exams coming up.'

Caroline shrugged. 'They're no longer important to me.'

Sue sat up. 'But what are you going to do instead?'

'Find myself work.'

'Well, heaven knows what kind of job you'll get with no qualifications,' Sue said with asperity. 'Honestly, Caro, you're the family bluestocking. You can't let us down like this.'

'Perhaps I want to change my image.'

'And maybe it isn't that easy.' Sue's gaze was frankly disbelieving. 'What in the world's come over you, Caro? Have you told Mother and Father what you're contemplating?'

'Not yet.'

'Then let's hope they can make you see sense. You had a career all planned.'

'I had one planned for me, certainly,' Caroline retorted. 'Now I'm thinking of a future instead. And not as a spinster schoolmarm, either.'

'And just how do you intend to begin?'

Caroline pushed her glasses up her nose. 'With cosmetic surgery,' she said, and walked out of the room.

And I did, Carly thought, remembering the long, painful and expensive months which had followed. She'd used part of her godmother's legacy to have her nose shortened, and her teeth straightened and capped. She'd had the shape of her chin fractionally altered, and learned to use contact lenses instead of her glasses. She'd joined a modelling school, and learned how to walk and stand and use her brand-new face and body for the camera. She'd still been a student when Clive had spotted her.

Since which, she hadn't looked back. And, if being a success had been all she'd wanted, then she would have been both happy and fulfilled.

Yet she had never let herself forget why she was doing this. Each time she looked in the mirror, she thought of Saul Kingsland, and promised herself that one day—one day they would meet again. She knew the opportunity would arise, and all she had to do was be patient. After all, natural justice demanded that she should be given the chance to ruin his life as surely as he'd ruined hers.

He'd destroyed the real Caroline Foxcroft, and replaced her with Carly North, the western world's most synthetic creation. An artefact who belonged nowhere, and was accepted by no one.

A plastic doll, she thought with contempt, who knew how to make the camera love her.

And a doll about to turn on her unwitting creator.

She laughed, and heard the sound splinter bleakly into a sob in the stillness of the room.

CHAPTER SEVEN

As THE bow of the caique cut through the water, Carly felt the cool misting of spray on her face, and drew a sharp breath of exhilaration.

Behind her, she could hear laughter, and the chink of glasses. Adonis, the boat's skipper, had produced a bottle of ouzo for the film crew and was pouring with a lavish hand.

She'd smilingly refused the offer of a drink. She needed to keep a cool head. She couldn't afford to be careless—to allow anything to go wrong now, at this stage in the game.

In the three weeks leading up to their departure for Thyrsos, Saul had been in constant touch with her. He'd been at her side when she'd signed the contract which bound her for a year to the exclusive promotion of Flawless cosmetics, and he was there, fending off awkward or too personal questions at the inevitable Press conferences which followed the announcement of the Flawless Girl's identity.

'You had the choice of every model in the UK,' a reporter asked Saul. 'So, why this particular girl?'

'You must be blind to ask a question like that,' Saul drawled. 'Miss North is an incredibly beautiful girl, and an angel in front of the camera— an absolute natural. As soon as I saw her, I knew she had to be my first and only choice.'

Carly forced herself to smile at his words, but under the shelter of the table they were seated at her hands clenched together in her lap until the knuckles turned white.

She wanted to scream aloud, But it wasn't always like that. When I was Caroline Foxcroft, I was too ugly—too grotesque to feature in his work. He rejected me totally.

Why don't I say it? she thought, the pain of it wrenching her apart. Why don't I finish it now—before it goes too far—before I'm in too deep?

And then, standing at the back, she saw Mark Clayfield. Their eyes met, and he smiled faintly, inclining his head. Carly looked away swiftly, her pulses thumping.

No, she thought. She had chosen what she was going to do, and she would see it through to the bitter end.

The tabloids the following day were full of gloating stories about ' "My One and Only," says playboy Saul', their columns listing the glamorous women he'd escorted on both sides of the Atlantic, commenting on the fact that he'd been lured back across the Atlantic to spearhead the Flawless campaign, and speculating openly about his relationship with Carly.

Carly reacted furiously when she read the more lurid pieces. Nor was her temper improved by Saul's amused acceptance of the gossip and innuendo which permeated most of the stories.

'Money and sex,' he told her succinctly. 'That's what sells newspapers. And although no actual figures are available, everyone knows that the Flawless campaign is going to be the most expensive cosmetics launch ever. So they can say we're not only being paid vast sums, but are heavily involved with each other as well. Rather like having your cake and eating it.'

'Don't you care what they say?' she asked hotly.

He shrugged. 'Why should I?' The look he sent her was faintly edged. 'We both know how far from the truth those stories are.'

Carly bit her lip and turned away.

Since that night at her flat when she'd come so perilously near to surrender, she had been ultra-careful where Saul was concerned.

Not, she was forced to admit, that it had been totally necessary. Although she saw him so often, there had been no further attempt on his part to make their relationship a sexual one. And, if she was completely honest, the last occasion hadn't been his fault.

I did throw myself at him, she reminded herself ruefully. And after that the situation—snowballed.

But she had not made that mistake again, and Saul himself seemed content to let the situation develop at the pace she dictated. When he greeted her, or said goodbye, he invariably kissed her, but more often than not it was a light touch on her cheek. When he kissed her mouth, she was aware that he was holding himself rigidly in check, allowing his lips merely to brush her own.

So far, it was all going to plan. She wanted him hungry, his entire attention focused exclusively on herself.

And he was being clever about it too, letting her see that, although he might be starving for her, he was capable of keeping his appetite within bounds.

He thought, of course, that patience and forbearance were all that he needed. That sooner or
later her own needs, her own sexual curiosity, would
drive her into his arms.

He believed, she had come to realise, that they
would be lovers on Thyrsos. And now they were
almost there at the island.

She heard a step behind her on deck, and tensed
involuntarily, knowing who it would be. Filming
for the campaign had started in earnest almost as
soon as the ink was dry on the contract. She had
found herself whisked from one location to
another, from a château in the Loire valley to the
grounds of an English stately home, where a small
Georgian gazebo overlooked a lake afloat with
water-lilies.

The emphasis of the campaign, as Septimus
Creed had made clear, was sheer romanticism, designed to appeal to every woman's secret dreams.
And at any other time Carly would have revelled
in the exquisite costumes chosen for her, appreciated the care that had selected the elegant
background for each commercial, and enjoyed the
professionalism of the director and film crew.

As it was, the knowledge of what she was about
to do haunted her. Her nights were plagued by
troubled dreams, and she awoke more than once to
find tears on her face.

And, whenever and wherever the shooting was
taking place, Saul was always there, a yard or so
behind the camera, watching every movement and
every expression, his eyes never leaving her.

He had taken numerous shots of her already, but the major part of his work on the campaign would be completed on Thyrsos.

Everything, Carly thought, would come to completion on Thyrsos.

As Saul's hands descended on her shoulders, his fingers warm and strong through the flimsy Indian cotton top she was wearing, she forced herself to relax, to lean back against him.

'Adonis says we'll be there in half an hour.'

She flung a smile over her shoulder at him. 'British time or Greek time?'

'Does it matter?'

'Not at all,' she said. Although it might, she thought, in the not too distant future, when I want to make a swift getaway. 'It's a wonderful day for a sea trip.' She paused. 'I'm testing the Flawless sunblock cream.'

'I hope you've brought plenty,' he said wryly. 'Sunbathing is definitely out while we're shooting. We can't handle a piebald model.'

'I could always go for an all-over tan,' she said lightly, and felt his fingers tighten on her shoulders in response.

He thought that was a signal, she thought with satisfaction. What was the phrase he'd once used to her? 'A declaration of intent.' Well, he would find out how wrong he was.

'Once work is finished, we might be able to steal some time to ourselves—maybe spend a few days on Mykonos,' Saul said softly into her ear. 'Did you like Mykonos?'

She shrugged. 'I liked what I saw on the way from the airport to the boat.'

'That's not giving the place a chance. It's beautiful, and it can be a little crazy. I'd like to show it to you. May I?'

'Maybe.' She made the word husky with anticipation.

After all, she thought, the more she promised, the more devastated he would be when she brought the world crashing down around him. And that was now only a matter of time.

She suppressed a shiver. She'd waited so long for this, manipulating events to her own ends, and now, suddenly, she had the feeling that she was no longer in control of circumstances—that she was being swept along by a current, too strong and too malignant for her to restrain. That there was now an inevitability about events which frightened her.

I must be weakening, she thought in self-derision. I've let his kisses get to me.

It was all part of life's unfairness—that, in spite of everything, Saul Kingsland's lightest touch on her hand had the power to stir her to her soul. But at least it meant she did not have to pretend—to fake a response when he came close to her—held her—because intuition told her that Saul was too worldly, and too experienced not to know.

Everything has to be paid for, she thought, even vengeance. And perhaps this harsh torment of yearning which Saul awoke in her was the price to be exacted from her in frustration, bitterness and tears.

Septimus Creed was waiting on the small stone jetty as Adonis manoeuvred the craft to its moorings.

'Welcome to Thyrsos,' he called. He summoned forward a stocky, smiling man in an immaculate white coat. 'This is Kostas, who'll be looking after us at the villa with his wife Penelope. If you can get your luggage ashore, Kostas will have it brought up to the house by donkey. In the meantime, we climb up these steps. I suggest you take them by degrees until you get acclimatised.'

The steps were steep, bordered by a low wall to the seaward side, and rough, as if they'd been hewn out of the tall cliff-face itself.

As they probably had, Carly thought, as she started up them. She soon outstripped the film crew, whom she could hear grumbling and cursing good-naturedly behind her, but she was aware of Saul at her shoulder, keeping pace with her easily, no matter how fast she climbed.

His voice reached her laconically. 'If this is a race, what's the prize?'

'Wait and see,' she tossed back at him.

'In that case——' Saul said, and overtook her easily, his long legs carrying him further and further ahead.

The first mad impetus which had taken her up the steps at a gallop was beginning to subside. It had been cool on the water, but here on land the sun seemed to beat down on her unprotected head, its heat reflected back off the cliff's bleached rock.

She thought, I should never have started this.

But the impulse to run had been too great. She'd been confined for too long, on the plane, in the car, and finally on the boat, with Saul never more than a few feet away from her. The word 'escape' had been drumming in her mind, and as soon as she felt solid ground under her feet she'd just taken off.

She paused for a moment, her hands pressed to her waist. A lizard lay on the wall beside her, its colour blending with the dusty parched stones, its only sign of life the swift, rhythmic panting which distended its small sides.

She said aloud, trying to catch her breath, 'I know how you feel,' and the little creature vanished in a blur of movement.

Saul was waiting for her at the top of the steps, where a huge terrace had been built overlooking the sea. Pride made her take the last few steps two at a time.

He said, 'Why all the hurry? Thyrsos is a small island. There's nowhere to run to...'

She stared at him for a dazed moment. It was as if he was warning her—as if he knew. *Nowhere to run to.* She swallowed. But that was nonsense. Saul knew—suspected nothing. How could he? And there was always somewhere to run—some escape—some refuge. Always.

He added, 'Unless, of course, you were rushing to see this.'

He took her by the shoulders, and turned her to face the bay and the horizon.

Carly caught her breath. The sea was a myriad of colours from amethyst to turquoise, crested here and there with tiny caps of white foam. In the distance she could see an island, and another beyond it, both fringed in green, the grey of their rocky interiors deepening to mauve in the intense light.

'Oh, how beautiful.'

'Flawless,' Saul agreed, an odd note in his voice.

She glanced at him, standing beside her, and re-alised he was looking not at the view but at herself, his eyes brooding and intent. For a moment his gaze held hers, then it shifted, sweeping down her body from the small, high breasts, frankly outlined against her thin top by the flurry of her breathing, to her pink-tipped toes in the rope-soled sandals, and then back to her parted lips.

He said, quietly, 'I claim my prize,' and took a step towards her, cancelling the small space which separated them.

A shaft of pure sensation pierced her, clenching her inner muscles like a fist. It was so painful and so sweet that she wanted to cry out, but no sound came from her dry throat. She was trembling suddenly, in anticipation and need, and she lifted a hand, pushing her sunglasses further up the bridge of her small nose in the small, nervous gesture she hadn't used for years.

And saw him stop, the dark face suddenly puzzled, his brows snapping together in concen-tration as if he was trying to recapture some elusive memory.

Sudden panic assailed her. If he thought hard enough, he might just recall the gauche, plain adolescent who'd created that silly, restless little movement. And she couldn't let him do that. She had to stop him thinking...

She made herself move, step forward towards him, so that their bodies were almost touching. Made herself smile, the tip of her tongue flicking along her lower lip. Made herself whisper, 'I'm glad you won,' as her hands reached up to his shoulders.

Immediately, Saul's arms went round her, drawing her fully against him in a way he had not allowed himself to do since that night at her flat. The sharp, arrested look went from his face, to be replaced with the starkness of a desire he could no longer conceal. For a long moment, he held her against the aroused warmth of his body, as if he was imprinting her on his flesh for all eternity, then he bent his head, and his mouth took hers.

She couldn't resist—couldn't push him away, after the explicit invitation of her words and actions. She would have to endure it—somehow.

But mere endurance was impossible. As Saul's lips parted her own, and she felt the thrust of his tongue against hers, her whole body was invaded by a startling, melting sweetness.

She thought frantically, This is dangerous, I can't let it happen. And she tried to retreat from him by sheer effort of will. But it was too late. Control was giving way to imperative instinct.

As Saul's kiss deepened inexorably, Carly found she was pressing her body against his, her breasts aching against the hard wall of his chest, her hips grinding slowly and languorously against his own. The sun was all around her, scorching her to her bones, dazzling her. Its heat was inside her too, burning her up, but Saul's mouth on hers was cool, like the first rainfall on some desert, and she drank from his lips, from his tongue, as if they were her sole salvation.

'I want you.' They were his words, breathed against her parted, eager lips, but they could have been her own, because they were there, unbidden,

in her mind, struggling for utterance. And that was not just danger, but madness...

The cough, quiet, apologetic but definite, separated them. A woman had emerged on to the terrace, and was standing, her black eyes sparkling with interest and amusement, waiting for their attention. She wore a dark dress covered by a spotless white apron, and held a list.

'*Me sinkhorite.* I ask your pardon.' She looked at the list. 'Who are you, please?'

'My name is Kingsland.' Saul's voice was ragged as he sought to control his breathing. 'And this is Kyria North.'

'I am Penelope, me.' Her smile was broad and welcoming. 'Come with me, please, and I will show you where you will sleep.'

Carly wasn't sure that she could move—that her legs would support her. Only a kiss, she thought feverishly, yet her pulse-beats were deafening her, and every inch of her body was quiveringly awakened.

'Are you all right?' Saul was staring at her, his face suddenly concerned.

She took a breath. 'Sep Creed was right.' She managed, somehow, to sound rueful, even amused. 'I should never have tried to run up those steps in this heat.'

'Let me help you.' Before she could protest, Saul had lifted her deftly into his arms, as if she was a child. 'Lead on,' he told Penelope.

She gave them an arch look, then, with a murmured, *'Po po po,'* she took them round the side of the villa to where a flight of steps, almost masked by flowering vine, led to the upper floor.

'Your own entrance,' she announced beaming. 'Only your rooms are here.'

Carly felt herself swallow as Saul carried her with seeming effortlessness up the steps. Events—the whole situation seemed to be out of her control. Certainly, she hadn't bargained for this—neither for the isolation, nor the proximity of their rooms, and the intimacy this implied.

Both rooms, she saw with alarm, had sliding glass doors which gave on to a joint balcony. There wasn't any kind of dividing wall or screen to give even an illusion of privacy between them.

Her room was cool and shadowy after the glare of the sun. The floor was tiled in marble, and the walls were covered in a pale blue wash. The furnishings were simple enough—a cupboard for clothes, a chest of drawers in some dark wood, and a wide bed invitingly made up with plump pillows and snowy sheets—and never in this world intended for single occupation, Carly thought numbly.

Saul put her down in the middle of the bed. He was very gentle, but his hands lingered on her, and she had to resist an impulse to cower away.

'You like, *ne*?' Penelope glanced around her with evident satisfaction. 'There is one bathroom only, which you share.' She gave them a droll look. 'But no problem, maybe.'

Carly's hands clenched at her sides. She could foresee all kinds of difficulties...

'Everything's fine.' Saul smiled at the housekeeper. 'And you are the wife of Kostas. Have you worked here long?'

She nodded emphatically. 'Since Kyrios Athol first built this house. He is a good man, and I like to welcome his friends.' She paused. 'I am also the sister of Adonis, who brought you in the boat. And my other brother, Yannis, has a good taverna in the village, by the edge of the harbour. There he cooks the swordfish which he catches himself.'

'Then, we'll be sure to pay him a visit, won't we, darling?' Saul looked down at Carly. 'Swordfish is a favourite of mine.'

She moistened her lips with the tip of her tongue. 'I—I don't think I've ever tasted it.'

'Then you've a treat in store.' He paused. 'Now, take it easy until dinner. Sep Creed's calling a short briefing meeting after the meal, but until then our time's our own.'

He gave her a swift smile, then followed Penelope out of the room.

Carly lay back against the pillows. Her breathing was beginning to return to its normal pace, and her inner weakness was dissipating. But there was no real reassurance to be gained from this. It was only a temporary respite, she thought feverishly, wrapping her arms round her body.

How could her body respond so wantonly, drowning in sensation, to a man her mind hated and rejected? she asked herself with a kind of despair. What was wrong with her?

This is what you planned, said a small, cold voice in her brain. You wanted him in your net—caught—trapped—obsessed by you here on Thyrsos. Well, you have your wish. Only, traps can sometimes be double-edged.

She shivered. There was one commercial to shoot with the film crew, then they would be returning to Britain, and she and Saul would be working virtually alone together.

She was geared for that. She'd rehearsed the role she would play, driving him slowly crazy in the sunlight.

But all her ploys were daytime ones. She hadn't reckoned on the fact that he would be spending his nights only a few paces away from her.

'Nowhere to run to.' The words returned to torment her, and she rolled over, pressing her hands to her ears.

Not long to go, she told herself. You can't weaken—chicken out now. You started this. You have to finish it.

But the truth was, she hadn't realised how many other people would be involved—hadn't stopped to think how far-reaching the repercussions of her private vengeance might be.

She'd forgotten her own innate professionalism which had responded joyously to the demands made on her during the filming of the commercials. It had been hard work, but fun, too, and a real camaraderie had built up among them all. And the commercials were undoubtedly some of the best work she'd ever done. The director and Sep Creed had worn smiles of quiet satisfaction at the end of each day's shooting.

Yet all that time, all that money, all that artistic and creative effort was going to be totally wasted, she thought with regret.

What she was about to do would never be forgotten or forgiven. She had to make up her mind to that. She was facing the deliberate sacrifice of her career.

Goodbye, Carly North, she thought with a tinge of sadness. You served your purpose. Now you can vanish back into well-deserved obscurity, and Caroline Foxcroft can take over again.

She was aware of a strange, panicky sensation in the pit of her stomach. Was it possible for her to do that—to wipe out the new face, the new persona she'd created for herself? Or would she find herself for the rest of her life caught in a kind of limbo between the two identities?

She moved restlessly, pressing her face into the pillow.

Pull yourself together, she adjured herself impatiently. You're just tired after the flight.

She would sleep for a while. Then, after a shower, she would be ready to face the final battle in her secret war against Saul Kingsland. She dealt with her contact lenses, then lay back, closing her eyes, emptying her mind quite deliberately, letting the warmth and her weariness have their way with her.

But there was no immediate peace to be found. Saul's face seemed to burn against the inside of her eyelids, his presence as real as if he'd been actually there in the room, bending over the bed, his hands reaching down for her...

She sat bolt upright with a little cry, staring round her. But she was alone. Only the shadows were there, deeper than they had been. Peering at her watch, Carly saw with astonishment that she'd actually been asleep for two hours.

Had she really dreamed about Saul all that time? she asked herself, her heart thudding uncomfortably. Surely not? Dreams were odd, stretching a few seconds into what could seem a lifetime. There would have been other fantasies, other recollections in her mind, but her subconscious was playing tricks on her, submerging them beneath an all-pervading vision of Saul.

She became aware of other things—the sound of voices in the distance, the rustle of leaves on the balcony as the evening breeze quickened, the splash of water closer at hand.

Saul, it seemed, had beaten her to that shower. She found it a disturbing thought, and for a moment an image assailed her, unbidden but potent, of his body, lean, tanned and wearing nothing but a few drops of water.

She dismissed it instantly and angrily, conscious that her skin had warmed involuntarily, as if she'd entered the bathroom without thinking, and found him there, in reality, naked.

Carly bit her lip. She could only hope that, when it was her turn, there would be at least a bolt on the communicating door with his room that she could use.

Someone, she saw, had brought in her case while she was asleep, and she would be far better employed unpacking something to wear for dinner than indulging in—ridiculous erotic fantasies.

Impatient with herself, she reached for her contact lens case, and began the familiar routine. But, as she positioned the first lens on her fingertip and raised it towards her eye, a stronger than usual gust of air from the open window lifted the tiny, transparent disc and flicked it into infinity.

'Oh, no!' Carly wailed. 'I don't believe it.'

She remained totally still, peering down at herself, praying that the errant lens had blown down on to her lap, and was trapped in a fold of her clothing, but there seemed no sign of it.

She said again, 'Oh, no,' and scrambled off the bed, trying to cause as little disarrangement of its covering as possible.

She had a spare pair, of course, but they were in the bathroom cupboard in her London flat. And tucked away inside her suitcase were the despised glasses which she'd promised herself she would only ever use in the direst emergency. She flung herself at the case and began to tug at its strap.

From the bathroom doorway, Saul said, 'Is something wrong?'

He was leaning there, very much at his ease. One brief, shaken glance told her that the water had darkened his hair to the colour of midnight, and the towel he wore draped round his hips did little more than preserve the decencies. That swift fantasy of a few moments ago had only told half the story, she realised, feeling the betraying colour surge into her face, and hating herself for it.

She said shortly, 'Everything's fine.'

He shrugged. 'Then I apologise for intruding. I thought I heard you call out.'

He was already turning away when she said reluctantly, 'As a matter of fact, there is something. I—I've let my contact lens blow away. And...'

'And you can't see well enough without it to find it,' he supplied drily. 'I get the idea.'

He walked across the room, slowly and carefully, staring down at the mottled tiles.

'This bloody floor doesn't help,' he commented.
'You've no notion which direction...? No, of course
you haven't.' He went down on one knee and began
a minute examination of the floor round the bed.
'What we really need is a miracle, but in case there
isn't one, how much of a problem is this going to
be for you? I mean, how much can you see without
them?'

'Not enough.' She had her spectacle case in her
hand now. Saul would soon be wondering why she
didn't do the obvious thing—put on her glasses and
join him in the search.

But, after her previous slip with her sunglasses,
she dared not risk it. The colour and shape of the
frames were too reminiscent of those she'd worn as
a girl. She'd jogged his memory once. Twice might
be too often.

He said, 'So how many more secrets have you
for me to discover?'

Tension gripped her. 'I—don't understand.'

'I usually notice things like lenses, but with you
I didn't.' He sounded rueful. 'Shows how hard I
find it to be objective about you.'

Her flush deepened hectically. 'I—forget I wear
them half the time. I feel so stupid—letting one
blow away like this.'

'I always understood that was a natural hazard
of the things.' Saul paused abruptly, and leaned
forward, frowning. He said softly, 'Good lord!
Wonder of wonders, I do believe...' He gave her
a swift grin. 'Hold your breath, sweetheart. I think
I've found it. Pass me a tissue.'

'Oh!' Carly sighed in gratitude and relief. 'Oh,
I don't know how to thank you!'

Saul's smile became faintly oblique. He said quite gently, 'I could suggest any variety of ways,' and put the lens, safe in a fold of tissue, in her out-stretched hand.

A sudden silence descended—pressed on them, closed them in together. He was so close to her that she could even see the faint dampness lingering on his chest hair—smell the scent of the soap he'd used. It would be so easy to reach out to him again—offer her lips. So easy, and so fatal.

She swallowed, dry-mouthed, desperately aware that she must break the tense expectancy of the moment. 'You—you said—no pressure.'

He said, 'And I meant it, heaven help me.' He got lithely to his feet, adjusting his towel as he did so. He looked at her levelly. 'But my patience has limits, and I'm fast reaching them.'

Her voice shook. 'You make that sound like a threat.'

Saul shook his head. 'No,' he said. 'Only a warning.' His smile was brief, almost impersonal, then he turned and walked away, back to his own room.

For a long moment, Carly stayed where she was, on her knees, staring after him. Then, slowly, the rigidity dissolved from her slim body, and she began to tremble.

CHAPTER EIGHT

THE three remaining columns of the little temple reared in apricot splendour against the azure of the morning sky.

Carly waited in the shade of an olive tree for the director to signal the start of the take. It was simple enough. They'd shot the close-ups already, the camera lingering lovingly on every plane and contour of her face, highlighted by the Flawless cosmetics.

Now all she had to do was walk slowly across the crumbling slabs of the pavement, and stand with her hand resting against one of the columns, looking down at the sea.

She reached down and smoothed the folds of the filmy white dress she was wearing. It had been designed on the lines of a Greek *chiton* and had a graceful simplicity that lent itself perfectly to its surroundings.

Her hair had been wound into a smooth coil and pinned on top of her head, with one long curl allowed to hang down over the shoulder her dress left bare.

It was much the same style as the one she'd worn to the Flawless reception, she thought. That was the night which had begun it all—when she'd made her quest for vengeance into a reality. And now, here on this small and sunlit island, it would finally reach its culmination.

The breeze came snaking across the small plateau carved out of the stark hillside where they stood, and Carly shivered slightly as she glanced towards the temple ruins. No one seemed to know to which of the ancient Greek deities the little sanctuary had been dedicated.

Maybe, she thought, it could even be Nemesis, the dark goddess of retribution herself.

She leaned back, feeling the roughness of the tree's bark beneath her fingers, staring up through the rustling silver leaves towards the sky.

The past week had been easier to cope with than she could have hoped for. She had worked with the film crew early each morning before the real heat of the day began, and afterwards they'd all stayed together as a team, enjoying the small sand and shingle beaches near the villa, or lounging beside its swimming pool.

Saul had not always joined them. He'd rented a motorbike in town, and gone on a photographic exploration of the island. He'd suggested once, casually, that she should accompany him, but had applied no further pressure when she'd demurred.

Even when darkness came, it had brought none of the problems she had frankly envisaged. In spite of his warning, Saul had been almost studious about avoiding any invasion of her privacy, in their shared part of the villa, although it had taken two anxious and sleepless nights before she'd realised that he had no immediate intention of persuading her to let him join her in that wide lovers' bed.

And thank heaven for Flawless cosmetics, she thought derisively, which had disguised the resulting shadows of restlessness beneath her eyes, and softened the line of strain along her cheekbones.

All the same, she was aware, as she'd been from the first, that he was only biding his time where she was concerned.

And now this was the last day of filming, she thought, touching her tongue delicately to the curve of her bottom lip. Tonight there would be a celebration at Yannis's taverna, and tomorrow she would be left here, alone with Saul.

Her stomach constricted nervously at the thought. Yet all her plans had been building inevitably, relentlessly, to just this moment. To having Saul at her mercy at last. To destroy his masculine pride, as surely as he'd ruined her vulnerable girlhood.

'Is something wrong?'

She had been so lost in her own thoughts that she hadn't heard his approach, and the quiet question made her start wildly.

'Wrong? No.' She found herself stammering. 'I—I'm fine. Everything's terrific.'

He studied her frowningly, his eyes missing nothing. 'Is it more of a strain that you expected, being the Flawless Girl?'

Carly shrugged. 'Perhaps. But nothing I can't handle. Although I'll be glad when this final shot is in the can.'

'So will I.' There was a note in his voice which made her pulses sharpen. A note of need, of anticipation. She stared down at the dusty ground, avoiding the intensity of his gaze. There was a silence, then Saul said more gently, 'Yet there's really nothing to worry about, darling. Sep Creed is delighted with you. So, just relax, and walk across the temple like the goddess you are.'

She attempted a little laugh. 'I don't feel much like a goddess. Besides—Aphrodite—wasn't she a blonde?'

'I wasn't thinking of Aphrodite,' Saul said. He took a small tissue-covered parcel from the pocket of his jeans and unwrapped it. 'This is for you. I saw it in the jeweller's shop in the village.'

A silver clasp shaped like a crescent moon lay in the palm of his hand.

Carly's lips parted in a small soundless gasp. 'It's—beautiful. But I can't take it.'

'Yes, you can.' Saul's voice was inexorable. 'It's to wear in your hair, like this.'

She had to struggle with herself not to recoil as he fastened the clasp into the gleaming mahogany strands.

'There you are.' His smile held a faint grimness as he surveyed her. 'Artemis personified.'

'Why Artemis?' The intimate brush of his fingers against her hair had produced its own devastating effect, she realised with dismay. Under the veiling of the white bodice, her breasts had tautened, the rosy peaks proud and all too visible beneath the thin material. A detail which, she saw, had not been lost on him.

'Because it seemed appropriate.' He paused, his eyes lingering almost ruefully on this unmistakable evidence of her arousal, then lifting to her flushing face. 'Artemis was a cool lady, too. One man who tried to get too close to her was torn to pieces for his trouble.'

Her mouth was suddenly dry. 'That sounds—incredibly violent.'

'They were violent days,' he said. 'Now we commit mayhem in a far more civilised manner, but the lasting effect is still the same.' His gaze held hers, challenging her suddenly.

He knows, she thought. But he can't, unless he's remembered that stupid trick with the glasses. And ever since then I've been so careful . . .

She said with a catch in her voice, 'And is that what you think I intend—mayhem?'

He said harshly, 'Lady, I'm damned if I know any more. You tell me.'

As he turned away, she heard the director call her name, and nerved herself, forcing the professional model to take over from the suddenly tremulous girl.

She moved across the uneven slabs of stone without faltering, using the smooth, half-floating walk she had learned so painstakingly, feeling the breeze tug effortlessly at her wispy draperies, making them cling ever closer to her slim body. She heard one of the crew whistle under his breath, and as she reached the tall pillar of stone, and placed her hand on it, she allowed herself to smile faintly, a woman secure in the conviction of her own beauty, her own sexuality.

There was a charged silence, then a brief spontaneous round of applause.

Jim, the director, said, 'I don't think we can better that, but we'll have to do another take as insurance, all the same.' He paused. 'Can you give it to us again, Carly, my love? That same combination of ice and sex?' He grinned at her. 'If it has the same effect on the viewing audience as it had on us, Flawless should sweep all the other cosmetic brands into oblivion.'

They were all so pleased with her, she realised with a heart-wrenching pang. So delighted with the way the project had gone. So excited with the campaign as a whole.

And, because of her, no one would ever see it. Oh, there would be a new campaign, and another Flawless Girl, but it wouldn't have the same quality, the same impact as this.

In fact, nothing would ever be the same again.

She thought, This will be the last time...

And, in that knowledge, Carly North retraced her steps, and gave the camera exactly what it wanted.

For their party that night, Yannis had barbecued a lamb, serving it with fresh crusty bread, still warm from the oven, and a variety of spicy, garlicky sauces. He'd strung coloured lights among the vine which twined across the taverna's roof, and placed candles in little glass holders on all the tables.

There was ouzo waiting for them, too, on the house.

'We drink,' Yannis beamed at them. 'To success, and to happiness—and that one day you all come back to Thyrsos.'

There was laughter and a muffled cheer as the toast was drunk. Carly only pretended to drink, keeping her fingers clamped for concealment round her glass. When no one was looking, she poured the ouzo away on the dusty floor beneath the table.

She couldn't drink that toast. She couldn't be such a hypocrite.

As she put the glass down, she saw Saul watching her, his brows drawn together. Had he seen what she'd done? she wondered feverishly. If so, it was time to divert his attention. Down the length of the table, she smiled at him, her face lighting up, her eyes sparking with mischief and frank seduction, and watched his expression relax, then change to a very different kind of tension.

Carly sent him one last provocative look under her lashes, then turned her attention to Septimus Creed's personal assistant, Julie, who was sitting next to her, openly bemoaning the fact that she was going home the next day.

'You're so lucky,' the other girl sighed. 'I bet it's raining non-stop in London.'

'I'm staying behind to work,' Carly reminded her, and Julie pulled a face.

'Some work,' she remarked naughtily. 'I wish providence had sent me a job like that. You wouldn't care to swap assignments?'

Yes, Carly thought savagely. Yes, I would. I'd give anything at this moment to have an ordinary job—to be happily engaged to a solicitor as you are, and be planning a summer wedding. To have no problem except finding a flat with enough room for your David's hi-fi and record collection.

She said quietly, 'A model's life isn't all it's cracked up to be. I've been lucky so far, but soon there'll be a dozen younger, prettier girls fighting their way past me.'

'And what will you do when that happens?'

Carly shrugged. 'My life's changed direction once. It can happen again.'

'You're not thinking in terms of marriage? You're so gorgeous, you must have loads of men after you.' Julie's tone was not flattering, merely stating the obvious.

Carly bent her head. 'Not as many as you'd think,' she said.

'Hm,' Julie said drily. 'Well, one obviously comes to mind, and not a million miles from this table, either.'

Colour stirred under Carly's skin. 'I don't know what you mean.'

Julie gave a soft hoot of laughter. 'Of course you do. He's absolutely obsessed by you—anyone can see that. I heard him saying to Jim that he felt he'd known you before—that he'd known you always.'

Carly's nails fastened painfully in the palms of her hands. Her throat tightened in alarm. She managed a laugh. 'Oh, dear. That sounds almost spooky.'

'Maybe,' Julie shrugged. 'But I thought it was really romantic.'

She turned to talk to someone else, leaving Carly alone with her thoughts.

They were far from comfortable.

When the meal was over, the tables were pushed back and there was dancing, led by Yannis and his sons. One by one the television crew were inveigled on to the floor, to receive a crash-course in the dipping, swaying movements and intricate footwork of the dance. Carly watched for a while, then slipped away out of the taverna on to the harbour wall, letting the music and laughter follow her.

The moon had risen, and was shining over the water in a rippling ribbon of silver.

Carly put up a hand and touched the crescent moon in her hair. She was wearing it loose this evening, letting it spill over her shoulders, with Saul's clasp keeping the heavy waves back from her forehead. Everyone had admired it, and she'd seen more than one smothered smile and significant glance being exchanged when she'd explained where it had come from.

Most of them, she realised, assumed that Saul and she were lovers already, and that the silver moon was some kind of intimate avowal—a token of long-term commitment. Whereas she knew it was just something else to be left behind in the ruins when the time came.

Pain slashed at her swiftly, and she drew a deep breath.

She thought, If Saul and I had met, in truth, for the first time that night at the Flawless reception— if there had been no burdens, no shadows from the past—it could all have been so different. It would have been so good—so right . . .

She stopped right there, her throat closing in shock and bewilderment bordering on panic, as she assimilated the tenor of her thoughts.

All this time she'd been telling herself that Saul had merely been the focus of her first tumultuous adolescent yearnings, and that was why his cruelty, his rejection of her had hurt so much—had damaged her so violently. That it was because of his treatment of her at that totally vulnerable time of her life that she'd found it impossible ever since to relate to any other man, however kind, caring or attentive he might be. Because Saul had smashed her dreams, and blighted the burgeoning impulses of her young sexuality.

He'd made her nothing, when she'd wanted to be everything to him.

But now the tables were turned, and suddenly she was in confusion.

She'd gone to meet him that night, hating him, deliberately using her face and body as the instruments of her revenge. What she hadn't allowed for was the residue of feeling lurking unacknowledged somewhere deep in her psyche. She hadn't bargained for the emotional charge that being with him would engender. She hadn't realised what would happen when he touched her—took her in his arms—kissed her. She hadn't known how he could make her feel.

She might look like a woman, but beneath the façade she was still the same vulnerable child she'd been when she first saw him—first loved him.

A groan of sheer anguish rose inside her, and was instantly stifled. What was she doing, allowing herself even to think like this? It was Julie's fault— talking all that sentimental nonsense about marriage.

Making her confront for the first time what might have been. The kind of happiness she could have had, if only...

No! The word was like a scream in her head. She hated Saul Kingsland, hated what he'd done to her. Her whole life had been based on that, dedicated to revenging herself on him.

Oh, dear heaven, surely she couldn't have been deceiving herself all this time? It just wasn't possible.

Oh, please, she prayed, as the moonlight on the water blurred, please don't let this be happening to me...

'Aren't you coming back to the party?'

Her whole body stiffened. She might have known that he would follow—seek her out. He was standing so close behind her, she knew, that all she'd have to do was turn and she would be in his arms.

She reached for a control she wasn't sure she possessed. 'I'm not really in a party mood.' *Heaven help me.* 'I hate the ending of things—goodbyes. I thought I might just slip away, back to the villa.'

'Shall I come with you?'

She shook her head. She was going to say, 'There's no need,' but the words stuck in her throat. Because there *was* a need in her, a necessity, an agony of yearning which filled the world.

And this man—this enemy whom she'd vowed to destroy in any way she could—was the only one who could satisfy that necessity, heal her and make her whole again.

Slowly, she turned to face him, taking one step backwards so that there was distance between them. Trying to make it safe. Failing.

She said, 'No—not now. Not tonight.'

'But soon.' He wasn't asking. He was telling her that the waiting was over.

She said his name on a little shaken sigh, and went from him, out of the moonlight to the darkness of the steep road back to the villa.

And, when she knew she was out of sight, she began to run.

Carly stood on the quayside, waving as Adonis manoeuvred his laughing, cheering boatload out towards the open sea. She had said goodbye, until she hated the sound of the word. She had smiled until her facial muscles ached with the strain.

And now it was over, and she was alone at the villa with Saul.

She swallowed thickly, aware that that deep inner trembling had begun all over again. It had plagued her throughout the previous night, keeping her from sleep, and this morning, she thought candidly, she looked a wreck.

Perhaps Saul thought so, too, because although he had made no overt comment, he had suggested they should take a day off, and spend it on the beach, relaxing.

It was a recommendation that fitted her own plans entirely.

The doubts that had assailed her last night had been deliberately relegated to some far corner of her mind. That had just been some inexplicable moment of weakness, she assured herself. And it meant nothing. All that mattered was achieving what she'd set out to do. That was what she had to remember. Not some nonsense about love and 'might have been'.

'They're a great crowd.' Smiling, Saul now came to stand beside her. 'It's good to think we'll be working with them again on the second stage of the campaign.'

Carly nodded, biting her lip.

'That, of course, is if there is a second stage,' he added, grinning.

'What do you mean?' She stared at him, eyes wide and startled.

He said ruefully, 'I meant if you survive the ride on the back of the bike down to that beach I mentioned to you. It was intended as a joke, but it was obviously a bad one.' He put a hand lightly on her shoulder. 'Loosen up, darling. Thyrsos was meant to be a relaxing experience for you, but most of the time you're so tensed up I'm afraid you'll snap.'

She shrugged slightly, moving away, releasing herself. 'I've never been the pivot of a campaign before. Maybe I am feeling the pressure, as you said.'

'Well, now the pressure's off—in every way,' he said quietly. 'I couldn't sleep last night for thinking about you—your face as you left me. You looked—stricken, as if I'd pronounced sentence of death. Darling, you know I want you, but it has to be mutual. Haven't I made that clear?'

Her heart skipped a beat. He was letting her off the hook again, and playing right into her hands.

She bent her head. 'Of course you have. I'm such an idiot.'

'No.' His voice was gentle. 'You're just much younger than you look, my sweet, and heartbreakingly innocent. Lord knows how you've preserved that in the rat race we both belong to, but I hope it's something you never lose, or not emotionally, at least,' he added, his mouth twisting wryly.

Carly bent swiftly to retrieve her beach-bag in order to conceal her rising blush. 'Well—shall we be going?'

Her hair streamed behind her as she rode on the pillion behind him to the beach. The bumpy road with its pot-holes, little better than a track, was hardly the ideal introduction to motorbike riding, she decided breathlessly, but the beach itself was idyllic, and well worth the jolting.

It was probably the only stretch of pure sand anywhere round the island, and totally deserted. Saul left the bike in a grove of olive trees, and they walked together down the path, bordered by scrub which led to the beach.

She said teasingly, 'I see you've brought your cameras. I thought today was going to be a holiday.'

He grimaced. 'They're like an extension of myself. I never seem able to abandon them entirely. Do you mind?'

'Not a bit.' Today, after all, it was no more than the truth.

Carly spread out her towel, then began to unbutton the black thigh-length muslin shirt she was wearing. She took her time, aware that Saul, already stripped down to brief trunks, was watching every movement. Underneath the shirt she was wearing a bikini, also in black. She had searched London until she'd found exactly what she wanted.

It was the least she'd ever worn in her life, the bra top so minimal that it barely contained the thrust of her firm breasts, and the briefs consisting of two skimpy triangles which tied with strings on her slender hips.

There was incredulity as well as hunger in Saul's eyes as he studied her, and her body warmed involuntarily under the frankness of his scrutiny.

'Do you approve?' She smiled with enforced gaiety, trying to hide her sudden self-consciousness.

He said slowly, 'I think approval is hardly the right word. I'm—overwhelmed.'

'I think you're exaggerating. You must have seen and photographed hundreds of girls wearing this amount—or less.'

'If so, I don't remember.'

Think back, she adjured him silently. Think back a few summers to a country wedding, and a girl called Katie, who stripped for you in the sunlight before you—you . . .

At the thought, as always, she felt the lash of the old familiar pain, the surge of nausea she had no defence against. Her hands clenched harshly into fists as she fought for control, and won.

She laughed. 'I don't think I'll be very flattered if you forget me as easily.'

'You,' Saul said, 'I can never forget. You're etched on my consciousness for all eternity, and beyond.'

There was a note in his voice which sent an almost feverish ripple of excitement shivering through her body. She crushed it down.

'Wouldn't a photograph be a simpler way of keeping the memory intact?' She sent him a demure look under her lashes.

He grimaced, half-wryly, half-humorously. 'At this moment, my sweet, I doubt if I could hold the camera steady. I think I'll go for a swim, and cool off a little.'

Carly watched him walk down the narrow strip of beach to the edge of the water.

There's no hurry, she reminded herself. There's plenty of time. Take it easy.

She put some more sunblock on her arms and legs, then lay down on her towel, face downwards. To her surprise, she found her thoughts beginning to drift. The peace of the place must be getting to her, she thought drowsily, or maybe it was just her disturbed night catching up with her. Whatever it was, closing her eyes for a few minutes couldn't do any harm. No harm at all.

She woke some time later to a familiar sound—the click and whirr of a camera's shutter. Saul was sitting a few yards away, his face intent as he focused on her.

She sat up with a gasp. 'What on earth are you doing?'

'Photographing Sleeping Beauty,' he said promptly. 'I'm sure the Prince would have done so, if cameras had been invented then.'

'Well, for her sake, I'm glad they weren't. I think you've taken an unfair advantage.' She pouted at him. 'I bet I had my mouth open, and was snoring.'

He said slowly, 'You looked like a little girl again.'

Something clenched in the pit of her stomach. 'You don't know that. You've no idea what I looked like when I was a little girl.'

'People don't change that much, surely,' he said. 'I could make an educated guess.'

Carly looked at him, held his gaze, smiled at him, moistening her lips with the tip of her tongue. 'But I'm really not a child—not any more.' She ran her hands lightly over her body. 'Look.'

'I'm looking.' His voice was suddenly grim.

'You don't seem totally convinced.' Her heart was
hammering. She was excited and frightened in equal
proportions at the prospect of what she was about
to do. 'Maybe I should offer you proof that I'm a
woman.'

She reached up, undid the clasp of her bikini top
as she'd seen Katie do that day, and let the scrap
of material drop to the sand beside her, every
movement a deliberate imitation of the scene which
had seared itself into her consciousness like an open
wound. She was playing with fire. Surely—now—
he must remember? Or was Katie just one in a line
of nubile girls taken cynically, and discarded
without a second thought? The possibility sent
anger mingled with anguish scorching through her
body.

Oh, she would make him pay, not just for
himself, but for all men who thought they could
use women lightly, then walk away.

She damped down the flare of rage inside her,
and stretched, lithely, provocatively. She said softly,
'Is that better?'

'Exquisite.' His tone was raw.

'Then why not make the most of me?' Her voice
deliberately teased him. 'Wouldn't you like your
own personal and private portfolio of the Flawless
Girl?'

'I wouldn't express it in quite those terms.'

'Then how?'

He said slowly, 'The beginning, perhaps, of a
lifetime's study.'

Her mouth was bone-dry, the muscles in her
throat tautening painfully. This wasn't the reaction
she'd expected. That wasn't what she'd wanted to

hear. She said with an effort, 'That sounds—
serious.'

'It was intended to.'

She tried to laugh, to lighten the moment, but
no sound would come. Suddenly there was silence,
enclosing them, cocooning them. An intense, deafening silence, containing nothing but the beat of
her heart and his.

His gaze held hers, sending a message of stark
yearning, of almost helpless need.

Carly felt as if invisible cords had tightened round
her, drawing her to him, her mouth on his, her
hands on his body. She seemed weightless,
suddenly, boneless, as if her entire physicality had
been poured, concentrated, into some central core
of sensation which was crying out for appeasement.

She was drowning in honey, entangled in some
warm, sweet, golden web, caught in the spell of her
own devising.

And that could not be.

She dredged up some forgotten reserve of will-
power, and moved, curving her body with deliberate seduction, forcing herself back into control.

She said, and was amazed to hear how normal
her voice sounded, 'You're keeping me waiting, Mr
Kingsland.'

He said quietly, menacingly, 'Am I?' and picked
up his camera.

She had never experienced anything like it before.
Within seconds, she knew that somehow, yet again,
she'd lost the whip hand, and that Saul was back
in command. He was totally merciless, making her
give as she'd never done before, his voice sometimes husky, often harsh as he encouraged and de-

manded. Before the session was half over, Carly
felt emotionally limp, the sweat pouring from her
body, but there was no rest, no respite. She had
offered herself as an object to be photographed,
and as such he took her.

'Had enough?' he flung at her at last.

'Have you?' She wiped the perspiration from her
eyes.

'It would take eternity for that.' There was no
humour in his smile. 'But I think we've exhausted
the possibilities of this session.'

'Not quite.' She knelt upright, composing herself,
letting the flurry of her breathing steady, resting
her hands on her waist. She said, 'You'd better
reload the camera,' and allowed her fingers to slide
with slow deliberation down to her hips, where the
little black bows waited to be untied. 'Won't you—
help me?'

'No.' The denial came from him with such force,
such a surge of uncontrollable emotion, that Carly's
head snapped back as if he'd hit her. Her fingers
stilled.

She said, stammering a little, 'What's the matter.
What's wrong?'

His voice was molten. 'You dare ask me that?'

'You've photographed nude women before.'
There had been an exhibition of his work in con-
junction with some other contemporary photographers at a London gallery. Saul Kingsland's
nudes and the erotic charge they conveyed had been
one of the talking points. She'd looked at them,
and remembered, and used those memories to fuel
her bitterness, her vengefulness.

'That was different.'

'How?' she hurled back in challenge.

'We are not,' he said, too softly, 'talking about an exercise in aesthetics. The first time, lady, that I see you naked, it will not be through the lens of my camera. That I swear.'

There was a brief, electric pause, then he added, in a tone that permitted no argument. 'Now get your clothes on. We're going back.'

Her fingers shook as she fastened her bikini top, and slid into her shirt. Out of the corner of her eye, she watched Saul stow the used rolls of film away in his canvas bag. Noted carefully and exactly where he put them. Took a little shuddering breath.

She hadn't achieved the whole of what she'd set out to do, but it was enough, surely, to bring the Flawless campaign crashing down, and Saul's career with it when those pictures of her appeared as the next Sunday Siren in Mark Clayfield's *Globe*.

I've won, she thought. And found herself wondering why, at the very moment of triumph, she should feel such an odd sense of defeat.

CHAPTER NINE

THE villa was very quiet. Carly sat on the edge of her bed, listening to the silence with growing unease.

It had been a strange, solitary afternoon. She'd spent most of it by the pool. But Saul had not joined her there. According to Penelope, who had appeared at intervals with iced drinks, Kyrios Saul had gone off once more on his motorcycle. It was clear she disapproved of such intense activity in the full heat of the day. It was also obvious that she regarded Saul's defection as thoroughly unloverlike behaviour. Although Penelope had more reason than most people to know that she and Saul were not, in fact, lovers at all, Carly thought, biting her lip.

But at least Saul's absence had meant that she'd had a chance to speak privately to Adonis on his return, and arrange for him to take her in his boat to Mykonos at first light the following day. She'd invented a story about arranging a surprise for Kyrios Saul—'A special surprise, Adonis'—and had little trouble in enlisting his support.

And by the time Adonis received the message she planned to leave for him at the harbour—that she had decided to spend a day or two on Mykonos—and returned to Thyrsos without her, it would be too late for Saul to come after her. And, even when he did follow, he wouldn't find her, she thought, her nerves tightening.

Because by then she would be safely back in London, and Mark Clayfield would have those sexy, damaging rolls of film, fully attributable to Saul Kingsland, to use just as he wanted.

And after that . . .

Her mind closed off. She didn't want to contemplate what would happen after that. It frightened her to realise what she'd set in motion. Some kind of serious legal action was only one possibility. Whatever the outcome, even if Saul proved that he hadn't given permission for the pictures to be used, his professional integrity would still be severely damaged.

Among those who would also inevitably suffer in the aftermath were Clive and Marge, and the realisation of that tore at her. They were the last people she wanted to hurt.

And her family too would writhe in the glare of the unavoidable publicity, once those pictures appeared, she thought drily. So it would be no use seeking sanctuary from Saul's anger at their home. She would not be welcome there. Might never be welcome again.

So many boats to burn in this, her personal holocaust.

But it will be worth it, she told herself, in a kind of panic. It has to be worth it. Doesn't it?

She waited for the inner reassurance that never failed; for the small, stony voice which told her that the end justified the means, no matter what other harm might be done. The voice that said Saul Kingsland deserved everything that was coming to him, and more.

But this time there was only that brooding silence.

Carly shivered, folding her arms defensively across her body. For the first time she found herself facing the fact that the person who might be most seriously damaged by what she was planning was herself.

Flawless would undoubtedly sue her for breach of contract, but she was prepared for that. What she couldn't predict was what psychological scars her quest for revenge on Saul might leave on her. She had only looked forward to the moment when he realised she had betrayed him totally, as he'd once betrayed her. Never beyond.

She had never considered the fact that, when it was all over, she would have to live with herself. Not merely build some kind of new life, but come to terms with what she'd done.

Why am I thinking like this now? she asked herself wildly. Why this moment—when I've achieved what I set out to do?

Not quite, she reminded herself. She still had to retrieve the rolls of film from Saul's bag. But that wouldn't present any great difficulty.

She glanced at her watch. Only a few more hours, she thought, swallowing. Only a few. No wonder I'm so tense.

She got up, and went towards the window. On the small dressing-chest, something glinted, cool and silver. Carly picked up the moon clasp, holding the crescent in the palm of her hand, staring down at it. Then, obeying an impulse she barely understood, she fastened it into her hair.

Penelope had set a table on the terrace overlooking the sea. Carly perched on the wall, and stared towards the horizon. Thyrsos was really

Paradise in miniature, she thought. If only things had been different, she could have been so happy here. With Saul.

She tried to block the words out, to deny them, but it was impossible. Whether she wanted to or not, she had to face the fact that Saul Kingsland was the only man in the world she had ever wanted, or ever would want. The bitter irony of it screamed at her.

How many times had it been said that there was only a thin dividing line between love and hate? It had become a cliché, but it also contained a terrible truth.

She had loved Saul, and then she had hated him with a kind of devouring madness. And now the two emotions were so inextricably confused in her mind that she didn't know what to think—what to feel.

The night was warm, but she felt cold, chilled to the bone, and she was trembling inside again, a prey to sensations she could neither explain or rationalise away. Saul was her enemy—the man who'd betrayed her—driven her to the extreme of changing her life completely. That was simple. That was what had motivated her all this time. So how was it possible that she could want him—need him, this enemy of hers—with such devastating completeness?

Penelope brought her retsina in a little copper pot, and she poured some into a glass and sipped it gratefully. She'd grown to like the strong resinated flavour of the wine. She wanted the warmth it engendered to drive the cold and the trembling away. But tonight, it seemed, it was not the panacea she needed.

'I'm sorry if I've kept you waiting for dinner.' Saul's voice was as formal as the words as he came to join her. He was wearing close-fitting cream trousers and a black shirt, left casually unbuttoned at the throat. His hair was damp, and Carly was aware of the sharp fragrance of soap and cologne commingled with the warm, intensely personal scent of his skin.

Her mouth went dry. It was so long—too long—since she'd been in his arms, she thought crazily. She wanted to be close to him, held by him, her face buried in the hollow between his neck and shoulder, breathing him, absorbing him through every pore.

And she couldn't—couldn't . . .

'Did you have a pleasant afternoon?' he went on, after a pause.

'Restful.' They were talking like polite strangers.

'I'm glad.' Another silence. Then he said, quietly, 'I'm sorry I allowed everything to get so fraught this morning. From the first moment I saw you, I wanted you. But you know that already. What I've never told you before is that it was like a home-coming—as if I'd found the other half of myself. But I kept telling myself that it would be all right— that I could work with you, and remain impersonal and professional about it all.' He laughed in self-derision. 'Well, now you know I can't. That's why I cleared out this afternoon. I knew I couldn't be with you—spend any more time with you, and not—touch you.' His voice was uneven suddenly.

'More than touch. So I rode around the island on the bike, and did some serious thinking.'

A shaky smile touched the corners of her mouth. 'No photography?'

'I didn't even take the cameras,' he said wryly. 'I couldn't see anything but you, anyway. You're inside my head, under my skin.' His hand lifted, and the long fingers touched the curve of her jaw, slowly, tentatively. He whispered, 'What are you doing to me? What are we doing to each other?'

She said his name, half under her breath, feeling it torn out of the ache in her chest, of the pain deep within her.

She saw some of the strain, some of the rigidity leave his face. Saw his mouth curve with a new gentleness as he bent towards her.

Then the shadows of the terrace were invaded, put to flight by light from within the villa, and Penelope was bustling out with a tray holding two steaming soup bowls.

'*Avgholemono,*' she announced, beaming, waving a hand at the pale, creamy liquid. 'You both eat good.'

Saul grinned at Carly, his expression both humorous and rueful. His mouth shaped the word, 'Later.'

The meal seemed endless, although they did not attempt to hurry it in any way. A covenant between them had been made, and would be kept. Carly knew that now, knew that it had always been inevitable, and with acceptance came a kind of peace. There would be no regrets, no wondering to pursue her into her new life. She would possess, and be possessed, and after that she would be free.

In the meantime, there was a strange, tantalising pleasure in facing him across the small lamplit table, and enjoying the food with him. And tonight Penelope had surpassed herself. The soup with its rich lemony flavour was succeeded by vine leaves stuffed with rice and meat, and then fish, baked in the oven. For dessert there was fruit, luscious peaches nestling among dark green leaves, and purple grapes, large as plums and sweet as honey. They drank white wine, dry and cool, which lingered on the palate, and ended the meal with tiny cups of thick Greek coffee, and a liqueur, redolent of tangerines.

As Carly drained her cup, she was aware of a tingling anticipation, half-pleasurable, half-fearful. Like the sensation, she thought, when the car of a rollercoaster reaches the crest, just before that wild plunge downwards into the unknown.

Saul pushed back his chair, and came round the table to her. He took her hand and pulled her gently to her feet, his eyes searching hers for any sign of withdrawal. With his other hand, he unpinned the crescent moon from her hair, and left it on the table. He said quietly, 'No virgin goddess tonight.'

He led her from the terrace to the steep, vine-shadowed steps, and up to the balcony above. The air was very still and warm. She could hear the rasping of the cicadas in the garden and, looking up, saw the full moon rising over the sea, like a serene face bestowing a pagan blessing. She thought, I'll remember this always . . .

She had half expected Saul to stop at the open window of her room, but he didn't even pause there.

Instead he took her to the end of the balcony, and his own room, where she had never been.

There was a lamp lit beside the bed, bathing the starkness of the snowy sheet and pillows with a soft radiance.

Her heart thudded in sudden alarm. Like a set for a play, she thought stupidly, staring at the bed. Only I don't know any of my lines. I don't know what to do. I don't know...

She didn't realise she'd said the last words aloud, until Saul said gently, 'We'll learn together, darling. Trust me.'

He kissed her softly at first, barely moving his mouth on hers. But soon, so soon, it was not enough. Carly wound her arms round his neck, pressing herself against him, feeling her soft breasts bloom to aching life against the hard wall of his chest.

She felt the stroke of his tongue along her lips, coaxing them to part for him, and she obeyed as a sweet delirium invaded her veins, turning her blood to fire.

They clung together, mouths and tongues searching and demanding almost frantically. She felt Saul's hands begin a slow, intimate pilgrimage down the length of her body. He touched her briefly, caressingly through her dress, his fingers lingering on her breasts, adoring the surge of her hardening nipples against the friction of the thin fabric, forcing a small, harsh sound of pleasure from her throat.

His hands moved down, as if memorising the planes and contours of ribcage, waist and stomach, and she swayed in his arms, oblivious to everything but the passage of those lingering, tormenting fingers. He traced the outline of her hips and the gentle swell of her buttocks, and a new, moist heat flared inside her. She moved against him in silent pleading, experiencing the stark urgency of his arousal through the minimal layers of clothing which separated them, but that was no appeasement for the hunger that tore at her. Her need was as fierce as his own.

His hand parted her thighs and found the cleft of her womanhood, and she cried out, her body convulsing in a pleasure she'd never before known, or even imagined.

He whispered her name against her mouth, then lifted her and carried her to the bed. He lay beside her, cupping her face in both hands, kissing her with a hot and hungry urgency. Carly held him, her slender body straining against his, her fingers gripping his shoulders. Her eyes were tightly closed, and little golden lights danced behind her lids.

When he lifted his head, she looked up at him dazedly. Saul smiled into her eyes, then slid one hand down to her waist to find the sash that fastened her simple wraparound dress, and tug it free.

The dress fell open, and he drew a sharp, uneven breath as he looked at her. He let his hand venture slowly, almost teasingly, down the valley between her breasts, then began to brush the creamy swell very gently with his fingertips. It was the simplest of caresses, but her whole body responded fiercely and wantonly to his touch.

His eyes fixed on her face, Saul began to trace a finger round each swollen dusky aureole in turn, his touch delicate and very exact. Never, even accidentally, did he allow his hand to stray to the aroused and aching peak. Yet she wanted him there—oh, so badly. She tried to speak, to tell him so, and he bent and silenced her with his mouth, before continuing his sweet, erotic torment.

She pushed her hands inside his shirt, feeling a button tear, but not caring as she slid her palms across the hair-roughened skin of his chest, then up to the broad, muscled sweep of his shoulders.

He felt so good, she thought, the breath catching in her throat. So strong, and utterly male. And she'd been waiting so long for this moment—all the days of her life...

He kissed her again, without haste, flicking his tongue sensuously across her parted lips, then bent his head, kissing each soft, scented mound before taking one proud, rosy nipple into his mouth.

She made a small, inarticulate sound as she felt the stroke of his tongue against her tumescent flesh, exciting, inciting sensations she had not known existed until this moment. She cradled his dark head in her hands, holding him to her breasts, her body arching in painful delight as he sucked more deeply, and she felt the faint graze of his teeth against her skin.

She thought crazily, I can't bear this. I can't... But if he stops, I'll die.

He slipped an arm underneath her, lifting her slightly so that he could free her completely from the hampering folds of her dress. He let it drop to the floor beside the bed, then sent his shirt to join it. He knelt over her, spreading her arms wide so that he could trace, with his lips, the whole of their

slender length. She felt his tongue exploring her
palms, the pulses going crazy at her wrists, the bend
of her elbow, the hollow of her armpit, and the
curve of her neck and shoulder.

She began to touch his back, running her hands
over his shoulderblades, then down the curve of his
spine, and he whispered his pleasure into the whorls
of her ear, biting at its lobe.

He kissed her mouth, then caressed her breasts
softly with his lips as his hands stroked down her
body.

Deftly, gently, he removed her last flimsy
covering, and for a moment shyness overwhelmed
her as he looked at her, and she tried to turn her
head away.

His fingers reached out instantly, capturing her
chin, making her face the burning intensity in his
eyes.

'No.' His voice sounded raw, suddenly. 'You can't
hide from me now, my darling. It's too late. You're
too beautiful.'

Tenderly, his hand found the warm moistness of
her, and began a new and devastating exploration.

All the breath seemed to leave her body.
Awareness receded to some far, dangerous distance. Nothing existed for her, except the silken,
tantalising stroke of Saul's fingers. She was no
longer in control, she recognised as she began to
move wantonly and crazily against his caressing
hand. She didn't even belong to herself any more.
She was his creation, half-toy, half-animal. An instrument of pleasure of his designing, and made
for him, only him.

There was a dark, savage ache—an over-whelming need—building, spiralling inside her. Every sense in her being seemed to be channelled suddenly and sharply—driven inexorably towards the fulfilment of that need.

Then she was there, at the edge of the unknown, and for a moment she was afraid. The spiral rose inside her in a final crescendo that was half-agony, and half-delight. She found herself taken, con-sumed by it, wrenched apart, and then released, as her body was racked by convulsion after con-vulsion of quivering, burning pleasure.

She lay dazed and drained, listening to the hammer of her own pulse-beats, hardly able to be-lieve the maelstrom of sensation which had pos-sessed and almost destroyed her. Reality returned slowly, languidly.

And reality was Saul lying next to her, naked himself now as any pagan god. He gathered her to him, and his mouth claimed hers, deeply and passionately. She clung to him, kissing him back without inhibition. She felt the heat and power of his maleness pressing against her pliant thighs, and realised, almost with shock, that what she had ex-perienced was only a beginning. Suddenly, and starkly, she wanted him inside her. Had to have him there.

She touched him in wonderment, shaping the power of him with her fingers, and his hand covered hers, halting her.

He said huskily, 'Darling, I can wait.'

'Why?' Acting on pure instinct, she lifted her legs to enfold him. Saul gasped, and heated colour flared along his cheekbones. He said her name on a shaken breath, and entered her with one deep, fluid thrust.

There was no pain. Just a sense of total completeness, and for a while they remained still in each other's arms, mouths gently brushing, bodies locked together in the final intimacy.

When Saul did begin to move, it was slowly at first, tempering his needs to her inexperience.

Her body felt like some fathomless cavern of the ocean, and he was the strong tide which ebbed and flowed within it. The kisses they exchanged were warm and languorous. Saul's hands cupped her breasts, fondling the nipples into vibrant, aching life, making her moan softly.

The sound of her voice, hoarse with desire, seemed to tip him over some brink. He was holding back no longer, his body plundering hers with harsh and fevered hunger, and she surrendered eagerly to the delicious, brutal rhythm of his possession, echoing each heated thrust, arms and legs gripping him fiercely.

This was for him, she found herself thinking. Solely and wholly for him.

But even as the thought took shape in her mind, it was already too late. The first, intense spasms of delight were overtaking her once more, tearing her slowly into a thousand, minute, shimmering pieces and flinging her out into some blinding golden cosmos where the last thing she was aware of was Saul's own triumphant cry of fulfilment.

This time, the descent from the heights took longer. She found there were tears on her face as she lay in his arms, and he kissed them away.

'Did I hurt you?' he whispered. 'Darling, did I hurt you?'

'No.' Sated, relaxed and more at peace with herself than she could ever remember, she lifted a hand and stroked the line of his jaw. 'Oh, no. I'm just—so happy, that's all.' She paused, shy again. 'Saul—I—I never knew—never thought it could be like that.'

'Then that makes two of us.' He cuddled her closer.

'But that can't be right,' she said slowly. 'You've had so many women...'

He propped himself up on one elbow, and stared down at her, visibly startled.

'What gives you that idea? I'm far from being a virgin, it's true, but reports of my conquests have been greatly exaggerated. I've had a few fairly serious relationships, but I've never gone in for casual sex, or one-night stands.'

She wanted to cry out, And what about Katie? Does your encounter with her qualify as a serious relationship? The cocoon of joy and peace enclosing her was shattered. She was remembering, if she had ever forgotten, what she had to do.

She said, 'I suppose these days, it just isn't safe.'

'There's that aspect,' he agreed levelly. 'But I'd already decided how I intended to live my personal life, long before the AIDS scare.' He paused. 'And while we're speaking with such frankness, may I ask if you, my darling, are on the Pill?'

'Of course not,' she denied indignantly. 'I've never needed to be...' Her voice trailed away. 'Oh.'

'Oh, indeed,' Saul mocked, running a lazy hand over her flat stomach. 'I wonder, now...'

'It couldn't possibly have happened,' she said, half to herself.

'Couldn't it?' He dropped a kiss on her hair. 'I rather go for the idea myself. Don't you?'

'No.' The sound was like a yelp of anguish, and Saul's brows lifted.

He said very evenly, 'I love you, Carly, and I want to marry you. If you don't need that kind of commitment, what are you doing in my bed?'

Exorcising a personal demon, she could have answered. Instead, she remained silent, gnawing at her lower lip.

At last, she said feebly, 'I—couldn't fulfil the Flawless contract if I was pregnant.'

'I've seen some radiant pregnant women. Photographed them, too.' He paused. 'But if you feel strongly about it, then we'll take precautions from now on. Your contract doesn't have a clause forbidding marriage.' He tilted her chin up, making her look at him. 'Well?'

'It's too soon.' Her lips felt dry, and she moistened them with the tip of her tongue. 'You don't really know me...'

He gave her a faint grin. 'I was under the impression that I'd just known you as intimately as it's possible to do and still go on living.'

'I didn't mean that,' she said desperately. 'You don't know the kind of person I am—my background—all that kind of thing.'

'I know you have a pretty weird family, who don't seem to give a damn about you,' he said bluntly. 'I also know you've been hurt in the not-so distant past.' He stroked an errant tress of hair back from her forehead. 'I intend to make up for the one, and heal the other.' He stretched. 'Think about it while I take a shower. Unless, of course, you want to join me.'

She shook her head. 'It might be better if I—I went back to my own room now.'

'I'd rather you stayed here.' His mouth twisted wryly. 'Under the circumstances, I won't make love to you again, but I'd like to hold you while we sleep.'

Her heart skipped a wild beat. 'Saul—please, I'm so confused. I need some time on my own to think—to decide.'

'Have it, then,' he said, letting her go with obvious reluctance. He smiled at her. 'Just as long as you reach the right decision in the end.'

He got out of bed, lithe and naked. A beautiful, graceful animal, Carly thought, as unlooked-for hunger awoke within her again, and in the hunter's sights...

She said, 'Saul, those pictures you took this morning—you won't get them muddled with the other films, will you?'

He stopped at the bathroom door, and stared back at her. 'No, of course not. They're just between the two of us.'

'I couldn't bear anyone else to see them.' She knew she was gabbling. 'Couldn't I have them—look after them, just in case?'

He went on watching her, a slight frown twisting his brows, then he shrugged. 'If it'll make you happy, help yourself.'

She waited until she heard the water running, then she left the bed, pulling on her dress, and tying the sash anyhow.

She took the small canisters out of his bag, and looked down at them. In the end, how simple it had been. She'd only had to ask.

'If it'll make you happy.' The words seemed to reverberate in her brain.

And later, as she lay alone and sleepless in the darkness, waiting for dawn and the arrival of Adonis with his boat, she knew, sadly, and finally, that with Saul she'd been given her only chance of happiness. And that now she had lost it forever.

CHAPTER TEN

THE offices of the *Sunday Globe* were housed in an anonymous glass and concrete building near the docks.

Mark Clayfield was on the telephone when she arrived, and Caroline had to wait in his secretary's office.

'Couldn't I just leave the films with you?' she asked, wishing that she'd sent them over by messenger. 'I'm in rather a hurry.'

'I'm sure Mr Clayfield will want to speak to you.' The woman gave her an impersonal smile. She was neatly dressed, and rather staid-looking—the last person in the world Caroline could imagine working for a rag like the *Globe*.

But then, who am I to talk? she thought, feeling faintly sick.

Her departure from Thyrsos and the flight back to the UK had gone like clockwork. All the Fates seemed to be conspiring with her. And although she was tired from the flight, and wanted a bath and a change of clothes, she'd decided to make a detour on her way from the airport, and drop off the films to Mark Clayfield.

She wanted to be rid of them, she told herself defensively. Once she'd handed them over, that was the end of it. Her life as Carly North was finished, and she was free to begin again. And that was all there was to it. There was no question of being

tempted to change her mind, which was the case
the longer the films remained in her possession, and
renege on her bargain with the *Globe*.

She glanced at her watch, wondering what time
it was in Greece, and whether realisation had yet
dawned on Saul that she was not coming back. She
bit her lip. She could only count on a few more
hours' leeway. Somehow she had to vanish, and as
yet she had little idea where or how.

The buzzer sounded on the secretary's desk, and
she rose. 'Will you go in now, please?'

Mark Clayfield was standing in front of a VDU
screen as Caroline entered. He turned, the pale eyes
flicking down her body, missing nothing.

'The films, as promised,' she said, putting them
down on his desk.

'I can't wait to see them.' He smiled at her. 'Are
they nude or just topless?'

'You said topless would be sufficient,' she reminded him evenly.

'So I did,' he said. 'But a man can dream, can't
he?' He paused. 'Profitable session, was it? Did
you and the dashing Mr Kingsland—get on all
right?'

'You asked for photographs,' Caroline said
curtly. 'Salacious details I'm sure you can invent
for yourself, as usual.'

He laughed. 'We're on the same side, sweetie,
remember?' He gave her a speculative look. 'I don't
doubt Mr Kingsland's talent, but his work generally
errs on the side of good taste. I hope these pictures
will be raunchy enough for our readers.'

'Can they actually read?' Caroline felt suddenly as if she'd been dipped in slime. 'I thought they were merely voyeurs.'

'Heavens, we are sharp today.' He put the films in his desk drawer. 'What I was going to say was—if we require some—additional material to spice up the spread a little, where can we contact you?'

'You can't,' she said icily. 'What you see is what you get. Goodbye, Mr Clayfield.'

'I hope it's *au revoir*,' he called after her as she walked to the door. 'If we get a good response to you on Sunday, I'm sure we'll want to use you again—persuade you to bare all for us next time.'

Suddenly her stomach was heaving, and there was a hot, acrid taste in her mouth. She managed to say to the secretary, 'Is there a ladies' room somewhere?' and just made it to the toilet cubicle before she was violently sick.

'Are you all right? Would you like a glass of water, or some coffee, perhaps?' The secretary was hovering, clearly anxious, when she emerged.

Caroline gave her a pallid smile. 'I think the flight must have upset me,' she said mendaciously. 'I'd just like to go home, if someone could call me a cab.'

The flat was empty when she got in. Caroline walked into the sitting-room and looked round. There were flowers on the table by the window, and a certain amount of cheerful clutter, which meant that Lucy was back from abroad.

Caroline was thankful that her flatmate was out, probably at the television studios. She didn't want to have to talk to anyone—to pretend, or offer explanations.

She took her travel bag into the bedroom, and emptied it more or less piecemeal into the linen basket. She would cope with that at some future time, she thought, as she went into the bathroom and began to run water into the tub.

It was like some ritual cleansing ceremony. Caroline scrubbed herself from head to foot, until her skin was pink and glowing. She even shampooed her hair, digging her fingers into her scalp.

As she dried herself, she caught sight of herself in the mirror. Saw the taut lines of her mouth, and the shadows under her eyes.

Is it enough? she thought. Will I ever be really clean again?

Somehow, she doubted it.

She felt tears stinging at the back of her eyes, and rigorously dammed them back. It was too late to worry about that now. All her bridges were burned. There was no way back. Perhaps there never had been.

She should be rejoicing, she told herself, as she put on fresh underwear, and tied back her still-damp hair with a black ribbon bow at the nape of her neck. She should be in a champagne mood, not feeling deathly cold and sick like this—and somehow—desperate.

Perhaps this is how you feel when you've murdered someone, she thought, as she dragged on jeans, and fastened a white cotton shirt. This terrible feeling of hopelessness.

Because in a way, I am a murderess. I've killed Saul's love for me. It's the only thing I've ever been offered that I wanted, and I've strangled it at birth—thrown it away.

Her whole body clenched in grief and longing as she remembered her last glimpse of him.

It had been stupid and dangerous, because he might have woken and seen her, but she hadn't been able to resist the temptation to go back to his room to say a silent goodbye.

He'd been asleep, lying on his side, face and body relaxed and defenceless, one arm thrown across the space in the bed beside him. As if he was seeking her, she'd thought with a pang. And he was smiling slightly as he slept. It had taken every atom of will-power she possessed not to reach down and kiss that smile.

Her whole being, mind, body and spirit, seemed to be crying out to him, urging him to wake and prevent her from ruining both their lives.

Instead she had stood in the window, with slow, scalding tears running down her face, trying to remember why she'd hated him—why revenge had seemed so overwhelmingly, so all-consumingly important. She'd watched him until she could bear no more. Then she'd gone, like the thief in the night that she was.

She found her weekend case, and packed it economically and methodically with the minimum she would need for her few days in hiding. When the *Globe* came out on Sunday with her pictures, there would be no point in remaining in seclusion any longer. She would have to face the music.

All she could hope was that Saul would be so angry—so bitter—that he would never want to see her again. She couldn't bear to face him, to see the condemnation in his eyes.

She tied a sweater across her shoulders. The skies over London were grey, and after Thyrsos the wind had an edge to it. She picked up her case, then paused. There were two last things she still had to do before she was free to run.

She wrote a brief note to Lucy, explaining she'd gone away for a little while, but would be in touch, and left it propped on the kitchen table.

Then she took the photograph of herself as a young girl out of its frame, and took one final, steady look at the gauche, vulnerable face. She tore it across, then tore it again, and dropped the fragments into her waste-basket.

'The end,' she said aloud. 'That's the end.'

She took her case, and carried it down to the car.

The inn's car park was nearly full when she arrived. Caroline slotted the Polo neatly between a Porsche and a Range Rover, and sat for a moment, looking around her.

She still wasn't sure why she'd come here. She'd found herself driving on autopilot most of the way. It seemed almost Freudian to have chosen this, of all villages, but the inn would do as a refuge for the night at least. She doubted whether she was capable of driving on further.

She got out and retrieved her bag, then, hunching her shoulders against the persistent drizzle which had followed her from London, she sprinted for the door marked 'Accommodation'.

She found herself in a carpeted passage with a neat reception desk facing her at its end. She rang the bell, and a girl in a dark skirt and white blouse appeared, and smiled at her.

'Can I help you?'

'I'd like a room. I suppose I should have phoned, really...'

'Oh, we're rarely that full midweek, and it's still early in the season.' The girl found a registration card and handed it to Caroline with a pen. 'How long were you wanting to stay?'

Caroline shrugged. 'My plans are fairly fluid. Could we just play it by ear?'

'Whatever suits you.' The girl paused. 'They're all double rooms, but we'd only charge for single occupation.' Briskly she ran through the tariff, and got Caroline to show her credit card. 'We've got quite a crowd in for dinner tonight, but if you wanted to eat, we could probably squeeze you in about nine-thirty.'

Caroline shook her head. 'I'm really not very hungry. I've been travelling a lot, and what I desperately need is sleep.'

She was taken up to a charming old-fashioned room, furnished in Laura Ashley prints, with a low, raftered ceiling and a window which looked across to the church, and the lych gate, and the yew tree beyond, where a lifetime ago Saul had photographed her for the first time, and called her Primavera.

And Persephone too, she remembered. Persephone, who'd condemned herself, through one rash act, to spend half her life in the darkness of Hell.

Well, her own sentence in Hell was just beginning, and perhaps this was why she'd come back to this of all the places in the world. To start her own private and personal torment.

And also because, she realised, this would be the last place Saul would ever think of looking for her. If, indeed, he wanted to...

With a slight shiver, she drew the curtains, took off her clothes, dropping them on the floor, climbed into bed, and went almost at once into the deep sleep of sheer exhaustion.

She was eventually awakened by a light tapping on the door.

She sat up. 'Who is it?'

'It's Karen from reception. I've brought you some tea. The boss, Mrs Bennett, was getting anxious about you.'

'Oh.' Caroline stumbled out of bed, found her robe, and opened the door. 'There was really no need.'

'I told her you said you were tired.' Karen handed her the tray. 'But you've slept the clock round.'

'My goodness.' A swift glance at her watch told Caroline this was no more than the truth. She forced a smile. 'I'm sorry. I didn't realise.'

'Not to worry.' Karen gave her a friendly, if slightly speculative smile. 'Will you be eating in the dining-room tonight?'

'Yes, please.' Caroline hesitated. 'And I'll be staying on, at least until Sunday. Will that be all right?'

'It'll be fine.' Karen's smile widened into a beam. 'It's even stopped raining at last.'

It was still too early for the bar and a pre-dinner drink when Caroline came downstairs, so she decided to go for a brief stroll instead.

The clouds had vanished, and a strong evening sun was coaxing a hot, damp smell out of the wet earth and foliage. Obeying an impulse, Caroline skirted the church, and set off down the lane towards the cottage. It was as beautiful as ever, with the climbing roses coming into full bloom. But there wouldn't be any azaleas remaining down by the river. Not unless time could run back, undoing, wiping out in some way the events of the past weeks. But that, of course, was impossible. Flowers bloomed and died. Love bloomed and died. Time moved on. Time, they said, was also a great healer. But not if you were determined to keep your wound open and bleeding.

If I could have one wish in the world, she thought, it would be to walk down the path at the side of the cottage, and find the azaleas still blossoming there. Because that would mean I had the power to make a choice—to change things.

It would mean I could be back on Thyrsos with Saul, working with him each day, sleeping in his arms at night. Planning our life, our future together.

As she reached the cottage gate, she almost hesitated. Then, just in time, she saw movement in the garden, and realised that the inhabitant had returned.

She was a tall, angular, elderly woman, with strongly marked features and a mass of white hair pushed untidily under a straw hat, and she was carrying a basket and a pair of secateurs. She'd been bending over a shrub rose, and as she straightened she frowned a little, her eyes going over the girl standing by her gate, as if in some way she knew Caroline had already been an intruder on her domain, and had dared to contemplate, however briefly, a further intrusion.

She wouldn't mind, Saul had said. But this wasn't a woman who looked as if she viewed uninvited and unwanted guests with indulgence. Caroline wasn't sure what she'd expected the cottage's owner to be like, but it certainly wasn't this formidable person.

'Good evening.' The tone was resonant, with a touch of the autocrat. 'Are you lost? This lane leads only to the farm, you know.'

'I didn't realise. I'm staying at the Black Horse, and I thought I'd explore at bit—work up an appetite for dinner.' And why the hell am I explaining myself—excusing myself like this? Caroline asked in silent vexation.

'I believe it's a very popular place for tourists. Sylvia Bennett is an excellent cook.'

'Yes, well...' Under the older woman's keen, unwavering stare, Caroline found herself sorely tempted to blush and shuffle her feet. She felt like a pupil suspected of a misdemeanour in the presence of her headmistress. She tried an unconvincing smile. 'I'd better get back and sample dinner.'

'Forgive me, but are you sure you are quite well?' The other's scrutiny had sharpened, measuring her.

'I'm fine.' Caroline found she was backing away. 'Fine, really. I'm sorry I disturbed you. It's such a lovely evening.'

She had to subdue an impulse to run as she retraced her steps. She probably thinks I've escaped from somewhere, she thought wryly. And if I go on behaving like a hermit, Mrs Bennett will probably think so, too. I'm supposed to be a tourist, so I'll start acting like one.

In the morning, after breakfast, she asked the ever-helpful Karen for some details of local beauty spots, and set off with a packed lunch to look at some of them.

Over the next days, she visited gardens and toured stately homes. She tramped round potteries and craft centres, and spent an afternoon at a wildlife sanctuary.

But no amount of activity could stop her thinking, or remembering and hurting inside. Or could prevent the fact that suddenly, almost before she knew it, the following day was going to be Sunday.

She slept badly that night, and woke too early. She made herself wait almost till breakfast-time before she rang down to reception to ask if there were any Sunday papers.

'We've got an *Express* left, and an *Observer*. Oh, and a *Telegraph*. Shall I bring one up?' Karen asked.

Caroline hesitated. 'Actually the one I wanted was the *Sunday Globe*.'

'The *Globe*?' Karen's astonishment was unmistakable. 'We've never had any call for that, I'm afraid. But I could pop down to the newsagents and see if they have one,' she added doubtfully.

'Oh, please don't go to all that trouble.' Caroline bit her lip. 'I can go myself.'

'No trouble at all,' Karen said cheerfully, and rang off.

Caroline sat down on the edge of the bed. She'd had her bath. She supposed she should get dressed—go down to the dining-room. But she was reluctant to face people. In spite of Karen's assurance, someone might have seen the *Globe* already that day, and could recognise her.

If I wear dark glasses, she thought, and no make-up. And if I put my hair up...

Her reverie was interrupted by a knock at the door. She got up, tightening the sash of her robe as she moved to answer. Karen, she thought, must have flown to the newsagents and back.

She forced a smile on to her taut lips as she opened the door. She began, 'You've been quick...' then stopped on a gasp of pure terror. 'You,' she said hoarsely and began to back away. 'But it can't be. It can't be...'

'Hello, Caroline.' Saul followed her into the room and closed the door behind him. He reached into the briefcase he was carrying, and produced a copy of the *Sunday Globe* which he tossed on to the bed. 'The paper you wanted, I believe. I was able to save the receptionist a journey.'

'What are you doing here? How did you find me?'

'Oh, that was the easy part. My grandmother recognised you outside her cottage. She'd seen the photographs of you among her azaleas, and knew you were the girl I was planning to marry. But she also knew you were supposed to be in Greece with me, and she felt concerned about you—about the fact that you looked ill. So she telephoned my flat, and left a message on the machine.'

He paused. 'I didn't get it at once, unfortunately. I was with Clive, going quietly off my head. I'd found out eventually that you'd flown back to

England, and assumed there'd been some
emergency. I tried your flat first, but there was no
one there, so Clive seemed the next best bet. Only
he was as much in the dark as I was. You'd vanished off the face of the earth, it seemed, with two
rolls of very personal film.' His face was unsmiling, almost expressionless as he looked at her.

'When I mentioned the films, Marge went very
quiet for a few minutes. Then she told us about
your cosy tête-à-tête with Mark Clayfield at that
party they gave, and how uneasy she'd always felt
about it—among other things. She said she'd always
felt you had another secret motive for becoming
the Flawless Girl, and that she was sure now there
was something desperately wrong with the entire
situation.'

In a voice she didn't recognise, Caroline said,
'Marge was always—too shrewd.'

'We went back to your flat,' he went on, as if
she hadn't spoken. 'And this time your flatmate
was there, and she let us in. She showed us your
note, and I went in your bedroom to see if you'd
left any clues about your ultimate destination. And
I found this.'

The torn photograph had been hastily taped back
together again. She looked obscene, she thought,
like a gargoyle. She swayed slightly.

'Sit down,' Saul said peremptorily. 'You're not
going to faint. You're going to listen to the rest of
what I have to say, and then you're going to explain why you tried to wreck the Flawless
campaign.'

'Not the campaign,' she said quietly. 'Just you. I had to destroy your life as you destroyed mine.' She began to laugh. 'I had to—had to...'

The laughter was stifled with the sharp sting of Saul's fingers against her cheek.

'No fainting,' he said icily. 'And no hysterics, either. So this was a one-woman exercise to bring me down. I congratulate you. You played your part brilliantly—right to the end. Some people might say that sacrificing your virginity to add extra credibility was going over the top, but I thought it was a master-stroke. No man who'd had a woman as completely and exquisitely as I'd had you would easily believe any wrong of her.'

She put up a hand to her tingling cheek. 'Don't— please don't...'

'But I've hardly begun,' he said gently. 'I can't— compartmentalise. Not yet, anyway. Even when I knew exactly what you'd tried to do to me—to us all—I could still only remember the way your hair looked spread across my pillow. How you trembled in my arms. How you looked when you lost control.' He drew a savage breath. 'That beautiful body that only I'd seen—known.' His laugh was harsh. 'Until, of course, you handed my films to the *Globe* to develop.'

He picked up the paper, and thrust it into her hands. 'So—take a long look at the centrefold, my sweet, sexy lady. See for yourself what you've achieved. Enjoy your big moment.'

Her hands were shaking so much that the paper rattled as she opened it.

The pictures danced in front of her eyes, and she blinked in shock, trying to focus, trying to come to terms with what she saw. 'Meet shapely Donna Pride', said the caption. 'Donna, 18, from Esher, takes Pride of Place this week as our Sunday Siren.'

Donna, Caroline saw dazedly, was a busty blonde with a come-hither smile who'd had no compunction at all about what she revealed for the camera.

She said, 'I don't understand.'

'It's quite simple,' he said. 'It's called pressure. Sep Creed was in on the act by this time, and he tried to contact Clayfield to find out if our suspicions were justified, but Clayfield wouldn't take his calls. So then Sep went right to the top—to Athol Clement himself. You remember him, don't you, sweetheart? He's the guy whose hospitality you've been enjoying on Thyrsos. It turns out that the proprietor of the *Globe*, Andrew Beresford, is an old friend of his and owes him a very large favour. So your appearance in the *Globe* was summarily cancelled, and all prints and negatives were duly returned.'

Tears began to trickle down her face. 'Thank heaven,' she whispered. 'Oh, thank heaven!'

'You hypocritical little bitch.' The contempt in his voice cut her to the bone. 'You're crying because your rotten scheming hasn't worked.'

'You're wrong.' Her voice shook. 'You don't understand.'

'I've been trying to,' he came back at her grimly. 'When I found that bloody photograph and pieced it together, I could hardly believe what I was seeing—what it was suggesting. I remembered the wedding where I'd met you, and while Sep was doing his stuff I drove down there to make some

enquiries, to find some motivation for this lunacy.
The Foxcrofts are a well-known local family. You
weren't hard to trace, now I knew who I was looking
for,' he added glacially.

'I had—an illuminating talk with your parents.
They told me in fascinating detail the exact lengths
you'd gone to in order to alter your appearance.
They seemed to take it as a personal insult. What
they didn't know—and what I'm asking you now
—is for goodness' sake, why?'

She pointed at the photograph. 'You see how I
was.' Her voice was high and strained. 'I was a
caricature—a laughing-stock. I was entitled to
change the way I looked, if it could be done.'

'But you changed everything,' he said too softly.
'Even your voice is different.'

'That's because of my teeth,' she said quickly. 'I
used to lisp.'

Saul came across to her, and took her by the
shoulders. 'Tell me why you did this.' His voice was
molten. 'Tell me why the sweet, happy child I met
at that foul wedding should have put herself
through this kind of ordeal. Tell me, Caroline,
before I bloody well shake it out of you. Tell me
why you wanted so badly to destroy me.'

His touch sang through her bones, turning them
to water. Her body clenched in desire and yearning.
And on the heels of that came anger.

She tore herself free and stood up. 'I'll tell you
why,' she said between her teeth. 'It was because
of the pathetic, childish crush I had on you, that
you probably weren't even aware of. You were in
the rose garden with a girl called Katie Arnold,
taking pictures of her, supposedly. But you were

talking about me—saying I was grotesque—an object lesson in how not to look. You said cruel, vile things. You laughed at me because I was ugly, and then—and then...'

'Yes,' Saul prompted, his eyes never leaving her face. 'What then, Caroline Foxcroft?'

Her voice thickened, broke. 'I—saw you with her. She took off her clothes—all of them. And you—you made love to her.'

There was a long silence. Saul said quietly, 'Oh, dear heaven, are you telling me I did this to you? I turned that radiant child into a monster because of something you thought you heard and saw?'

'Radiant?' she bit at him. 'How dare you say that—after the things you called me, after what you did?'

'How else would you describe yourself?' He took his wallet from his back pocket, and extracted a photograph. 'Recognise this?'

She stared down at herself. The girl she'd once been, smiling, her face shining with happiness as she played with a dog on a riverbank.

Saul said harshly, 'It's the only photograph I kept from that damned wedding. You were so sweet, so gallant and innocent, totally separate from all the bitching and manoeuvring round you. I've carried it with me ever since as a kind of talisman, to remind myself at intervals what a truly decent, lovable human being can be like.'

Her eyes blurred. She said stonily, 'You say that now. But I saw you with her. I heard you...'

'Then I'm very glad I'm not on trial, with you as a witness for the defence,' he said wearily. 'I remember that afternoon and Katie's charming striptease very vividly. I remember too that she really had her knife in you—she was clearly piqued because I preferred your company to anyone else's. I'd seen the way they all treated you, and it occurred to me that if I leapt to your defence, gave her the hard word, you'd probably suffer for it later. So I kept quiet and let her get rid of the poison inside her. At least she wasn't venting it directly on you. Probably I was wrong, but it seemed the best thing to do at the time.'

He shook his head. 'And, yes, I said you were an object lesson in how not to look, because it happened to be true. No one had ever bothered about you—paid any attention to your hair, or your skin, your posture, or the clothes you wore. It was all pretty Sister Sue, and that made me bloody angry.'

'But you wouldn't take my photograph,' she said wildly. 'You didn't want me in any of the groups.'

'Because you were so obviously the odd one out.' His voice had gentled. 'It was cruel and thoughtless of them to have asked you, knowing that your height alone made it impossible for you to fit in. And the dress was wrong for you—style, colour—everything. I didn't want to draw even more attention to the fact.'

He paused. 'I never did that book about the wedding, Caroline. I was just too disgusted with the whole scene. I simply produced some pretty-pretty conventional pictures on the day, and left it at that. However, I did wonder about you and your out-of-the-blue virus. I wondered if Katie had had a go at you, after all. In fact, I rang your house to enquire if you were better. I was going to drive over and see you, but your mother said you were resting and you couldn't be disturbed. I got the strong impression that she didn't want me around. She probably thought I was lusting after your sister. If she'd only known.'

She said, her lips moving stiffly, 'Are you pretending that you—cared about me?'

'No,' he said. 'I was certainly concerned about you—about your well-being, and what was going to happen to you. But that was as far as it went.' He gave her a straight look. 'I'd like to say that I fell in love with you, as you were then. But it wouldn't be true. All I knew was that you had an incredibly appealing personality which touched some chord in me. I wanted to protect you, and I couldn't, and that also made me angry.'

Caroline lifted her hands and pressed them to her face. 'I do remember what happened.' Her voice cracked piteously. 'I can't have got it wrong. I can't . . .'

'Think back,' Saul said quietly. 'But before you do, let's talk about what you think you saw. You watched Katie take off her bikini.'

'With your assistance.'

'I untied a couple of strings,' he said with a shrug. 'I seem to remember you invited me to do the same for you when . . .' He stopped abruptly, some of the colour draining from his face. He said, 'Of course, that whole scene was intended to be a re-run of the Katie episode, wasn't it? If I hadn't been so lost, so crazy about you, so totally turned on by what you were doing, I might have remembered.'

'Why didn't you?'

'Because it wasn't that bloody important.' Saul slammed a fist down on the chest of drawers.

'Look, Katie Arnold may have been a friend of your cousin's, but she was basically a slut and an exhibitionist. She was dying for me to photograph her nude. She'd been hinting at it from day one.' His mouth curled. 'She also presumed the sight of her body would drive me so frantic with lust that I'd have to have her there and then. But she was wrong. If I want a woman, I do my own chasing, and I made it brutally clear to her that I did not want her. She was good-looking, but she was also a spoiled, vindictive, egotistical little bitch, and I wouldn't have wished her on my worst enemy.'

He took her chin in his hand, making her look at him. 'Caroline, you may have seen the offer being made, but if you'd stayed you'd also have seen it rejected. I was no one's lover at that wedding. I was there to take pictures—and hold out a hand to a child who seemed to need a friend.'

He smoothed her hair back from her forehead. 'Now, tell me the truth. Which really mattered most to you? The comments about your appearance, or the fact that you believed I was Katie's lover?'

She said in a muffled voice, 'I ran away and was sick. I couldn't see anything, I couldn't think of anything but you—with her. I was so unhappy, I wanted to die.'

'You said it was just a childish crush,' he reminded her evenly. 'It seems to have been rather more. Crushes fade. The kind of revenge you planned needs a stronger emotion to feed on.'

She flushed dully. 'What do you want me to say? That I—loved you?'

'Only if it's true.'

She said slowly, 'Perhaps I was mistaken about that—as I was about so many things. And what does it matter, anyway, after all this time?'

'I think it matters a great deal. When we made love the other night, I asked you to marry me. You didn't give me a straight answer, which under the circumstances is understandable. But I want an answer now. Did you build this monster inside you because you loved me, and thought I'd rejected you for Katie?'

She was silent for a moment. Then she said on a sigh, 'Yes.' She released herself and moved away to sit on the edge of the bed. She stared down at the carpet. 'I was so jealous, and so angry. I—wanted to believe it was you who'd said all those things, because it made it easier to hate you—easier to blame you—for spoiling my life.' Her throat constricted painfully. 'My family didn't really care about me when I was plain—you saw that. But they liked me even less when I—changed. I was an embarrassment to them.' She gave an uneven laugh. 'I held you responsible for that, too.'

Saul knelt beside her, and took her hands in his. 'You were a hurt child hitting out in pain,' he said quietly. 'But that's behind you now, and you're a woman in every sense of the word. It isn't the past that matters, but the future.'

Her voice shook. 'But I have to go on wearing this face.'

He said patiently, 'Caroline, be honest with me. Has your life really been spoiled by your change of looks? Your family don't approve. So what? You're so lovely that you take my breath away. You have a career. You have friends who care about you. You're a success. You're the Flawless Girl.'

She shook her head. 'Not any more. Not after— all this. Clive—Sep Creed—they all know I tried to blow the campaign. They won't want to use me after this.'

He said drily, 'On the contrary, darling. You're a valuable property, and one of the reasons I'm here is to find out when you'll be ready to start work again.'

'I can't face anyone,' she said in a low voice. 'Not after what I've done.'

'After what you failed to do,' he corrected. 'The cover story is that you were naïve, and let yourself be conned by one of the *Globe*'s smooth operators. Then you got uneasy and confessed all to Sep Creed and myself, and we put a stop to it. It's as simple as that.'

'As simple as that,' she repeated, and began to cry in great, gusty sobs which clawed painfully at her throat and chest, tearing away the last remnants of bitterness and hurting. The man at her feet didn't move. He just knelt, holding her hands until the paroxysms quietened, and eventually died away.

At last, she said huskily, 'It sounds so inadequate, but I'm sorry—for everything.'

'I'm sorry too,' he said quietly. 'I'm sorry I allowed your mother to put me off that day. If I'd insisted on seeing you, perhaps it could all have been sorted out.'

'But then Carly North might never have existed.'

'Oh, I think there would have been some kind of metamorphosis, though maybe not quite such a drastic one. Carly North has cost you a great deal, in human terms particularly.' He paused. 'Anyway, it's Caroline Foxcroft that Gran is waiting to meet. She ordered me to sort everything out with you, then bring you to lunch.'

Caroline shrank. 'It's too soon. I—can't.'

He was silent for a moment, then got to his feet, shrugging. 'Then I'll have to go alone.'

He was at the door when she said, hardly breathing, 'Saul?'

He turned, his face enigmatic. 'Yes?'

She ran her tongue round her dry lips. 'You said—that you reached out a hand once to a child who needed a friend. Don't walk away—please. I—I need a friend now.'

'I need more than that,' he said. 'I need a lover, a wife, and a mother for my children. And any reaching out has to be mutual.'

She got slowly to her feet. 'You can't still want me. Not after this.'

'Listen,' he said, 'even if the *Globe* had published colour photos of you today stark naked in three dimensions, I would still love you. And I would be here with you now, helping to pick up the pieces. You are mine, and I am yours. Nothing will ever change that. And it's the woman inside you I love, not the image. Now, will you put some clothes on before I go crazy, and come and meet my grandmother?'

She began to loosen the sash of her robe. 'On the other hand, it isn't nearly lunchtime yet.'

'And guests who arrive too early are almost as bad as those who are late,' Saul agreed solemnly, watching the movement of her fingers with open fascination. 'Perhaps we should find something else to occupy us for the next hour or so.'

'It's—difficult.' The robe was loose now and, delicately, she let it slip from her shoulders and pool round her feet. 'This is a very quiet village. There isn't a great deal to do.'

'You amaze me,' Saul said, too evenly. 'I can think of any number of activities, and we don't even have to leave this room.' He reached behind him and turned the key in the lock. Then he leaned back against the panels and smiled at her. 'Say the words, lady. I need to hear them from you.'

She said quietly and clearly, 'I love you. I think always have, and I know I always will. And I'll marry you whenever you want me to.'

He came to her then, lifting her against his heart.

He said softly, 'My sweet—my flawless love.' And his mouth sought hers in tenderness and promise.

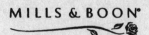

MILLS & BOON®

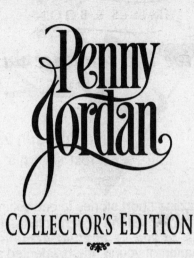

Penny Jordan

COLLECTOR'S EDITION

Mills & Boon® are proud to bring back a collection of best-selling titles from Penny Jordan—one of the world's best-loved romance authors.

Each book is presented in beautifully matching volumes, with specially commissioned illustrations and presented as one precious collection.

Two titles every month at £3.10 each.

DEBBIE MACOMBER

Married in Montana

Needing a safe place for her sons to grow up, Molly
Cogan decided it was time to return home.
Home to Sweetgrass Montana.
Home to her grandfather's ranch.

*"Debbie Macomber's name on a book is a guarantee
of delightful, warm-hearted romance."*
—Jayne Ann Krentz

1-55166-400-3
AVAILABLE IN PAPERBACK
FROM AUGUST, 1998

RONA JAFFE

Five Women

Once a week, five women meet over dinner and
drinks at the Yellowbird, their favourite
Manhattan bar. To the shared table they bring
their troubled pasts; their hidden secrets.
And through their friendship, each will find
a courageous new beginning.

Five Women is an *"insightful look at female
relationships."*

—Publishers Weekly

1-55166-424-0
**AVAILABLE IN PAPERBACK
FROM AUGUST, 1998**

JAYNE ANN KRENTZ

A Woman's Touch

He was her boss—and her lover!
Life had turned complicated for Rebecca Wade when she
met Kyle Stockbridge. He *almost* had her believing he
loved her, until she realised she was in possession
of something he wanted.

"...one of the hottest writers in romance today."

—USA Today

1-55166-315-5
AVAILABLE IN PAPERBACK
FROM AUGUST, 1998

They were only watching...

ERICA SPINDLER

Shocking Pink

A chilling psychological suspense from the critically
acclaimed author of *Fortune, Forbidden Fruit* and *Red*.

Spindler delivers *"a high adventure of love's triumph over
twisted obsession."*

—Publishers Weekly

1-55166-415-1
AVAILABLE FROM JULY 1998

LaVyrle
SPENCER

Spring Fancy

No-nonsense, Winn Gardner was maid of honour at her
best friend's wedding. She never dreamt she could be
tempted by the handsome, teasing best man. Her own
wedding was only three months away. But the initial thrill
of their first meeting quickly turned into a sensuous blaze.

"Spencer leaves the reader breathless."

—New York Daily Times

MIRA

1-55166-397-X
AVAILABLE FROM JULY 1998

LAURA
VAN
WORMER

❦❖❧

Just for the Summer

Nothing prepares Mary Liz for the summer she spends in
the moneyed town of East Hampton, Long Island. From
the death of one of their own, Mary Liz realises that these
stunningly beautiful people have some of the ugliest
agendas in the world.

*"Van Wormer,...has the glamorama Hampton's scene down to
a T. (Just for the Summer is) as voyeuristic as it is fun."*
—Kirkus Reviews

MIRA

1-55166-439-9
AVAILABLE NOW IN PAPERBACK

EMILIE RICHARDS

RUNAWAY

Runaway is the first of an intriguing trilogy.

Krista Jensen is desperate. Desperate enough to pose as a young
prostitute and walk the narrow alley ways of New Orleans.
So it's with relief that Krista finds herself a protector in
the form of Jess Cantrell. Grateful for his help,
she isn't sure she can trust him.

Trusting the wrong man could prove fatal.

MIRA®

1-55166-398-8
AVAILABLE NOW IN PAPERBACK

DEBBIE MACOMBER

The Playboy and the Widow

A confirmed bachelor, Cliff Howard wasn't prepared to
trade in the fast lane for car pools. Diana Collins lived life
hiding behind motherhood and determined to play it
safe. They were both adept at playing their roles.
Until the playboy met the widow...

"Debbie Macomber's stories sparkle with love and laughter..."
—*New York Times* bestselling author, Jayne Ann Krentz

1-55166-080-6
AVAILABLE NOW IN PAPERBACK